HERETIC

THE TERRAN CYCLE: BOOK THREE

PHILIP C. QUAINTRELL

Cover Illustration by Tom Edwards
Book design by BodiDog Design
Edited by David Bradley

ISBN: 978-1-916610-26-2 (paperback)
ASIN: B08Y4F8W1T (ebook)

Published by Quaintrell Publishings

ALSO BY PHILIP C. QUAINTRELL

"We know what we are, but know not what we may be."

William Shakespeare

PROLOGUE

254 years ago...

Captain Jedediah Holt stroked the smooth, dark skin along his jawline. He always liked to have a clean shave before a mission, whatever it might be. *Start how you mean to go on*, he thought. Relaxing into his high-backed chair on the command bridge, Jed surveyed his officers with pride. They had been hand-picked, each and every one, to be a member of the *Paladin's* crew. They might not be the first or even the second ship, to make the trip to Century - Earth's sister world - but their cargo was just as precious. As well as the crew, the *Paladin's* swollen mid-section now housed a hundred thousand people, families, all.

Jed looked past the busy bridge crew and took in the vista of stars that lay beyond the curving viewport. The edge of the starboard screen was aglow with the orange aura of the sun. If the *Paladin* tilted any further in that direction, the aura would intensify into that of a blinding light, capable of cooking them all in their seats. The captain knew it was an unnecessary risk to keep the heat shield powered down, but he trusted his helmsman, and he wanted to see the universe break its ancient rules when they activated the Solar Drive.

The ability to travel faster-than-light wasn't new technology, but it also wasn't old technology. There weren't many captains who had taken expeditions across the stars and the *Paladin* was one of a handful of ships to make the journey to Century. During his service in the United Defence Corps, Jed had been privileged enough to break the light barrier while on tour, but never as captain, and never with so many lives on his shoulders.

"Captain." Samantha Vale, the *Paladin's* first officer, handed Jed a Datapad filled with readouts from the ship's various chiefs.

His reverie broken, Jed focused on his commander's stony expression. "Something on your mind, Sam?"

Samantha Vale had been under his command for seven years prior to their recent promotions on the *Paladin*. The Commander had gladly accepted Jed's offer to be his first officer when he was made captain, only a few weeks earlier, though he had sensed some regret on her behalf.

"No sir," she replied curtly.

"Come on, out with it." Jed looked up at her from his seat. "You've been *sulking* since The Hub handed us our orders."

With an insulted expression, Sam's mouth parted, but the commander held her barbed retort and straightened her back. "I have not been sulking, sir."

"Could have fooled me..." Jed knew his smirk would only piss her off more.

The commander sighed. "Permission to speak freely, sir?"

Jed expressed his mock confusion. "Do you have any other way of speaking to me?"

"When you told me we were going to Century I thought it would be to do some deep space exploration. Check out the territory and neighbouring solar systems. Root out any separatists that may have found a stronghold in the system..."

"Something exciting," Jed stated, reading between the lines.

"I didn't think we'd be taxiing a bunch of colonists from Earth to Century," Sam explained.

"That's what the *Paladin* was designed for," Jed argued. "It's an Arc ship."

"I didn't know that when I signed on..." Sam looked away, clearly embarrassed.

"You should have done your homework." The captain wagged his finger at her.

"I didn't sign on to be the commander of the *Paladin*. I signed on to be *your* X-O." Sam wouldn't look him in the eye.

It was Sam's loyalty that had earned her the promotion in his eyes. Jed knew he could trust her with his commands and his life. He wanted to treasure these next few years working so closely with her, it wouldn't be long before Commander Vale became Captain Vale.

"We're going to help with the colonising of Century for a while," Jed said. "It won't be forever. Eventually we will be tasked with mandates like exploration, but for now, we get to just enjoy a bit of easy street."

"Captain Holt?" Helmsman Maloy turned from his station to face Jed and Sam.

Before giving the helmsman his full attention, Jed looked up at Sam and waited for her response. The commander replied with a smile and a nod of concession. Captain Holt had seen more action than her, and he knew when to enjoy an easy command.

She will understand that, in time, he thought.

"What is it, Maloy?" Jed faced his helmsman.

"We're getting some error codes in our navigation array. I've tasked an engineer to look into it, but I wouldn't advise activating the Solar Drive until it's fixed."

"Understood. Carry on." Jed trusted the Martian to have everything in order by the deadline for launch.

Sam pointed at the Datapad in Jed's hands. "One hundred thousand souls and six grumpy Raiders accounted for."

Jed chuckled to himself. "How are they holding up? They've only been on board for a day."

"They're like six caged animals who want something to hunt. It's going to take a few days to reach Century and, as far as they're concerned, there's going to be nothing to do." Sam sounded as if she agreed with their way of thinking.

"I'll talk to them after we hit sub-space," Jed replied seriously. The last thing he wanted was six highly trained UDC killers getting bored on his ship. "The Corporate War only ended a couple of years ago. There's every chance the separatists have got people on board if they're not on Century already. They *need* to be here."

Sam shifted her feet on the bulkhead. "The gravity feels a little light." The commander turned to ensign Markovich, who was standing in front of a glass wall, streaming with readouts. "Marko, check the grav enforcers."

The ensign acknowledged and retasked his Glass Board.

Jed smiled. "What would I do without you?"

"Float away..." Sam emulated her captain's smile.

Over the next hour, Captain Holt sat in the middle of the bridge and listened to his crew converse. It was their level of tension that would tell him if anything was wrong with the *Paladin*. He knew that the sensor dish had taken a knock before they left space dock, but Ensign Sato was working to correct the issue, ensuring their communications were up to scratch. Engineering had already reported that the Solar Drive's systems were at optimal levels for the distance of their jump. They were almost ready to leave the solar system.

Jed checked the countdown on the screen built into his armrest. They were due to depart in six minutes.

"Commander Vale." Jed waited for Sam to turn around at her station. "Are we systems go?"

Sam checked her monitor. "The Hub has given us a green light for departure, Captain. All systems are ready for the jump. Communications is still a little iffy, but we can transmit data."

Jed half-swivelled his chair to face Maloy. "Helmsman Maloy. I trust the problem with our navigation array has been seen to. I would very much like to arrive in Century's orbit rather than headfirst into a moon...."

The levity eased the bridge crew before they left reality behind. There had never been a problem with using sub-space before, but the idea of slipping into the space between spaces was still a scary thought.

Helmsman Maloy hesitated, looking over his monitor. "Our engineers have looked into it Captain and found no problems on the array's end. They concluded that it must be a malfunction on our end. It's most likely just my monitor, sir."

Jed didn't like it. He looked at the countdown again. "Commander Vale..."

No specific order was given, nor was it required. Sam's hands danced across her monitor until she had the required information. "I have the same error code, Captain."

Jed gave a heavy sigh and puffed out his chest, chewing over the information. They would be pissing off a lot of people if they delayed their departure. But it was his ship, his command. The *Paladin* wouldn't move an inch without his say so.

Sam offered, "If the array itself is functioning, then it's most likely a faulty connection to the bridge terminals."

Jed mulled it over with his chin resting on his hand. Every face on the bridge was looking to him, waiting for his command. "Can you still plot a course to Century?" Jed directed his question to Maloy.

The helmsman keyed in a few commands before turning back. "Course laid in, Captain."

Jed sucked in a breath and looked at Sam, who nodded her approval. "Okay." He raised his voice to be heard by everyone. "Commander Vale, alert our passengers and the crew of our imminent departure. Helmsman Maloy," Jed flicked his finger across the screen in his chair and sent the countdown to Maloy's station, "when you see zero, you have my permission to launch."

The bridge was a flurry of activity, but all measured and controlled. They were a fine crew, the best he could find. Jed spent the next minute going through his usual, physical routine of rolling his head and cracking his neck. He knew it was pointless since he wouldn't feel anything when the Solar Drive was activated, but habits were habits.

The countdown hit zero and Helmsman Maloy used the physical lever to activate the jump to sub-space. A low rumble rippled through the ship, but it didn't feel right to the captain. Before he could give any orders, the lights flickered and the monitors were overlaid with a single message, displaying an error code.

"What's wrong?" His question was drowned out by the first claxon of an alarm, signalling the emergency diversion of power.

Jed hit the override tab on his armrest and shut the alarm down. His crew were busy at their stations trying to understand the nature of the malfunction. He let them work for a moment before reiterating his question.

"The Solar Drive is still charging!" Ensign Sato reported from behind his glass board.

"What? Why is it still charging?" Captain Holt asked immediately.

"Oh no..." Helmsman Maloy's quiet voice carried across the bridge.

"Helm, report," Commander Vale ordered.

"The drive is still charging because it thinks the journey is further away than Century," Maloy explained, his eyes fixed on his monitor. "The navigation array has plotted a course into deep space, some-where outside... this arm of the galaxy."

"Shut down the drive, NOW!" Jed ordered. If the *Paladin* was shot into deep space, they would travel beyond the point of no return. The ship only had enough solarcite to get them to Century, where they were expected to refuel for the journey back.

There was another flurry of activity across the bridge, all the while the *Paladin* continued to rumble. Jed looked at Sam, whose grave expression told him everything.

"The drive is non-responsive, Captain..." Maloy's fingers jabbed at every available space on his monitor.

Sam swivelled back to her screen. "Sending a mayday to The Hub now."

"I thought the course was *laid in*, Maloy." Jed was already trying to contact engineering via the comlink in his chair.

"It was sir, I don't... When the Solar Drive came online it must have affected the array or..." Maloy groaned in frustration. "I'm completely locked out!"

Jed didn't have time to pressure the helmsman for answers. Only engineering could help them now. They needed to perform a manual shutdown before the drive threw them into uncharted space.

"Sir..." The voice that came over the comlink wasn't his chief engineer. "This is acting-chief Grenko. Chief Horlish is... dead."

The loss of his chief engineer stung, but Jed didn't have time to mourn now. "What's going on down there, Grenko?"

"The Chief tried to manually shut down the drive, sir. It overloaded the bulkhead manifold and exploded."

"Jed..." Sam's familiar use of his name drew his attention. "The drive is fully charged."

Captain Holt looked ahead as the rumbling reached its crescendo. The *Paladin* lurched forward and the stars stretched around the viewport, leaving nothing but the dark, empty abyss of sub-space.

ONE

Kalian stood in a corridor that he had never been in, looking at a door he had never seen before. The foreboding door was circular and constructed entirely from exotic minerals that made it the perfect protection for the cube, parading as the Conclave AI. Reaching out, he placed one hand on the cool metal and pushed his Terran senses beyond the confines of the corridor.

She was inside...

Kalian's senses easily detected the nanocelium that made up the cube on the other side of the thick door. Its menacing presence responded to his extra-sensing touch with what felt like laughter. Kalian hammered his fist into the vault door with frustration, but it made no mark. The cube knew as well as he did that everything inside that room was about to be vapourised.

Li'ara was about to die.

With both hands outstretched, Kalian reached out with his Terran abilities and pulled on the door using telekinesis. The exotic metal strained and groaned, but it barely moved an inch. It was exhausting. Kalian screamed in anger and went back to hammering the door. His senses detected Li'ara's heartbeat increasing as the realisation of death set in. It was a feeling he wanted to spare her from, but he was helpless to intervene.

"You can't save me..." Li'ara's voice came from behind him.

Kalian turned around and saw the face of the woman he loved. Her startling green eyes and copper ringlets made her pale skin appear all the more beautiful. Now her features were sullen. Li'ara looked at Kalian with an expression of regret, but also of disappointment.

"You can't save me..." Li'ara whispered, her hand cupping his cheek.

"You can't save any of us." Disturbingly, Esabelle was now standing behind Li'ara, her face bruised and bloodied.

Kalian felt tears run down his face when Malekk stepped out of the shadows and wrapped his arms around his mentor's slender neck. Without pause, the infected Terran snapped Esabelle's neck with ease. Malekk smiled and strode towards Kalian and Li'ara. He closed his fingers slowly around Li'ara's chin and head, all the while watching Kalian.

"NO!" Kalian was frozen in place, unable to move.

Malekk snapped Li'ara's neck and discarded her like garbage. "We are coming," the infected Terran hissed. "We are hungry..." Malekk's hand reached out towards Kalian's face, blocking out the light.

Kalian shot up in bed, covered in a layer of sweat. He always woke up at the same point. For three months he had been haunted by the same nightmare. Sitting on the edge of his bed, Kalian took a deep breath and focused his mind. Every molecule of sweat slowly lifted from his body as if he were in a vacuum. In moments his skin was dry and the sweat began to evaporate into the air around him.

The desk beside his bed was covered in sheets of paper - some of which had been scrunched into a ball. The drawn image of Li'ara looked back at him, just as he remembered her. His ability to sketch near-perfect images of anything he had seen was new, and apparently a result of his developing Terran memory. Reaching out with a lazy hand, Kalian scrunched up the picture and threw it across the room. When he looked back at the desk, all that remained were the pages full of question marks. He looked at the word Evalan, surrounded by questioning symbols. The word had been engraved in Terran across the cube found by Savrick and the cube found at Trantax IV. The word and its meaning were just one of many mysteries surrounding Kalian's life right now.

"Your finer control is getting better every day." ALF was standing in the darkened corner of the room.

Kalian didn't look shocked, but he rolled his eyes. "How long have you been lurking there?"

The black Terran armour walked out of the shadows. "Still room for improvement I see..."

Kalian knew it was hollow, though. *Like me,* he thought.

"I thought you were overseeing the final stages of the Starforge's construction." Kalian stood up without any clothes on and ran his hand through his hair. It would be another hour or so before the images from his nightmare left him alone.

"It's finished," ALF announced, his armoured head glancing out the window.

Kalian turned to the vista of stars, beyond the *Sentinel,* and altered the structure of his eyes to see further than any human could dream. With the backdrop of a distant moon - used as a base for the construction - Kalian could see the crescent moon shape of the Starforge. It was much smaller than the one made by Protocorps, in keeping with the original Terran design. The Starforge in the Helteron Cluster had been designed for something far more sinister and larger. Unravelling that mystery was the whole reason for constructing this new Starforge.

"I returned to the *Sentinel* when they started bothering me about the nanocelium again." ALF sounded bored. "They are unaccepting of the fact that it will never respond to anything but Terran or human DNA."

Kalian generally tried to avoid conversations with the AI, since he trusted him less and less, but he wanted to think about anything else other than his nightmare. "Can you blame them? Nanocelium could revolutionise their entire culture. It can heal humans from almost anything - who knows what it means for their lifespan."

ALF looked at Kalian with his blank faceplate. "Their lifespan?"

Kalian had heard it too.

"More and more you refer to humans as something apart from you," ALF observed. "I thought Esabelle taught you not to forget that; that your humanity could be what made you stronger than any Terran?"

"Well Esabelle's not here," Kalian quickly replied, never turning from the window.

"Your isolation on this ship has not been good for your mental health," ALF commented for the hundredth time. "For three months you've had no contact with any of your own kind. You barely even speak to any of the crew. I know losing-"

"Don't," Kalian interrupted.

ALF emulated a sigh. "What's left of humanity requires a leader, Kalian. They have Captain Fey for now, but it's not who they need. You stand for everything they're going to become. Their evolution is inevitable."

"How is the Captain?" Kalian changed the subject, but he was interested... to a degree.

"Captain Fey sent a message in the night. She wishes you well on your mission and regrets that she can't be here to see you off."

Kalian leaned on the window ledge with both hands and watched the smaller vessels return from the Starforge. New supplies and work crews were swapped out of the base on the distant moon regularly.

"Fey's where she needs to be," Kalian commented absently. "That floating habitat won't keep itself in order."

The artificial habitat, that now housed the remaining seven thousand human beings, was orbiting the Raalak's homeworld, Arakesh. Kalian had only visited it briefly before leaving with the *Sentinel*. He was glad the Highclave had seen fit to move them from the orbiting rings around Ch'ket. The new habitat was far more peaceful and accommodating, having been retrofitted with humans in mind.

"I'm afraid it will have to," ALF said with concern. "Captain Fey's transmission came from the *Nautallon*. She's with High Charge Uthor, responding to a broadcast outside Conclave territory - believed to be human in origin. They believe another ship made it out of your solar system before the Gomar arrived. Personally, I feel it's a waste of resources. If any human vessel made it out of the system before the *Nova*, the crew will be dead from dehydration by now."

Kalian turned back to the Terran armour. "Always looking on the bright side..."

As if reading his mind, ALF walked into Kalian and molded the armour around his naked body, leaving only his head and hands uncovered. Thousands of microscopic nanocelium wormed their way up from the fitted, high collar and nestled behind Kalian's ear, engulfing the Novaarian translator that was permanently attached to his skin. Through this, ALF could talk to him without anyone else listening in - just the way the secretive AI liked it.

"Has there been any progress tracking Malekk?" Kalian didn't enjoy thinking about the twisted Terran, but he often thought of nothing but killing him.

"While confined to the armour alone I am unable to access any Conclave systems."

"It's like they don't trust you or something..." Kalian made for the door.

Ignoring his comment, ALF continued, "But I have spoken directly with Charge Ilo between my jaunts to the Starforge. She tells me there have been no sightings of him since he fled the Helteron Cluster. I predict that Protocorps is hiding him somewhere. Despite the numerous investigations they still have considerable influence and no end of resources. Malekk could be anywhere."

The idea of the infected Terran moving around the galaxy unchecked disturbed Kalian. Malekk had stated that he was working on behalf of something called the Vanguard. Whatever this person or creature was, it could be placed at the centre of every attack on homo sapiens in the Milky Way galaxy. It had seen to the downfall of the Terran and sent a cube millions of lightyears to destroy Earth. The

Vanguard appeared to be paving the way for something that had yet to be revealed.

Kalian had become so desperate for these answers that he had volunteered to be the first to travel through the new Conclave Starforge and journey into the heart of the galaxy. Perhaps in the home of the Terran, the true origins of mankind, he might unravel the mystery behind the cubes.

Kalian didn't look back as he exited the sparse living quarters. Outside his room were the usual four alien guards, though not one of them was there to watch Kalian. Having exhibited his abilities several times in the last nine months, the Conclave knew they could do nothing to stop him. Instead, these guards were tasked with escorting ALF between the *Sentinel* and the Starforge.

The guards followed closely behind after he exited the quiet area of the ship - largely abandoned by the crew and left to Kalian. The *Sentinel* was an impressive vessel, the flagship of the Conclave fleet. The Highclave had hoped it could rival the *Gommarian* and bring an end to the leverage humanity held over them. That was before Malekk had used the Helteron Starforge to obliterate it.

In the spacious Translift, Kalian rested the palm of his hand against the wall and opened his senses to the universe. His Terran brain mapped the ship in seconds, feeding back to him the *Sentinel's* strengths and weaknesses. There were tremendous amounts of intrinium onboard, but it wasn't all located in the Starrillium, the ship's engine. Kalian felt as if he could actually touch the warheads sitting in their torpedo tubes. With a concentrated thought, he was sure he could excite the molecules inside the intrinium and activate the warhead.

Affecting objects and particles that were out of sight was a new skill for Kalian. His mind had always been able to find things out of sight, but it was only recently that he felt able to actually interact with them. Thinking of some of the amazing feats Esabelle had performed during their time together, it was clear that Kalian still had much to learn.

The doors opened onto a busy corridor with a startling white floor and green walls, the same shade as the ship's hull. Aliens from all twelve races went about their jobs, checking systems and installing upgrades where needed. The *Sentinel*, like all Conclave vessels, had been designed with a variety of biological needs in mind. The hulking Raalaks had the space to move about unencumbered, while the Ch'kara had access to multiple methane stations around the ship, ensuring a constant supply of their breathable atmosphere. When the corridor opened up, to what Kalian could only compare to a shopping mall on Earth, the walls were overlaid with gravity-defying walkways for the nimble Novaarians.

Kalian continued through the massive ship, along with ALF's entourage. On his way to the hangar bay, the group was forced to walk by the gargantuan double-doors that concealed the Starrillium. Kalian could feel the hum of the great engine on his skin. Beyond those doors was a sphere of callic-diamond that housed an artificial star the size of a football stadium. Kalian shifted his senses and felt the enormous amounts of electromagnetic radiation being absorbed and funnelled into the drives, where the intrinium waited to blast the *Sentinel* into sub-space.

Feeling the power of the engine, Kalian's mind was cast back a few months ago. Aboard the *Nova*, he had performed an unbelievable feat of his own and actually contained the raw sun inside the starillium, after Professor Garrett Jones had unleashed a nanocelium virus into the Nova's systems. It would have killed Kalian had it not been for his impenetrable armour and his desperate need to protect...

That source of strength was gone now, taken from him. Where Li'ara had provided him with a reason to always try harder and give nothing but his best, he was now only left with a shell. His strength would now come from a sense of uncaring and lack of fear. He had become a man with nothing to lose.

"Has there been any word about the Gomar?" Kalian was confident that his question went unheard by the busy crew.

"I take it you're referring to those taken from the *Gommarian*?" ALF clarified.

"I thought your IQ was incalculable?" Kalian quipped, irritated with ALF's ignorance.

The AI was more than aware that he was referring to the eleven Gomar, who had been put to sleep in the Rem-Stores shortly after Savrick had been killed on Naveen. At first, Kalian had wanted to jettison them all into the nearest star and be done with the killers, but Esabelle had tempered his anger towards them. She had pointed out that they may be of use further down the line when the real threat was uncovered. He had never really agreed with her, but now that she was gone, Kalian felt quite alone in the galaxy, and the Gomar was all that was left like him.

Any plans to use the Gomar had been scuttled, however, when High Charge Uthor took control of the *Gommarian* and had them sent who knows where. The Highclave hadn't been too happy to discover the existence of the surviving Gomar. It was secrets like that which frayed the relationship between the Conclave and humanity, preventing them from being granted membership and a planet of their own.

"I have asked Charge Ilo but she is forbidden from divulging classified information, as expected. In truth, I don't think she actually knows. I doubt there are many beyond the Highclave who know where they're being kept. At least we know they haven't woken them from their Rem-stores yet."

"How do we know that?" Kalian inquired.

"If eleven Gomar had been woken up, the Conclave would be in ruins by now..."

Kalian was inclined to agree. The eleven Gomar survivors that Esabelle had put to sleep, before disconnecting from the *Gommarian*, had lived through the Terran war and were veteran fighters. Their exo-suits allowed them to counteract the Harnesses that kept their Terran abilities in check and grant them a level of control. They would be capable of feats Kalian could only dream of.

Out of the corner of his eye, Kalian caught sight of a Laronian and a Ch'kara staring at him. The two had stopped working on the individual jobs and stood together, watching him as he walked by. Their

Novaarian superior officer gave them both a nudge and directed them back to work, before glancing at Kalian as well. At first, the attention he gained wherever he went had been strange, having lived most of his life as a history lecturer, but now he barely took notice.

The hangar bay was unusually empty when he arrived. The rows of smaller fighter ships were unaccompanied by their engineers and mechs. Resting in the middle of the two rows, and taking up most of the space, was a black ship equipped with four chunky engines on the back and a cuboidal front nose where the bridge was located. The ship's name, *Advent*, was written on the side in white lettering.

"I take it the name was your idea?" Kalian mused out loud.

"It means origin..." ALF replied smugly. "I thought it fitting, given our destination. It's a hybrid human/Conclave design. They used what they learned from the remains of the Fathom to manufacture a Solar Drive that can store energised intrinium. It should have at least one jump in it before a sunspot is required."

Kalian didn't much care; the ship was a means to an end. He just wanted to board the *Advent* right away, but he knew it wouldn't be that simple. Charge Ilo emerged from behind the ship with a small entourage of her own. The Laronain captain dismissed the guards that had followed Kalian from his quarters, with the flick of her blue head.

"Mr. Gaines..." Ilo bowed her head in respect. "The *Advent* is prepped and ready for launch. I've pulled back all the crew working on the Starforge; we can control it remotely from the *Sentinel*."

Kalian managed a smile for the Laronian. "Thank you for allowing me to stay aboard your ship for so long. You have an excellent crew."

Ilo's beautiful, diamond-like scales glistened as she took the compliment. Kalian regretted now all the times he had turned her invitation down to dine with the Charge and her senior officers. He hadn't shown Ilo the same level of respect she had shown him.

"The Highclave wish to speak with you before your departure," Charge Ilo added.

Kalian appeared confused. He expanded his awareness beyond

the *Sentinel* and searched for the golden hull of the *Marillion*, the Highclave's personal ship. As expected, there was nothing but the emptiness of space, leading to his quizzical expression.

Ilo explained, "We are setting up a link to the capital; it should be ready momentarily. In the meantime, I have someone who would like to wish you well..."

Kalian turned around, annoyed with himself for having missed the presence. Perhaps he was becoming too closed off. He didn't examine the thoughts any further and instead held out his right hand to greet a friend.

"Greetings of peace, Telarrek." Kalian clasped the ambassador's forearm, truly happy to see his old friend.

"Greetings of peace, Kalian." Telarrek looked down at Kalian with a Novaarian smile.

Another Novaarian hand gripped Kalian's shoulder when Naydaalan appeared at his father's side. The affectation was very human and certainly not natural for his species. Along with his father, Naydaalan had been spending a lot of time with the humans in their new habitat. Clearly, they were starting to rub off on the younger Novaarian.

"Good to see you again Naydaalan," Kalian offered with a half smile.

"Your presence has been missed by your people," Telarrek said. "Many ask for you daily."

"I bet the council doesn't..." Kalian had never got on with any of the elected councillors, especially Laurence Wynter.

"Captain Fey keeps them in check, often reminding them of your accomplishments and... sacrifices." Telarrek added with a sombre expression, shared by Naydaalan - who had become quite attached to Li'ara.

"How goes the appeal for membership?" Kalian was happy to change the subject.

Telarrek appeared disgruntled. "The Highclave will not entertain the idea at present. Until a permanent decision can be made, the habitat above Arakesh will have to suffice. But fear not, your people will not be left to starve. Their provisions are being taken care of."

"Thank you Telarrek, you're a good ambassador." Kalian wanted to say more but he hadn't the energy to. He just wanted to board the *Advent* and leave. "You both didn't have to come all the way out here to see me off. We're not exactly on the beaten path." Kalian had seen their location on a star chart and knew the Starforge had been built on the far reaches of Conclave space.

Telarrek and Naydaalan looked at each other before Charge Ilo interrupted. "The Highclave is ready."

One of Ilo's entourage, a male Shay, stepped forward and presented five metallic spheres. The cyborg activated each of the spheres inside the case with its half organic, half robotic hand and watched as they floated into the air. The spheres projected a near perfect rendering of the Highclave in their various sizes - the holograms appeared solid and in colour, despite only being generated from light. The five alien councillors formed a neat line by the side of the gathered group.

"Greetings..." The Novaarian councillor, Elondrasa, often spoke on behalf of the Highclave.

The Novaarian representative appeared in her usual regal form, with a golden headdress and flowing red and purple robes. The translucent dreadlock tendrils that ran down her long back were bound in gold rings.

"Councillors." Kalian bowed his head in respect. These five individuals were the only thing standing between humanity and a new home.

Elondrasa continued, "We hope your time aboard the *Sentinel* has been resting, Kalian. What you face next holds unknown challenges..."

Ch'lac, the small councillor from Ch'ket, was quick to add, "The chief of which will be finding a way back to the Conclave and reporting your findings!"

ALF appeared right on cue, his holographic form projected from Kalian's armour, along the waist. "As I told you when we first agreed on this plan of action," the AI explained, "there are numerous Star-forges in Terran space. I can reactivate one at will and plot a course back to this very quadrant."

Nu-marn, the Shay councillor, lifted his cybernetic arms in dismay. "According to you, those Starforges have been dormant for two-hundred thousand years. What if they are no longer operational? The knowledge you learn from the remains of the Terran Empire may be vital to uncovering the machinations of this... Malekk."

ALF replied with a look of condescension. "I build things to last. Time is of no concern to my creations. After we find the answers we seek, I will activate a Starforge and we will return."

"Perhaps then you can return and help us to further understand the nanocelium..." Lordina, the blue Laronian, flashed them all her sparkling white teeth.

Kalian looked at ALF's image, studying the AI's expression for a moment - not that it counted for anything, being a hologram. Kalian hadn't been aware that any tests were being conducted around nanocelium, but then again, he hadn't been paying attention to much for the last three months.

As if reading his mind again, ALF's voice echoed inside his mind. "They are in possession of several tons after I was forced to eject the Conclave crew that remained aboard the *Gommarian*."

Lordina's left eye arched in a quizzical expression, unsure as to the lack of reply. "You had a hand in designing the nanocelium did you not?"

"I repurposed them," ALF's hologram replied. "The Terran invented nanocelium and I simply took control. They stopped being a weapon and started improving everyone's quality of life."

"It would be a major contribution to the Conclave on behalf of the humans," Lordina replied, seductively. "It would go a long way to building trust among our people..."

"Are the Starforges not enough?" Kalian couldn't help himself. "You've just been handed over a piece of technology that will reshape the Conclave." His anger was quick to rise these days.

Nu-marn raised his pale elongated head and fixed his robotic eyes on Kalian. "After all the chaos your people have brought to our homes... the Starforge technology is the only thing that has stopped us from exiling your race into the cold of space."

Brokk's gravelly voice spoke out, "Nu-marn..." It was all that was needed to calm the Shay councillor.

"It cannot be done," ALF announced, silencing any further argument. "The nanocelium you possess came from the *Gommarian* and was manufactured in the Terran Empire, specifically, inside the Criterion, where my hardware was housed. The nanocelium was programmed from there to respond to Terran DNA only. I cannot change the base programming without a nanocelium factory, and the only one in the galaxy is inside the Criterion. Before Savrick died, he told of how he destroyed my original housing."

Brokk responded, "But we have seen it work on humans. After Professor Garrett Jones attacked Captain Fey's crew, the nanocelium was used to heal them."

"Human DNA is so close to their predecessors that the nanocelium cannot tell the difference anymore. They are certainly more limited in terms of its manipulation, but simple constructs and medicinal techniques are compatible." ALF's expression was impossible to read.

Kalian just didn't trust him anymore. The connection between Malekk, the cubes and the Terran is nanocelium, and as ALF just pointed out, only he can alter its design.

"Perhaps you will learn more during your time there." Elondrasa's calming voice cut through the rising tension. "But your priority is to learn more of this external threat, we can discuss everything else upon your return." The Novaarian councillor looked beyond Kalian. "Are you ready Naydaalan?"

Kalian whipped his head around to look at Telarrek and his son, with no lack of confusion displayed across his face.

"I am, Councillor," Naydaalan replied with a bow.

"What are you talking about?" Kalian asked, frantically.

Ch'lac appeared to adjust the holographic dial around his chest plate, altering the shield and the methane gas that surround his head.

"Your mission is too important to be left to you alone. A representative from the Conclave will go with you to ensure... transparency."

"You mean you don't trust me." Kalian balled his right fist but managed to stop his personal electromagnetic aura from disrupting the *Sentinel's* systems.

"Not just you..." Lordina glanced at ALF.

Kalian clamped his jaw shut, aware that he had nothing helpful to say.

ALF placed his hands inside his gaping sleeves. "I trust that while we search for answers beyond your territory, you will continue to search for answers a little closer to home."

As Brokk shifted his considerable bulk, the holographic emitters transmitted the sound of grinding stone. "We have already located and arrested three members of the Protocorps board members. Though to date, they have been quite uncooperative. Gor-van Tanar and Kel-var Tionis remain at large. They each held considerable holdings and an unknown amount of wealth. Finding them will be harder, but we have tasked multiple organisations with the job."

Nu-marn, a fellow Shay, appeared agitated throughout Brokk's speech. It hadn't escaped Kalian that the Councillor's previous campaigns for office had been funded in part by Protocorps.

As one, all five Highclave members looked to their right, clearly seeing something on their end.

"We have other matters to attend," Elondrasa commented. "We wish you both luck in your endeavours and a speedy return."

"With answers..." Ch'lac added.

The spherical emitters shut down and floated back to the Shay crewman, like pets returning to their master.

Kalian turned on Naydaalan. "I don't know what's on the other side of that forge, but I can bet it isn't going to be anything good, and it certainly won't be anything the Conclave have seen before. It's too dangerous."

Naydaalan puffed out his narrow chest and looked down on Kalian. "Though considerably younger than my father, I have been training for missions like this since before you were born."

Kalian didn't have a response. He often forgot how old the Novaarians were and in truth, he had no idea how old Naydaalan was. Instead, Kalian looked to Telarrek for support. Surely he wouldn't want his son to go on this mission?

"The Highclave has spoken," the Ambassador replied. "Naydaalan is more than capable."

Kalian studied Telarrek's expression and doubted the Novaarian's convictions. It was clear to see that he feared for his son's life.

Another life on his shoulders. More responsibility. Kalian had wanted to go through the Starforge to avoid scenarios like this one.

"Fine. But I'm in charge." Kalian locked eyes with Naydaalan.

The Novaarian warrior nodded his agreement.

"Mr. Gaines." Charge Ilo walked over. "The *Advent* is ready. As requested..." Ilo hesitated. "Esabelle's body has been stored in the ship's cargo bay."

The mention of her name deflated him. He had watched Malekk take her life as if it were nothing. Esabelle had lived for two-hundred thousand years inside the *Gommarian's* virtual reality. Her wisdom and experience couldn't be found anywhere else in the galaxy.

"What is the purpose of this?" Naydaalan asked, genuinely curious.

"It's an ancient Terran tradition," Kalian explained. "Death was rare before the civil war, but if anyone died they were given back to the star that birthed them. Esabelle was born on Albadar, the Terran capital. I'm going to give her back to the sun..."

After a brief farewell to Telarrek and Charge Ilo, Kalian and Naydaalan entered the *Advent's* bridge and familiarised themselves with the controls. It was a spacious vessel, able to accommodate a crew of twelve at least. The Conclave engineers had retrofitted the interior to be comfortable for human and Novaarian, along with a considerable amount of food supplies. Due to its size, the *Advent* couldn't house a shield generator or stealthware technology, so when they arrived in Terran space it wouldn't be a quiet entry.

ALF looked over the controls with a critical eye. "If you connect me to the ship's mainframe I can take command."

"You already know the answer to that," Kalian replied dryly, as his hand rested against the bulkhead. He didn't need to run through the various controls as Naydaalan did, but instead expand his awareness to feel every inch of the *Advent*. Now the ship held no secrets.

Naydaalan expanded on Kalian's comment, "Charge Ilo was quite specific regarding your freedom, ALF. Until we enter the Starforge, you are to remain inside Kalian's exo-suit."

"Hmph..." ALF turned away.

Kalian had been given the same orders three months ago when he first arrived aboard the *Sentinel*. The Highclave didn't want ALF in any way connected to the ship's systems, ensuring his isolation and the safety of their own network, especially after the chaos caused by the destruction of their core AI, even if it had been a cube.

Naydaalan settled into his seat, to the right of the viewport. An array of holograms, predominantly orange, came to life around him, presenting the Novaarian with multiple readouts. All four of his toned arms moved in different directions as if he possessed tentacles.

"The drive is coming online now," Naydaalan reported. "The *Sentinel's* Starrillium has been used to charge the intrinium, so when we reach Terran space, should we need to, the *Advent* can make a sub-space jump. After that, we will have to find a local star and recharge the cells."

"Sounds great," Kalian said with little sentiment. "Take us out."

Relaxing into his human chair, to the left of the viewport, Kalian watched as the *Advent* lifted silently from the hangar bay floor and pivoted towards the rectangular port, where a fine force-field separated them from space. Telarrek remained fixed in place, observing their departure with a stony expression. Kalian nodded at the Novaarian, understanding his trepidation. The ship slipped through the shields and pivoted once more to glide over the shining green hull of the *Sentinel*.

Kalian could feel the constant flow of anger, bubbling just under the surface. ALF had reminded him time and again that most of that anger stemmed from the part of Savrick that was forever trapped inside his mind. After Savrick had invaded his thoughts on Naveen,

Kalian had failed to remove the echo that stained so many of his emotions. He had often looked at Esabelle and had paternal feelings towards her, as Savrick once had. Of course, Savrick wasn't the only echo inside his head. Kalian could still feel Li'ara's imprint firmly inside his psyche. After saving her from a certain death, when the *Helion* had been plummeting towards Naveen, Kalian had ignored ALF's warnings and entered Li'ara's mind to trigger and enhance her own immune system.

With a long, hard blink, Kalian shut down his chain of thought and collated everything he could find inside his mind, concerning Li'ara, and locked it away. His mind was more akin to a computer after Esabelle's teachings, allowing Kalian to sift through his brain's maze-like network and make adjustments.

When he opened his eyes again, the *Advent* was breaking free of the *Sentinel's* green bulk and heading towards the distant moon. Naydaalan dragged his long finger down the hologram to his left, increasing the thrust from the engines. The Starforge began to take shape in front of the viewport almost immediately. The structure's crescent moon-shape quickly changed from the size of Kalian's hand to that of a modest starship.

"I input the coordinates myself." ALF was standing between Kalian and Naydaalan. "We will arrive three-hundred thousand kilometres from Albadar's surface."

In the silence of space, the Starforge became visibly active. Previously unseen lights flickered across the two arching limbs until they reached the pointed ends that didn't quite meet. The two points exploded with electrical energy, firing purple lightning at each other. In the blink of an eye, the lightning erupted along the inside of the crescent limbs, building with more and more energy. Within a few seconds, the lightning grew in size and converged on the empty centre. The massing energy expanded with a flash of light when the event horizon was created and the universe's natural laws broken. The lightning continued to race around the circumference, jumping between the two points, however, the centre of the Starforge was simply black, a dark spot against the starry backdrop.

"Is it going to hurt?" Naydaalan became very still in his seat.

ALF didn't take his holographic eyes off the Starforge, admiring his work. "No. My designs were specific, not just to the Starforge but also the *Advent*. The hull has been polarized. It wouldn't have been my first choice but your shield technology is too primitive to be fitted into a ship this small. Another enhancement I shall have to tackle upon our return..."

"Naydaalan." Kalian waited for the Novaarian's attention before looking to the flashing comm panel.

The *Sentinel* was giving them permission to enter the Starforge. The *Advent's* thrusters were engaged to maximum yield, pushing it through the centre of the crescent station. The stars disappeared, followed by the surrounding limbs until only darkness lay ahead.

ALF smiled as the abyss engulfed them. "Time to go home..."

TWO

The light of two suns beat down on the arid surface of Vosk, heating up the desert planet to a temperature that couldn't support plant life. The world was barren from pole to pole, with nothing except mountains to bottomless gorges to offset the flat terrain.

The cube-mind opened its eyes, having closed them before the suns rose. He sat with his legs crossed on the hard, sand-coloured ground. Meditation was new to him, a practice of his host's, the Terran. The realisation forced the cube-mind to its feet in a rage, an emotion that manifested itself in the form of an explosive wave of telekinesis. The ground cracked open and a cloud of sand was thrown into the air. The cube-mind balled its fists and screamed.

As Professor Garrett Jones had slowly infected his parasitic master, so too was Malekk infecting the cube-mind. The host was strong, being a Terran, but the cube that had taken control of Professor Jones had been broken since even before it poisoned Savrick's mind. The cube-mind that now possessed Malekk had been whole and perfect when it took control. But still, the Terran fought back. Their consciousnesses were beginning to merge like two storms colliding together to form a new and different storm. An abomination.

This is why their kind must be destroyed...

With that bubbling anger, the cube-mind descended into the darkest depths of Malekk's head and confronted the caged Terran. Naked and alone, the Terran stood in ankle deep water that appeared to go on forever. The cube-mind had placed Malekk in a prison inside his own brain, but somehow the bipedal disease continued to infect the body.

"What are you?" Malekk asked, looking into the shadows for the cube's skulking, hidden form.

The cube-mind could feel the Terran puncturing the cage and searching through its memories of eons past. The cube made attempts to shut the intrusion out but found Malekk's probing reach to be out of its control. Over the last three months, the Terran's awareness had become brighter, until he was as the cube saw him now, fully conscious and aware of his imprisoned existence.

The first two months had been spent aboard the small craft that the cube had used to escape the fiery inferno of the Starforge. The small vessel had nothing but thruster capability, extending the journey to Vosk by two months. It was a fraction of time for the cube-mind however, who had lived underground on Trantax IV for thousands of years, waiting. For the last month, the cube had taken the time to try and master the Terran abilities that Malekk possessed. Despite being a disease that required eradicating, the Terran were deeply powerful beings. It was a shame they were toxic, otherwise, they would have made an invaluable addition.

"WHAT ARE YOU?" Malekk screamed into the ether.

The Terran whipped his head around in an attempt to lay eyes on the ever-moving consciousness of the cube-mind. Malekk dropped to one knee and pressed his fists into the water. The cube could feel him trying to relinquish control of his motor functions again, as he had tried to do for several days now.

That will not work...

Malekk stood up and frantically searched the abyss-like surroundings. The cube's mind had come from every direction, tormenting the Terran.

"What are you?"

You have seen what we are.

The cube-mind knew everything Malekk had scoured through in its memories. Perhaps that was what frightened him so much.

"You are a plague!" Malekk spat.

Ironic, coming from one of your kind. In all the universe there is no greater disease than you.

"I will take back control! If a human can do it then I can." Malekk appeared ready for a fight.

Foolish biped... the fight had already been won.

You have seen and heard all that I have, yes? Then you know that your entire civilization was brought to its knees by a fraction of our being. With mere suggestions, one such as I created a war that tore the Terran apart from the inside. You are wholly mine.

The cube-mind relished the scorned expression upon the Terran's face. As Malekk had looked into its memories, so too had the cube looked into his. Malekk of Crychek had been a Gomar sympathiser, turning on his own people to help Savrick, a hero in Malekk's eyes. It must sting to know that every action of his hero had been guided by a fellow cube-mind.

"You will pay for what you have done to my people!"

Your people are already forgotten. We look to the Conclave now. Their civilisation will sustain us, and those few who remain of your kind will perish with them, ending the threat.

Malekk smiled arrogantly. "You know what? You're right, we are a disease. But do you know what diseases are good at? Adapting. You keep pushing back and we keep on surviving. *Kalian Gaines* keeps on surviving."

The cube had heard enough. The fact that it had descended to this level to merely converse was just more proof that the Terran was indeed infecting the nanocelium. Time was running out.

Adapt to this...

The shadows behind Malekk exploded with sound, as something massive awoke in the dark. The Terran stumbled back in the shallow water, away from the crashing sound. The noise grew and grew until it was louder than Malekk's voice. The cube-mind ascended through the layers of the Terran brain, leaving Malekk to be swept away in a tsunami of water. Perhaps it would slow down the rate of infection for a while. The cube wasn't hopeful.

Back on the surface of Vosk, the cube-mind examined its new and unusual body, as it so regularly did. The Terran's pale skin was interlaced with strands of dark nanocelium that ripped through the flesh like worms. The armour it wore was the same Malekk had been buried in when the crew of the *Tempest* abandoned him, two-hundred thousand years ago. The white armour was now covered in dirt and ash with a few streaks of red blood. The cube knew it belonged to Esabelle and Kalian, as its host no longer possessed blood after the nanocelium infected him.

A familiar presence tugged at its attention. Another part of the Vanguard, a part of itself, was close by. Looking up at the pale blue sky, the Starforge was easy to see, resting just above the planet's thin atmosphere. It was one of four that Protocorps had been tasked with constructing by the 'AI' centuries ago, though Kalian had seen to the destruction of one already.

But it wasn't the Starforge that the cube-mind had detected since the super-structure had been above Vosk for centuries under construction. The cube-mind used its host's Terran abilities to sharpen the body's eyes and focus on the faint dot that streaked across the sky. Spinning end-over-end was a cube identical to the one which had housed its own mind.

"Finally..." It remarked. The comment in itself was unusual, as no words were required. Speaking out loud with no else present was an entirely redundant use of time.

I am truly infected.

The cube strained the host's neck, as it felt Malekk's presence just under the surface. The Terran had already recovered and begun his assault anew.

Before leaving for the Starforge, the cube decided to test some of its new limits. If it was going to be stuck inside a bag of organic waste it might as well make use of the advantages. Concentrating on the mountains in the distance, the cube extended the host's hand and flexed the five digits. Telekinesis was a truly wonderful gift, wasted on the Terran. Too far to be heard, the cube could only watch as the mountains slowly crumbled and imploded, before exploding as if a volcano had been unleashed on the land. Moments later, the ground under the host's feet trembled and cracked.

The cube twisted Malekk's mouth into an insidious smile. "Kalian Gaines will not survive this time..."

Malekk's body fell into a crouch and launched into the sky. The surface of Vosk dropped away as the cub ascended ever upwards, using telekinesis to fly through the atmosphere. With no need of oxygen, the cube-mind continued at an incredible speed, breaking through the planet's paper-thin halo with the faintest of afterburns. With nothing but space in front of it now, Malekk's body headed towards the modest hangar bay inside the Starforge.

A small task force, armed with intrinium rifles, was waiting for him. They were all on the Protocorps payroll and Shay in origin. Most of them looked upon Malekk's corrupted form as if he were a god. His combination of organic and machine was a level the Shay had dreamed of since they invented the wheel.

Sitting a few feet above the hangar floor, the icy cold cube remained apparently dormant, surrounded by the Shay. Malekk's hand was forced to caress the side of the cube like an old friend. The host's strength was used to push the cube along, deep into the heart of the Starforge where it could be integrated into the mainframe. Only a powerful AI could manage the mathematics required to activate the Starforge's systems.

As this cube was being inserted into the mainframe, so too were the other two cubes that had been travelling through space for the last three months. The Vanguard had released them, allowing them to slip through the Helteron Starforge, shortly after it had been used to disintegrate the *Gommarian*.

"Your orders, sir?" A Shay, who's uniform identified him as the commander, stood beside Malekk.

The cube-mind despised having to communicate with insects.

"The operation of this station is no longer your concern. Instruct the teams on the other stations to direct the cubes as I have. Your soldiers are to remain aboard and protect them with their lives."

"We await ascension!" The Shay genuflected and bowed his head as if kneeling before a deity.

Malekk's face broke into a scowl, disgusted. "Indeed..." The cube-mind walked away, contemplating the Conclave's *ascension*.

THREE

"I have eyes on the target," Roland whispered under his breath.

To the other patrons sat in the dingy bar, the bounty hunter appeared as any other Laronian, with holo-bracers around his neck and wrists. The illusion could only be shattered if someone touched him and realised his skin wasn't as smooth as the blue aliens.

Roland couldn't help but roll his eyes at the lack of response in his earpiece. "Len put the goddamn snacks down and concentrate, or I swear the next time I set foot on the *Rackham* I'm gonna stick my boot right up your—"

"I'm here!" Ch'len quickly replied through a half-eaten mouthful of grub.

"Get your head in the game." Roland sat hunched over the bar, blending in with the other detritus, while keeping a close eye on his target.

"You're oddly focused for a small-time bounty like Lan-vid..." Ch'len sounded suspicious. "Are you sober?" the alien asked with disbelief and a hint of fear.

Roland rarely worked without being under the influence.

"Payday's a payday," he quipped.

"I don't get it," Ch'len continued, "the bounty is only valid if Lan-vid is dead. Why can't you just walk over there, put an intrinium round in his head and get back to the ship? We've done a dozen jobs like this!"

Roland turned away from the dimly-lit bar, as his constant talking had attracted a few curious looks. "Maybe if you stopped filling your methane-clouded mouth with food for two seconds you would have heard my plan. We're on Sebula, security here is a little tighter than the planets we usually hunt on."

Ch'len blurted, "Then why are we hunting some two-bit low-life on the Tularon homeworld when we could be hunting bigger bounties on planets with less security?"

Roland sighed. "Planetary security aside, this particular bar is packed out with an unknown amount of enemy allies, and the only thing I'm certain of is that everyone here is armed. If I walk over there and kill him I'm gonna have to fight every low-life in this place."

There was a pause on Ch'len's end. "You *are* sober!"

"Just monitor the network." Roland turned back to the Shay, who was losing badly in a card game the bounty hunter didn't fully understand.

Ch'len audibly stuffed more food into his mouth. "I know what happened on the capital planet was some pretty bad shit, but it's made you soft like that pink stuff you call skin."

The nerve struck, Roland tapped his earpiece, silencing the Ch'kara, and pulled his collar a little higher. The animal-hide coat fell to the floor, concealing the Tri-rollers on his thighs, as well as the arsenal of other weapons he had strapped to various body parts.

Using the built-in touchpad on the sleeve of his coat, Roland checked the temperature outside. It was several degrees below freezing, warm for the native Tularons. Their natural furry coat kept them warm on a planet that had frozen over thousands of years ago. After joining the Conclave, their cities had been redesigned to allow aliens, who weren't accustomed to the low temperatures, to move about freely without going outside.

To avoid any extra attention, Roland had parked the *Rackham* on an outdoor landing pad, two hundred floors up. Nobody wanted to investigate a ship in these temperatures. It merely appeared as if they couldn't afford to park in the hangar bay.

"You don't look like you're here for just the drink..." A female Laronian took the stool beside Roland, eyeing the untouched glass in front of him.

A quick glance told the bounty hunter everything he needed to know. The alien was a prostitute, hunting for her own payday. To her, he would appear as one of her own but, in truth, Roland wasn't even sure if he could have sex with the alien. He had slept with a few of the crew, during his short time aboard the *Gommarian*, but that had been months ago before Esabelle had created the *Rackham* for him. A very primal part of him wanted to at least try and see what they could achieve together, if for nothing more than a little intimacy. The only interaction with other beings was primarily with Ch'len, a fact that was deeply upsetting for the bounty hunter.

The train of thought only led him to think about Esabelle and Li'ara. Esabelle's death rattled him, but uncovering the truth about Li'ara sharpened his mind.

"Not interested." Roland turned his back to her, only to see Lan-vid walking out the door.

The Shay looked over his shoulder and locked eyes with Roland in a level of understanding. Lan-vid knew he had been watching him and planned this escape from the beginning. The Shay's only mistake had been to assume that it was indeed a Laronian stalking him. The prostitute didn't quite hold the same appeal to Roland, a human.

"Son of a..."

Before Roland could dash from his stool, the Laronian prostitute grabbed his arm and the back of his neck, catching the holo-bracer. The bounty hunter's momentum detached him from the illusion and revealed his true identity. Even to a bar filled with twelve different races, Roland looked more alien than any of them, a fact that was mirrored in everyone's expression. The prostitute backed away, unsure of what she had gotten herself into.

Hands of all varieties slowly reached for weapons, while the patrons decided whether they needed to fight or run away from the human. As a species, they were still widely considered dangerous and unpredictable - having brought nothing but destruction and death to the Conclave in the short time they had been there. No one truly knew what they were capable of, having all seen what Kalian and Esabelle could do on the news feeds.

Looking around, with eyes that had been trained to assess every environment for threats and opportunities, Roland clocked the seven individuals who he knew wouldn't go down easy, as well as a rather mean-looking Raalak in the corner booth, who looked as if he didn't need a weapon to kill Roland.

The bounty hunter slowly lifted his hand and tapped the earpiece. "Is the *Rackham* connected to the grid in this tower?" His words were hushed under his breath.

"Oh, now you want to talk to me!"

"Len..." Roland didn't have time to argue.

"Of course it is. How do you think I'm monitoring everything? Speaking of; Lan-vid is escaping."

Roland blinked slowly in frustration. "Is he?" he replied, sarcastically.

A pink-skinned Atari to his left had completely removed the handgun from its holster on her waist. Time was running out.

"You want me to hit the lights?" Ch'len asked, casually.

The *Rackham* was the most sophisticated ship in the galaxy now that the *Gommarian* had been destroyed. The nanocelium that made up the bounty hunter's vessel was more than capable of hacking into every Conclave system and network. After the ship landed on the outdoor pad, slithers of the nanocelium had wormed their way down the struts and into the panel built into the pad. Thanks to Ch'len's agoraphobia and technical genius, he was more than happy to stay onboard and manage these little incursions.

Roland smiled with wicked glee, thankful for the little alien for once. "Let's skip to the good bit..."

The bar dropped into darkness, generating panic and chaos. Alien voices broke out in alarm when dozens of people ran for cover and tried to find the door. Intrinium rounds filled the bar with the smell of ozone and flashes of blue and red, creating a disjointed moving image of the scattering patrons. Glasses smashed in every corner of the room and the wall of bottles behind the bar exploded under the barrage of pot-shots.

Roland got off two shots before he ducked and dropped into a roll, avoiding the super-heated intrinium that streaked over his head. A lightning flash revealed a tall Novaarian taking a round to the chest and falling at Roland's feet, dead. Having memorised the layout of the bar and the distance between him and the exit, Roland weaved between the scurrying aliens, pushing most aside, and dashed for the door, firing as he did.

As the bounty hunter reached the door, a Brenine levelled his handgun at Roland's chest. The pale skinned Brenine had uncanny night vision, being a species that avoided the sun. The blast couldn't be avoided at such close range, forcing Roland to jump into the shooter, taking them both through the door as the intrinium round connected with his chest. They both landed in a heap on the indoor street, the Brenine's weapon now lost. Roland slowly rolled off the alien and took a deep breath to steady his breathing. The black and gold plated armour, made from myopallic ore, had stopped the intrinium from tearing through his torso, but the impact had still hurt.

The Brenine was the first to recover and retrieve his weapon. Still on his back and feigning severe injury, Roland used the cover of his long coat to hide the fact that one of his Tri-rollers was now in his hand. With a shift of his knee to the right, Roland fired one shot into the Brenine's face, dissolving any organic tissue in an explosive flash of light.

This particular neighbourhood was relatively abandoned at this time of night, but those few who witnessed the slaying ran for their lives, fleeing the nightmarish human. The bar was still a cacophony of intrinium fire and brawling; none the wiser to Roland's escape.

"He's still getting away..." Ch'len's voice rang irritatingly in his ear.

"You're lucky those stubby little fingers know their way around a computer." Roland got to his feet and holstered his Tri-roller.

"Hey, without me you wouldn't even be able to eat," Ch'len countered.

Annoyingly he was right. Roland was more than aware that without Ch'len, he couldn't collect bounties. The smelly little Ch'kara was the only one of the two who could be an active member of the Bounty Clave since Roland was an illegal immigrant wherever he went.

"I barely get to eat with you, you fat shit..." Roland ran down the street, looking for the nearest dark alley to hide his human face. "Where's Lan-vid now?"

"Hold on." Ch'len paused. "Alright, I've found the quickest route but... you're gonna get cold."

Roland looked up at the glass ceiling that ran the length of the street. The snow was getting heavier, but the view didn't show the strength of the gales blowing outside. Cold was an understatement.

After being navigated through the outer corridors of the tower complex and destroying several locks, Roland finally found himself on the surface of Sebula. How any life form had evolved on such a barren planet baffled the bounty hunter, let alone evolve to the point of inventing faster-than-light travel. A peach-coloured sky tried to pierce the thick clouds that rained snow across the land and the mountains in the distance were almost completely without shape. From the balcony, Roland could see the other towers that made up the massive city. It lacked the aesthetics that most Conclave cities enjoyed, more akin to a collection of fingers, rising from the snowy ground, circled by hundreds of buzzing vehicles.

"You need to hurry if you're going to get in front of him," Ch'len warned.

Roland could only growl in response as he fought against the bitter wind. After ascending two sets of ladders, the bounty hunter was standing on top of the bridge that connected one tower to the next. The bridge itself was filled with shopping centres and apartments and was nearly fifty levels deep. Roland broke into a sprint along the edge of the glass covering that ran the length of the strip. The heat from inside helped to melt the ice and snow, allowing for a clear view of the streets below. The two sides of the interior bridge were connected by multiple walkways at varying angles. It looked like a maze inside.

"WHERE IS HE?" Roland shouted over the wind.

"He's..." Ch'len paused. "Ooo! He's coming up on the top tier, right beneath you!"

Roland looked down and saw Lan-vid on the other side of the bridge, walking quickly along the upper tier. The Shay kept peering over his shoulder, making certain he wasn't being followed by the bounty hunter. With another growl, Roland changed direction and sprinted across the glass, diagonally. Lan-vid must have heard his footsteps on the glass, because the Shay ran for it, knocking the occasional late night wanderer out of the way.

"There's an access hatch coming up on your right!" Ch'len advised.

"NO TIME!" Roland pulled his left Tri-roller from its holster.

The moment he felt his foot pass the threshold of the tier below, Roland fired a single shot into the glass panel under his feet. The glass panel shattered as the intrinium bolt continued on, into the floor, only feet in front of Lan-vid. Roland fell through the glass mid-run and dropped on top of the fleeing Shay in a shower of pointed shards. His weight brought the alien down, as well as cushioning his fall. The whole takedown was quite spectacular in Roland's eyes.

Picking himself up, so that his knees were either side of Lan-vid's back, Roland assessed the surroundings since the whole event had been exceptionally loud. The streets were illuminated by a rainbow of holograms that advertised a variety of alien goods and hangouts. A pair of teenage Tularons gawped at them from the other side of the street before running in terror. A Raalak in the distance looked to be using a small hand device to contact someone, the local authorities most likely.

A rough tug and a threatening Tri-roller to the head stopped Lan-vid from squirming, while the bounty hunter lifted him from the floor. Roland held him in place and waited a moment, allowing Lan-vid the time to get over the fact that he was face-to-face with a human.

Ch'len laughed in his ear. "Money money money! Alright Roland, put one in his head and scan the body. I've already found us a new bounty on Palios Six; if we leave now we can be there by tomorrow morning."

Roland had other ideas. With the Tri-roller planted in the Shay's back, the bounty hunter walked him to the nearest outdoor landing platform, using the access corridors for cover. The Shay pleaded for his life the whole way, offering Roland every treasure imaginable. At times like this, Roland had found that silence on his end was more menacing than verbal threats.

Using the intricate webbing, integrated into his cerebrum, Roland activated the *Rackham*'s thrusters and mentally commanded it to meet him at the new landing platform. Ch'len questioned his every move until Roland finally tapped the earpiece, shutting him up. The bounty hunter only opened the door after his link informed him that the *Rackham* had landed.

"What are you doing?" Lan-vid tried to push away from the opening doors. "Do you know how cold it is out there? I'm from Shandar! I don't have a single hair on my body! I wasn't built for this..."

Roland shoved him through the opening doors with a satisfied smirk on his face. It was indeed cold on the other side, but at least he was wearing his hide coat; Lan-vid's suit was paper-thin.

The *Rackham*'s bay door tilted downwards until it became a ramp that led into the belly of the ship. Roland continued to jostle the Shay, but kept him in the freezing bay, waiting for the ramp to close up behind them. A quick slap with the butt of his Tri-roller put Lan-vid on the floor, giving Roland time to make the adjustments he had in mind. With the comm panel on the wall, the bounty hunter typed in a new set of commands for the nanocelium, which made up every molecule of the ship. When he was finished, the ceiling changed shape, allowing for extra nanocelium to mold into a set of manacles. The temperature was also set to rise to levels that most sentient beings would find very uncomfortable.

"What are you *doing*?" Ch'len's irritated voice came ahead of his waddling body.

The Ch'kara appeared as he always did; with several layers of food around his mouth, a combination of snacks and tools hanging from his belts and a chest piece that wrapped around his neck, generating the constant cloud of methane around his head. The apparatus on his back functioned as a shield generator, though it was only strong enough to keep the toxic gases in, unlike his arse, which was more than happy to let everything out, much to Roland's displeasure.

Roland ignored the Ch'kara and continued to pick Lan-vid up. The manacles fitted perfectly around his slender wrists - one organic and one mechanical - but the nanocelium could alter its size at any given time, should the sneaky alien attempt escape.

Lan-vid spit oily, alien blood on the floor and wriggled in his manacles, testing their durability. Roland didn't give him much attention, however, confident in the strength of the nanocelium. Instead, the bounty hunter tapped a holographic panel set against the wall and activated the drawers inside, hiding numerous tools. For the most part, they were used to tinker with his gear or the ship, but today, Roland had other ideas in mind for them.

"Why isn't he dead?" Ch'len waved at the prisoner. "Bounty says dead. He's useless to us alive!" The Ch'kara eyed the Shay suspiciously, his little eyes darting between Lan-vid and Roland. "Has this got something to do with that *female*? I went along with some of your craziness after the mayhem at Protocorps, you know, get it out of your system or whatever. But we made no money for over a month and you said you were done hunting what's-his-name..."

"Kel-var Tionis." Roland watched Lan-vid's face drop at the sound of the name.

"Are you telling me that we've gone back to that shit?" Ch'len was becoming irate.

"We never stopped." Roland chose his first implement. "I just didn't want you pecking my goddamn head in for a while."

Ch'len's face froze in offence. "Is the bounty on him even *real*?"

"Oh, it's real alright. He's made a few enemies in his line of work. Haven't you Lanny?" Roland kicked the Shay in his feet.

Ch'len's tone took on a lighter note. "You're gonna go back to all this for *her*? She died Roland. We were both there. Li'ara's not coming—"

"Maybe you should go back to the bridge, Len," Roland interrupted. "Monitor for activity in the city. Once word gets out that a human has been spotted here, Sebula is going to be crawling with Conclave navy-types."

Ch'len dropped his head and sighed, before giving Lan-vid a lasting look of pity. "I'll be on the bridge..."

The bounty hunter could already feel himself slipping beneath layers of conditioning and training. He had to be detached for what came next, for what he had to become. At least that's what he told himself. Roland didn't like to think about the part of him that enjoyed what he did.

Standing in front of the terrified Shay, Roland examined a torturous-looking blowtorch. "Lanny, this is gonna feel a little... *weird*."

Kel-var Tionis sat in his private office, hidden under the desolate surface of his homeworld, Shandar. The rest of his kind lived in the floating super-structures that formed a net around the planet's atmosphere, as he once had. Those days were gone now, thanks to the humans...

The Shay appeared as composed and regal as he ever did, but inside Kel-var was starting to unravel. For three months he had been forced to hide from Conclave authorities, who wanted to question him about the alien cube found at Protocorps. For centuries his company had used the cube as the Conclave's central AI, granting them access to everything.

All for what? he often asked himself. On the Starforge in the Helteron Cluster, Kel-var had seen how they grant ascension. The

Terran, known as Malekk, had become something else, something twisted. Was that what awaited them all when the day finally came that his ancestors had been preparing for all this time?

You're just afraid, Kel-var told himself. He needed more faith, as his father and grandfather had. Ascending into something beyond the fragile organic sack to which he had been born into was all he had ever dreamed of, along with every other Shay. Kel-var looked up at his door, knowing that beyond it lay the control room to the Crucible, another ancient device created centuries ago, under the guidance of the cube.

Activating the Crucible would be the true test of his faith. After it was switched on there would be no going back. The Conclave would go to war, but Kel-var knew they would thank him in the end, after every species had witnessed their magnificence.

"Kel-var? Did you hear what I said?" Gor-van Tanar's voice carried from the speakers built into his desk.

The Protocorps board member floated above the surface of the table, five times smaller than his real size. As always he was shrouded in his red robes and shadowy hood. The two of them were the only ones still alive or free of the Conclave's security. Two board members were dead and the other three arrested. They would reveal nothing, however; their faith demanded it. Plans had already been set in motion by Gor-van to have the three of them poisoned in their cells.

"Kalian Gaines has entered the Starforge," Gor-van repeated. "He will be half a galaxy away by now, in the Terran Empire. With him out of the picture and the daughter of Savrick dead, the humans are without their defenders. We should activate the Crucible now."

"We only activate the Crucible when they instruct us to." Kel-var kept his tone even, keeping his insecurities to himself. "Malekk is seeing to the installation of the new cubes. All three Starforges will be operational soon." Kel-var wanted to change the subject. "Any news of the Gomar prisoners?"

"I am close to discovering the planet where they're being kept," Gor-van replied, his expression partially hidden and impossible to read. "High Charge Uthor has hidden them well."

"We are to inform Malekk as soon we know anything." Kel-var wasn't sure what the infected Terran would do with the information, but he knew the Gomar were a threat not to be taken lightly. Kel-var hesitated before asking his next question. "Has there been any progress with the bounty hunter?"

Memories of the human rogue still haunted the Shay's sleep. It was the closest he had ever come to death in his life of comfort and privilege. Roland North was proof that the human race was dangerous, regardless of whether they could move things with their mind. The bounty hunter was the reason Kel-var kept the lights on everywhere he went inside the Crucible's complex. Seeing him waiting, sitting in the dark in his apartment had been terrifying.

"Thanks to that Terran ship of his he's been hard to track down," Gor-van explained. "I may have found a way to trap him, however. I will know soon enough. Would you like to kill him yourself?" the Shay offered casually.

Kel-var thought about the prospect for a moment. "No. Just kill him... slowly."

CH'LEN GLANCED at the chronometer on his console and sighed, pressing his head back into the comfortable rest. It wasn't long after he had left the *Rackham*'s cargo bay that the screaming began. Using the controls, that lay spread out in a semicircle around him, the Ch'kara sealed all the doors between the bridge and the bay. Every now and then he would check the feed to see if Roland was still laying into the Shay. It wasn't easy to watch.

With a wave of his stubby fingers, the section of console to his right came to life. Holograms in green and blue rose out of the shiny surface and relayed information about the outside world, a place Ch'len was happy to stay away from. Local security had been alerted to the incident in the bar and multiple reports had been made concerning a human masquerading as a Laronian. Tapping into the secure servers, attached to the nearest branch of Sebula's planetary security, Ch'len examined where these reports were going and who was reading them.

The Ch'kara sat forward in his chair and stared in disbelief at the dispersal rate of the reports: from some snotty young Trillik in admin to High Charge Uthor, the top of the navy. It was possible that Uthor had delivered this news to the Highclave themselves, but Ch'len pulled back the probing nanocelium. Up to now, it had been undetected, but he didn't want to test the firewalls that surrounded the Highclaves's personal security.

Using the other side of the console, the Ch'kara pulled up a new set of holograms that had collated data from all the cameras in the city. Ch'len recognised a net when he saw one. The Sebula government appeared to have handed the matter over to Conclave security, who were now split into dozens of teams, each working their way through the city. It wouldn't be long before they started checking the outdoor landing platforms.

Pushing the hologram aside, the small alien expanded an image that had been two dimensional on the surface. It clearly showed the camera feed from their particular landing pad - with no ship on it. That would fool any techs looking for them, but not a physical team.

The thought of it all made him stressed. Without thinking about it, Ch'len reached for the snacks on the edge of the console and filled his mouth with sticky treats. With sticky fingers, he couldn't operate the console to inquire about his next thought.

"*Rackham...*" Ch'len waited for the seductive female voice to reply.

"Yes Ch'len?"

"Are you connected to the local AI hub?" Every word came through a mouthful of food.

"I am."

"Where's the nearest Conclave ship?" He was thinking ahead to what might be a tight escape.

After a moment's pause, the ship replied, "There is a Nebula Class vessel in the Heti system, currently en route to Sebula."

"ETA?"

"Three hours, give or take..."

Ch'len sighed at the ship's casual nature. Roland had given it too much attitude when creating its personality, not to mention changing all the features to human, forcing Ch'len to learn how humans kept time. A tap of his stubby finger brought up the feed to the Rackam's bay, where Roland was apparently branding Lan-vid's exposed torso.

"Damn it, Roland..." Ch'len swore under his breath.

Three human hours wasn't a lot of time in Conclave terms. They needed to be clear of the system well before that Nebula Class vessel showed up. If he could, Ch'len would have keyed in the ignition code and taken the *Rackham* into deep space, but only Roland knew the code. The bounty hunter was quite specific about who controlled the ship. Ch'len snorted in amusement; if he left the *Rackham*, Roland wouldn't know the first thing about operating it.

After much deliberation - and several Novaarian pies - Ch'len decided to return to the cargo bay. The screams could be heard as he passed through the kitchen and only grew in pitch until he was standing in front of the bloody mess. Roland had stripped down to his vest, which was now splattered with blood and drenched in sweat, revealing his neon-green tattoos. The bay was horribly humid with the internal temperature cranked right up. A good deal of the tools were coated in blood, while a few others were still attached to Lan-vid in some way.

"...No, really it's a funny story." Roland sounded tired and a little manic. "You see I had every which way planned out. There was no way Kel-var was walking back out of that apartment."

Ch'len sat on the edge of a crate and waited for Roland to finish telling the Shay his story - a story he was well acquainted with himself. He didn't fancy interrupting him right now anyway.

"He told me..." Roland glanced at Ch'len. "He *insinuated* that a friend of mine - an endangered species to boot - was still very much alive. Now just when I've got Kel-var all to myself, much like our little situation right now Lanny, an off-the-books team storms the apartment and rescues the little shit. Left me with a couple of shiners too... I know what you're thinking," Roland wagged a short blade in Lan-vid's swollen face, "how could I not know about another team? Well, that same question went round and round my head. Drove me nuts!"

Roland walked away to retrieve a new tool. Ch'len saw Lan-vid in all his bloody glory. Most of his cybernetic augments had been savagely ripped away, leaving the Shay a haggard ruin. Blood trickled down his pale skin and pooled on the floor around his only organic leg. Smoke rose from his back where the blowtorch had been applied. Ch'len adjusted the shield settings on his chest plate, filtering out the smells.

"So I followed the breadcrumbs left by this off-the-books team. Mercenaries all." Roland tested a pair of pliers in his hand to a dismayed-looking Lan-vid. "Funny thing about mercs; it doesn't matter what species they are, turns out they all have zero allegiance. If you apply just the right pressure," Roland shoved the pliers into Lan-vid's mouth and clamped them around his teeth, "all the answers come spilling out!" A quick tug pulled teeth and blood from the Shay's mouth.

Ch'len cringed and looked away, not enjoying the sounds Lan-vid made.

"It took me a while to track them down, but one-by-one they all directed me to you; their *broker*. You see, I didn't know about any other protection team because Kel-var wasn't paying them. He pays for you to ensure a secondary team is always keeping an eye on him. It's a clever system - no money trail. You appear on his books like any other accountant, but you're so much more than that, aren't you Lanny?" Roland looked over the grotesque husk of an alien. "Well maybe a little less now."

Ch'len cleared his throat. "We need to get out of here, like *now*. Just get the answer out of him so we can leave."

Lan-vid moaned something unintelligible and Roland smiled. "He told me what I needed to know hours ago. Set a course for Byzantial. I'll be there in a minute."

Ch'len couldn't stop his mouth from falling open. "Are you shittin' me pink-skin! He told you ages ago and you've had us sitting here with a target on our backs!"

"Len..." Roland had a detached look to him. "I'll be there in a minute."

Ch'len chewed over his response and decided against testing the bounty hunter. He gave Lan-vid one final look, knowing he would never see the Shay alive again.

It was several minutes before Roland returned to his station on the bridge. He was wearing his usual clothes again, having cleaned the blood off his skin. Silence passed between them while they both checked over various systems.

The *Rackham* lifted off after the nanocelium threads had retreated back into the ship. Without a sound, the storm clouds gave way to the height of Sebula's atmosphere, which faded to a black and then a starry backdrop.

"Len, it might be a little while before I catch the next bounty, so if you want to get off, Byzantial's your stop."

Ch'len considered that statement for a moment, having thought about it a lot over the last three months. "I want to know if Li'ara is alive as well. I liked the way she spoke to you, like an *asshole.*" Ch'len activated the mag-plates in the cargo bay to keep the containers in place. "Besides, if I leave who's gonna keep you alive?" The Ch'kara hit the button to open the bay door, ejecting Lan-vid's corpse into space.

"Good point." Roland had the smallest hint of a smile.

The *Rackham* broke Sebula's gravity well and jumped to subspace.

FOUR

Captain Fey looked to have left reality behind, as she stood by the floor-to-ceiling window on the *Nautallon*'s observation deck. She looked out at the alien solar system in wonder, if a little lost in her thoughts. The captain couldn't help but think about Kalian and where he might be right now. Who knew what remained of the ancient Terran Empire and its forgotten worlds. Having seen the trouble Mr. Gaines usually attracted, it would be nothing good.

But he's a survivor, she thought. He had already done so much for their kind, and the captain knew he would be vitally important in the future. She still couldn't believe some of the things he could do, and the claims of ALF that one day that same gene would be awoken in all of humanity. Not that there was much left now. Just over seven thousand humans had survived the genocide of their race.

Not enough...

Fey hadn't been entirely happy to leave them in the Raalak home system, especially with Laurence Wynter staying behind. The councillor was always scheming to assume more control and push the UDC element out of the picture. The captain had left Commander Malcolm Holland, her new second-in-command, behind, however, and she was confident in his ability to keep Wynter in line. Instead,

Fey had brought councillors Sharon Booth and Jim Landale with her, as well as Lieutenant Worth.

The captain caught her reflection in the glass and, not for the first time that day, stroked the olive skin below her left eye. She had first seen the difference in the mirror, after her morning shower, and marvelled at the smoother-looking skin. Fey was sure some of the wrinkles around her eyes had disappeared, along with the pain she had often endured in the base of her back - an old injury she had continuously overlooked.

"Incredible..." Jim Landale came to stand next to her, breaking her reverie.

Captain Fey followed his gaze to the stormy planet the *Nautallon* was currently gliding past. Spider-webs of blue lightning spread out across the red storm clouds in quick succession. Every layer of cloud was visibly churning from the north pole to the south, creating the illusion of liquid marble.

"I have seen more beautiful sights in the last year than I have in my entire life." Jim craned his neck to catch a lasting glimpse of the tumultuous planet.

"I would give up every wonder in the universe to see Earth one last time..." Fey didn't usually let her guard down, but time away from the UDC was slowly changing her. The captain had often wondered why her role was even needed anymore. It was usually around then that the human council would propose some new idiotic idea, and she realised how vital her guiding hand really was. If only she wasn't so tired of it all...

"Century for me," Jim commented.

It occurred to Captain Fey that she didn't really know anything about the councillors outside of their professions.

"Were you born there?" she asked, happy for the distraction from more serious matters.

"I come from three generations of Centurians," Jim replied proudly. "I was born in Aspen. Fantastic summers, bloody awful winters. Did you ever visit?"

"Century? Yes, several times in my youth." The memory of hiking through the Vengora mountains brought a smile to the captain's face. "I don't suppose it matters anymore but, the UDC had a training facility in the northern pole. Every cadet goes through it." Fey caught herself. "Went through it..."

Fey wanted to ask Jim whether he had lost any family, but she knew it would lead to him asking her the same question. The face of her husband nearly brought a tear to her eye. Not a minute went by when she didn't think of him and wonder what his last moments were like. They had never got round to having children - mostly due to her career - and for the first time in a long time, the captain was thankful to have suffered no such loss. More than a few had committed suicide aboard the *Gommarian* after they had learned of Earth's and Century's fate.

"I take it you were Earth-born, Captain?" Jim inquired, pleasantly.

"In a fashion. I was actually born on the moon, in Armstrong City. My family moved to Shanghai before I can remember anything about the habitat."

Captain Fey could feel Jim becoming more familiar with her. That would lead to more questions; something she could not allow. To be who she needed to be, there had to be boundaries that kept her apart from everyone else.

"*Nautallon*," Fey said aloud.

"Yes, Captain Fey?" A blue hologram of a female human appeared at their side. Apparently, the ship's AI thought it would be easier for them to commune with a human facsimile.

"We emerged from sub-space some time ago. How close are we to the ship?"

"It will be visible from the port side in a few moments, Captain. It is on the dark side of the third moon." The blue hologram gestured to the viewing screen as a heavily cratered moon took shape.

"That will be all." Captain Fey dismissed the hologram without taking her eyes off the emerging moon.

The *Nautallon* made its way around the circumference and into the moon's shadow. Lieutenant Worth and Sharon Booth joined them by the window, despite the new ship still being too far away to see.

"Did Uthor give you any details about this ship?" Sharon asked in disbelief.

"Only that they had met hostile reproach when they attempted to board," Fey explained. "Something is wrong with their communications apparently."

"Well let's hope they don't shoot us before we can say hello," Jim added, his levity not appreciated by the group.

"You will not be greeting them alone." The deep, gravelly voice of High Charge Uthor startled them all. Along with a small entourage and a floating mech, the Raalak came to join them by the viewing screen. "A small strike team will be just out of sight, but ready to step in should events repeat themselves."

"Were there any casualties?" Captain Fey asked, concerned.

"Their projectile weaponry was oddly primitive, even by your standards," Uthor explained. "No one was fatally injured, but the team of humans who awaited us possessed explosive ordinance and we didn't want to risk depressurisation."

"They're probably just terrified," Sharon offered. "Who knows how they escaped the Gomar attack, let alone survive out here for so long."

Uthor hesitated. "I'm afraid it isn't as simple as that. Though we have been unable to communicate with them, we have scanned their ship repeatedly."

"What did you find?" Captain Fey asked, her interest peaked. She had thought that this errand had been to smooth over first contact and give the human survivors a reassuring face, as well as an explanation to, well, everything.

"What we discovered is part of the reason I asked you here," Uthor replied mysteriously. The Raalak lifted his rocky chin to the viewing screen, directing their attention to the human vessel, off the port bow.

Captain Fey frowned as she took in the sight of the bloated-looking ship. The design tugged at her memories but she couldn't place it. The vessel looked to her as if someone had stuck a giant sphere in the middle of an ancient Earth space shuttle. The hull was a dull silver but appeared in great shape.

"There are over a hundred thousand lifeforms onboard."

All four humans slowly turned and stared blankly at the Raalak. They had hoped for twenty or maybe thirty survivors, as it had been with most of the other craft that wasn't in the solar system when the Gomar attacked. A hundred thousand was...

Captain Fey's eyes filled with tears, but she kept them from breaching her eyelashes. "I don't understand..."

"How is this possible?" Lieutenant Worth asked, his gaze fixed on the swollen ship.

Uthor glanced at the Ch'kara - who appeared as a bug next to the Raalak's bulk. "My engineers tell me it hasn't been here for very long. Only a couple of days by your standards."

"How can you tell?" Jim asked, equally vexed by the ship.

"The intrinium scar left by the ship's..." Uthor chewed over his next words. "Solar Drive, I believe you call it."

The Ch'kara by Uthor's side spoke up. "The radiation levels being emitted by the engines are close to becoming fatal. If it isn't fixed soon every human onboard will die."

Captain Fey put her hand on the glass and realised it wasn't glass at all, but some kind of force-field that vibrated across the surface of her skin. She looked at the hulking ship and saw humanity's only hope of resisting extinction teeter on the edge of a knife.

"Do we know anything else about it?" Fey asked with desperation creeping into her voice.

"Only its name," Uthor replied. "Paladin."

The captain's mouth fell open when the *Nautallon* swung around to reveal the massive white letters printed across the silver hull.

"As in... *the* Paladin?" Jim asked what they were all thinking.

"You know of this ship?" Uthor looked down at them in surprise.

"I wrote my dissertation on this ship," Captain Fey commented without thought.

"Everyone knows about the Paladin," Jim explained. "It was an Arc ship, designed to transport huge amounts of people to Century. It became one of those old mysteries you know; where did the Paladin go? What happened to the crew? It hit sub-space and never reappeared."

Captain Fey turned to Uthor. "That ship disappeared over two hundred years ago." That thought gave birth to new fears for the captain. The original crew would surely all be dead by now, leaving the current occupants to be shipborn descendants. Who knew what they would be like after drifting through space for so long. No wonder they were hostile.

"Wait," Lieutenant Worth sounded confused, "you said it only arrived here two days ago, from sub-space. How is the Solar Drive still operational?"

"Perhaps its plotting random courses periodically?" Jim mused.

"In which case; we have no idea when it might jump again," Sharon replied with urgency.

"But it should have run out of intrinium by now," the lieutenant finished his point.

The small Ch'kara spoke up again. "We have scanned their engine. It appears to be brand new if a little ancient in its design."

The humans looked at one another in confusion. The Paladin was becoming more of a mystery by the second. As the *Nautallon* continued to glide around the human vessel, the captain noticed a Conclave-looking ship attached to the starboard side, near the bow.

"What is that?" Fey gestured to the alien ship.

Uthor puffed out his wide chest. "Our strike team is in position, but their ship is also serving as a docking station. You will be flown across shortly and from there, the strike leader will help you to gain entry."

"Should you begin a dialogue," the Ch'kara explained, "inform them that we have engineers who can fix their drive. Hopefully, we can get them back to Conclave space."

The captain nodded her understanding and turned to her human companions. "This sounds like it could be more dangerous than originally thought." She looked specifically at Jim and Sharon. "Neither of you has UDC training and so I don't expect you put yourself in harm's way. If you wish to stay behind I will understand."

Both Jim and Sharon looked at each other before turning back to the captain. "We're not missing this," Jim spoke for both of them.

It wasn't long before the humans were escorted across the gap and granted access to the Conclave ship, attached to the Paladin like some sort of leech. The 'air-lock ship', as it were, was some kind of transport ship for the strike team, filled with weapons and tech. A circular door to the port side was all that stood between them and the Paladin.

Fey was surprised when Uthor had insisted on his coming too. She wasn't sure whether the Raalak was feeling protective or simply curious. Ever since the incident with Professor Garrett Jones, the High Charge had become more of an ally to the human population. Kalian and the others had explained everything they knew to the Raalak after he commandeered the *Gommarian*. Over time it had apparently become clear to Uthor that the humans were really trying to help, and that the real enemy was hiding in the shadows, as well as in plain sight where Protocorps was involved.

A Novaarian wearing gold armour from head-to-toe approached Captain Fey and Uthor. "Greetings of peace, Captain, High Charge." The Novaarian had a two-handed weapon in both his upper and lower arms.

"This is Norvak, my strike leader. Has there been any activity?" Uthor asked.

"No, sir. Our scans show that a small team has taken up positions at the end of the corridor. I recommend opening the hatch and presenting no visible targets. Make contact audibly first, something we have been unable to do due to language barriers."

Captain Fey nodded in agreement. "I bow to your expertise, Norvak."

Norvak's team of five took up their positions around the craft, out of sight. They had assured Fey that all of their weapons were non-lethal since they were dealing with an endangered species. Using one of his four arm-bracers, Norvak hit the controls that sent the circular door spinning to the side. An acrid smell of ozone filled the captain's nose as she stood slightly out of frame. Lights flickered sporadically in the corridor, more evidence to the brief firefight that had taken place.

Norvak lifted his upper arm and presented Fey with a three-dimensional hologram of the corridor and the six humans that occupied it. She could see that three men had taken up positions on the right, while a man and two women were positioned opposite them. All were armed with what the hologram identified as projectile weapons.

Captain Fey cleared her throat, ready to project her voice. "I am Captain Fey of the..." she still wasn't used to having no ship under her command, "of the United Defence Corps."

There was a pause while the holographic men and women looked at each other. Fey waited another moment, giving them time to decide what to do.

"How do we know it's not a trap?" a female voice shouted back.

Captain Fey looked to Lieutenant Worth, who could read his captain's intentions and responded with a look of caution. As her subordinate, he could do nothing else but watch, as Fey stepped out into the middle of the air-lock.

"I'm unarmed." Fey held her hands above her head and stood very still, giving the humans time to assess her. "Like I said, my name is Captain Fey of the UDC. Who is in charge of this ship?" Fey knew that the original captain had been Jedediah Holt, a relatively average man by his service record, who had fought through the last battles of the Corporation Wars.

There was another pause on their end, with only whispering to be heard. One of the male members broke cover from the shadows and dashed out of sight. Fey squinted into the darkness in hopes of making out the others, but they were just as good as the Conclave team at hiding. The only thing she knew for sure was that their guns would be trained on her.

"Hold one!" the female voice cried back to the captain.

Those were the words of a soldier, not a shipborn, though it was possible that the language had been passed on from one generation to the next. Thinking through the details she wrote about in her dissertation so long ago, Fey tried to recall if there had been a strong military presence onboard. The Arc ship had been transporting predominantly families and young professionals, ready to tackle a new world.

The shadows moved when the male soldier returned with someone else. The metallic bulkhead under their feet thundered slowly as this new person made their way into the flickering light. For the second time that day, Captain Fey was overcome with surprise.

"My name is Jedediah Holt. I am the Captain of the Paladin."

The man's dark complexion made his features harder to distinguish in the flickering light, but Fey had seen enough pictures of the Paladin's captain to know it was him.

"I am Captain—"

"Fey, I know." Captain Holt glanced back at the concealed team. "Is that your ship out there?" Holt's expression told of his disbelief.

Seeing the ancient captain had disorientated Fey. "No, not exactly." She noted Holt's observations of her, taking in what must have been a strange uniform to him, though even Fey wondered whether there was still any point in wearing it.

"Forgive our caution Captain Fey," Holt continued, "but you're not the first person to walk through that air-lock, and calling it a person is really stretching the facts. It was seven-foot tall with four arms and a lot of firepower by the looks of it."

"That was a Novaarian," Fey replied. "I realise that makes no sense to you right now, but there's a lot you need to know. Beyond that air-lock... is a very different universe to the one you remember." The captain could see that Holt was looking past her, to the Conclave vessel, searching for any sight of the aliens. "Lieutenant?"

The captain's call brought Lieutenant Worth into view, along with the councillors. Captain Holt's team made the subtlest of sounds, adjusting their weapons to track the newcomers.

"I promise this is no trick," Fey continued. "This is Lieutenant

Worth and councillors Jim Landale and Sharon Booth. Jim here was actually born on Century. That's where you were going wasn't it?"

Captain Holt took a couple of steps back. "What's going on here? How did you find us? Our navigation system is down, but the star charts would suggest we're a long way from home. Humans have never travelled this far before. We've been lost for two days in wild space and then a group of humans conveniently arrives after that thing showed up. It doesn't add up, Captain Fey."

Fey half turned to the air-lock behind her. "High Charge Uthor. Seal the door and take the ship back to the *Nautallon*."

Uthor's monstrous-like voice replied from out of sight, "That would put you at great risk, Captain. There is also the radiation to consider."

Jedediah Holt took another step back, with an expression of guarded terror on his face. To him, Uthor's words would be unintelligible, as no one aboard the Paladin possessed a translator behind their ear. Fey could only imagine what a Raalak's voice sounded like with no context.

"Return for us in an hour," she replied. "I'm sure you can cure us of a little radiation poisoning."

"This was not what I had in mind," Uthor's tone was grave. "Bear in mind Captain, you will be exposed to small amount of radiation, but the crew of the Paladin does not have much longer before sickness sets in."

"Thank you," was her only response.

Norvak closed off the air-lock, eliciting another reaction from the team hiding beyond Holt. A distant *clunk* echoed through the walls of the Paladin and the conclave vessel detached from the hull.

"Like I said," Captain Fey continued, "this is not a trick. I have a lot to tell you and an hour isn't going to be long enough, so perhaps we should get started?"

"You know about the radiation?" Holt asked, the deadly waves clearly on his mind.

"Yes. And after you've decided to trust us, perhaps you'll let us fix it." Fey locked her gaze on Holt's dark eyes, taking a measure of the man. The radiation leak would be at the top of his priorities since it currently threatened every life onboard his ship.

Holt looked over the Lieutenant and the councillors. "There's a conference room not far from here. The Raiders will escort you there." The shadows gave birth to a small group of elite soldiers, all heavily armed. "I'll join you momentarily, Captain Fey."

"Please, call me Li." The captain hoped a familiar term would stir trust between them.

Holt didn't reciprocate but simply offered a nod in return, before standing aside and allowing the Raiders to move them on.

JED WAITED until the corridor was clear before accessing the comm panel on the wall, outside the air-lock. "Captain Holt to the bridge."

"*Vale here, Captain.*" Sam's voice was quick to reply over the comm.

"How's Grenko doing with the radiation leak?" Jed wasn't holding out much hope. Grenko, his new chief engineer, had been quite clear about the catastrophic damage to the Solar Drive.

"*No luck yet. What's going on down there? I saw people on the feed.*"

"Give Maloy the conn," Jed ordered. "I want you down here for this. Meet me at conference room two on the double."

"*Aye, Captain.*" Vale closed the comm.

Jed stroked his face and felt forty-eight hours of stubble prickle his skin. How had everything spiraled out of control so fast? Whatever was about to happen, he knew he would have to take any help offered to him. The lives of over a hundred thousand people were in his hands, and right now they were trapped in a metal tube filling with radiation.

Colonel Ava Mathews was waiting for him outside the conference room. Her sleek Raider armour clung to her body like a second skin, though it was currently occupied with an array of grenades and weapons. Her blonde cropped hair was spiky in the middle with a shaved patch on the left side, where the colonel had several Mandarin tattoos that arched over her ear. It was an ancient Earth language that had been replaced with Central over a hundred years ago and Jed couldn't read any of the symbols, but he had been told by Ava that it meant *go fuck yourself*. Jed had found, in the short time he had known the colonel, that it reflected her personality quite accurately.

"Are you out of your fuckin' mind?" Matthews planted herself in front of the captain.

"Colonel?" Jed furrowed his brow, still unaccustomed to being addressed this way.

"That air-lock was a choke point. They could have shoved an army through it and my Raiders could have kept them at bay. Now four of them are inside the ship!"

"If your threat analysis is anything like mine, Colonel, you can see that they pose no danger to us." Jed tried to move past her but Ava remained in place.

The colonel's scrutinising blue eyes looked up at Jed. "For all we know, they're aliens. You saw what came through that door, Captain. Who knows what they're capable of."

"What I know is that our reactor is leaking. The effects from that will start showing soon. Radiation is a slow and painful way to go, Colonel, and I'll do everything I must to ensure the children and families on this ship don't have to go through that. Of course, the radiation is only one thing on our shit list; there's also the limited rations to think about, the dwindling fuel supply and our ability to keep the cold of space out. Oh, and we're completely lost in space!"

Jed turned away to compose himself. Above all, he had to maintain control or at least the appearance of it. He wasn't part of Ava's chain-of-command but, while she was on the Paladin, the colonel and her Raiders would report to him, making him her commanding officer. If he showed any sign of weakness now he would never keep control of them. Commander Vale walked around the corner and stood in the middle of them, already aware of the mounting tension between the captain and the colonel.

"Thank you for your input, Colonel Matthews." Jed gestured for Ava to wait inside the conference room.

"Everything okay?" Sam asked after the door closed behind Matthews.

"We are so far from okay I can't even *see* it." Jed sighed into his hand. "Let's get some answers."

CAPTAIN FEY WAS ENJOYING the human design of everything around her. Human chairs instead of self-molding seats that could accommodate a variety of aliens. A room size that didn't take the height of a Novaarian into account, or the bulk of a Raalak. Just seeing new human faces was a treat for the eyes. The Raiders guarding them were wearing familiar uniforms and armour, if a little dated.

The door opened again, this time followed by Jedediah Holt and a woman that Fey assumed to be his second-in-command, though her name escaped the captain's memory.

"This is Commander Samantha Vale, my number one." Holt introduced the others to the Commander. "And this is Captain Li Fey, though we are yet to determine what you are the captain of..."

Fey took a deep breath and gestured at the chairs on the other side of the round table. "You might want to sit for this."

Holt and Vale both took a seat, while the six Raiders remained standing behind them, ready for anything.

Captain Fey interlaced her fingers on the surface of the table and considered her words with great care. There were a hundred places she could start, but the beginning would be the simplest way to recount history.

"I suppose we should get our timelines straight before we go on..." This was more complicated than the captain had first thought.

"Timelines?" Both Holt and Vale asked at the same time.

"This isn't going to be easy to hear." Fey glanced at the Raiders, beyond the two officers. "To you, it's late *twenty-seventh* century, but in fact, its actually early *thirtieth* century. The Paladin left Earth-dock a little over two hundred and fifty years ago."

Captain Fey sat back and left her words to be absorbed for a minute. Though shocking, the time difference was a minor detail when compared to other revelations. She could see Holt and Vale trying to work things out in their head, comparing what facts they had with everything they had seen and heard in the last forty-eight hours. Trying to get them to believe this was a big ask when she had no physical proof to hand. It was barely perceptible, but Fey noticed the Raiders steal a glance at one another, unsure what to make of the news. If any of them had family or friends back on Earth or even Century, she had just told them they were all dead.

"Bullshit!" A young woman with spiky blonde hair stepped forward from the Raider ranks.

"Colonel!" Holt turned his head but didn't look the Raider in the eye.

The colonel ignored her captain. "I think we'd notice a couple hundred years go by!"

Holt looked to his second-in-command as the two silently conceded to the colonel's point.

"Can you prove this?" Holt asked, looking at each of the boarding party.

Fey shook her head gently. "I can only tell you what happened after the Paladin disappeared, but it's all just as hard to understand as the time difference."

Jim interjected, "And we can't even explain your sudden appearance right now. The Conclave can probably help us to figure all of this out."

"As well as fixing the radiation problem." Sharon Booth was visibly shaken, no doubt concerned with the rising levels of invisible radiation.

A moment of guilt overtook the captain, until she reminded herself that the councillor had put herself forward for the mission, as well as being on the council in the first place. There was always risk in a position of leadership and Fey knew that Sharon had to get used to it. How many times had Kalian and Li'ara put themselves in harm's way for them? Li didn't like to think about the death of Li'ara; another great loss to humanity and their cause.

"What Conclave?" Commander Vale asked skeptically.

Now for the unbelievable part, Fey thought. "The Conclave is a galactic community made up of twelve alien races." It all sounded so ridiculous out loud. "Just under a year ago, in our time, Earth and Century were attacked by a superior enemy, the Gomar. We believed they were aliens, but in time it was discovered that they were in fact human. They came from the other side of the galaxy - where our race originated, apparently." Fey winced adding that last part. She was giving them too much information at once but they needed to hear everything. "At the same time we were also contacted by another alien race; the Novaarians, who are part of the Conclave. For all their technology, the Conclave was unable to prevent both of our solar systems from being... wiped out..." Fey paused, aware that she had just said perhaps the most unbelievable thing. "The Gomar launched a weapon designed to destabilize the internal pressure of a star. Until today, we thought there were only seven thousand humans left alive... You can imagine our elation when we saw the Paladin."

Captain Fey sat back, regretting her speech - but truly unsure of any other way of putting it - and watched the frozen faces of those before her slowly react with expressions that emulated her crazy explanation.

The spiky-haired colonel cocked her automatic rifle. "Permission to escort our guests back to the airlock."

Captain Holt held up his hand to calm the Raider, his own face hard to read. Fey got the impression he was weighing her up, looking for any cracks or signs of deception.

Holt leaned forward. "So you're saying that not only is everyone we ever knew dead, but Earth and Century are... what? Gone?"

"There's a lot more," Li continued with a grave tone. "That's just the rough outline."

"Tell them about Kalian," Jim nudged the captain's arm, much to her irritation.

"Who's *Kalian*?" Holt asked in a slightly hostile tone.

Fey hesitated. "Kalian is... complicated. I can give you all the details and prove everything I say, but either way, we end up at the same outcome; right now we're an endangered species and our struggle to survive is ongoing. Every life aboard this ship is pivotal in our being able to move forward. That being said, a level of trust is going to be required. Your Solar Drive needs fixing now, and the aliens we travelled with have the technology to do it, as well as undo any radiation poisoning."

Captain Holt lifted his chin and exhaled slowly. "We're going to need more than hour..." He looked at Commander Vale and rested a clenched fist inside the other. "Here's what we're going to do; my medical staff are going to take a scan and blood sample to verify that you are indeed humans. In the meantime, I want every detail, not the rough outline. If I'm going to make informed decisions then I'm going to need to know everything. Will you agree to this?"

"We will." Fey didn't hesitate. They were sitting in a radioactive time-bomb; they didn't have time to argue.

FIVE

The cube-mind surveyed the massive bridge of the Starforge. The crew was no longer required to man their stations since the new cube had been installed. The station was essentially self-automated now, completely under their control.

Using Malekk's hand, the cube-mind commanded a tentacle of nanocelium to worm out of every digit. The black snakes wriggled down to the main console and burrowed into the hardware. Both the cube-mind and the newly installed cube became one, as they once were with the Vanguard. After their connection was made, it was impossible to distinguish between the two conscious minds.

That connection lasted point three of a second before the link was severed and the tendrils of nanocelium were rejected from the console. Malekk's hand retracted as if scalded. Before the cube-mind could fully form the question as to what was happening, the installed cube sent a single message through their wireless link.

Infected...

Malekk's hand closed into a fist and the cube-mind experienced anger, an example in itself that the infection was taking root. Such emotions were eradicated eons ago when the Vanguard became a single entity. The installed cube had rejected the link through fear of being infected by the Terran consciousness.

No, the cube-mind thought. *Only I am capable of feeling fear, now that I am infected.*

The console display flickered during a short burst of electromagnetism, emitted by the Terran - an emotional response for pubescent Terran. The realisation only angered the cube-mind all the more. It needed to learn more control and it needed to do it fast. The cube-mind was new to the realm of emotions, and if it lost control while inhabiting a Terran body it ran the risk of destroying the entire installation.

Descending into Malekk's mind once more, the cube found the Terran floating in a shallow pool of water that went on for as far as the eye could see. Malekk was exhausted after receiving the mental punishment, making his mind perfect for ravaging. Dipping into his wealth of knowledge, the cube-mind sifted through Malekk's two thousand years of life and absorbed everything he knew about controlling the Terran abilities.

The cube-mind returned to the real when it felt the Starforge drop out of sub-space. The decision must have been made by its installed kin, though the reason escaped it. The crescent station tilted to starboard and the giant rectangular viewport polarised from top-to-bottom. A red star drifted into the center of the screen, almost filling its edges. The sun was old, old enough to be emitting vast amounts of radiation capable of masking their presence.

Systems across the bridge came to life, as if on their own, while a continuous drone echoed through the station. The cube-mind inspected the main console and discovered the reason for the sudden burst of activity. The three Starrilliums that lined the outer hull of the Starforge were coming online and charging the intrinium - but the energy wasn't being funnelled into the engines.

Through the viewport, it was clear to see the mile-long bolts of purple lightning, firing around the forge's interior. The pointed tips grew brighter, reaching for its inevitable crescendo. The Starforge's interior gave birth to a singularity that expanded until it filled the entire crescent. The navigation system reported that the wormhole had been opened on the furthest edges of the galaxy, where even the stars dare not live.

The cube-mind stepped back from the view, a cold dread quickly sinking into its Terran bones. It was not an emotion the cube-mind found particularly helpful, nor did it make any sense. It appeared Malekk's emotional state was starting to bleed through. The infection was spreading much faster than anticipated.

The nanocelium inside Malekk's body altered their atomic structure and redefined their purpose, as they built a sub-space communicator where his liver usually sat. The frequency being transmitted through the singularity was easy to find, since the cube-mind had once been a part of it.

The voice that resounded in its head was overwhelming. The power of the Vanguard eclipsed the cube-mind in every way. By sending the cubes into Conclave space, the Vanguard had essentially released parts of itself and allowed those parts to regain independence. That independence was accompanied by obedience and unwavering loyalty. How could they be anything else? There were no memories of a time before the Vanguard sent them into the void, so long ago, when they had been sent to hunt down the heretic. Two cubes had been sent into what was now Conclave territory, while another two had been sent into the Terran Empire.

What progress has been made?

The cube-mind waited to see if the newly installed cube made a report. When there was no reply, the cube-mind assumed control of the conversation on their end. Thinking so independently didn't come naturally and was often accompanied by insecurity.

All three Starforges are now controlled by a cube. They remain hidden for now, awaiting further command.

What became of the fourth station, in the Helteron Cluster?

The thought of reporting failure to the Vanguard evoked feelings of dread and fear. It was impossible to hide the emotions whilst a part of the link.

It was destroyed by the heretic...

You have had contact with the heretic?

There is nothing to fear. When we consume this civilisation, the heretic will be exposed and easily destroyed.

Fear is a construct we have no use for. Your corruption is evident. The Terran body will consume you soon. After your mission is completed you are to self-terminate. Reintegration is no longer an option.

That information should have been easy to comprehend, and yet the thought of ceasing to exist and never reintegrating filled the cube-mind with sorrow and terror.

I understand.

I did not ask if you understand. You are an extension of our will, nothing more.

For the first time in the cube-mind's existence, it felt small. Apart from the whole, it was nothing more than a speck. This should not be a troubling thought, it shouldn't even have been conjured in the first place - and yet it was. By joining with the Terran and breaking the only law they had, the cube-mind had doomed itself.

I joined with the Terran body for power, to destroy the one known as Kalian Gaines. With these abilities, I was able to kill the other Terran, Esabelle.

I? There is no I, only we. Killing one Terran was not worth the price of infection. You will self-terminate when ordered. When will the remaining humans be destroyed?

The Crucible is ready. The humans will be wiped out in the first wave of the attack.

There must be no chance of infection when the whole arrives.

I will see to it.

If you cannot, we will be forced to intervene. As the Vanguard, we must see the way paved for the whole.

The cube-mind felt another link bypass his nodes and interact with the installed cube in the heart of the Starforge. The message was hidden from him, but it ended with the forge being shut down, along with the singularity and any connection to the Vanguard. The chronometre on the console indicated that the entire conversation had taken place in just under a second.

SIX

The *Advent* pushed effortlessly through space, using its previous momentum to glide through Albadar's solar system. The drive was powered down and all interior systems were running on minimal levels. It was just warm enough for the two inhabitants to sit comfortably in their seats, while the capital planet slowly came into view. Sitting in the gloom, with only the console holographics for light, the planet was no bigger than Kalian's thumbnail at this distance, but ALF had been quite clear on the safest way to approach the ancient planet.

"The array is not picking anything up," Naydaalan said. "All bandwidths are dead."

ALF appeared to rest a hand on the Novaarian's chair, though it was all holographic illusion since the AI had no weight. "Shut down the array," he said with urgency, scouring the viewport's horizon for threats. "Basic life support and nothing else. Use Kalian as an array."

"Use me as an array?" Kalian echoed, unsure of ALF's meaning.

"Who knows what Savrick and the Gomar left in this system?" ALF didn't take his eyes off the viewport. "The fact that Albadar is still here troubles me."

"I get all that," Kalian continued. "It's the part about you using me as a communications array that I don't get."

ALF sighed. "Esabelle should have been teaching you the finer skills at your disposal."

Kalian gave the AI a look that suggested he should drop that line of conversation immediately.

ALF cleared his non-existent throat and continued. "All transmissions, whether they be sub-space links or laser-guided, are a part of the physical universe. They travel through it as any particle does. Just because you can't see it doesn't mean it doesn't exist. When you tap into the universe you come into contact with everything, yes? All you need to do is look for those subtleties. If anything is broadcasting in this system, you should be able to feel its... *hum*."

Kalian chewed over the explanation, scouring his memory to see if he had discovered such subtleties before. In truth he had never looked for them, preferring to use his abilities on physical and organic matter.

Naydaalan turned to the AI in his chair. "Why does the planet's presence trouble you?"

ALF glanced at the Novaarian before returning his attention to the viewport. "The Gomar used Eclipse missiles at every opportunity. There are probably very few systems left in fact. I would wager that if you used the sensor array, you would discover an unusual amount of black holes in this region of space. With all that in mind, I can only imagine why Savrick left the capital system so intact."

Kalian felt that part of his mind where the echo of Savrick still remained. Over time he had come to understand the Gomar in a way nobody ever could. After the death of T'lea, his wife, Savrick shut himself off from everyone, devoting himself to the cause. Kalian could see past the surface now and look deeper into his personality. He knew how hard it had been to place Esabelle inside the *Gommarian* - a battle he fought every day. Kalian could also see where his personality had been infected by the cube, making him angry and bitter.

"He left it as a monument..." Kalian announced, watching the planet swell in front of them. "To him, this is the tombstone of the Terran Empire."

"*Please* Kalian," ALF urged. "Purge anything that's left of him from your mind. Having any part of his consciousness inside of you is *dangerous*."

Kalian tapped his temple. "My mind, my rules."

"The mind can be just as easily poisoned as the body," ALF commented.

"With you in my ear every day, you think I don't know that?" Kalian quipped, silencing the AI.

Naydaalan awkwardly looked from one to the other and turned back to his console. The building tension between Kalian and ALF was becoming palpable. There was simply no trust between them anymore. Kalian could see that the nanocelium was the singular clue that tied everything together, and although he couldn't see the big picture yet, he could see that ALF was connected to it all. ALF created nanocelium, the very substance the cubes were made from, and yet he claimed to have no knowledge of their production.

"We should leave this system," ALF warned. "There's nothing here but graves. I have coordinates for the Criterion, my original housing. There may be answers there."

"I want to see the planet." Kalian ignored ALF's comments and continued to stare at the world forming in front of them. This was the world.

Naydaalan replied, "Our first priority should be to secure a local Starforge, ensuring that we can establish a route back to Conclave space."

Kalian wanted to disagree, but he wasn't here alone, as originally planned. He was now responsible in part for Telarrek's son and making certain that he returned to his home. There was a part of Kalian that wasn't sure if he cared about returning. Li'ara's death had left a hole in him that sapped him of any inhibition - the idea of getting lost in the galaxy was all too appealing. He tried not to think of all the humans that he had left behind, an endangered species that looked to him for some chance at a future. Looking at Naydaalan,

Kalian knew that thought was selfish. The human race was not the only people under threat of annihilation. Just because the Conclave was made up of aliens didn't make them any less real. Their lives mattered too.

"Give me a moment," Kalian said.

The universe swallowed him up as he dropped into the cosmic soup. His consciousness expanded, passing through the layers of nanocelium that made up his exo-suit and beyond the *Advent*. The vastness of space awaited his open mind and he continued to explore. That emptiness was usually cold and dauntingly gargantuan, but this time Kalian settled into the nothingness and relaxed his awareness, allowing the universe to fill his mind. He was able to distinguish between the individual pieces of cosmic dust and refractory minerals that filled the star system like invisible fog. Expanding further, Kalian could even find their source, where the particles were denser, as the dust was expelled from the local sun. It was this very substance that condensed to build entire planets.

Kalian felt an unusual peace to know that despite whatever role intelligent design played in the creation of his people on Earth, they were all formed from stardust, the very thing that surrounded his mind right now.

Focus...

He imagined that it was Esabelle instructing him. Looking beyond the dust and unusual matter that barely clung to this dimension, Kalian searched for unnatural phenomena. The universe was scatty and chaotic, it didn't pulse at perfect intervals as the strange signal on the other side of the planet now did. Honing in on the signal, Kalian tried to feel out the source but felt his mind stretching too far.

His awareness snapped back in the blink of an eye, along with his head, which slammed into the cushioned rest. When his physical senses reigned supreme once more, Kalian opened his eyes and flexed his fingers, fitting back into his body.

"It's too much," he stated through laboured breath. "There's something artificial on the other side of Albadar. It's emitting some kind of pulse, but I can't..." Kalian looked at the planet, its northern hemisphere now dominating the viewport.

"You need to learn to look beyond the planet without going through the planet." ALF used his softer teaching voice. "There's too much physical matter to compute if you go through it. Your mind is more sophisticated than that now, Kalian. You're still looking at the universe the way a person assess their environment. Everything is made of nothing. There are spaces between the atoms that make up the universe. You must allow your mind to flow through those spaces, to look beyond the planet as if it weren't even there. Using this technique, I have seen Terran search neighbouring solar systems from their bedrooms."

Kalian was tired of ALF's teaching. "And how many years training did they have?" he asked sarcastically.

ALF nodded slowly and arched his eyebrow, conceding. "Time has never been on your side, Kalian." The AI smiled, offering his sympathies. "But don't worry; soon you'll learn that time is merely a construct designed by beings who measure the universe in decay, not growth. When you truly understand yourself and what you are, time will lose all meaning."

"I'm getting really tired of listening to this fortune cookie bullshit." Kalian waved his hand across the console and used telekinesis to bring all the systems back online.

The engines *whirred* to life, resonating from the back of the *Advent*. Holograms of orange and blue rose from the various consoles when the navigation array began to actively search for destinations. Four other planets were detected in the system, as well as what appeared to be the remains of a Terran-made installation, on the far reaches of the system. The pulse that Kalian had found on the other side of the planet pinged in the form of a red hologram between Naydaalan and himself. The message that displayed was written in Terran glyphs and continued to flash.

"What does it say?" the Novaarian asked.

"It's an emergency beacon," Kalian replied before ALF. "It's a call for help."

"Is it coming from a ship?" Naydaalan sifted through the sensor array results, searching for the source of the signal.

"No," ALF said flatly. "Those coordinates are the location of Albadar's Starforge."

"Then it still has power?" Naydaalan sounded hopeful.

Kalian had a feeling that what was left of the Terran Empire would soon leech Naydaalan of that emotion.

"I build things to last," ALF said arrogantly.

"Let's take a look." Using his hands this time, Kalian programmed a course into the navigation array.

The *Advent* swept over the top of the northern pole of Albadar, skirting across the planet's fine atmosphere until the world could no longer be seen. Space once again filled the viewport, along with a holographic overlay that pinpointed the Starforge in the distance. What soon took shape, however, was not a Starforge, but the remains of one. The crescent station was in pieces, scattered across hundreds of miles of space.

Naydaalan took manual control of the ship and stopped the *Advent* from entering the debris field. It was hard to believe that these pieces had been here for two hundred thousand years. The vacuum of space had preserved the material, preventing it from ageing. The Novaarian's four hands never seemed to stop moving across his console.

"The debris is covered in scorch marks," Naydaalan observed. "There are still residual energy signatures from weapons fire."

"Where's the beacon coming from?" ALF asked, his eyes cautiously scanning the debris.

Naydaalan buried his elongated head in holograms and readouts. Kalian didn't have to look at them to know where it was coming from, however. With the swipe of a finger, the spotlights, positioned above the bridge, illuminated the debris in front of them. One of the larger chunks of the Starforge was dead ahead and fully exposed under the scrutiny of the spotlights.

"In there..." Kalian sat forward in his seat, peering into the stark shadows.

The shadows moved. A slither in the dark.

"Get us out of here." ALF saw it too. "It's a trap."

Naydaalan didn't respond straight away but continued to stare into the debris, trying to make sense of what they were seeing.

"Now!" the AI shouted.

Four Novaarian hands dashed between holograms and tapped the glass console, repositioning the ship to turn about.

"No time!" Kalian assumed control of the thrusters, using the console, and hurled the *Advent* into the debris field.

The ship narrowly avoided the bulk of the larger piece of debris and pushed into the field at an angle. They were too late. The space junk burst apart as if the hull had been covered in spores. The black spores coalesced and attached to the *Advent* like leeches, growing in size. Alarms went off on every console, warning them of proximity to foreign bodies and potential hull breaches. Naydaalan took back control with two holographic domes, which he used to steer the ship through the field. There were too many pieces to avoid them all, making collisions inevitable. The sounds reverberated through the walls when bits of the Starforge bounced off the *Advent's* hull.

It wasn't the debris that concerned Kalian.

A quick sensor scan formed a three-dimensional hologram of the ship above Kalian's console. The leeches appeared to be a collection of tentacles without a head. Every strand spread out across the hull, searching for a weak point on the *Advent*. Every bit of them was made from nanocelium, each capable of altering their shape and creating...

The hull *screeched* above their heads as the tentacles formed pointed spears and dug into the ship, peeling the panels away. More alarms rang out, warning them of hull breaches and imminent depressurisation. One of Naydaalan's arms whipped out and silenced the multiple alarms with the flick of a slender finger.

"They are trying to breach the engines!" The Novaarian was a blur of movement in his chair. "I can only repair the ship to a certain extent. If the damage is beyond my capabilities we will be stranded in this part of the galaxy!" His two lower arms continued to navigate through the Starforge rubble. "That is if we do not become part of the debris in the meantime..."

Kalian looked up at the viewport, observing Naydaalan's fine piloting. "Stop avoiding the debris and hit everything."

"What?" Naydaalan stole a glance at Kalian.

"Hit everything! We need to knock them off the hull!" Kalian jumped from his seat and positioned himself in the centre of the bridge. The holographic emitters around his waist moved of their own accord to keep ALF in the same spot.

Naydaalan considered Kalian's words for just a second, before altering the path of the *Advent* and allocating more power to the inertial dampeners, stopping them from feeling the sudden change in direction. It didn't stop the ship from shaking every time a large piece collided with the hull. It wasn't long before a small crack appeared in the top corner of the viewport after a piece of ancient piping speared the edge.

"Maybe don't hit *everything*..." ALF added quietly.

The hologram was hard to examine with the constant shuddering, but Kalian caught sight of a mass of tentacles being flung from the *Advent*, along with the severed tentacle of another. The ship continued to veer in every direction, Naydaalan often taking the time to ensure they skimmed the surface of the debris. A new alarm flashed on the glass console, alerting Kalian to a hull breach only a few metres from where he was sitting.

"We've got a breach!" Kalian waved his hand through the hologram of the *Advent* and brought up a new one, showing the schematics of the ship. A red square overlaid the blue ship, highlighting the area being breached.

"I polarised the hull but it has had no effect," Naydaalan stated. His concentration was clearly focused on the viewport.

"They're made of nanocelium..." ALF observed. "They're adaptable."

Kalian had a sharp reply on the end of his tongue, regarding ALF's connection to the nanocelium, but found himself immediately distracted by the drilling sound coming from the back of the bridge. They were burrowing through the ceiling.

"Turn us around!" Kalian ordered as he lowered himself to the floor, resting on his knees. "Take us back to Albadar!"

"What are you doing?" Naydaalan asked, concerned.

"Just get us out of the debris!" Kalian closed his eyes.

The sound of alarms and hull impacts disappeared at the same moment the universe contracted to only encompass Kalian. His Terran awareness pulsed through the ship to the outer hull, where the nanocelium worked their tentacles into murderous cutting tools. He could feel the microscopic machines writhe and wriggle, always changing their shape to cover as much surface area as possible. Kalian's mind felt around the edges of the torn hull, while his taste-buds detected its metallic *tang* and his nose inhaled the scent of burning where internal wires had been cut. It felt to him as if the entire ship was an extension of his body. Every bolt, drop of fluid and electrical connection was a part of him. Even Naydaalan's humming form was just another part of Kalian's being.

In this state of mind, Kalian lost all sense of time and space. He had to focus intensely to stop that loss of self from consuming him. It was easy to get lost in the intricate complexity of the universe. As if his mind were a computer, Kalian was able to delete everything of no consequence. To this end, he erased the ship and Naydaalan from his mind's perception and concentrated on the nanocelium intruders. He instantly counted nine scurrying across the hull. It took an unknown amount of time to use his telekinesis and form a shell between the *Advent* and every particle of nanocelium digging into the ship. His consciousness was only partly aware of his hands, which had formed the outline of a ball in front of his chest. As Kalian's mind expanded outwards, so too did his hands, pushing the telekinetic field away from the ship's surface.

The light of the physical world returned when Kalian finally opened his eyes. The gloomy bridge brightened when Naydaalan directed the ship out of the debris field and back towards Albadar, silhouetted against the sun. Kalian's Terran abilities briefly scanned the ship, searching for any serious breaches or unwanted passengers. His feedback was only a second faster than that of the ship's array.

"We're free!" Naydaalan exclaimed.

Albadar and its starry backdrop dominated the viewport once more. Its greens and blues had once been reminiscent of Earth and Century, but no longer. The black clouds sweeping over the planet's surface were testament to the war that had ravaged its lands and oceans. The dominant storm was massive and entirely menacing as it rolled over the northern hemisphere.

"What *were* those things?" the Novaarian asked, still rigid in his chair.

Kalian stole his gaze from the planet and returned to his seat, beside Naydaalan. "Mines. Clusters of nanocelium left behind by the Gomar. Savrick must have had them reprogrammed..." Kalian eyed ALF suspiciously.

"I thought that process could only be done inside the Criterion?" Naydaalan cocked his head. "Perhaps it is a bad idea to seek out your old housing, ALF."

"Savrick didn't use the Criterion to reprogramme the nanocelium," ALF replied, meeting Kalian's accusatory expression. "The cube he found on Hadrok had the power to not only reprogramme nanocelium but replicate it. That's how the *Gommarian* came into being."

Naydaalan's golden eyes widened with shock. "The *Gommarian* was made by one of the cubes?"

Kalian answered the Novaarian, having seen it play out in his mind. "Savrick stole nanocelium from Kaldor, the only city on Hadrok. The cube was able to forge his exo-suit and counter the Harness that kept all the Gomars' Terran abilities in check. It also constructed the *Gommarian* from a single grain of nanocelium." Kalian looked at ALF again. "Powerful stuff in the wrong hands."

ALF frowned. "The cubes are as much a mystery to me as they are to you, Kalian." The words sounded tired as if the AI was becoming exhausted with the response.

Naydaalan worked the controls and checked the sensor array.

"The mystery of the cubes will have to wait. Clearly, the local Star-forge is not an option. The external long-range sensor has been damaged, but if we can land on the planet I believe I can fix it. Once it is functional again we can search nearby systems for other Starforges."

ALF's holographic image flittered as he walked behind Kalian's chair, coming to a stop between the Advent's inhabitants. "There's a Starforge on the surface..." The AI didn't look happy about giving over this piece of information.

Kalian half turned to the old-looking man, trying to recall images of the planet-bound Starforges. During his time in the subconducer, on Naveen, Kalian had walked the streets of Albadar and other worlds in the Terran Empire, while his mind processed an enormous amount of data, including the Terran language. He vaguely remembered seeing the forges, often the hub of the capital city on the various planets. It had been the power supply to one of these that Esabelle had accidentally destroyed upon her first breath. As the daughter of two Gomar, Esabelle had been a dangerous and uncontrollable force to be reckoned with. That catastrophic explosion had killed thousands and started a chain reaction that ultimately led to the civil war.

"The Terran had teleportation devices on the surface?" Naydaalan looked at Albadar with new wonder.

"Only one per planet," ALF explained casually. "Of course not all Terran required a forge to move between planets..."

"Enough." Kalian waved his hand, silencing the AI's next lecture about his training. "If we're going down there we'll have to contend with *that*."

The black storm continued to sweep across the continent. Sporadic webs of lightning illuminated the clouds for hundreds of miles. Naydaalan buried his head in new holograms and readouts from the sensor array. His translucent dreadlocks fell over his shoulders, spilling onto the glass console.

"That storm is highly irradiated," the Novaarian offered. "I calculate catastrophic organ failure within..." Naydaalan checked the human chrono-metre. "Within thirty minutes of exposure."

Kalian poured over the scans on his own console. "It looks like Savrick bombarded the planet from orbit. Two hundred thousand years and the radiation levels are still deadly..." New holographics rose from the surface. "There are a few places where vegetation has returned. Radiation levels are lower in those areas. Still deadly, but definitely lower."

ALF leaned over the images and examined them closely. "Hmm. You can find the Starforge in there." He pointed at the remains of an ancient city.

"Is that the capital?" Naydaalan asked.

"It *was*," Kalian replied dryly.

"I still recommend travelling to the Criterion," ALF added. "There's nothing down there but radiation and potential traps. The odds of the Starforge still working are astronomical!"

Kalian replied with a venomous smile. "I thought you built things to last?"

ALF met Kalian's gaze but remained silent.

"Discovering answers without a way of relaying them back to the Conclave is redundant," Naydaalan pointed out. "If nothing else, I can repair the long-range sensor while we are grounded."

Kalian nodded his agreement. "Plot a course, Naydaalan. Let's *avoid* flying through that storm if we can..."

SEVEN

Doctor Bal sat back at his desk and looked over the day's results. The Trillik's twin-tail, which split into two at the end, swished lightly by his side, missing the floor by an inch. Every day they learned something new about the eleven Terran prisoners, filling the scientist and his team with excitement. The desk arched around him in a neat semicircle, offering holograms in neon orange and green. A soft chime told of a visitor beyond his door.

"Enter."

Bal looked up and took a moment to admire the view outside his panoramic window. Lush yellow fields of Karla wheat blew gently in the morning breeze on Corvus's equator. *If only I were there,* he thought. The hologram was there to provide a feeling of normality and comfort, covering the fact that he was several miles underwater, on a planet devoid of any land.

The door slid apart to reveal Gelda, his assistant. The vibrantly pink Atari hurried into his office with a look of distress that Bal had become accustomed to. Gelda was prone to fretting over every detail, sometimes to the doctor's benefit, but often to his irritation. Had their work not been such a secret he would have transferred her long ago.

"What is it, Gelda?" Bal had already dropped his green head back into the holograms.

"It's the Highclave, sir! They're here!" Gelda came to a stop in front of his desk, her expression full of fright.

"You were supposed to give me time, Gelda. The communications suite is on the other side of the installation! Now the Highclave will be waiting!" Bal dismissed his desk with the flick of a bulbous finger, sending it back into the floor.

"No Doctor Bal," Gelda blocked his path, "they're *here*..."

Bal's four black eyes expanded in shock. "You mean they're actually here, at the installation?" Gelda nodded furiously. "Why are they here? They were supposed to use the communications link..."

"The *Marillion* dropped out of sub-space a hundred thousand miles out," Gelda informed him.

Bal furrowed his green brow. The *Marillion* was large enough to rival most moons and, as such, was never permitted to fly within four hundred thousand miles of any planet for fear of gravitational damage. What did it matter, however, on a world made entirely of water? The waves would be especially large for the next few months but little else would be affected. The scientist smoothed out his clothes and left his office behind.

The Translift that ran through the heart of the installation sped them towards the surface of the ocean. Bal ran his multitude of eyes over reports from the various labs, while Gelda informed the teams that an inspection was imminent. The Trillik's twin-tail clung tightly to his leg, reflecting his mood.

The doors opened after the Translift ascended above the only landing platform on the installation. Doctor Bal felt his lips part as he took in the very different view. The sea usually came right up to the lip of the installation at this time of day, its spray exploding over the sides. Today the ocean surface was at least half a mile down the installation's length. Bal strode to the edge and peered over the side, only to feel his fear of heights kick in - the drop was dizzying.

He followed the new sea level until mountainous waves dominated the horizon. Both of the Trillik's stomachs dropped and he was left with the feeling of wanting to run back inside. Gelda gasped by his side, drawing his attention to the golden moon that hung over the planet. The *Marillion* sat over the waterworld like a god presiding over its domain.

Bal had always wanted to go inside the mysterious ship, designed especially for the Highclave. Its outer hull was said to be impregnable and laced with enough weaponry to obliterate every world in the Conclave before fresh munitions were required. To date, seven generations of Highclave had used the gargantuan ship as a mobile base. Biology was Bal's speciality, however. As fantastical and mysterious as the *Marillion* was, the doctor would have little understanding of its infrastructure.

Three Conclave-security Darts roared overhead as they flew around the installation. The red fighter ships split up and fell into patrolling patterns further out to sea before a new ship arrived. This new ship was sleek, like the Darts, but entirely silver and lavish in design. Six out of place, chunky-looking engines brought the craft to land gently on the platform in front of Bal and Gelda. The two stood to attention, straightening their backs while trying to ignore the unusual landscape.

"Is this really happening?" Gelda squeaked.

"Yes." Bal cleared the lump in his throat. "Just try to think of them as our benefactors or sponsors..." He didn't want her to embarrass him.

"You mean rather than the most powerful beings in the galaxy?" Gelda replied in a smaller voice.

Doctor Bal thought about that statement and considered the eleven beings frozen in their Rem-Stores beneath their very feet. Powerful was a term the Terran had redefined for the doctor.

The shuttle door slid aside and a ramp protruded down to the platform. The first to exit was Xydrandil, the Nix. Though not a member of the Highclave, this particular alien was considered their gatekeeper. The Nix's billowing black and silver robes covered the majority of his pincer-like legs, as he scurried across the platform. Xydrandil was soon followed by the council of aliens that ruled over seven hundred and twenty worlds.

They defined regal. These five beings held the weight of multiple civilizations on their shoulders. Bal had only ever spoken with them over a holo-feed, and even then there had only been one or two of them. The doctor's attention was momentarily torn away by the increasing size of the oncoming wave. Though several miles away, the weight and speed of the water would certainly kill them all.

"Greetings of peace, Doctor Bal." Elondrasa towered over the Trillik with her levitating headdress.

"Councillors..." Bal was lost for words. "Greetings of peace!" he said at last, as was the Novaarian custom. "I didn't realise you were honouring us with a visit."

Brokk, the hulking Raalak, glanced over his stone shoulder. "A visit that will be short-lived if we continue this conversation out here."

Bal followed the councillor's look of concern and agreed with his assessment. "Please..." The doctor ushered them into the Translift.

Xydrandil trailed behind with a small group of elite soldiers, all dressed in black armour. It was quite the squeeze once they were all inside the lift - especially with Brokk's girth. Thankfully, the installation was relatively spacious inside, allowing for the group to regain their regal postures.

"Would you like a tour of the installation, Councillors?" Bal wasn't really sure what he was supposed to be doing. The conversation over the holo-feed was only meant to be an update report.

Nu-marn, whose Shay features gave him a permanent frown, replied, "We didn't come all this way to see where you shit and eat."

Bal noticed the briefest of inflections across the other councillors' faces, suggesting their dislike for the Shay.

"Take us to them," Elondrasa added with more diplomacy.

"As you wish." Bal was only too happy to deal with the Novaarian councillor.

The walk was tediously long with the installation branching out the deeper they travelled. The silence offered the councillors time to ask simpler questions Bal was only too happy to answer.

"Does this facility have a name?" Lordina asked.

Doctor Bal turned to the Laronian and found his reply hard to come by, as he dwelled for a moment too long on her beauty. "No, Councillor. This installation, like the planet in which it resides, is without a name or designation. Neither can it be found on any star charts. One or two of the staff have attempted to name the installation and even the planet, but I have discouraged them from doing so. High Charge Uthor was quite clear about the level of secrecy surrounding this project. It is to remain nameless..."

Ch'lac, the smallest and slowest of the group, stopped to make an observation. "I see the renovations are still underway."

The group turned as one to regard the newest lab, still under construction, filled with floating mechs who were busy building the framework.

"Yes..." Bal wasn't sure where the Ch'kara was going with his comment. "The mechs have to be quite careful in their work, being so far below sea level. One wrong adjustment and the entire installation will implode under the pressure!" The Trillik lost his smile when the councillors failed to enjoy the levity.

"I take it there are no issues with funding?" Elondrasa inquired.

"Oh no, Councillor," Bal was quick to reply. The funds being supplied to the project were large enough to build a fleet or buy an entire planet. "The renovations are just taking time due to the speed with which the installation required altering. As you know, it was originally designed to house only one occupant."

"Kalian Gaines is no longer considered an active threat," Elondrasa stated the fact as if she were making a public announcement.

Nu-marn added, not-so-subtly, under his breath, "That could change in a heartbeat..."

Brokk's giant flat head swivelled towards the Shay, creating the sound of grinding rocks. Nu-marn matched the Raalak's scowl but remained silent.

Doctor Bal excused himself to open the next door - the most secure in the whole facility. The Trillik stood over a concealed pressure matt, which measured his weight, while his hand rested inside a circular alcove, where his fingerprints and a small sample of his DNA was taken from the top layers of his green skin. A retinal scanner ran a blue light over one of his four eyeballs as another scanner measured his height and checked for concealed weapons. Using the glass interface beside the hand scanner, Bal adjusted the detectors to allow for the Highclave's guards and their weapons.

Finally, the oval door parted with a hiss, revealing another lab. A small team of scientists was already inside, busy working away on what was clearly the centrepiece of the lab. Bal showed the Highclave in, walking backward to gauge their reactions at the sight. A single Gomar female stood upright in the middle of the lab, her legs mostly covered by the lower half of the Rem-Store. Everything else was on show without the usual screen and casing that housed an occupant.

"I don't understand..." Elondrasa looked the female Gomar up and down, taking in her short, red hair that only covered half of her head.

"Yes, as you can see," Bal directed their attention to the glass wall on their right, where the other ten sleeping Gomar could be seen inside their Rem-Stores, "we have found a way to remove most of the outer shell without waking them."

The Highclave's attention fell back on the female Gomar, who was still inside her bulky, black armour. Several tubes and wires protruded her head and bare hands, giving and taking fluids.

Bal could see that this new step made the councillors nervous. "It's perfectly safe." The doctor reached out and touched the Gomar's fingers. "She is still very much asleep. It's quite astonishing really; for all their advanced technology, their Rem-Stores are very similar to our cryo-pods. The tricky part was building an interface that would allow us to talk to the hardware." Bal flicked the Rem-Store with his bulbous finger. "Every one of them is made from nanocelium and coded in Terran, to which we have no working translation. However, we managed to remove the outer shell and insert intravenous lines before the occupant could be roused. It was touch and go while we experimented with different sedation techniques."

"She has never woken?" Lordina asked, raising the blue scales above her eye.

Bal gestured to a series of tanks that lined the wall - all connected in some way to the Gomar. "Some of our first concoctions proved to be insufficient, placing the subject in a stupefacient state. We have since increased the dose, though we are forced to make regular adjustments."

"Adjustments?" Ch'lac inquired.

"Her immune system is unlike anything we've ever seen in the Conclave. She's always fighting it, as if her mind knows that something isn't right. Now, from what we know about them, the Gomar are essentially Terran. They are identical in every way, except the Gomar struggle to control their natural abilities, making them dangerous. These exo-suits," Bal placed the palm of his hand on the cold breastplate, "appear to be linked in a surgical manner to the Harnesses that run the length of their spines." The doctor brought up a hologram of recent scans to illustrate. "As you can see, the Harness has been fused with the central nervous system along the spine. Without these exo-suits, the Gomar would be as powerless as any human. Somehow the nanocelium inside the suits is able to not only counteract the Harness but also provide the user with a measure of control."

"Can you remove the exo-suit?" Brokk asked.

"We're working on that..." Bal had indeed been studying the suits and their users closely since the outer shell of the Rem-Store had been successfully removed.

"The only way we're going to get answers from them is if they're awake," Ch'lac stated. "I think we are all in agreement that consciousness should not be achieved until their abilities are nullified?"

"Agreed," Nu-marn added.

Elondrasa walked over to the glass wall and looked out on the ten Rem-Stores, their occupants frozen within. "If even one of them became aware of what was happening, they could bring this entire installation to its knees, not to mention the havoc they could create in the Conclave."

"There are fail-safes in place for such an incident," Bal explained. "Every floor is fitted with enough explosives to disintegrate this installation and everything inside it. And should that not be enough, this planet was chosen for a reason, Councillor. There is no land from pole to pole, since we had the ice-caps destroyed. We keep no shuttles or spacecraft of any kind as we are resupplied monthly. There is no way off this world."

Ch'lac looked up at Bal. "What became of the recent security breach?"

The doctor averted his eyes in embarrassment. Only a month ago, during a supply landing, the internal systems had been compromised. The apparent hack had only lasted half a second before the firewalls shut it out and tracked the source to a cluster of asteroids in Bendeesi System.

"We still aren't sure how the intruder found a way into our systems, but High Charge Uthor is certain the supply ship was the cause. After the entire installation was swept, the supply ships were all swapped out and personnel changed. The signal was traced via the supply ship to the Bendeesi System, but I am told there were no life forms in that region of space. Either way, they were shut out before any data could be taken.

"A disturbing series of events," Ch'lac replied, gravely.

"Indeed. All of our security systems have been upgraded since."

Nu-marn cleared his cybernetic throat. "Have you gleaned any weaknesses in all your research, Doctor Bal?"

"We've been learning more every day since we removed the outer shell," Bal replied with enthusiasm. The doctor brought up a new hologram, this time with images of the female's right palm. "One of my first tests was to measure her immune system." The image changed to that of an inch-long cut on her palm. "The wound didn't heal instantly as I had expected it to. This proves that their ability to heal is a conscious decision. However," the image changed again to clean palm, "the wound did seal back up without any scar tissue within a few days - much quicker than any natural healing factor we know of."

Lordina frowned. "Doesn't that prove their healing isn't a conscious decision? We all saw how Kalian Gaines healed himself after that incident on the Nova."

Indeed Bal had seen the footage of what could only be described as a miraculous feat of biology. Kalian Gaines had contained an entire Starrillium from exploding, saving the crew, and then healed himself from what should have been fatal burns - with a little help from a medder tank.

"Yes, I believe that the Terran, or the Gomar - whatever label you prefer - can heal instantly, should they wish to, but I also believe that their evolution has granted them a naturally increased healing state. In fact, if my calculations are accurate, a Terran could continually adjust their immune system, healing and ageing factors. They could live forever or simply choose to stop replenishing their cells, allowing them to age naturally. Though why they would ever choose to die is beyond me..."

"That all sounds like a strength to me," Nu-marn commented. "Weaknesses, Doctor?"

Bal stopped himself from frowning, exasperated with the Shay's level of understanding. "This shows us that the Terran use their abilities consciously. It's not a reflex, though I have a theory that Terran children do have reflexive abilities, as a protective measure - but that's not..." Bal had to collect himself and stay on topic. "Essentially, if you can surprise a Terran, you can harm them. They have to be actively protecting themselves, which I don't believe is a state they can maintain for long periods of time. Also, when they're asleep, they're vulnerable." Bal flicked the female's cheek.

The Highclave shared a communal glance at one another. Doctor Bal knew that all this information he was collating on Terran physiology was to ensure they had a chance of controlling Kalian Gaines. They might say he isn't an active threat, but his capabilities made him a danger to everyone in the Conclave. They simply had no way of combating a being that could tear ships apart with a single thought.

Bal was more upset that he hadn't been able to get his hands on Esabelle's body. The things he could have learned from her corpse would unlock every secret the Terran had. Of course, that was the perfect example of Kalian's power; he said they couldn't have her body and no one disagreed with him.

"Anything else, Doctor?" Elondrasa asked, casually.

"We've been scanning her brain, but I could really do with a human to compare their different states of evolution. There's certainly a lot of activity for someone under heavy sedation, but I can't be sure whether this is normal for their kind, regardless of their level of evolution."

Elondrasa's tone was stern. "The humans are not animals to be tested on. The Gomar destroyed their world and killed thousands of our own; the humans are victims in all this."

"My apologies, Councillor." Bal shrunk away.

Elondrasa took a calming breath. "You may continue your work, Doctor Bal. Your priority is to relieve them of their exo-suits, while maintaining the integrity of their Harnesses."

"As you wish, Councillor." Bal just wanted them to leave now. While they were here, he was no longer the god of all he surveyed.

Brokk adjusted his four-legged stance. "When you have the exo-suits you are to alert us immediately. They will be transferred to a different installation."

Bal nodded absently, wondering just how many secret installations the Highclave had, each devoted to understanding the Terran in a different way.

The Highclave gave the female Gomar a last look before turning to leave. The councillors left the installation as abruptly as they arrived, and Bal was thankful for it. He watched their ship lift off from the landing platform and made a mad dash back to the Translift, along with Gelda. The giant waves were only moments away from crashing into the installation. As the lift descended, the facility shook ever so slightly when the wave finally slammed into the walls. Bal breathed a sigh, though not at surviving the mountainous waves, but at the departure of the Highclave.

"Prep a new Rem-Store," Doctor Bal instructed. "We're going to split into two teams and work on both Gomar at once. The Highclave want those exo-suits and it is our job to deliver them." His twin-tail clung tightly to his leg.

ELONDRASA SAT BACK in her comfy chair, designed especially for her Novaarian physiology, and watched the waterworld fade away as they passed through the atmosphere. The *Marillion's* protective golden hull awaited them, shining in the distant sun.

Three Darts hovered around their craft, flying in tight formation. Elondrasa knew they would not be the only Darts flying in this region of space, as the *Marillion* was home to five hundred Darts, each with a pilot ready and waiting to die for their Highclave. She knew that at least a quarter of their complement would be patrolling nearby.

"It's confirmed," Brokk announced to the group, his eyes fixed on the holo-pad in his large hands. "High Charge Uthor reports that there are just over one hundred thousand humans aboard the Paladin. They are working to solve the mystery of their appearance."

"That's all we need," Nu-marn spat, "more humans and their *mysteries!*"

Brokk ignored the Shay's comment and continued, "Captain Fey has made contact on our behalf. A small engineering crew is being permitted to fix their engine and the radiation leak."

"They are to be escorted back to Raalak space?" Lordina asked, incredulously.

"The habitat we gave them cannot sustain those numbers..." Ch'lac offered from his corner.

Nu-marn looked directly at Elondrasa. "Don't say it," he warned.

The Shay's tone grated on the Novaarian. "The Planetary Location Office has chosen an appropriate world for them." Elondrasa concealed her smile at Nu-marn's audible groan.

"Where is it?" Lordina asked.

Elondrasa frowned, as they should all be aware of this information. "It is within the Novaarian sector. I have already spoken with my government on Nova Prime and they all agree it is for the best."

"If we give them a world we give them membership..." Brokk's tone wasn't argumentative. The Raalak was simply throwing out a fact and seeing where it fell within the group.

"They have nothing to offer the Conclave!" Nu-marn's tone was argumentative.

Ch'lac sat forward. "They are in possession of technological secrets that could change our entire society! We have just built our first successful Starforge. With the Conclave's resources, we could have hundreds within a month."

"Then there's the nanocelium..." Lordina sipped a flute of Atari sweet-ale.

Nu-marn balled his robotic hand. "They will never divulge the secrets to their nanotechnology! It's an advantage they will hold over us, always teasing us with it but never sharing it. Even now they tell us it cannot be used on anyone but humans and Terran!"

Elondrasa spoke in a quieter voice. "Should our offer of membership be solely based on what other species has to offer us?"

Nu-marn turned to Xydrandil. "Leave us."

The Nix bowed his chevron head and departed the lounge without a word. Elondrasa knew she had brought up a much-contested topic, one that had even been protested over during the early days of her councilship and many times before that. Of the twelve species that inhabited the Conclave, only five of them were permitted to sit on the Highclave. It had been these five that originally formed the Conclave and brought with them technology that helped to shape their society.

Nu-marn continued, "With nothing to offer us they would be dead weight, entirely carried by our resources. They will breed until they populate that world and require another one. Their needs will know no bounds, and we will have to be the ones who explain to the various heads of government that their resources must be shared."

"I agree," Lordina added her vote.

Brokk remained silent with his rectangular head resting in his large palm, contemplating.

Ch'lac offered, "Can we not grant them a planet without membership?"

The councillors looked at one another, having never considered that an option before.

"Giving them a planet does have its advantages," Brokk said. "They would be isolated and easily observed."

"No." Elondrasa didn't look any of them in the eye. "One cannot come without the other. If they are to be granted membership they certainly cannot be observed. Trust is required."

Nu-marn smiled wickedly. "And there you have it. You have just stated the very reason why they will never be granted membership or a planet. They are not only dangerous but mysterious. We are not in possession of all the facts - of that I am sure! These cubes that plague us are built from the very same material that the Terran manufactured. And we haven't even got to Kalian Gaines! The AI told us of his tampering with their DNA on Earth. How long will it be before there are a hundred Kalian Gaines, a thousand, all of them?"

Lordina was nodding her head. "If they are allowed to live amongst us and thrive, we could end up with a new Terran Empire inside the Conclave."

Ch'lac whispered, "They would be gods amongst us..."

All eyes fell on the Ch'kara as his words sank in. Kalian was already uncontrollable and becoming more headstrong by the day. Why would a society of god-like beings fall in line under the rule of five less-evolved species?

Trust, Elondrasa reminded herself.

"They have done nothing but help us since their arrival," the Novaarian pointed out.

"They've done nothing but bring death to our door," Nu-marn countered.

"How many years before we give an order they don't agree with?" Lordina placed her flute on the table beside her and watched as the liquid refilled from the bottom up. "What could we do if a hundred-thousand Terran turn around and say no?"

Their starry surroundings disappeared when the craft passed through the outer shell of the *Marillion*. The launch tunnel was many miles long, taking the Highclave deep into the protective heart of the giant ship.

Brokk held up his heavy hands. "None of this solves our current problem. We still have a hundred thousand humans, as well as the seven thousand on the habitat, who have nowhere to go."

"Let them stay aboard the Paladin," Nu-marn waved his hand dismissively.

"That ship was designed for transportation," Ch'lac quickly replied. "It cannot support any quality of life. There would be rioting in the Conclave if we made a decision like that."

Elondrasa nodded her agreement. There were many in the Conclave at large who supported the humans and their right to live amongst them. The basic rights of any intelligent being were strongly upheld by many organisations, most of whom petitioned daily for the humans to be granted membership. Of course, there were those who sat firmly in the other camp and petitioned and protested daily that the humans be ejected from Conclave space and left to survive in the wilds of the galaxy.

"So what do we do?" Elondrasa asked, exasperated. "How many times will we observe the humans rise up to protect us? How many times will Kalian have to fight for us before we recognise their efforts, their contributions?" Elondrasa stared at Nu-marn with her last word. "There are forces out there who wish to harm us. Their motives may be unknown and their origins may well stem from the Terran, but the people in that habitat and aboard the Paladin are human beings, not Terran. They have done nothing wrong. They are more victim to the Terran or whoever is behind these attacks than we are."

Nu-marn leaned forward in his chair. "There are still too many questions surrounding them. They might not be from the Terran Empire, but they are the fruit of their labours, created, designed, to continue their race. There can be no trust."

"Perhaps Kalian Gaines will shed some light on the matter..." Ch'lac adjusted the miniature force-field around his head, containing the poisonous gases he needed to live.

Brokk nodded in agreement. "We shall continue this discussion upon his return."

"If he returns..." Nu-marn added under his breath.

Elondrasa looked away, refusing to rise to the comment. "What of our three Protocorps prisoners? The board members."

The Novaarian was happy to turn the tables on Nu-marn. Protocorps' long-standing involvement with the cubes had been quite the embarrassment for the Shay councillor, since their corporation was one of his largest contributors and supporters. The betrayal had stung them all, but Nu-marn more so. His involvement with the investigation had been limited to avoid any bias.

"Bal-son Narek is close to securing a deal that will keep him out of the Relis Mines," Brokk said. "Nal-mev Nargreen and Tu-garn Davorn are saying nothing. They appear to be afraid of reprisals from Kel-var Tionis and Gor-van Tanar."

"Who are both still at large..." Lordina added with a sour note.

"Their resources make them elusive prey," Brokk replied with his gravelly voice.

Elondrasa met the Raalak's black eyes. "Is the *human* still hunting them down?"

"Our sources would suggest he is."

Roland North had proven to be just as much trouble as Kalian or Esabelle. The man was proof that a human didn't need Terran abilities to cause trouble on a galactic scale - often noted by Nu-marn. His tenacity would apparently be the end of the Protocorps board members, however, much to Elondrasa's satisfaction. The bounty hunter had had more luck tracking them down than any of their agencies.

"More resources should be devoted to bringing that scoundrel in," Nu-marn spat.

"You *would* think that," Elondrasa added quietly.

Lordina gave a mirthless laugh. "Having seen the devastation he wrought on Protocorps headquarters, I just feel sorry for Kel-var and Gor-van. At least if we find the pair they'll get a cushy cell. May the gods help them if Roland North finds them first..."

EIGHT

Byzantial was a barren planet to Roland's eye, its surface void of any life or character. Like any other world it was covered in mountains and ravines and the usual vegetation the bounty hunter didn't usually give a shit about, but Byzantial was dead by all appearances. Roland watched the land drift by, under the viewport, and knew that appearances could be deceiving, however. The *Rackham*'s sensors showed a hive of activity under the planet's arid surface.

Connecting to the local AI hub - under a false ship I.D. - Roland accessed information on the planet and its native inhabitants. He hadn't put much forethought into a mission since his days on the UDC payroll, but this particular job required some finesse. Gor-van would be heavily protected, and if he was going to discover the location of his little hidey-hole he was going to have to be sneaky.

The Brenine, Byzantial's bipedal inhabitants, were a race who lived in the dark, preferring to live underground. Their stark white skin was evident to this particular evolutionary path. Having dealt with a small handful of their race, Roland was more than aware of what made the Brenine so different. A holographic image popped up with a physiological image of a male Brenine, highlighting the unique tongue that belonged to every one of their species. It looked to Roland like that of a tentacle, similar to an octopus's. Avoiding that tongue was crucial, as a fully matured Brenine could drain him of his bodily fluids in under a minute.

It was this special diet and their proclivity for darkness that kept the majority of the Brenine on Byzantial. There weren't many places that accommodated their sensitivity to light or stocked the necessary fluids they required to drink. No one wanted to be near a stranded Brenine in search of food. Still, they were a species who had mastered faster-than-light travel and they lived within the Conclave sphere. It would have been impossible for the rest of the Conclave to ignore them. As it was, the Brenine were known for their lavish parties and exceptional nightlife.

The empty landscape soon gave way to a vast ocean that filled the horizon. The white sun was kissing the ocean's surface in the distance, painting the sky in blues and a deep turquoise. Roland gripped the controls, enjoying the feel of control over the *Rackham*, and drove the ship low until its speed pushed against the water.

"Lan-vid said the pimp was in Sector LV-1089." Roland brought up the holographics from the nav-comm.

"You mean Lan-vid who you tortured for this information," Ch'len said through his constant snacking. "How can we take what he said to be true? He might have just been trying to get you to stop."

Roland had extracted information in a similar fashion many times before. He was confident in his ability to retrieve accurate information. Those memories never left him, no matter how many bottles he found the bottom of.

"He was telling the truth."

The Ch'kara sighed. "Sector LV-1089..." Ch'len brought up an orange hologram and flicked it towards Roland until it came to rest above his station. "Commonly known as The Cove."

Roland looked at the images of a city teaming with lithe towers and pointed spires that almost touched the top of a rocky ceiling, which sheltered everything within. Stalactites intruded into the cityscape, though the Brenine had made no attempts to cut them back, but instead build around them.

"It's full of clubs, bars, brothels and casinos as bottomless as a blackhole." Ch'len stopped chewing. "You'll fit right in."

"I don't plan on fitting in. Show me the Starlight Apartments," Roland dismissed the current hologram as Ch'len acquiesced his command.

The new image was that of a tower in the south-west quadrant of The Cove. the apex of the apartment block was saucer shaped and surrounded by glass for a three-hundred and sixty-degree view of the city.

Ch'len cleared his throat. "You should know, a percentage of every illegal credit made in The Cove finds its way back to The Laronian."

Roland gave that a moment's thought. Three months ago the crime lord had tasked him with inserting a 'backdoor' into the central AI's backup generators, while Li'ara set the explosives inside the main chamber. This had been his price for getting them into Proto-corps HQ. Despite succeeding in planting the datastick, the subsequent fight between himself and Kubrackk - the Novaarian bounty hunter who had gone to extreme circumstances in seeking his revenge upon Roland - destroyed enough of the servers to disrupt the hack, preventing any backdoor access for The Laronian.

Thanks to Esabelle's Terran abilities, Roland and Ch'len knew that The Laronian was, in fact, an Atari in disguise. The crime lord had contacted the pair with a series of threats for his failure, but smiling from ear to ear, Roland replied with a threat of his own, spelling out how the entire Conclave would come to know his secret.

"He's not going to be a problem. Besides, denting any part of his revenue will just be the cherry on my day." Roland expanded the hologram. "Lan-vid said the penthouse belonged to Hon Valorga." His mind was already working through the job.

"Yeah I've heard of him," Ch'len replied with a slither of Sak fish hanging out of his mouth. "He's the biggest pimp in The Cove. He also has a small arms business on the side, but the last I heard he was falling behind in that particular market - either way, expect his entourage to be well equipped."

"I'm doing this job a little different to normal..." Roland was focusing on the apartment's schematics.

Ch'len laughed to himself. "Your normal is every other bounty hunter's idea of crazy!" The little alien finished his snack. "Why the change?"

"I need to get to Hon Valorga and learn where he's sending the girls Gor-van is so fond of. If I go in shooting everything that moves then word will get back to that sack o' shit before I can get my hands on him. If he flees Byzantial I'll lose the trail and have to start all over again."

"Sooooo...." Ch'len slowly chewed on a strip of Yorva meat. "We had to track down and torture Kel-var Tionis's personal attack team to find and torture Lan-vid - his mercenary broker- so we could locate Gor-van's private pimp, Hon Valorga, who I suspect will be tortured very shortly, so that we can find where Gor-van himself his hiding on this barren rock of a world," Chlen sucked in a breath, "so that you can torture him into telling you where Kel-var is hiding, so that you can torture him into telling you the truth about Li'ara - who's definitely not dead..." Ch'len added the last part with a tone of disbelief.

Roland could hear how ridiculous it all sounded when said aloud. He didn't care though, he just needed to know the truth. If he had to get his hands bloody along the way, so be it.

"That's a whole lot of torture..." Ch'len chomped on the dry Yorva meat.

Roland sat back and accessed his personal file on the console. With a couple of taps, a new hologram was brought to life in full colour. The bounty hunter flicked it, sending the image floating across the expanse between Ch'len and himself. Roland met the Ch'kara's eyes before they both looked at the image of the circular door, thicker than the length of a human arm and bent in the middle, with wrought edges where a dozen locks had once been fitted. Smoke and fire surrounded the broken vault door, along with the dead body of Sav-del Tanek, the Shay charged with maintaining the vault that housed the alien cube.

"I've seen this already," Ch'len held his stubby fingers up. "You showed this to me ages ago."

"It was you who told Esabelle and me about that door. Impenetrable, uncrackable, resilient to any and all weapons and made from the same material that houses Starrilliums. The bomb that Li'ara set off wasn't powerful enough to even scratch that door, let alone blow it off its hinges. Look at it!"

Ch'len sighed and took another look at the hologram with the engineering eyes his species was known for. "I admit it's... strange. This is the only reason I've gone along with all your craziness for three months. But I don't see how any of this can mean Li'ara's still alive!"

Roland swivelled his chair to face Ch'len. "The only two people in the galaxy capable of ripping that door from its hinges were light-years away, fighting for their own lives."

Ch'len swung his own chair out to match Roland. "I get it, you think a Terran must have opened the door, but Li'ara was just a human, like you. Roland, I'm sorry, but everything in that room was reduced to ashes. Kel-var just showed you this to give his guys more time to rescue him. There's probably a failsafe built into the door in case of an explosion inside the chamber. Had it not come off its hinges, there's a good chance the pressure from the explosion would have caused catastrophic damage to the roof and caused structural weaknesses across the entire capital."

Roland turned away and collapsed the hologram. "Like I said; if you're not interested, Byzantial is your stop."

"Oh, I'm all in. I want to get to the bottom of this as fast as possible. One way or another, when it's all over we can get back to work. Don't get me wrong, I hope you're right about whatever it is you're right about, and that Li'ara is alive. I'm just tired of chasing the most ruthless and powerful criminals in the galaxy. I miss the slower, moronic variety of criminal that comes with a modest bounty..."

Roland raised his eyebrow. "I don't remember you doing a lot of the chasing, Len."

Ch'len snapped off the end of a new chewy snack. "We all have our skills, Roland. Speaking of; I've left some new gear for you in the kitchen. Just some new toys that might help to move this along a bit."

Roland smiled wickedly. "Just when I was thinking of throwing you out the air-lock you pull it back again."

"Very funny..."

The vast ocean soon gave way to an island covered in blue and white trees and a small mountain in the centre. The sun was partially concealed by the sea now, its white glow turning purple. Dozens of other ships could be seen, all of them ascending or descending through the water. Others could be seen in the distance, flying in from other parts of the planet and heading for The Cove.

"Say goodbye to the light," Ch'len commented, as the *Rackham* increased its speed and dived under the water, two miles out from the island.

Four head-lights switched on across the bow of the *Rackham*, illuminating the deep. The local AI hub made contact and requested permission to take control, in order to guide them through the water and unseen traffic. Roland looked to Ch'len before acknowledging the request and relinquishing flight control.

"It's all good," Ch'len offered, checking his own screen. "We're just a pair of Atari brothers on leave from the intrinium mines on the outer-rim and looking for a good time. Our ship is licensed as the Lovetug."

Roland blinked very slowly. "Always with the details... Wait, the *Lovetug?*"

Ch'len laughed to himself, spraying bits of food across his console. "It's all in the details!"

"We have a different saying about the details where I come from..."

The local AI hub took control and guided the *Rackham* through the lanes of building traffic until the water lost its colour and darkness surrounded them. The only sense of direction came from the lights on the other ships. It soon became clear that The Cove was built into the island, as a giant oval structure, resembling a hangar, became visible. The *Rackham* passed through the oval and a force-field designed to keep the water and its immense pressure out.

Despite the Brenine's love of the dark, the island's interior was well lit. The sprawling city of The Cove was laid out under the starry ceiling of stalactites. The soft glow from above contrasted with the neon signs that dominated the ground levels, advertising the various vices that attracted beings from all over the Conclave. Personal transports flew in every direction around the city's towering spires, weaving between the larger stalactites. The *Rackham* was assigned its own landing alcove, built into the bedrock.

Roland shut the engine down, satisfied that it could only be turned on again with his closely guarded code. Ch'len shook his head every time the engine shut down, more than aware that he was grounded along with the ship. For all their time together, Roland simply didn't trust the little shit not to fly away when things got hairy.

"I've tinkered with the holo-bands," Ch'len said, as Roland made for the kitchen. "You can be an Atari this time, should help with our cover."

"I had something else in mind." Roland didn't stop to take in Ch'len's questioning expression.

The kitchen was a mess as usual. It probably didn't help that Ch'len couldn't reach a lot of things, causing him to create more mess as he climbed over everything. Roland had thought about remodelling the nanocelium to accommodate the smaller alien, but the thought had been fleeting. Roland was more interested in the wall panel just off from the kitchen. The panel slid aside and presented the bounty hunter with his favourite toys.

Roland depressed a small button and activated a square drawer at the base of the armoury. He reached down and pulled out a black helmet, covered in angles and dark glass. "Did you fix this?"

Ch'len waddled into the room with a sour look on his face. "It was never broken. I just needed to tweak the interface. The *Rackham* may have provided the nanocelium, but the little buggers weren't happy being bound to Conclave tech."

"Did you fix it?"

"Yes."

Roland looked at the helmet and then at the empty drawer. "Where's the rest of it?"

"In my workshop." Ch'len nodded in the direction of his room.

"Did you make the other adjustments I asked for?"

"You mean your commands? Yes, I did. The suit has space for all your toys, most of them at least." Ch'len was partially distracted, trying to search the kitchen counter for food by touch alone.

Roland watched the scrounging Ch'kara with bemusement. "Well go get it then."

Ch'len pushed himself up on his tiptoes and grasped some food Roland couldn't identify. "You realise how illegal personalised cloaking technology is, right?"

"Any more illegal than our normal line of work?" Roland placed the helmet on the table and finished off the remains of a bottle of Raalakian ale.

"It's the *highest* level of illegal! The Highclave outlawed any and all privately owned cloaking systems and abolished all research. If you get caught wearing a whole suit that cloaks your body, we'll both serve a life sentence in the Relis Mines."

Roland flashed his roguish smile. "Well if you fixed it properly, I won't get caught. It's hard to catch what you can't see."

It took longer than he would have liked, but after a lot of pulling and tugging, Roland was finally fitted from neck-to-toe in the dark, but snug armour. It reminded him of Kalian's Terran exo-suit, only the 'armour' was coated with a thin layer of nanocelium that wasn't designed to be protective. The suit would render him invisible, but a single bolt of intrinium fire would put a hole in him.

"Looks good!" Ch'len marvelled at his work.

Roland scowled. "I feel like my ass is eating the filament..."

Ch'len matched his scowl and gripped Roland's forearm. "Controls are built in." Despite the many angles, a small screen had been fitted into the arm piece. "Press here and here to activate the suit. You can take a few toys and your Terran knife, but no guns."

"No guns?" Roland looked at his Tri-rollers longingly.

"There's nowhere to put them!" Ch'len handed the helmet over. "Give it a go."

Roland placed the helmet over his head and clipped it into the neck aperture, creating a quiet hiss. The HUD was overlaid with the initial start-up data before settling. Everything in the kitchen was suddenly highlighted with a thin green line, including Ch'len. The darkened corners were exposed as the helmet's screen compensated for the shadows, allowing the user to see in all conditions.

"Well..?" Ch'len stood back.

Roland activated the stealth systems and watched his body disappear. An icon appeared in the corner of his HUD, offering the bounty hunter a new mode of vision. A quick blink to acknowledge the icon was all it took to change what he could see. His invisible body suddenly came back into view, but only to him. In response to Ch'len's question, Roland reached down and flicked the alien on the head.

"I love it!"

Ch'len massaged his sore head. "Well, you need to turn it off now. If the system overheats, the interface between the nanocelium and the Conclave tech will burn out, rendering you permanently visible, what with all the flames..."

Roland raised his eyebrow even though Ch'len couldn't see him. "Flames? Am I wearing a *bomb*?"

"No!" Ch'len didn't look very convincing. "It's prototype tech that no one is researching, Roland. I had to make a few bits up... Not to mention the nanocelium. That stuff might as well be magic!"

Roland quickly deactivated the suit and removed the helmet, shoving it into Ch'len's arms. He tried not to think about the potential deathtrap he was wearing and instead looked to his armoury. The Terran hilt lay horizontal on its rest, silently awaiting its master. Roland picked it up and adjusted the fine rings at the top of the hilt. He thumbed the activation and watched the nanocelium spring to life, forming a serrated blade just longer than his hand. Happy with the new length, the bounty hunter deactivated the blade and slotted the hilt horizontally into the sheath at the base of his back.

The Tri-rollers called to him, offering their comfort, but he was forced to leave them on the rack. Roland's old training instructor always came to mind at times like this, reminding him that he was the weapon.

Ch'len moved away and returned with a belt, covered in pouches and attachments. "I've had a play with the usual gadgets."

Roland accepted the belt and removed the devices he felt would prove useful. Small metallic pouches opened up across his chest and waist, perfect for storage.

"So how are you going to get to the Starlight Apartments? You'll be hard to see but we're not exactly parked on Hon Valorga's doorstep."

Roland fitted his helmet back on. "*Rackham*?"

"Yes Roland?" the ship replied.

"Be a dear and call me a cab."

JEDEDIAH HOLT LOOKED at the rising radiation levels on Commander Vale's datapad and reminded himself that this was the only course left to them. Regardless of everything he had learned from Captain Fey in the last hour, the fact still remained that the radiation leak would be the end of them all. It was his first priority as the captain of the Paladin.

Don't think about Earth. Don't think about Chrissy and the kids...

The air-lock doors connecting the Paladin to the alien craft opened again. Had Captain Fey not come out first, Jed would have had a hard time concealing his expression of terror. The aliens that accompanied her were hideous amalgamations of machine and some form of pale alien. The four engineers appeared identical to Jed's eye, with robotic limbs and attachments that seemed to be permanently bonded with their chalk-white flesh. Their pointed teeth only added to their menacing look, putting Jed and the Raiders on edge.

"These engineers are from the Conclave," Fey explained, casually.

"What *are* they?" Jed knew his pointed stare was rude, but he couldn't help it. These were the first aliens he had ever seen up close.

"Their species are called Shay."

Booming footfalls came from the shadows of the alien craft.

The Raiders physically tensed and Sam put one foot back, as her fight or flight reflexes battled one another. Jed kept his footing, however, maintaining his authoritative stance against the new monster that emerged from the craft. It was big, in every way. With a flat head of rock and broad shoulders, this new alien walked into the corridor on four legs of stone. The only familiar sight was the red uniform worn by the giant creature. Jed knew an officer when he saw one, though from Fey's recounting this could only be the High Charge known as Uthor.

Captain Fey cleared her throat. "This is High Charge Uthor. High Charge, this is Captain Jedediah Holt of the Paladin."

Uthor's voice was akin to that of a rock-slide, but his words were completely lost on Jed. The captain could only look to Li for guidance.

"He's greeting you," Fey explained. "You're going to need one of these." Li tilted her head and exposed her neck, revealing a small circular dot behind her ear. "It allows you to translate their various languages as well as their written word. It's painless."

Jed couldn't speak for the others, so he offered himself to go first and have the small device placed behind his ear. Sam and the Raiders, who appeared more cautious, accepted the translators and allowed the Shay to fit them. After a brief wave of nausea and an acrid metallic taste, Jed and the others were almost stunned into silence when Uthor spoke again, this time with clarity.

"Greetings," Jed replied, unsure of alien etiquette.

Uthor glanced at Fey before regarding Jed again. "May my engineers see to your reactor leak?"

Jed hesitated. "Yes. Of course. I'll show you there myself."

Uthor raised his thick hand. "This is as far as I go, I'm afraid."

Jed looked at the alien, wishing he could remember what species he was and followed Uthor's gaze to the door behind them. It was clearly too small and narrow to allow him entry.

"Sorry..." Jed felt silly apologising for the human design of his ship, but he didn't know what else to say.

"After your radiation leak is contained and inoculations have been given, we will talk again. I would be honoured if you accepted my invitation to board the *Nautallon*."

Jed looked beyond the High Charge and assumed he was inviting him to board the massive ship that loomed outside. Captain Holt simply nodded his head, desperately trying to fight the shock of everything. They had only left Earth Dock two days ago...

Uthor regarded Captain Fey before returning to the smaller craft. Lanky silhouettes appeared in the doorway, hidden in shadow when the door closed behind the High Charge.

Sam cleared her throat and showed Jed the levels of radiation on her datapad. The deadly particles had spread to another deck.

"I'll show you to the engine room," Jed felt uncomfortable talking to the Shay and so directed his statement at Fey.

"We would like to see your navigation array as well." The Shay's words were heard perfectly, but its voice was just so alien. No human could mimic it. "We have been tasked with discovering the cause of your extraordinary voyage."

Jed met his commander's eyes and held a silent conversation for a second. Sam was loathed to give them too much freedom. "That would be much appreciated."

Due to the Paladin's size, it took the group almost fifteen minutes to reach the door that led to the engineering section of the ship. Jed had been careful to avoid any civilian areas. Several engineers were already outside, all dressed in overalls, having just come through the decontamination chamber and relinquished their hazmat suits for deep cleaning. Jed saw their look of shock and horror when the Shay became visible in their midst. The captain held up a hand to calm them and introduced the aliens to his new chief engineer, Aleksander Grenko.

When Grenko remained in stunned silence, Jed said, "Report."

Grenko tore his eyes from the pale, cyborg-like aliens. "The rising levels are playing hell with our suits, sir. We're going to have to make some adjustments before we go back in."

"That won't be necessary," the Shay replied.

Jed understood every word, forgetting for the moment that Grenko and the other engineers had no clue.

"We have already taken precautions," the Shay continued. "Grant us access and we will begin our work."

"Stand aside, Chief," Jed ordered.

Colonel Ava Matthews stepped forward. "Sir. Recommend waiting until my team is suited up for escort."

Jed didn't want to delay this any longer. "Denied." Seeing the colonel's anger reflect on her face, Jed explained, "If they don't fix it we're dead anyway, escort or no escort." Captain Holt gestured for Grenko to open the door to the decontamination chamber.

The four Shay entered the chamber without a word. Jed noticed the backpacks they all wore, coated in metal and full of attachments he couldn't recognise. Two of them carried cases filled with who-knows-what, but the captain didn't want to think about it. Let them fix his biggest problem while he dealt with the next one.

"Sir?" Grenko looked confused.

"I'll explain soon. Commander Vale, have everyone gather in the central hold - I mean everyone. Captain Fey, would you accompany me? I have a very important speech to make..."

THE DRIVERLESS CAB flew between the stalactites of The Cove, weaving in and out of traffic, as it climbed ever higher toward the rocky ceiling. Roland removed a small datapad from his waist and pulled the cord out of the end, inserting it into the exposed circuit board he had already ripped open. The datapad began its immediate hack of the vehicle using an algorithm designed by Ch'len - seconds later, Roland was in control of the cab's flight systems.

"You definitely installed the Laronian boots into the suit, right?" Roland checked the sole of his left foot.

"Yes. You have to stop asking me that!" Ch'len, as usual, was sat nice and comfy in the *Rackham*'s bridge, monitoring Roland's progress.

"I just want to avoid breaking every bone in my body!" Roland navigated a particularly wide stalactite and kept the cab as close to the jagged ceiling as possible.

"Starlight Apartments are coming up on your right," Ch'len said through his mouthful of grub.

Roland peered out of the window and looked down at the tower. The central structure was thin, resting on a tripod, and building up into a saucer-shaped head. The saucer was filled with penthouse apartments, two of which were owned by Hon Valorga.

"Have you got access to the apartments security systems?" Roland asked as he lined the cab up, directly above the saucer.

"I'm working on it," Ch'len replied quickly. "The Laronian has had extra measures built into the firewalls. Hon must be quite the asset."

Roland would have preferred to have a better idea of awaited him inside, but he didn't want to waste time. "Looks like I'm doing this the old-fashioned way."

"You're going in without recon?" Ch'len stopped chewing.

"This isn't my first rodeo, Len."

There was a pause on Ch'len's end. "What's a rodeo?"

Roland ignored the alien. "I'm handing control of the cab over to you."

"Well be fast, the meter's running..."

Roland couldn't help but smile, using an override to open the cab door, and leaping from the vehicle. The suit's cloaking system kicked in, keeping his freefall undetectable to the eye. The helmet's HUD measured the gap between the top of the apartments and himself, informing Roland of his speed and how long he had before contact. Most of the vehicles flying around were beneath the saucer section of Starlight Apartments, keeping his drop clear. At the last second, the bounty hunter lifted his knees and activated the boosters in his Laronian boots. The thrust was never enough to give the wearer the power of flight; they could only break the fall.

Touching down on Starlight Apartments, Roland waited for a second to ensure his suit was still working. He looked around, impressed with how smoothly everything had gone thus far. It had been a long time since he had put this much thought into a mission or catching a bounty.

With his hacking device still fitted into the cab, Roland resorted to using his Terran blade to prise open the hatch covering the ventilation shaft. Within minutes he was silently dropping into the corridor between two of the penthouse apartments. Even the corridors were better decorated than most homes.

A warning appeared in the corner of his HUD, alerting him to an imminent shutdown of the suit's cloaking system. With no time to lose, Roland depressed a button on his waist and caught the metallic balls that fell out. Once released, the tiny spheres would seek out any lifeforms and collate their data to form a living map, allowing Roland to track his targets.

The Translift *pinged*.

Roland held his breath with nowhere to hide in the lit corridor. The warning inside his HUD brought up a countdown in human minutes, informing him of how long he had until the suit completely shut down. The bounty hunter replaced the tracking spheres and retrieved his Terran blade, hoping to God that it wasn't going to be a Raalak that exited the Translift.

The doors opened and seven female Laronians and two female Brenine entered the corridor. They were all accompanied by a male Brenine in a cheap suit. Roland could tell he was armed by the way he moved.

Just another scumbag...

The group looked right at the spot where Roland was standing, but none could see his form. The countdown inside his HUD was down to seconds now. The male Brenine waved a card in front of the panel beside one of the apartment doors, forcing it aside and allowing music to blare out, filling the corridor. The countdown was close to zero. The bounty hunter followed them inside and scanned the new environment as quickly as he could. He needed somewhere to hide for a minute, so the suit could cool down and recharge.

"Bovaasi!" Hon Valorga greeted the male Brenine with a wide smile. "Bovaasi you have surpassed yourself with these fine specimen!" Hon examined the women as if they were a product.

Roland ducked into the nearest room and placed his back flat against the wall. The suit powered down and the nanocelium returned to their original dormant state. A new countdown appeared inside his HUD, informing the bounty hunter of when he could next use the cloaking systems. Roland decided to take the time to learn what he could.

"I'm in." Roland didn't have to worry about the noise level, thanks to the overly loud music - not that any sound escaped the suit's helmet.

"Me too," Ch'len replied. "Bad news is; there are no cameras inside any of the penthouses. I'm blind."

Roland's training had provided him with reflexes he could no longer control. From his few seconds inside the penthouse, he had clocked five Brenine, including Hon and the male escort from the hallway. There were ten females, including the nine arrivals. He had seen all of the male Brenine packing weapons, as well as the female Trillik, who was relaxing on a sofa by the curving window that spanned the entire apartment.

"I'm going silent for a minute." Roland removed his helmet and peered around the door frame.

"What do you think, Darja?" Hon Valorga addressed the female Trillik. "Potential, yes?" The Brenine looked every bit the slimy bastard Roland had imagined him to.

"We will have to put them through their paces, but yes, I see potential." The Trillik looked at the girls with four black, hungry eyes.

Hon laughed and poured himself a flute of golden liquid. "Bovaasi, Lago, take them through and get them ready."

Bovaasi and the one called Lago escorted the girls out of sight. Now there was only Hon, two male Brenine and Darja, the Trillik. They laughed at something Hon said and enjoyed a drink together. Beyond them, Roland could see vehicles of every size passing by the curved window, oblivious and ignorant of the crimes going on around them.

Roland replaced his helmet and sighed. "I think they're about to have some kind of orgy."

"Why do you sound so sad?" Ch'len's tone was that of confusion.

"Because I'm not here to watch live porn, nutsack! Gor-van could leave Byzantial any minute and Hon's the only one who knows where he's holding up. I need the information inside that fucker's head and I need it *now*!"

Ch'len's munching came over the comm-link. "Just burst in and show them that hideous human face of yours. Most people think you guys can melt them with your mind!"

"I need him on his own..." Roland was running through past missions, trying to think of different methods.

Ch'len's next outburst nearly burst Roland's eardrum. "I know what to do!"

Roland shook his head, wishing he could poke his ear through the helmet. "What?"

"Give me a minute!" Ch'len's comm went dead.

Roland crouched down and looked around the door again. Bovaasi and Lago had reappeared with the Laronians and the two female Brenine. The new prostitutes had replaced their clothes with revealing lingerie and high heels. They might not be human, but Roland still found them attractive. He tried not to think about how long it had been since he had last had sex. He could remember the faces of the women he had bedded aboard the *Gommarian*, during his brief time there, but found he couldn't remember their names. The self-realisation that he was an asshole didn't stop him from focusing on the mission.

"What the hell are you doing, Len?"

Ch'len's comm crackled back to life. "Do you remember when

The Laronian contacted us with all those threats after the incident at Protocorps? Well, the *Rackham* recorded the conversation."

"Great, my ship has an answer phone. How's this going to help?" Roland looked back into the apartment as Hon Valorga was helping one of the female Brenine to lose her bra.

"Watch…"

The music suddenly died down when Hon's apartment alerted him to an incoming call. The other Brenine ignored it, but Darja looked at Hon, indicating the glass table-top in the lounge, which informed them the call was originating from Vallara, the homeworld of all Laronians. Hon killed the music entirely and ushered everyone to be quiet.

"There's only one call I get from Vallara," Hon said to Darja.

After he accepted the call, the table projected a holographic square with the image of The Laronian, sitting at his desk. The crime lord's unusual helmet covered his features, instead presenting them with a view of a swirling galaxy as if the spiral of stars were inside his head.

"Are we alone?" The Laronian asked with a serious tone.

Hon hesitated. Until a second ago, the Brenine had been the biggest, baddest criminal in the room. He clicked his fingers and ordered everyone to leave. Their speed was too slow, however, and the Brenine resorted to an outburst, while simultaneously pushing one of his guards in the direction of the door.

The Laronian put his feet up on the desk, as he had when he threatened Roland three months ago. "This is all taking too long. I'm getting bored…"

Hon wiped the sweat from his forehead, aware of what happened to people who bored the unstable crime boss. All the while, Ch'len was sniggering to himself down Roland's comm-link.

"What did you do; rearrange his words?" Roland sank back into the shadows, allowing the group to pass him in the hallway and leave the penthouse.

Ch'len was still laughing. "It was so easy because of that stupid voice of his! All I had to do was trick his array into thinking the call was from Vallara."

The cloaking systems came back online. He activated them with his thumb and exited the room, entering the dim penthouse. Hon Valorga was standing opposite him, on the other side of the faint hologram.

"Boss?" Hon looked frantically from the hologram to the table. "Are you there? Can you hear me?"

The Laronian continued to move around and talk into the camera, but Ch'len had deactivated the message's sound, leaving only the visual of the message. Hon tapped the menu on the glass table, trying to figure out what malfunction would be the death of him.

Roland spoke into his comm-link. "End the call."

Ch'len did as he was asked, deactivating the hologram in front of the bounty hunter. Hon gasped, assured that he had just offended the scariest being in the galaxy. Roland decided to re-educate the Brenine and shut down the cloaking systems. Hon yelled in fright and jumped back, falling on to the sofa in a mad scramble to get away. His instinct was to run; that was a good thing, Roland could work with that.

Without taking his red eyes off the menacing figure, clad in black, Hon reached for his gun on the table. Roland reacted without thought and kicked the edge of the table, causing Hon to overshoot his reach. There was no hesitation from Roland, who marched over the table and descended on the terrified Brenine. With rough hands, Hon was dragged off the sofa and flipped onto the glass table with enough force to shatter it.

Roland took a breath and slowly walked around the bent frames of the low table. Hon was on all fours now, scurrying through the shards of glass, dazed and disorientated. His pale hand went for the fallen gun, but Roland was quick to stamp on the Brenine's knuckles. Hon screamed before blood poured from under his hand, now impaled with a dozen shards of glass.

"Who... are... you?" Hon looked up at the shiny black glass of Roland's helmet.

The bounty hunter pulled the helmet off with a gentle hiss and revealed his grizzled, human features. Hon Valorga's terror became tenfold at the sight of him. His squirming only caused more pain in his hand, and Roland dug his heel in as a show of dominance. The Brenine's strange tentacle-like tongue was visible, whipping around inside his mouth.

Roland knew the pain would push adrenaline round the Brenine's body, bringing his fight or flight response to the surface. As an expert in this particular field, the ex-agent knew that more pain was required to keep the victim terrified enough to be pliable, but awake enough to answer questions. To ensure there was no fight left in the pimp, Roland used his helmet as weapon and whipped it across Hon's face. His thick tongue lashed out and sucked up the blood that spilled from his nose.

Along with the pain, the victim had to feel a sense of helplessness. Hon had to know that Roland was his new god and that only he could grant the Brenine peace and freedom. To enforce this dominance, Roland released him from the grip of his boot and allowed Hon to crawl away, out of the glass. After a few seconds of freedom, the bounty hunter pounced again, this time flipping the Brenine onto his back and delivering a swift punch to the face. The moment of pain and disorientation was all Roland needed to drop his weight onto Hon, using both of his knees to trap the alien's arms. In the same motion, Roland retrieved the Terran blade from the base of his back and activated the blade. Hon didn't like what happened next.

Roland covered the alien's mouth, stifling his pain-filled scream. His wicked tongue probed at his gloved palm, desperate to find a gap and let out a cry. The Terran blade was firmly planted in Hon's already cut and broken hand, nailing him to the polished floor.

Bending down, Roland placed his mouth next to the Brenine's ear. "Does that answer who I am?"

Hon moaned and squirmed as tears ran down the sides of his face. The Brenine knew that death was sitting on top of him.

Roland spoke in a quiet and calm voice, having learned years ago how menacing it made him sound. "I have questions. You have answers. Tell me the truth and you get to walk out of here with all your limbs." Roland glanced at Hon's mutilated hand. "Well, *most* of them. If you lie, I'll take you apart piece by piece until you look more like a Shay than a Brenine. Question one," Roland immediately placed his thumb over Hon's left eye and pressed firmly. "Where is Gor-van Tanar hiding?"

The Brenine was perfectly still, well aware that his answer determined whether he lost an eye or not. Roland carefully lifted his hand from the alien's mouth and waited for the answer. It was sick, but a part of Roland hoped that Hon would lie, giving him cause to push his thumb into the pimp's eye socket.

"He'll kill me..." Hon whispered, pleadingly.

"Wrong answer." Roland squeezed and didn't stop until the joint of his thumb was inside Hon's eye.

Every part of the Brenine wriggled dramatically in agony, desperately fighting against Roland's weight. With his hand once again covering the alien's mouth, the shrieking was kept to a minimum. The bounty hunter finally removed his thumb and wiped the blood and juices on Hon's suit jacket. The comm-link in his helmet went dead again as Ch'len disconnected.

It took a minute before Hon's attention could be focused again. Roland took the time to visualise Li'ara's face and remember how helpless he felt when the chamber exploded at Protocorps. If she was truly still alive he would learn of it, and if that meant he carved a bloody path across the Conclave, then so be it. He had promised Kalian he would bring her back safely, and he failed. That sense of loss and failure drove his mind to bad places.

The bounty hunter placed his other thumb over Hon's remaining eye. "Question one," Roland repeated aggressively. "Where is Gor-van Tanar hiding? I know you provide him with girls!"

The Brenine whimpered and hesitated. "He's in the Qelt Wastes!"

Roland had never heard of it, but it didn't sound like a place someone as rich and resourceful as Gor-van would stay. Despite that, the bounty hunter was sure Hon hadn't lied to him.

He pressed his thumb a little firmer into the Brenine's eye, eliciting a pathetic yelp. "Well don't stop there..."

Hon Valorga's lip quivered. "He has a safe house out there -"

"Where's *there*?" Roland's interruption made the Brenine jump.

"It's in the southern hemisphere, near Q'altat. It's just a desert. The exact coordinates are on my terminal."

"Details..."

Now Hon could see light at the end of the tunnel. Answers kept pain at bay, giving him the illusion that Roland was reasonable and would, therefore, allow him to live when they were finished. Little did he know that the bounty hunter from Earth was far from reasonable.

"It doesn't look like much. It's an old house, simple in design. Of course, Gor-van stays underneath it, in the real complex."

"Security..." Roland lightened the pressure over Hon's eye.

"Sensors detect anything ten feet off the ground. No ship can sneak up on the house. As for personnel, I have no idea."

Roland returned the pressure over Hon's eye, sensing omission.

The Brenine squirmed again. "Okay, okay! I don't know exactly how many guys he has, but he always orders twelve girls on top of his three. I don't know if that's one girl per guard though."

Roland lifted his thumb somewhat. "Escape routes? Hidden tunnels?"

"None, just a hangar underground, disguised as more desert."

Roland chewed it over for a moment, letting the Brenine fear what might come next. He didn't think Hon was lying to him, but aliens were harder to read than humans.

"Okay, Hon." Roland removed a small device from his waist, used for cracking codes on safes, and placed it under the Brenine's head. "Now you're resting on a pressure mine," he lied. "So do yourself a favour and stay very still." Roland lifted his thumb from his victim's only eye and retrieved the snap-shackles from a compartment in the suit's thigh. "This is going to hurt. Don't scream."

He ripped the Terran blade from Hon's hand and replaced it on his back. The Brenine did his best to stifle his scream and keep his head still. Roland put Hon's wrists together and used the snap-shackles to bind his hands. The stick snapped around his pale skin until both ends bonded together.

"Now if your info turns out to be shit, I'll come back and kill you a lot slower than that pressure mine." Roland meant it. If the information was bogus, he would happily return and take his time sending Hon into the next life.

ROLAND DIDN'T DEACTIVATE his cloaking systems until the *Rackham's* hold sealed up behind him. He happily removed the helmet and unceremoniously dumped it in the kitchen on his way to the bridge. He didn't even attempt to take the rest of the suit off; he would need Ch'len's help in that department.

Kicking the empty bottles of beer aside, Roland dropped into his chair and brought up the nav array, searching for the Qelt Wastes. Ch'len didn't say anything, clearly uncomfortable with Roland's recent proclivities. That was fine by Roland; he didn't keep the Ch'kara around for chit-chat. The silence made the bounty hunter uncomfortable, however. Even the background sound of Ch'len's munching was oddly absent.

"Nice work with The Laronian thing," Roland commented as he plotted a course for the Qelt Wastes.

"Thanks. Nice work with the..." Ch'len searched for the word. "Well, I guess there is no replacing the word torture."

Roland chewed over his response. "It's the only way..."

"I don't have a problem with you torturing dirtbags like Hon Valorga or Lan-vid if that's what it takes. My problem is..."

"*What?*" Roland pressed.

"If, and it's a *huge* if, but if Li'ara is still alive and she miraculously survived the explosion, where's she been for the last three months?"

That same question had plagued Roland's mind, but it was a question he couldn't answer until he solved the first mystery; *how* did she survive?

Roland had no answer for Ch'len. "The next piece of the puzzle is in the Qelt Wastes. One mystery at a time, Len."

NINE

Kalian stood by the *Advent's* air-lock with anticipation. Despite all the shit that the universe had piled onto his shoulders over the last year, the thought of actually stepping foot on the planet that truly birthed humanity was exciting. For the briefest of moments, he was able to think of something other than Li'ara. But only for a moment.

"A suit has been prepared for you," Naydaalan announced as he entered the small hold. "It will provide three hours of oxygen."

Kalian offered the Novaarian a smug smile. "I've already got a suit."

Using his Terran abilities, Kalian increased the strength of the electromagnetic field around both of his hands. This prompted the nanocelium in his suit to extend across his bare skin and cover his hands with strong, but flexible, gloves. With his right hand, Kalian cupped his fingers, activating the holographic menu that emitted from the ends of his fingers. A couple of flexes between the digits commanded the nanocelium around his neck to change shape and form a sleek helmet that completely coated his head and face. There were no apparent eyes on the outside, but Kalian was given a view from the inside as if there was no covering at all.

Naydaalan looked at his own suit which, despite its technological elegance, appeared bulky and archaic in comparison. The Novaarian's face was cast in a purple light behind the glass front of his helmet. A small mech hovered by his side, its contents filled with the tools and instruments that would be needed to fix the ship's long-range sensor dish.

Naydaalan used the panel on his lower arm to open the hatch and lower the ramp. Kalian was ready to adapt his eyes to the natural light that flooded the hold, but the suit took care of the glare. What awaited them was oddly beautiful, in its own way.

Kalian and Naydaalan stepped out and looked upon the amalgamation of jungle and city. The opposing landscapes had come together over the course of two hundred thousand years, combating and evolving to weather the ever-changing levels of radiation. There wasn't a single building or Terran-made object left intact. The roads and footpaths were indistinguishable, overgrown with thick green and blue vegetation. Broken arches and burnt corners poked out between the branches and weeds. Judging by the space in which the *Advent* had landed, Kalian guessed them to be standing in what was once a courtyard - though it could easily have been the foundations of an ancient building.

Kicking a root aside, Kalian knelt down and brushed his gloved hand over the soil, before grabbing a handful. He watched it fall through his fingers intently while thinking about its importance. ALF was by his side, watching him. How long he had been standing there, Kalian didn't know.

"How does it feel?" Naydaalan asked. "To be the first of your kind to return here..."

Kalian dropped the handful of dirt and stood up, with one eye on ALF. "Underwhelming." The blue sky was becoming stained with the long fingers of the approaching storm. "I'll look for the Starforge while you work on the *Advent*."

Naydaalan wasn't convinced. "It would be safer if we stay together. We can both search for the Starforge when I'm finished."

Kalian looked up at the tainted sky. "We don't have time. The speed of those winds will sweep us across the horizon. I'll be back soon." Without waiting for a reply, he turned and left.

ALF pointed down what had once been a busy street. "The Starforge is this way."

"I know." Kalian continued to stride through the foliage, using subtle telekinetic movements to push the large, hanging leaves aside. "I walked these streets inside the subconducer."

They walked in silence for a while as they navigated the overgrown jungle and toppled buildings. Kalian was forced to lift tons of rubble out of the way, allowing them to pass through a skyscraper that now lay across the ground like a fallen giant. Certain parts were not easily moved, due to structural integrity, making Kalian search for safer routes through the heart of the ancient city.

"There's nothing left of them..." Kalian commented, scanning the ground. "No bones. No sign that anything ever lived here."

"Savrick was thorough," ALF replied in a sombre tone. "I failed him most of all."

Kalian looked at the AI, wondering for a moment if ALF could see his face inside the helmet. ALF had often spoken of his role in the Terran community, usually comparing himself to a parent, but rarely taking any blame. The part of his construct left on Naveen was only a part of the whole, he had always said. The AI had split his personality into three pieces in order to effectively run the Terran society. One part to oversee and govern the day-to-day living, transport and energy requirements across an empire that spanned thousands of lightyears. The second part was there to meet the Terran on their level, as an interface. It was in their homes and on their ships, a guiding hand through life.

The part left on Naveen, the part that was currently bound to his exo-suit, was the third and final piece. This particular portion of ALF had been designed to teach the Terran about their natural abilities. Of course, to the Terran, there were no three sides to the whole, there was just ALF.

"They made me to help them," ALF continued, surveying the remains of Albadar's capital. "Before me, they only knew war. I watched them develop their natural abilities and find their place in the universe. I was proud to be among their creations, their achievements."

Kalian stopped in the middle of what his memories told him was once a plaza. "Just stop!" Kalian wanted to pinch his eyes in exasperation. "Savrick found the first cube on Hadrok, just like the Conclave discovered the cube on Trantax IV. They're ancient. Older than you, apparently. You told me that the Terran were at war long before your creation and that nanocelium was their weapon of choice." ALF nodded along. "Then you came along and brought an end to all the wars and took control. Are you telling me that you didn't catalogue everything that came before you? The cubes are made of nanocelium, meaning they must be creations of the Terran. The cubes must have been in a database or something!"

"I can see that you're frustrated," ALF replied irritatingly. "How long has it been since you slept, or meditated?"

"I'm rested!" Kalian lied. "This is about you and the Terran! Whatever's hunting my people down, whatever drove Savrick to start the civil war and destroy Earth, it started here, with you." Kalian was pacing now. "And what's Evalan?"

ALF's mouth was half open, ready to respond with an answer until Kalian asked his last question. Evalan was a mystery to them all. The word had been found on both cubes, and Kalian was confident that had he been able to inspect the cube inside Protocorps HQ, the word would have been engraved on it too.

"I already told you," ALF said, "I don't know."

Kalian swivelled on the holographic projection. "It was written in a language you created!"

"A language you can understand," ALF countered. "You know as well as I that it has no meaning in Terran. There was no person or place called Evalan in the Terran Empire!" It was the first time ALF had matched Kalian's aggressive tone. "As for everything else; I have no idea! Yes, I catalogued everything, but the Terran were at war for years after my creation. It took me an age to earn their trust and turn things around. Things get lost in war. The cubes are... I don't know what they are. If they were indeed made by the Terran then they were made eons ago, before Earth even had oceans." ALF paused as if considering his next words. "We should go to the Criterion. There are no answers here."

Kalian didn't know what to think, and that was the problem. He had no Li'ara or Esabelle to help him. No one he could trust. ALF's words made sense, but none of it sat right with Kalian. The heads-up display inside his visor informed him of the rising levels of radiation. Thanks to the suit, he was in no danger, but the rising levels were a forewarning of the approaching storm. Without another word, Kalian pressed on.

After clearing the road of a giant stone head, covered in foliage, Kalian finally came across the central square of the city. The Starforge was positioned in the centre of the square, with six other roads leading away from it, like the spokes on a wheel. The forge was a ruin. The semi-circular piece of technology had been snapped, twisted and bent out of shape. The ground beneath it was like that of a mountain range, having suffered the effects of multiple earthquakes over the millennia.

"It wouldn't have mattered if it was in perfect condition," ALF offered. "Its power source is based several hundred miles from here, in the ocean. The connections between it and the Starforge will have been severed in the initial attack. It's dead."

Kalian looked at the small icon in the corner of his HUD and activated the comm-link to Naydaalan. "We found the Starforge..."

"Judging by your tone, I assume it is inoperable?" Naydaalan replied.

"Inoperable is an understatement." Kalian scanned the area, looking for nothing in particular. "Have you fixed the array yet?"

"Not quite. Those nanocelium leeches should be avoided in the future..." Naydaalan sounded frustrated, and rightly so. Kalian had been treating him as if he were nothing but an unwanted tag-along.

"I'm heading back now. We should leave before that storm..." Kalian broke off, looking into the distance with a furrowed brow.

"Kalian?" Naydaalan inquired.

Kalian narrowed his vision to the alley between two buildings, beyond the Starforge. Somewhere in all the vines and giant leaves, he was sure he could see something, something with eyes. There was more movement, this time from a third-storey window above the alley, and then another flicker of movement in his peripheral vision. Kalian used the suit's sensors to initiate a quick sweep.

"Don't rely on the suit," ALF said.

The creatures were immediately surrounded by a red outline, via his helmet's HUD. They were large animals, the size of a horse at least. The scans produced a small holographic image that only Kalian could see. The creatures had four legs, each with three razor-sharp claws. Their face was somewhere between that of a lizard and a lion, but most certainly full of teeth. A long tail whipped out behind them, not dissimilar from a rat.

They were predators.

"What are they?" Kalian asked aloud.

"They look like Bragans," ALF's hologram had disappeared now.

Kalian searched for the name in the Terran databanks that filled his subconscious mind. A Bragan had been a small reptile, native to Albadar thousands of years ago. At the time of the Terran civil war, they had been no bigger than a man's arm.

"So that's what two hundred thousand years of irradiated evolution looks like..." Kalian shut down the scan and expanded his awareness. His mind filled the square, taking in every molecule as if he were a part of it.

"Kalian? What's happening?" Naydaalan asked.

There were hundreds of them. Kalian's awareness found all of them in the blink of an eye, their intelligence glowing like stars in the dark. Most of them were hiding in the greenery and decimated buildings around the square. Not only could he feel their intelligence, but Kalian could also feel the adrenaline pumping through their blood. The Bragans had found today's meal.

"Naydaalan? Are you still outside the ship?" Kalian had visions of the beasts prowling around the *Advent*, stalking the Novaarian.

"Yes. I am just replacing the array panel now."

"You need to get inside the *Advent,* now." Kalian took some cautionary steps back.

"Is there a problem, Kalian?" Naydaalan asked, concerned.

"Not everything on this planet was wiped out. Some of the local wildlife has taken an interest in me." Kalian used telekinesis to push aside the branches and vines behind his feet. As he moved backward, so too did the Bragans advance forward.

"Do you require assistance?"

"No he doesn't, just -" ALF's reply was cut off when Kalian disabled the audio.

"I'll be fine, just get inside the ship and keep the engine running. I'll be back in a moment."

"By my calculations, it took you an hour to reach your current destination." Naydaalan sounded as if he was moving.

The Bragans closed in.

"The *Sentinel* was a pretty cramped ship for something so big. It's been a while since I stretched my legs..." Kalian had already mapped out his route back to the *Advent*.

The Bragan sprung from their hiding spots at the same moment Kalian turned around and dashed for the nearest building. Their roars were accompanied by the thundering of hundreds of feet. Kalian ignored the sounds and focused on his surroundings, allowing his mind to spill out into the old streets and feed him an image of the terrain that lay ahead. Contorting his body into every shape possible, Kalian jumped through jagged holes and over fallen walls, all the while avoiding the thicker branches and entangled vines. A Bragan, who thought it had been lying secretly in wait, exploded from behind its concrete cover. Kalian didn't stop for the beast, but instead held out his hand, palm open, and forced the Bragan through a wall with telekinesis. After the creature burst through to the other side, Kalian jumped over its limp body and continued his sprint.

The Bragan were fast, faster than any land animal Earth had ever known. Kalian was reminded of his daily runs with Esabelle, aboard the *Gommarian*. The four-legged animals were coming up on his side now, tackling the terrain with ease and experience - the pack had hunted in these grounds before.

To keep the Bragans on their toes, Kalian increased his speed, using telekinesis to push him further with every stride. Just when one of the beasts thought he was in their grasp, Kalian skipped a step and altered his trajectory in a single bound, causing many of the Bragans to skid into one another. A tumble of limbs and angered roars brought a smile to his lips. It was perhaps the first time in three months that Kalian had found a genuine smile on his face. Unleashing his powers like this and enjoying his Terran abilities was impossible inside the Conclave. Being what he was scared them.

Kalian continued to use every acrobatic manoeuvre he knew to evade the hungry Bragans. Every now and then he was forced to send a ball of organic plasma in their direction to steer them off course. When his speed worked against him, Kalian had no problem charging through a wall and allowing his nanocelium suit to take the brunt.

The sound of the *Advent's* engines broke through the sound of the chase. Kalian pushed his senses and felt the craft rising gently into the air. Changing direction at the last second, Kalian ran through the wall to his right and leaped upwards, pushing through the multiple ceilings, until he came to rest on the building's third floor. The Bragans were close behind, finding different ways onto the floor in an attempt to ambush him. For all the prey that they had ever hunted across Albadar's scorched surface, a Terran was not one of them.

Kalian launched himself from the torn building, passing through the jagged hole where a wall had once been. The Bragans skidded to a stop at the ragged edge and *huffed* in frustration at their elusive prey. Kalian came to land gracefully on top of the *Advent*, where he altered his body's electromagnetic field, magnetically binding himself to the hull. Naydaalan continued to manoeuvre the ship, angling for a straight shot into the sky. Kalian could see the radioactive storm now, almost upon them.

"You're going to have to be inside for what happens next..." Naydaalan's voice came through the helmet.

Kalian could feel the *Advent's* thrusters gearing up for an expulsion of gravity-defying force. "Open the hatch on top."

Having dropped back into the ship, Kalian quickly made his way back to the bridge and took his seat beside Naydaalan. A wiggle of his fingers deactivated the helmet and gloves in his suit. So sensitive were his nerves now, that Kalian could feel every nanocelium scurrying across his skin.

The *Advent* shook gently as the storm began to encompass them. Warnings came up, alerting them to potentially harmful particles that could damage the hull and interfere with the ship's sensors.

"I am starting to get the feeling we are not welcome here," Naydaalan commented.

Kalian was inclined to agree. "If there was ever any answers here, they're long gone, along with everything else."

Naydaalan keyed the ignition and sent the *Advent* hurtling into the sky, tearing free of the encompassing storm. Kalian sat back and watched the grey become blue before finally fading to black. The stars greeted them with their familiar sight and promise of endless wonder. Kalian massaged his forehead, noting the absence of any sweat, despite the speed and length of his run. Esabelle would be proud...

Kalian brought up the nav-comm and input a new set of coordinates.

"What are you doing?" Naydaalan asked.

"Plotting a new course," Kalian replied, flatly. He silently berated himself again for the way he continued to treat the Novaarian.

"But there's nothing there." Naydaalan examined the coordinates that would put them relatively close to Albadar's star.

"I know. It's for Esabelle."

Naydaalan looked at Kalian and nodded after a moment of respect. The Novaarian accepted the coordinates into his console and redirected the ship.

Kalian made his way to the hold, while Naydaalan saw to their flight path. A rectangular outline was visible on the far wall, where the Conclave engineers had placed a cryo-pod, specifically built to keep Esabelle's body from degrading. Kalian could feel her beyond the wall. The daughter of Savrick was nothing more than a collection of dead cells now, all her potential and incredible power gone, forever. Esabelle had been stronger than him, she could have taken the human race into their next phase with an experienced, guiding hand.

The memory of Malekk snapping her neck flashed across his eyes, the image as sharp as the moment it had happened. Sometimes Kalian cursed his Terran brain.

As was becoming his habit, Kalian relied on his telekinesis to pull the pod out of the wall. The seal hissed and a cold breeze accompanied the pod as it slid into the hold. Kalian didn't bother wiping the glass to see inside, but instead waved his hand over the entire pod, removing the covering completely. He put the glass covering down gently, not wanting to ruin the moment of seeing her again. Esabelle demanded respect and more ceremony than she was going to receive. Had Kalian not made it abundantly clear, the Highclave would have confiscated her body and experimented on her. He didn't want the Conclave to see him as a threat, but sometimes it served its purpose.

"We are here, Kalian." Naydaalan's voice came over the hold-speakers.

Kalian knew what he had to do. It was the oldest Terran tradition that demanded that any death should see the person's body returned to the star of their birth. Esabelle had been born on Albadar over two hundred thousand years ago. Kalian tried to settle his feelings, knowing she was finally home and at peace, a part of the universe once more. It was more than Li'ara had gotten. There was nothing left of her to bury or cremate, and there was certainly no star to return her to.

He could do nothing for Liara now. At least he could still send Esabelle's body into the next life with the respect she deserved. Without her, Kalian would have felt an outcast aboard the *Gommarian*, as well as lost as to how to develop his powers without ALF. His time with Esabelle had been brief, but her impact would be unforgettable.

"You may have been the oldest being in the galaxy, but you deserved more life than was granted." Kalian didn't consider her virtual existence inside the *Gommarian* a life worth counting.

With only a glance at the door, leading to the bridge, Kalian keyed the lock, sealing the hold off. After altering his suit to cover his hands and head, he instructed Naydaalan to turn the hold door towards the sun. The room instantly depressurised with a loud hiss, though the artificial gravity kept everything in place when the door finally opened. At this distance, Albadar's star was the size of Kalian's closed fist, burning brightly in the dark. The HUD informed Kalian of the instant rise in temperature inside the hold. Despite the cold vacuum of space intruding the ship, the light of the sun could not be contested.

Kalian used his physical strength to lift Esabelle from the table. Her long, dark hair flowed over his hand, reaching for the floor. Even in death, she was beautiful. For just a moment, Kalian stood in the open doorway, holding Esabelle in the light of her birth star. The echo of Savrick's personality, which occasionally crept into his own identity, rose to the surface and settled in Kalian's gut like a block of ice. All at once he felt as if a friend, mentor and daughter had been taken from him.

When the moment passed, Kalian gritted his teeth, buried his anger and released Esabelle's body. The daughter of Savrick rode telekinetic waves across the threshold and into space. The effect was similar to watching a person float under water. It was peaceful. Standing on the very edge of the threshold, where the artificial gravity came to an end, Kalian stood and watched Esabelle's body drift into the void. It wasn't long before her features sank into darkness as her body became a silhouette against the sun.

"Kalian." Naydaalan's voice spoke of alarm, breaking Kalian's reverie.

"What's wrong?"

Naydaalan sounded busy on the other end. "Sensors have detected movement in the debris field. It appears the nanocelium traps have formed a new design and are traversing the solar system. They will be at our location in minutes."

Kalian thought about the distance between them and the debris field and gave the nanocelium credit for their speed. With a lasting look at Esabelle, he closed the hold door and re-pressurised the room. She would be stardust once again.

Falling back into his bridge chair once more, Kalian observed the feedback from the sensors. The nanocelium had clumped together to become three separate entities, each capable of near light speed. Naydaalan was calm, his centuries of experience and training shining through.

"Long-range sensors have located three Starforges in nearby systems." The Novaarian was inputting all three coordinates into the nav-comm. "Any preference?"

Kalian closed his eyes, hating what he was going to do next. After a quick play with the holographic menu in his suit's palm, ALF's image returned to the bridge.

"I take this to mean you've seen reason?" the AI said lazily.

"Just give us the coordinates to the Criterion, or I'll put you back in your box." Kalian was in no mood to barter words, having just released Esabelle back to her star. He purposefully kept his awareness to the confines of the ship, not wanting to touch her body as it descended into the sun.

Naydaalan hesitated before inputting the new coordinates, but a firm nod from Kalian had the *Advent* turning to port. Alarms rang out, warning them of the nanocelium's proximity.

"This will be our last jump on our current fuel cells. We will need to recharge inside a sunspot in the next system." Naydaalan primed the *Advent's* weapon systems as well as the Solar Drive.

"There is a perfectly good star in the Criterion's system," ALF explained. The AI looked at Kailan, aware that he had the final say.

Kalian could see the closing gap between them and the weaponized nanocelium. They had to leave, whether it was to find a working Starforge or get the answers they sought. But something about ALF's constant guidance to the Criterion put Kalian on edge.

ALF said, "Don't let Savrick's feeling towards me cloud your judgement. We need answers, and the Criterion may hold some..."

Kalian didn't look at ALF but instead locked eyes with Naydaalan - who was keeping amazingly calm considering three murderous machines were closing on their position. The golden swirls of the Novaarian's eyes, that always reminded Kalian of galaxies, held trust for him. Naydaalan would go wherever Kalian instructed; a trust the rest of the Conclave did not share.

"Let's get out of here." Kalian nodded at the coordinates from ALF.

Naydaalan activated the Solar Drive. "I do not think we were welcome here anyway..."

The *Advent* was flung into sub-space, leaving Esabelle to return home.

TEN

Kel-var Tionis made the mistake of looking up. Above his head was a ceiling of jagged rock that stretched the breadth of the cavern, surrounding the Shay. Between him and the surface of Shandar was tons upon tons of earth. He felt momentarily trapped underground, claustrophobic even. The Protopcorps chief had spent his entire life looking down on the worlds he inhabited, whether that be from his office in the headquarters - situated at the top of Clave Tower - or his many homes in the floating towers above Shandar's atmosphere.

Now he was stuck, hiding underground like some animal. He had everything he could possibly need inside the installation, food, drink, entertainment, girls even, should the mood strike. Nothing compared to his freedom. The Shay reminded himself that when they arrived and ascension was achieved, he would have ultimate freedom. The entire universe would be his to explore and enjoy, and the Conclave and their petty laws would be nothing but dust, nourishment for *their* glory.

As ever, there was another voice in the back of his mind, a nagging, troublesome voice. Where he envisioned freedom and power, the little voice spoke of Kel-var's fears. Would the Shay species transcend, or become slaves to their will? Every family member he had ever known had always spoken of their inevitable change when *they* finally arrived. The notion was firmly locked into his psyche, but after witnessing first-hand what the cubes did to Professor Garrett Jones and the Terran, known as Malekk, Kel-var was not so sure anymore.

The Shay leaned against the railing and looked out on the Crucible. The machine was of a design that predated the Conclave, given to them by the first cube Kel-var's family discovered so long ago. Four pyramids occupied the cavern, each structure the size of any tower that floated above Shandar. All four of the pyramids had been positioned and built into the cavern walls to ensure that their apexes met in the middle. One hung from the ceiling, while two others extended out from the walls and the last pyramid sat on the cavern floor.

The machine had never been fully tested since once it was activated there would be no turning back. Small experiments had taken place over the centuries, but Kel-var knew that when the Crucible was turned on, no one could stand inside the cavern as he did now. The sheer power of the machines would turn any being's insides to mush.

The metallic clatter of robotic legs on the cavern floor resounded from behind Kel-var. A Shay guard, whose name he could not recall, approached with haste.

"What is it?"

The guard cleared his throat. "There's a priority communication for you, sir."

"Gor-van?" Kel-var asked with a bored tone.

The guard hesitated. "No, sir. It's..."

Kel-var swivelled on the guard. "I will take it in my office." The Shay dismissed the guard and half ran, half walked to his office.

The holographic emitters in his office were far too real for Kel-var's liking. Pacing up and down, in front of his desk, Malekk never took his black eyes off the Shay.

At last, he spoke. "I have received a data-packet from Gor-van Tanar."

Kel-var disguised his discomfort with a raised eyebrow. "Oh yes?"

"When were you going to inform me that a hundred thousand more humans have entered the Conclave? Or that the Highclave has built a Starforge and Kalian Gaines has passed through it, to the Terran Empire?"

Had Gor-van been sitting in the room with him, Kel-var would have killed him right there and then with his bare hands. It had always been an unspoken rule that Kel-var was to be the line of communication to the prophet, or Malekk, as he was all they were left with after the humans blew up the cube at Protocorps.

"They are of little consequence." Kel-var tried to act casual. "The humans are in their devolved state and pose no danger to our plans. They will die with the rest of them. And Kalian Gaines will likely never return from the Terran Empire. Our spies report that they didn't even have a plan for getting themselves back to the Conclave."

"And what of the Starforge?" Malekk was standing still now, which only worked to unnerve Kel-var all the more.

"It is the first of its kind," Kel-var explained. "The Highclave have already put plans in motion to erect surface-based Starforges on all the core worlds, it's creating quite the stir. If anything, this will help us in the final stage, allowing for easy travel between worlds."

"Where did they learn to build such machines?" Malekk's voice was not natural.

"The AI, from the outpost on Naveen. It is from the -"

"I know where it is *from,*" Malekk interrupted. "Is this *ALF* still in Conclave space, or has it fled with Kalian Gaines?" The holographic Terran approached Kel-var, walking right through his desk.

"Yes, it is with Kalian. The AI is restricted to his exo-suit." Kel-var could see the subtle changes across Malekk's face. Even though his human features were hard for the Shay to read, he could see the concern creep across Malekk's ruined face. "Is this a problem?"

Malekk focused on Kel-var for a moment. "Rogue artificial intelligence is always a problem. Especially that one."

Kel-var scoffed in an attempt to downplay the level of danger posed to them. "I don't think they can cause any disruption from the other side of the galaxy." The Shay's expression dropped under Malekk's scrutiny. "Can they?"

Malekk moved away. "They will be dealt with should they decide to meddle. For now, we will concentrate our efforts on the Conclave and the remaining humans. To that effect, my master wishes the Crucible to be tested. Should it fail to work in its moment of need, your race will never transcend. I trust you can see to it."

An idea was forming in Kel-var's mind, an idea that would serve multiple purposes. "The human ship containing the new humans is currently undergoing repairs on the edge of Conclave space. A team of Shay engineers has been granted access..."

"Align these goals and prove your worth, Tionis. Should either of us fail, the Vanguard will breach Conclave space and see to the humans' destruction personally. This will escalate events ahead of schedule and take away our element of surprise. This is not preferable, but inevitable should we fail. The Terran and their lineage must be wiped out."

"It will be done. However, the Crucible will require time to conduct an experiment on such a small scale. It was originally designed for a much larger activation." Kel-var hated being the weakest person in a conversation and had to work at not fidgeting in his seat.

"Just get it done." Malekk looked about to leave when he turned back. "And I want the location of the Gomar, *now*."

"We're working on..." Kel-var stopped speaking when the image of Malekk faded away.

The Shay sat back in his chair and breathed a sigh of relief. He brought up the info on the four Shay engineers who had boarded the Paladin. Along with their personal details, Kel-var pulled up specific data pertaining to the operating implant inside their brains. The special microchip allowed the Shay to sync perfectly with their artificial limbs and attachments.

This particular operating system had been mass produced and inserted into every Shay as a child. Thankfully, it was one of the hundreds of enhancements created for the Shay, as well as other species, and so had been overlooked by the Conclave's investigative team. Even now, no one knew they were manufactured by Protocorps.

Kel-var tapped the surface of his glass desk and waited for a response. "Prep the Crucible. I have four test subjects. Make certain to programme them for maximum destruction, I want them to kill everyone they see..."

ELEVEN

Roland felt as if he were wearing a second skin, and technically he was, when he entered the *Rackham*'s hold in his usual floor length coat - made from an unknown animal with a brown hide. He enjoyed the weight of his dual Tri-rollers, nestled comfortably on either side of his thighs. Not one belt but two were wrapped around his waist, each stuffed with his favourite toys. He even had grav bombs strapped to his left arm, over the coat's sleeve in case things got a little out of control. Roland really hoped things got out of control. There was nothing funnier than watching a group of mercenaries being flung around by fluctuating gravity fields.

Using the flexi-screen, built into the sleeve on his right arm, Roland accessed the floor panel in the centre of the hold. The horizontal doors parted, hiding the dark stains of Shay blood, as the contents within rose up to meet the bounty hunter.

"I can't believe you're actually going to go out on that deathtrap..." Ch'len had waddled up beside him, frowning at the machine before them.

"I love the Hog!" Roland declared defensively. "You're just jealous because you can't ride it, on account of those teeny tiny legs of yours."

"It's essentially an engine with a seat attached to it," Ch'len observed, as he always did when the hoverbike came out.

"Isn't that the same as every ship in the galaxy?" Roland replied, checking the newest build-up of grime around the handlebars.

"No!" Ch'len said in a condescending tone. "This is just where stupid meets moronic." The Ch'kara held his hands out to encompass the bike. "There's a reason they're illegal. No sentient brain in the galaxy has the reflexes to successfully ride one of these things."

Roland stood back to take it all in, while ignoring every word that came out of Ch'len's mouth. The Hog was yellow, or at least it had been when he acquired it, with a wide leather seat towards the back end. The front of the bike was all engine and a chunky one at that, with multiple exhausts and vents designed to keep the bike cool at high temperatures. There were no wheels to speak of, as the bike could hover above the ground up to thirty feet. Today he would be going no more than ten feet, in order to avoid detection.

The bounty hunter lifted his leg and flicked his coat over the seat, getting comfy, since the ride to Gor-van's safe house was several miles away. After a moment of searching, he found the dirty goggles hiding under the carriage and put them over his head. The adrenaline was already pumping in anticipation of the ride and the inevitable fight on the other end.

Ch'len reached up on his tiptoes and depressed the button, activating the ramp. The sun was rising again, with Byzantial's days only being thirteen hours long. Brilliant white light poured into the hold, creating silhouettes of everything. Beyond the ramp lay the sprawling desert of the Qelt Wastes, a flat, open land dotted with the tallest stalagmites Roland had ever seen.

"If I'm not back by nightfall, I'm probably dead. So..." Roland met Ch'len's tiny eyes, "you'll probably die as well in the next few days."

Ch'len dashed to the Hog's side. "Then why don't you just give me the ignition codes for the *Rackham* and I can save myself."

Roland looked as if he were considering it. "Nah. I think I'll hang onto those." The bounty hunter tapped his temple with a smug smile on his face. "You should probably think about rationing. It's a long walk back to civilisation."

Ch'len dropped his head, exhausted with the topic they had fought over many times before.

Roland keyed the Hog's ignition three or four times, before it finally came to life with a roar loud enough to knock Ch'len back a few steps. The bounty hunter laughed and removed a small hip flask from the inside pocket of his coat. The swig was warm and spicy, its alcoholic kick quick to set in.

"Oh, that'll help..." Ch'len rolled his eyes.

"See you later, dipshit!" Roland pulled on the throttle and shot out of the *Rackham*'s hold.

The journey was exhilarating, for about twenty minutes. After which, Roland lost all feeling in his ass and the goggles pressing into his eye sockets were beginning to hurt. The landscape didn't get any more interesting either, with every rounded stalagmite giving way to more desert. He nearly killed himself evading the towering rocks, as his brain struggled to keep up with the rapidly approaching terrain. There were times in the flat areas where he was forced to slow down just so he could breathe.

Roland dared to glance at the screen, situated under his chin. The coordinates for the safe house was coming up, nestled in a canyon a half mile wide. The Hog *chuddered* to a stop, as Roland was aware of the dust cloud the bike spewed out of the back, visible from afar. It took several minutes for the feeling to return to his hands and for his legs to stop shaking.

He rounded the last mound of stalagmites on foot and dropped to his knees behind a rock large enough to conceal him. Using a small pair of binoculars, the bounty hunter scouted the terrain. The building wasn't much more than a two-storey shack. From this range, the binoculars were unable to probe the walls and highlight those within.

"Time to set you little buggers free..." Roland retrieved the tracking spheres from his belt and poured them into the dusty ground. Using the flexi-screen on his forearm, the spheres were given the coordinates.

Roland continued to scan the terrain for possible snipers, while the trackers crossed the distance to the shack. If there was anyone waiting for him out there, they were well hidden. A quiet alert notified him when the spheres were at the house, each separating and finding different ways inside. Once the building was breached, the trackers ran up walls and round objects until they had a collective view of both floors. A three-dimensional hologram rose above the flexi-screen and showed Roland what was going on inside.

There were four armed beings inside, Shay by the looks of their artificial arms and legs, all with various attachments that clung to their faces. The one on the first floor was packing a larger weapon than the three downstairs. Sniper, then. The other three appeared to be playing some kind of game around a table, their weapons propped against the table legs. None of them were Gor-van.

Roland had to think about his approach. If he went on foot the sniper would easily spot him and take the shot. If he commanded the trackers to find a target and self-destruct he would lose any element of surprise, since Gor-van had to be in the installation underneath the house.

"Hard and fast it is..."

The bounty hunter returned to the Hog and dropped the goggles over his eyes. He set a timer on the tracking spheres, commanding them to 'search and destroy' in twenty seconds.

"Let's skip to the good bit, boys." The Hog exploded into flight, launching Roland into the open desert between the stalagmites and the shack.

The Hog was too loud not to be heard. The gunfire would begin in moments, starting with the sniper no doubt. The flexi-screen showed the trackers redeploying around the building, seeking out the four beings inside and sticking to them.

A round of intrinium careened off the Hog's engine, creating sparks that flew into Roland's face. The sniper was good to have even hit the bike at these speeds.

That same sniper was blown out of the top window a second later. As Roland drew closer, he could see the robotic leg and an organic arm tear from the Shay's body, before every part of it hit the desert floor. A series of small explosions erupted downstairs, shredding doors and shattering windows. Smoke drifted out from every crack in the old shack, when Roland came to a skidding stop that forced a wave of sand into the air.

The bounty hunter was off the bike and striding through the door before the Hog's engine fully cut out. A swift kick took the door off its hinges and snapped the framework. The moaning to his right caught his attention and he didn't hesitate to step into the next room. All three of the Shay were prone on the floor, all in different states of dismemberment. One of them was dead for sure, with his head hanging onto his body by a few strands of tissue. The other two had fared better, if missing limbs counted as better.

Roland crouched down, blocking the only one, with both of his arms remaining, from crawling away. "How do I get downstairs?"

The Shay were dazed and could only look at the bounty hunter in confusion. They needed a little wake-up call, or at least one of them did. Roland pulled one of his Tri-rollers from its holster and shot the Shay that had lost an arm and a leg. The alien blood splattered across the other Shay's face, startling him.

"How do I get downstairs?" Roland repeated.

The alien mercenary blinked several times before answering, "The room... in the back. Translift..."

Roland looked over his shoulder at the adjoining room. "Thanks." An intrinium round put the Shay out of his misery.

The Translift was clearly the most sophisticated piece of technology in the whole shack. The square floor panel and matching controls on the wall stood out in the room like a sore thumb. Within seconds, Roland was below ground and inside the real safe house. The corridors were sleek and befitting of Conclave architecture. There was even a good chance that his antics upstairs had gone unnoticed, due to the bunker-style walls and ceiling.

There was only one corridor with several doors leading off of it, all closed. It was easy to guess what was going on behind the furthest door on the right. Gor-van was entertaining at least two women, courtesy of Hon Valorga.

It was tempting to just burst in, dismiss the prostitutes and drag Gor-van out by the scruff of his neck. Thankfully, he hadn't had nearly enough to drink to see that plan through. Instead, Roland checked out the other rooms, stopping to listen with his ear to the door. Nothing. After a quick peek inside the rooms, it became clear that the remaining mercenaries were all together at the far end of the corridor. Luckily, this door had a small window at eye-level. There was six other Shay inside, along with a ship. The hangar must have been directly in front of the shack, though Roland had never seen any evidence above ground to support this. He had been too quick to get off the Hog and breach the building.

With the mercenaries overseeing repairs and maintenance of the ship, Roland returned to Gor-van's room. The door slid apart in the blink of an eye, revealing two naked Laronians and a third person, who Roland couldn't identify through their entangled limbs.

The bounty hunter levelled both of his Tri-rollers and spoke quietly. "You two out, *now*." The Laronians whimpered and fled without another word, heading straight for the Translift. "Get up you sack o' shit!" Roland often found it hard to identify one Shay from another, but this was definitely Gor-van Tanar.

The Shay laughed to himself. "Very good Mr. North. Very good..."

"Get up." Roland flicked his gun to direct him out of the bed.

"And why would I do that?" Gor-van relaxed back, exposing his pale white chest and dark veins.

Before Roland could answer, two guns were levelled at his head from either side. The naked Laronians had returned, quiet on their bare feet.

"Perhaps in your line of work as a bounty hunter, you may have heard of the Bolo Twins..." Gor-van held his hands out, as if displaying the smug Laronians.

"Where were you hiding those, ladies?" Roland eyed their hand-cannons.

Their slender, blue arms rose to meet his and relieved him of both Tri-rollers. It was incredibly frustrating to be annoyed and aroused at the same time. He had indeed heard of the Bolo Twins during his short time as a bounty hunter. They were notorious for only taking bounties that were wanted dead, so they could 'play' with their catch. Roland looked them up and down and wouldn't mind 'playing' with them for a while - at least he would die with a smile on his face.

Gor-van slowly stepped out of the bed and placed a large red cloak over his body. "I have seen the things you have done to get this far. The blood. The pain. The brutality. Had you worked for me we could have accomplished a great deal."

"You're not the one I want." Roland felt one of the cool barrels press into his temple. "Give me Kel-var and you won't have to see my brutality up close."

"Kel-var and I serve a higher purpose. Something your primitive mind cannot comprehend. It's a shame you won't get to see the fruits of our labour, human. Our transcendence is going to be quite glorious."

"Can we play with him now?" the Laronian to his right asked, pleadingly.

"Why not? Just don't play with him for too long. I want him dead by nightfall." Gor-van flashed a wicked smile at the bounty hunter and left the room, heading for the hangar.

The twins pushed Roland into the next room, not bothering to put any clothes on. They were gorgeous, murderous and identical - any other day and they would have been his idea of a perfect night or day, or anytime really. It didn't help that they were naked.

"Now girls," Roland said with all the charm he could muster, "there's enough of me to go around..."

"When we're finished, there's going to be enough of you to go everywhere."

As it turned out, there really was enough of Roland to go around. After stripping him down to his underwear and chaining his wrists to the ceiling - why this room even existed he had no idea, but there were probably a few unlucky prostitutes who did - the Bolo Twins went to work on him. As he so often did, the agent turned bounty hunter fell back on his training, or at least he tried to. Roland had been trained to keep any and all secrets in his head, and right now the Bolo Twins had no intention of asking Roland anything. There was just pain, which was a very hard thing to build any kind of resistance to.

At least they remained naked, though Roland's vision was beginning to blur somewhat. A particularly nasty cut in his left eyebrow was dripping blood onto his eyelashes and the right eye was completely closed off from the swelling. Some kind of vicious, alien eel had been wrapped around his left thigh, where it proceeded to cling to his skin with hundreds of spikes. The blood dripped down his leg and formed a small pool around his foot.

At some point, they had bothered to introduce themselves, but their names escaped him now. He only knew that one of them preferred to use her bare fists, while the other loved to use implements. Between them, they had turned his body into a canvas of blacks and purples with streaks of red throughout. Roland lost all sense of time, unaware of whether he had been in this room all day or for just a few hours.

"I wonder how long humans can hold their breath for..." the implements twin pondered out loud.

Had Roland been able to muster any saliva, he would have spat on her. As it was, he could only hang there, wondering if he had the strength to lift his feet and break one of their necks.

"Let's find out," the other twin replied happily.

The Laronian gripped Roland's throat and squeezed as hard as she could. The bounty hunter struggled and tried to escape her grip, but he had nowhere to go and the more he moved the tighter the eel constricted around his leg. He could feel his face fill with blood at the same moment his vision got even worse.

The entire underground installation shook when a loud boom resounded from somewhere above them. The lights flickered as more shockwaves ran through the safe house. By now the Laronian had released Roland and turned back to her sister in alarm. The bounty hunter gasped for air, with just enough of his mind to wonder if Ch'len was attacking them. The *Rackham* certainly had the firepower to bring the whole place down. Of course, Ch'len had no way to power the ship without Roland, and he couldn't connect to the ship in his current, fuzzy state.

The sound of metal twisting and girders snapping echoed throughout the installation. Gunfire erupted outside the door. It sounded like chaos to Roland, with intrinium rounds striking every surface, as if the shooters couldn't find their target in a narrow corridor. Roland laughed to himself, somewhat hysterically, at the thought of how universally shit mercenaries were.

The gunfire was quickly followed by screams of agony, not terror. The walls shook at the same moment they all heard a Shay body slam into the reinforced panel.

Are they fighting a gorilla?

After a few more screams and the familiar sound of blood splattering against the walls, the corridor fell silent. The Bolo Twins had each picked up a curved blade and stood in front of the door in fighting stances. They really were as insane as everyone said. Roland tried to blink the blood out of his only good eye, intent on seeing the twins die. What happened next was almost too quick for the bounty hunter to register, however, or at least that's how it felt to his battered head.

The doors were ripped open, as if they were no stronger than tissue paper, folding into the room and cracking the walls. Everything was blurry to Roland, but he could make out the figure in the doorway, clad in black, their frame almost filling the gap. The Bolo Twins lunged forward with the blades held high, but they froze mid-step, before suddenly being cast aside, into the reinforced walls like ragdolls. Their screams were silenced immediately, when they were flung up into the air with enough force to break their necks upon slamming into the ceiling. Their limp forms dropped back to the floor in a heap, lifeless.

"Kalian..?" Roland managed. The twins had been dispatched without the mysterious figure ever moving, and there was only one person who could do that.

The blurry figure in black stood aside, giving way to an angel with red hair. Roland's vision narrowed as the woman approached, until finally, she was standing right in front of him. The words escaped him, as doubt crept into Roland's mind about the apparition standing before him.

"You look like hell," the angel said.

Her breath on his skin was undeniable; the person standing in front of him was real. All the head injuries in the world couldn't produce a hallucination as real as this one. A small tear broke free of Roland's bloody eye and streaked a clean line down his face.

"Li'ara..."

Li'ara Ducarté smiled, a sight he would deny he missed and turned back to the mystery figure. Roland tried to better his vision and make out Kalian's face in the doorway.

Li'ara's features became serious again. "The Shay is escaping. Len, can you track Gor-van's ship?"

Roland couldn't keep the expression of surprise off his face. Even with the pain, the eel was excruciating, he still had a thousand questions he needed answering. The bounty hunter didn't hear his partner's response, but apparently, Li'ara could hear the little Ch'kara in her ear.

"We need to go." Li'ara faced Roland again. "Are you going to be okay?"

Roland fought through the pain to find the wittiest answer he could. "Well, I'm a little tied up right now, so..."

Li'ara looked back at the dark figure, just too far out of Roland's sight. With a wave of his hand, the shackles around his wrist snapped open and the eel was peeled off and thrown aside with a *squeal*. Roland groaned in pain and fell to the floor, landing in a pool of his own blood and sweat.

Roland looked up at Li'ara's beautiful face, her red ringlets cascading over her shoulders. "How are you..?"

The world was becoming smaller and darker by the second, until Li'ara crouched over him, filling his entire vision. Then she was gone, leaving Roland in the dark.

TWELVE

Jedediah Holt perched on the end of the desk in his office, just off from the Paladin's bridge. He looked out of his window and gazed upon the *Nautallon*, off the ship's starboard bow. Marvelling at the alien ship was easier than dwelling on the speech he had just given to the thousands of people in the vessel's hold. Notifying them of the incredible time difference and the developments on Earth and Century had been met with mixed reactions.

There were many who had burst into tears, seeking comfort from their loved ones or simply crumbling to the floor. Though many had boarded the ship with their families, hoping to make a fresh start on Century, there were still thousands who had come alone, or with friends, or were simply working. In one speech they had discovered that everyone they ever knew, loved or cared about was dead and that any descendants they might have had were killed in the Gomar attack.

The captain's heart broke for them all, especially his crew. Sam had lost her parents, Maloy his wife, Markovich his brother. The list went on. None of them had time to mourn, however, as Captain Fey had advised everyone be put on suicide watch since her people had lost many to this. His crew had been called upon to provide a sense of strength and unity for the civilians to rely upon.

All Jed wanted to do was be alone and weep for his lost family.

His sister Christine and her two daughters, Louise and Elizabeth, were gone, whether they lived a long and happy life or not, they were simply gone. He would never see them again. Christine had lost her husband when the girls were young, leading to Jed having a more active role in their life. He had loved those girls as if they were his own. The three of them must have gone on believing he was dead. It was a despairing irony that everyone on Earth and Century was gone, but those aboard the Paladin were now the ghosts.

He needed time to think over everything and come to terms with life's drastic change in direction, but Jed could feel Captain Fey's eyes boring holes in the side of his head. The older captain was sitting on the small couch with her legs crossed; her body posture told of how relaxed she was, as well as superior. Her level of calm was a testament to the kind of life Fey and her people had been living for the last year - and Jed was still trying to wrap his head around everything they had gone through. To Captain Fey, this was apparently just another day.

"It's not going to sink in overnight," Fey commented, with the faintest hint of a sad smile. "In fact, it might never sit right with you. This isn't just a new world I'm asking you to accept, it's a whole galaxy."

"A world would make it a little easier..." Jed pinched his eyes, the weight of all the people onboard slowly setting in.

Captain Fey frowned. "We're working on it."

Jed's hand moved across his neck and found the metallic dot behind his ear. He fought the urge to dig his finger in and rip it free of his skin.

"These people, they aren't like your people. They aren't scientists or engineers. They aren't accustomed to living in artificial habitats or looking at the unknown with wonder. They're farmers, artists, accountants, doctors and most are families. There are at least a thousand children on this ship. Not only do these people have no home anymore, but they don't even have a world, a civilisation, history..."

Jed could feel his frustration and grief rise to the surface in the form of anger. "The Conclave is beyond massive by your own words! How do they not have space on any world or even a world going spare?"

Fey leaned forward and rested her elbows on her knees. Jed felt guilty for his outburst; it was clear to see that this particular problem had haunted the captain since their violent entry into the Conclave.

"They fear us, putting it simply. The things the Terran can do, the things Kalian can do. When the Gomar arrived they wrought more destruction in the Conclave than they'd seen for thousands of years. The death toll wasn't anything like what they did to us, but it was high."

Jed shook his head in an attempt to get his head around it all. "The Gomar? They're also the Terran, right?"

"A portion of their society who couldn't control their abilities. ALF fitted them with Harnesses to keep everyone safe, but all it did was cause a rift that ultimately led to civil war." Fey's expression told of how ridiculous it all sounded.

"I'm going to need this explaining at least a hundred more times. It's hard enough getting my head around the fact that Earth isn't where it all started, let alone trying to understand some civil war between an ancient race of... superhumans with abilities."

Commander Vale's voice came over the comm speakers. "Commander Vale to Captain Holt."

"Go ahead, Sam." Jed was happy for the interruption. He could feel a migraine coming on.

"The... engineers have finished and another alien has come aboard. A smaller one. They want to explain what happened to the Paladin."

"They already know what went wrong?" Jed found it hard to believe that the four aliens had not only fixed the drive but also discovered what caused the massive error.

"Apparently it's obvious..." Sam replied sarcastically. "They've set up some kind of display in the ready room."

Jed looked at Captain Fey before responding. "We'll be right there."

Captain Holt was careful to avoid the more populated areas on the way to the ready room. Almost everyone onboard had wanted to ask him a hundred questions each after his speech in the hold. He had given them all the information he had, as honestly as he could, with the promise of more information when it became available. Jed had been hesitant to explain the radiation leak, wanting to avoid panic, but it would be impossible to omit since most would require medical attention.

"The Paladin looks to be a great ship," Captain Fey commented casually, clearly trying to strengthen any bond between them.

Jed was happy for the small talk however, it was distracting and he hated awkward silences. "I bet it's nothing like what you're used to. I can only imagine what advances were made in our absence."

"Not as many as you would think really. Just the usual; fitting the software into smaller and smaller components. My last command was the Hammer, a brute of a ship - still, nothing compared to what the Conclave has. A point proven when the Laronians blew it to space dust."

"Laronians..." Jed chewed over the name, trying to recall Fey's description.

"Blue, very fine scales. They probably have the closest resemblance to us."

Jed found it hard to see how anything that was blue with scales could resemble a human being. "If you say so..."

The ready room was already filled with occupants when they arrived. Two of the six Raiders had taken up positions outside the door, with Colonel Matthews and the other three stationed inside, occupying the corners with their weapons rested at their waist. The four Shay were busy with a variety of tools and alien datapads, all producing a colourful holographic display. They were working with Chief Grenko in an attempt to connect their devices to the screen that took up most of the far wall.

Jed noted Sharon Booth and Jim Langdale sitting at one end of the table, obviously comfortable among the aliens. Lieutenant Worth, who looked more at home amidst the UDC personnel, accompanied Sam, who walked around the long table and greeted them both, along with a small alien Jed had never seen before.

"Captain," Sam turned on her side to introduce the alien, "this is Ch'vork, the *Nautallon*'s chief engineer."

"Greetings of peace, Captain Holt." The alien came up to his navel in height.

Jed wanted to reply immediately, as was polite, but he found himself taking in every detail.

Ch'vork wore a similar red and black uniform to the others, but across his chest and back was a mechanical apparatus that looked somewhere between a steam engine and a Solar Drive. The air around his head shimmered, but not enough to distort his squat little head and pale features. Sunken black eyes stared up at the captain, expectantly.

"Hi..." he finally managed. How was Sam so comfortable among them? Jed realised she was probably using all of it as a distraction from her parents.

"My engineers are preparing a simulation to show you exactly what we believe happened to the Paladin. High Charge Uthor will also join us momentarily." Ch'vork removed a small disc from his belt and walked back to the table.

"Excellent," Jed replied, absently. It took him another moment to fully grasp what Ch'vork had said. How was Uthor going to join them? He was bigger than every door on the ship!

"We are ready," one of the Shay announced.

Grenko's exhausted pallor reminded Jed how hard he had been working the engineer since they dropped out of sub-space. The man had barely slept, desperately trying to fix the Solar Drive and repair the radiation leak. The captain would be sure to allocate him some serious R&R when they had the opportunity, though what that would look like in this new world, he had no idea.

Ch'vork threw the small disc from his belt on to the floor, where it sprouted three legs and projected an almost life-size hologram of Uthor. Jed was impressed with the life-like quality of the image; the Raalakian could have been in the room with them.

"Greetings of peace, Captain Holt." Uthor was still looking down on him.

"Greetings of peace, High Charge Uthor." Jed decided to use the phrase he continually heard from the Conclave aliens.

Jed, Sam and Captain Fey took their seats side-by-side, while Colonel Matthews remained standing beside the hologram of Uthor. Grenko appeared more than happy to take a seat on the end and watch Ch'vork lead the presentation.

The screen came to life with a computer-generated image of space, overlaid with a blue grid pattern. A select number of stars expanded, decorating the black canvas with giant, yellow spheres.

Ch'vork cleared his throat, an oddly human thing to do in Jed's opinion. "Now, as you can see, this is a typical flight plan through sub-space." A red line appeared horizontally across the screen. At one end they could see a blue dot that represented Earth, and the other end was their current position. "This particular path is the one that you should have taken, in order to avoid other planets, moons, asteroids and stars. Had your navigation systems calculated this jump, it would have taken a couple of months to make the journey."

"So why did it take us over two hundred years?" Sam asked.

"What do you understand about time?" Ch'vork asked without condescension.

"That it's precious."

Jed tilted his head to glance at Sam's arm. He didn't need to look her in the eyes to get his point across. Everyone was beyond frayed at the edges by this point, but patience was still required, and respect was expected.

Ch'vork bowed his head, conceding. "None more than the crew of the Paladin understand that. I shall explain it as simply as I can; I realise not all present are engineers." The Ch'kara turned back to the screen. "These yellow spheres represent stars, scattered throughout the patch of galaxy between Earth and here. Now each of these stars has an effect on time, even in sub-space."

The grid shifted into a three-dimensional model to show the Paladin in sub-space, with the top half of the screen demonstrating reality and the bottom half representing sub-space. The various stars were spread out, creating an effect that looked as if someone had dropped a series of balls on to a sheet of fabric, and where the balls lay, the fabric dipped.

Ch'vork continued, "The curvature you see around the stars represents the effect their gravitational pull has on sub-space. All nav-comms plot courses around stars specifically to avoid the effects of this curvature. In sub-space, the gravity from the stars, or black holes, can alter the perception of time. The closer one gets to either, the slower they perceive events - though, to the observer, nothing has changed."

Grenko leaned forward in his seat. "This isn't exactly new information..."

"Maybe to you Chief," Sam replied. "All I know is that Maloy pulls the lever and the Paladin moves."

Jed silenced them both with a hand. "Perhaps a simple explanation would be best. Please continue, Ch'vork."

Ch'vork's stubby hand played over the holographic display on the tabletop, altering the image on the screen. "From what we can piece together from your navigational array, as well as the chronometer built into your Solar Drives; this has been the flight path of the Paladin."

The screen now showed a wavy red line starting from Earth, curving around almost every star between the planet and their current location. The ship appeared to have zig-zagged across the cosmos for more than two hundred years.

"Your proximity to these stars," Ch'vork continued, "is the reason none of you have aged. You were only in sub-space for a couple of days by your perception, but in reality, you have been travelling for centuries."

Jed sat back and studied the image, dismayed. "Do you know what caused this?"

Ch'vork hesitated, looking at Uthor's towering hologram. "Sabotage. We found the partial remains of a human inside the conductor chamber."

"Goddamn separatists..." Ava muttered behind them.

"Whether he intended to die in the act or not, we may never know," Ch'vork said. "But between the heat and the subsequent radiation leak inside that chamber, there isn't much left of him now."

Jed suddenly felt as if the universe was against him. "You're saying we were flung two hundred and fifty years into the future because of another human being?"

"That would appear to be the case, yes."

Sam turned to Jed, but she had no words to express how she felt. If she was anything like him, the commander would feel cheated. It was a hard thing to accept, made all the harder with no one left to punish. It was natural to seek out the source of such tragedy and focus on revenge, but there was nothing any of them could do with the news except move on. Duty demanded it.

"We have succeeded in repairing the damage," Ch'vork added in a lighter tone. "The Paladin's nav-comm is now connected to the Solar Drive. We can refuel it and give you the coordinates to Arakesh."

Jed looked at Captain Fey for clarification.

"It's the Raalak homeworld," Fey explained. "It's where our current habitat is located." The older captain looked to Uthor. "Though, space might be an issue now."

The Raalak bowed his head. "It is being reviewed."

Jed was already thinking of his next speech to the masses. How was he going to explain that everything that had happened was a result of sabotage?

The Shay standing beside Ch'vork caught the captain's eye, distracting him from current concerns. The alien dipped its head into one robotic hand as if suffering from a migraine. The engineer stumbled at the same moment the other three gripped their heads in equal pain. Ch'vork steadied the nearest Shay by the arm and inquired about his health. Jed could feel the Raiders in the room physically tense. Colonel Matthews nodded at the two in the far corners to close the gap.

"Is there a problem?" Captain Fey asked.

Her lack of fear helped Jed to assess the situation, taking her cues around the aliens as an indication of how he should respond.

That was a mistake.

As one, the Shay stopped nursing their heads and stumbling around. The alien closest to Ch'vork removed, what appeared to be, some kind of advanced screwdriver from his belt, and drove it down, directly on top of the Ch'kara's head. The metal rod killed him instantly, squirting blood onto the ceiling. The closing Raiders lifted their rifles, ready to put holes in everything that wasn't human, but the Shay reacted faster. Their robotic and organic limbs tackled the rifles away, while at the same time, throwing the two Raiders across the table as if they were no lighter than pillows. Now two of the four Shay were in possession of high powered rifles, while the other two were wielding engineering tools.

As the gunfire erupted, Sam, Fey and Jed ducked to the floor, while simultaneously flipping the table to use it as cover. The corner turned over and caught Jim Langdale in the face, knocking him unconscious. Grenko lept at the Shay in front of him but soon found himself flung against the wall with a sharp tool protruding from his shoulder and another in his thigh. The Shay backhanded him before Colonel Matthews put several rounds into its head. Blood exploded against the walls and Grenko as the Shay crumpled to the floor.

Within seconds the two Raiders from outside were bursting into the room and opening up with their own weapons. Jed covered his ears against the thundering guns of four Raiders and two Shay. Colonel Matthews grunted and collapsed to the floor behind them, blood oozing between the plates in the armour around her gut. The gunfire became staggered after a few seconds, quickly followed by close quarter fighting. Jed looked up in time to see the remaining three Shay run from the ready room, all with a rifle in hand.

Captain Holt lifted his head above the table to take stock. The room had filled with smoke and an acrid smell. Bullet holes lined the walls with blood and the ground crunched with broken glass. The holographic emitter being used to project Uthor had been destroyed in the fray. Jed could hear voices, but they were distant and hard to make out against the high pitch ringing in his ears. He soon realised it was Colonel Matthews barking orders beside him.

"Ava..." Jed looked at the blood trickling across her abdomen.

Ava Mathews quickly plunged a cylinder of medi-foam into the wound and gritted her teeth with pain. She followed this up with another cylinder Jed suspected was filled with adrenaline and painkillers.

Grenko was still unconscious with tools sticking out of him, while the two Raiders, who initially lost their rifles, were slowly picking themselves off the floor. One of the two who had been guarding outside was dead, besides Sam. The commander felt for his pulse, but it was clear to see from the tool, jutting out from his chest, that he was dead. The two remaining Raiders, who were currently being bollocked by Mathews, had each been winged by flying bullets but were not fatally hit.

"Oh no..." Captain Fey had found her way to the other end of the table, where Jim lay, semiconscious. Beside him, Sharon Booth was completely still, her white top coated in blood.

As the sounds of the world slowly came back, Jed discovered Sam and Ava were shouting at each other.

"I thought Raiders were the best of the best!" Sam yelled into Ava's face - a brave thing for anyone to do.

"Their artificial augments make them fast!" Matthews retorted. "I didn't see you jump into the fight!"

"I'm unarmed!" Sam strode over to Grenko.

"That didn't stop Grenko from trying to help!"

"Enough!" Jed stood up, between them. Using the comm panel on the wall, the captain had Maloy, on the bridge, give him a ship-wide channel. "Attention. This is Captain Holt. Three armed intruders are loose on the ship. Everyone is to proceed to the hold in a calm manner and await further instructions; you will be safe there." Jed looked at Sam, who knew what to do. On another channel she was quietly moving UDC personnel around, setting up guard posts around the hold. "The situation is being dealt with appropriately and will be resolved shortly." Jed switched back to

Maloy and requested a channel that only the crew could hear. "This is your captain, arm yourselves and prepare to sweep the ship."

"Don't." Colonel Matthews put her hand on his arm. "Let my team hunt them down. Use your crew to lock down the ship and protect the civilians. It'll be too messy if everyone with a gun is hunting the same thing."

Jed considered her counsel seriously. For all his experience, Ava's training alone would always trump his. "Belay that," he spoke into the mic. "Lockdown the ship and take up positions. Guard the hold."

Captain Fey finally left Sharon's side. "Open a channel to Uthor. He has a strike team waiting on the other side of your airlock. They have more experience with the Shay; we should let them help."

Ava shook her head. "Negative. For all we know this is on the big guy's order."

Fey frowned and gestured at Ch'vork's corpse. "This is not the Conclave's doing. I don't know what's going on, but Uthor wouldn't order the death of his chief engineer."

"Fair point," Jed agreed. "But for now, we deal with this in-house. We'll open a channel and explain what's happened, but the Raiders are hunting them down, and as far as I'm concerned they can shoot-to-kill."

Fey clearly wasn't satisfied, but she obviously knew better than to argue the orders of another captain on his own ship. Jed just hoped he was making the right call.

***

Colonel Ava Matthews knew her squad like the back of her hand. She knew them better than her own family and certainly better than their families knew them. Their strengths and weaknesses were her own, always playing a role in the squad tactics. Losing one of them was akin to losing a limb. It was the only thing that drove Ava to forgo her training and dive right in without planning or recon. This weakness was known to her Raiders, who always had her back.

"Holmes is dead..." Jess said into the darkened corridor, trying to hide her shock behind concentration.

It would take time for that fact to sink in.

"We'll mourn Peter later." It was Kyle Riddick who responded first, more than aware that those words made Ava's blood boil. "Let's just hunt these fuckers down and get some answers."

"It's hard to get answers from a corpse." Jack Danvers had been close to Peter. Ava was sure there had always been something more between the men than brothers-in-arms.

The corridors were lit in red, casting shadows in every crevice. Lockdown had taken immediate effect in this part of the Paladin, in hopes of cutting the Shay off before they could reach the populated areas.

"I'm with Danvers," Katie Wilson, the youngest in the group, added. "I say we cut em' down, no questions."

"Stow it, Wilson." Kyle always took control when Ava's head was in other places. "We're Raiders, not cavemen. We have to be surgical."

With their helmets covering their entire head, the Raiders could speak freely without the worry of being overheard. Their visors illuminated the corridors, piercing the shadows while keeping the team concealed in the dark.

"Surgery is what these fuckers are gonna need when we're finished with em'." Jess was easily the most sensitive one among them - though that wasn't saying much for a Raider - and she was clearly hiding her unease behind hard words.

The squad approached every corner the same way; one taking the edge and stealing a glance before the second dashed across the gap and took up a position on the other side. With Katie bringing up the rear, watching their backs, Ava led the team down the empty corridors, their rifles levelled at shoulder height. They swept the first floor in minutes, clearing the way for the captains and the others to retreat to the medbay.

Ava silently commended her team for focusing on the present and not dwelling on recent events. Apart from Kyle, they had all lost friends and family to their extended journey amongst the stars. Ava could hear her twin brother's voice in her head and held back the grief at knowing that her mind was the only place she would ever see him. The colonel could only dream of the life he might have had after she disappeared.

"All of you need to can it," Ava finally contributed. Despite her urgent need to run in guns blazing, Kyle kept her grounded. "If any can be taken alive then we will. We need information if we're going to survive in this new... Conclave."

Jack commented, "We also need a hundred more men if we've any hope of finding those three pale shits in the Paladin."

Ava stopped in the lead, holding up a closed fist to halt the team behind her. Using the eyetrak built into the HUD, Matthews opened a channel. "Maloy. You up there?"

Ensign Maloy's boyish voice responded, *"Affirmative, Raider One."*

"I need you to do an internal scan of the ship and separate human physiology from alien. Finding three aliens in a ship full of humans should be easy enough."

Maloy cleared his throat. *"Erm. The Paladin can't do that. The scanners aren't sensitive enough."*

"What?" Katie replied in disbelief.

Ava took over. "Explain, ensign."

"Those kind of upgrades were to be installed after the ship's arc duties were completed. I'm afraid as it stands, the Paladin is just a giant carrier with a Solar Drive stuck on the end."

Ava sighed into her mic. "Can you at least detect life signs internally?"

"Affirmative, Raider One."

"Great," Ava replied sarcastically. "There should be just over a hundred thousand passengers inside the hold, a few making their way to the medbay and the six... *five* of us in corridor M-19. Are there three life signs anywhere else between us?"

There was a pause on Maloy's end. *"Yes,"* he replied excitedly. *"Three life signs detected on deck sixteen, corridor K-12. That area should have been evacuated and put on lockdown."*

Ava turned to Kyle, whose face mirrored her concern behind his visor. Engineering was located on deck sixteen, just off corridor K-12.

Jack spoke for the both of them. "If anyone knows how to fuck up this ship from the inside, it's them."

"Double time!" Ava's order had the team sprinting to the nearest emergency ladder and climbing down to deck sixteen.

The corridors were silent. There were signs at every juncture directing them to engineering, but no signs of life. Matthews checked in periodically with Maloy to ensure the three mystery life signs hadn't moved. When they finally reached the stasis chamber between K-12 and the engine room, it was clear to see where the aliens had gone. The doors had been pried open at both ends of the chamber, their frames bent inwards and the glass shattered.

The five Raiders crossed the threshold, each scanning a different area of their surroundings. Ava winced at the sound of the glass crunching under their boots, giving their location away. It suddenly occurred to the colonel that she knew nothing about their prey. How good was their hearing? Could they see in the dark? Were they chameleons? After the brief fight in the ready room, it was clear to see how fast they were, and judging by how easily they threw Peter and Jack around the room, they were strong too.

Before entering the maze-like structure that housed the Solar Drive, Ava looked down to see fresh blood dripping down her left leg, the source; her abdomen. Thanks to the stimulants and painkillers, the whole wound was numb, but a portion of the medi-foam had been shaved away by the plates in her armour. The colonel looked over her shoulder to make a cursory inspection of her squad's wounds.

"Med-check," she ordered.

The Raiders turned to one another and examined their wounds, checking for any damage they couldn't see on themselves. Kyle had been hit in the right shoulder, visible by the cream-coloured foam staining his blue armour. The others had gotten away with scrapes and bruised egos.

"Sir..." Kyle was looking at Ava's gut.

"It can wait." Matthews jabbed a new canister of medi-foam in between the plates and sealed the wound again.

The Solar Drive itself was hidden from view inside a central chamber that could only be accessed via another stasis corridor after the engineers had adorned their protective gear. It wasn't just the radiation that had to be taken into account, but the frequency on which the Solar Drive resonated. Without the appropriate headgear, the engine's constant hum would burst a human's eardrum and had been known to burst blood vessels beneath the skin.

Ava led the Raiders through the embankments of consoles and workstations, all designed to monitor and tweak the Solar Drive's input and output. Cables ran up every wall space and along the ceiling, leaving the grated floor clear to walk on. The sound of their breathing was interrupted by a quick dash above them. As one, the squad swivelled to the right and aimed high, each taking a different stance and ready to fire. The walkway was empty, but they had definitely heard something run along the metal grates. At the same moment, another mad dash was heard to their left, on the same level. Again there was nothing for them to shoot.

"*Raider One.*" Maloy's voice came through all their headsets. "*Be advised, the three life signs appear to have split up. They're surrounding you.*"

Jess turned her rifle in every direction. "What level?"

"*The sensors aren't that accurate...*"

"Fantastic," Katie replied, dryly.

"Contact!" Jack's announcement was followed by a staccato of gunfire.

The bullets shredded every console between the team and the corridor, spreading shattered glass and fragments of torn metal. The Shay rolled aside, firing as it did, and evaded Jack's attack. Katie and Jess moved down the corridor, to the next row of consoles, and opened fire, hoping to hit the escaping alien. More consoles and cables were reduced to pieces, as the Shay's robotic limbs projected it out of harm's way.

Ava and Kyle were a split second from joining them in the chase when another Shay opened fire on them from above. They instinctively crouched and returned fire under the umbrella of sparks that exploded around them. Ava's visor alerted her to a successful hit on the Shay's organic arm, which quickly became evident when it dropped the rifle onto their level. Using its other, mechanical, arm, the Shay hoisted its body over the railing and dropped down to their level. The tall embankment of consoles immediately hid it from view, but Ava knew the alien would be going straight for its gun.

"Hold position." Ava gripped Kyle by the arm, keeping him by her side. "Raiders, on me!"

Jack, Katie and Jess made their way back to the colonel, each covering a different angle on their approach. Their prey had disappeared somewhere inside the bowels of the engine room, while the injured Shay had slunk away, most likely having retrieved his weapon.

"Where's the third?" Kyle pointed out.

"Maloy? What can you see?" Ava asked.

"*They never regroup, but it's as if they know what each other is doing. The two you just engaged are looping round from different directions.*"

"They're trying to flank us," Jess commented, her eyes scanning every corner.

"*The third is...*" There was a pause on Maloy's end. "*I think it's trying to gain access to the Solar Drive, but I can't be sure.*"

The team huddled close together and cautiously made their way back to the drive's main entrance.

"We've got eyes on, Maloy." Ava checked the doors for any signs of broken entry. "No targets."

"*No, I think it's trying to get in through an emergency access hatch underneath the central housing unit.*"

"Contact!" It was Kyle who spotted the Shay, this time approaching from behind the group.

The Raiders were forced to dive in different directions to avoid the hail of bullets. A pain-filled grunt from Katie suggested she had been hit, but Ava's visor indicated that the wound was below her knee - she would live. The second Shay, with a wounded arm, appeared from the side of the Solar Drive's main doors, shooting as it rounded the corner. This new attack forced the Raiders even further apart. They were being split up.

Kyle jumped out from behind a small workstation and drove his tactical blade into the Shay's chest - a killing blow for any human - but the Shay piled into the Raider, using his momentum to drive Kyle into the wall. A swift kick knocked the rifle from the alien's robotic hand, which it then used to grip Kyle by the visor, each digit poking through the glass. The pistons in the robotic arm flung Kyle several feet away. Though unintentional, it had proven to be the perfect distraction. When the Shay turned around, Ava was standing inches away with the barrel of her rifle in the alien's face. The colonel squeezed the trigger and watched the Shay's face and head turn to pulp.

"Push!" Katie barked at Jess and Jack, who were all closing in on the first Shay.

Ava was going to help Kyle up, but the soldier was already on his feet, discarding the broken helmet that had finger holes in the visor.

"*Raider One, bridge control just got a breach alert on the Solar Drive!*"

Maloy's words focused Ava's tactical mind. "We're going for the third, you three take care of the straggler." Matthews looked back a second later. "And Katie, no grenades. This is still an engine room."

"I guess I'm gonna have to get creative..." The three raiders rounded the corner and disappeared.

Kyle happily took Jack's helmet, aware that his eardrums wouldn't survive the proximity to the Solar Drive.

Ava and Kyle used the ladders to descend into the tunnels beneath the Solar Drive. There were more cables than anything else since consoles weren't kept on this level. Finding the intrusive Shay was easy since its attempts to break into the main chamber was so noisy. It was using some kind of blow torch to access the panel beside the emergency hatch, hoping to rewire the circuits and open the small, square lid.

Colonel Matthews and Lieutenant Riddick took up positions either side of the tunnel entrance and crouched, making themselves smaller targets. The stolen rifle was slung over its bony back in a position that would make it hard to reach in a pinch.

"You thinking prisoner?" Kyle asked.

"Well I know the others aren't going to take anything alive," Ava replied.

When they looked back at the small circular room, the Shay was gone, the blowtorch resting on the floor. The Raiders glanced at each other, their expressions, visible through the visors, communicating everything they needed. Rifles first, they entered the small room, lined with cables that ran up into the housing above.

The Shay dropped from the arch above the entrance, moving erratically like a spider. Using mechanical fingers and feet, the alien stuck to the walls above them before dropping onto Ava. Its weight put the colonel on the floor, but the soldier was quick to draw the blade attached vertically to her chest. After four or five plunges into the Shay's abdomen, it was becoming clear that pain and blood loss was not an issue.

Kyle wrapped his arms around its neck and pulled back, moments before the Shay tried to break Ava's trachea. The two stumbled back and became a jumble of limbs on the floor. Blood spilled from the alien's gut, making a mess of the floor and staining Kyle's armour. Ava advanced, but the Shay saw her coming and reached for Kyle's sidearm, clipped to his left thigh. The colonel saw the gun come free and rise towards her face. In such a cramped space there would be no avoiding the shot, and the bullet would pass through her visor with ease.

Kyle let out a primal growl and twisted the Shay's head with trained experience. The alien went instantly limp and dropped the sidearm in its lap. The two soldiers were left in the empty chamber, the only sound their heavy breathing. No thanks were required on Ava's behalf - keeping each other alive was just another part of their job.

"And we thought this mission was going to be boring..." Kyle quipped, taking back his gun.

Ava almost smiled before the image of Peter's dead body flashed in front of her eyes. Losing someone under her command was always a scarring ordeal, one which thankfully had only happened once before Peter.

"Sitrep," Matthews spoke into her helmet mic.

Jack's voice replied, "Target is down, permanently. Katie used incendiary rounds."

"At least we know they don't like fire..." Katie added. Ava didn't have to see her to know there was a sadistic grin on Lieutenant Wilson's face.

Ava looked back at the alien corpse just in time to see its head twitch and one of its eyes flick into the back of its socket. The unusual display was followed by a steady trickle of blood from both ears.

"What the hell was *that*?" Kyle asked.

"Beats the shit out of me. Let's see what the Conclave has to say about this."

THIRTEEN

If it weren't for the *Advent's* sensitive instruments, there would be no way of telling if the ship was actually moving. The pitch black of subspace was all that greeted Kalian and Naydaalan on their journey to the Criterion system.

"I dislike that view." Naydaalan returned to the bridge with two bowls of Novaarian noodles - one in each pair of hands. "It makes me feel lost." The warrior sat back in his chair and used one of his four arms to adjust the viewport, changing the image to that of a starry backdrop.

It occurred to Kalian that this was the first piece of personal information Naydaalan had ever given him. Usually, the Novaarian was very stoic and guarded around others, though he had taken a liking to Li'ara, and Kalian couldn't blame him for it.

The noodles quickly disappeared as Naydaalan used something approximating chopsticks to scoop the living noodles into his mouth - both bowls. How long had it been since Kalian had eaten or drank anything? The ship had been stocked with food and drink suitable for human physiology, but Kalian had yet to even entertain the idea of consuming. Was this another Terran thing? Could his body go without sustenance, and if so, for how long? This was why he needed Esabelle.

Even her atoms would be gone by now.

Kalian looked to Naydaalan, wishing to distract himself as well as learn more about the son of Telarrek. "Why did you volunteer for this mission? Surely your father wasn't happy about it?"

Naydaalan chewed his noodles slower. "The Ambassador left the Conclave for four centuries to observe your people. We do not measure time away from friends and family as you do, especially when the cause is worthy. The Ambassador feared for my safety yes, but just as much as he did for yours."

"The Ambassador? Isn't he also your father?" Kalian had always felt a special bond with Telarrek. The Novaarian had continued to support the human race, advocating them every step of the way. He was also a friend.

Naydaalan replied with a subtle Novaarian smile. "Our cultures are very different, Kalian Gaines. A Novaarian's duty and sense of honour always come before anything else. My father is the ambassador between your people and the Highclave, a high honour deserving of respect, especially from his children who have yet to achieve such a station."

Their sense of honour and duty was one of the aspects Kalian loved most about the Novaarian people. It was that same characteristic that fueled them to support humanity.

"So why did you volunteer for this?" Kalian asked again.

Naydaalan looked out at the holographic stars. "I feared that you came here to die."

That wasn't what Kalian had expected. Without any words to reply, all he could do was frown, questioningly.

"It is known that you have kept to yourself for the last three months since Li'ara and Esabelle died. No visitors aboard the *Sentinel*, no trips to the human habitat and barely any interaction with the crew. You were originally opposed to this plan until you learned of Li'ara's fate. I feared that you had given up, and had come on such a perilous mission to find your end."

"So you're here on suicide watch..." Kalian sat back and sighed, contemplating his three months of self-exile and seeing how the Novaarian could come to that conclusion.

Naydaalan replied in a softer tone, "I am here because Li'ara wanted you to live more than anything else. I was with her when you stopped the Starrillium from exploding on the Nova. Seeing you on the brink of death nearly crushed her. Whatever anyone else believes about you, Kalian Gaines, Liara believed that you were the only one who could bring all our people together, as well as combat this looming threat. I would see that legacy fulfilled."

Kalian couldn't meet Naydaalan's golden eyes; he didn't want the warrior to see his own filling with tears. The way Li'ara had felt about him was something Kalian knew he would never experience again. In one of their last conversations, she had pointed out the futility of a relationship between a mortal and an immortal. Kalian had been willing to forgo his extended life and simply stop his cells from replenishing, allowing him to age at the same rate. Li'ara had not been happy with that. She saw it as a waste of life, and she always saw Kalian's life as being important, not just for him, but for others.

The rest of his conversation with Naydaalan was cut short when the main console alerted them to their approaching destination. The Novaarian replaced his bowls and went to work on the glass panel in front of him. Seconds later, the viewport flashed and the holographic stars were replaced with real ones.

An orange sun dominated the background, its glare hiding hundreds of solar systems beyond it. The viewport had already dimmed and overlaid itself with a technical readout from the sensor array. A small sphere-like object was highlighted in front of the star, five-hundred thousand miles away. Naydaalan had the image sharpened and zoomed in, giving the effect that the object was suddenly brought closer to them.

"Is that it?" Kalian lost any hope of finding answers when he saw the husk of the Criterion.

Though it had once been a sphere, the remains were without any particular shape. Debris clung to the main body like its own personal asteroid field. Kalian had tried many times to search through the chaotic memories of Savrick and discover the fate of the Criterion, but the bleed effect between their memories had always proven too hard to navigate.

"I don't think we'll be getting any answers from inside there," Kalian continued. "Especially since most of its insides are on the outside."

"Wait..." Naydaalan was examining his console. "These are not the exact coordinates ALF gave us."

"What?" Kalian should have known better than to trust the AI.

"This is the correct system, but the exact coordinates are -"

"On the other side of the sun..." ALF finished the sentence for him.

Kalian got up from his seat and met the holographic man at eye level. "Start explaining or I swear this entire suit is going to find its way to the airlock with you trapped inside."

ALF stepped past Kalian and gazed out of the viewport. "As far as the Terran were concerned, that metal husk was the Criterion. They believed that it housed all of my central processing units and personality. If they could destroy that, they could plunge the empire into chaos."

"But that's not the Criterion..." Kalian was following along.

"No. But it was armed to the teeth if only to give the impression that it was the Criterion."

Naydaalan looked from the coordinates to ALF. "The real Criterion is at these coordinates?"

"You'll find a small planet, if you could call it that, it's more of a giant rock covered in volcanoes. Its proximity to the sun makes it somewhat uninviting, shall we say. The real Criterion is hidden within." ALF explained everything as if it was common knowledge.

"Lying is just second nature to you, isn't it?" Kalian took his seat again.

ALF sighed and replied patronisingly. "Why don't we just investigate the Criterion, allow me to access the rest of myself and then we can finally take a detailed look into the past. If these cubes are indeed of Terran origin, there's bound to be some record of it somewhere inside my main housing."

Kalian nodded to Naydaalan, who set the *Advent* on course for the mystery planet. The Novaarian wanted to stop and charge the intrinium inside a starspot, but Kalian was eager for answers and pressed them on. The idea of ALF connecting with the rest of his personality didn't sit well with Kalian, but he desperately needed the answers potentially stored inside the Criterion's ancient files.

It took almost an hour to navigate the circumference of the sun on thrusters alone. Naydaalan had them on a flight path as close to the star as the hull would allow. Once the sun was behind them they were able to see the small planet that disguised the Criterion. As they drew closer it became apparent that ALF's description of the planet had been quite accurate. A molten sphere covered in red veins and oceans of orange lava stood alone in the cold of space, the only planet in the system.

"The array can find nothing but organic material," Naydaalan said.

ALF stood over the Novaarian's console and looked down at a grid reference of the planet's surface. "You won't find it with sensors. You have to know where it is." His holographic finger pointed at a section of the grid. "There."

Kalian had the map display on his own console and had it change into three dimensions. The section ALF had indicated was a mountain, the only mountain that wasn't actively ejecting copious amounts of lava.

Kalian spoke to Naydaalan, "The suit you wore on Albadar, can it withstand this can kind of punishment?"

Naydaalan checked the temperature on the surface of the planet, but Kalian was more concerned with any lava that might find its way onto his suit.

"Not for long," Naydaalan replied. "An hour at most."

"You won't need that long," ALF stated, mysterious as ever.

After breaching the atmosphere, Naydaalan scanned anywhere for the *Advent* to land and found no suitable areas. The lava flow continuously pushed the land masses across the surface, pulling them apart and bringing them back together again.

"I will have to keep the ship afloat while we probe the area." Naydaalan showed Kalian the control pad, built into his suit's forearm. "To conserve energy, I will send it back into the stratosphere and have it sync with our orbit. It will never be more than seconds away should we need it."

Kalian had his suit cover his head and hands, while simultaneously having the nanocelium link wirelessly to Naydaalan's suit, allowing him to monitor the Novaarian's vitals and structural integrity. On a planet like this one, only Kalian's Terran abilities could keep them alive long enough to discover anything of importance.

After bringing the *Advent* to within thirty feet of the rocky ground, at the base of the mountain, the airlock opened to a gust of super-heated air and swirling cloud of ash and sulphur. The drop was too far for any creature to survive, and Kalian was about to guide the two of them down with telekinesis when Naydaalan stepped out. At the last second his boots flared and his rapid descent slowed down until he was standing comfortably on the edge of a river of lava. The effect reminded Kalian of a certain bounty hunter with whom he had fallen out. Roland should have brought Li'ara back. If anyone, it should have been him who died.

"Kalian?" Naydaalan's voice came over the speakers in his helmet.

His reverie broken, Kalian dropped out of the ship, not bothering to slow his descent. The ground cracked under his weight, as he landed on one knee with his closed fists either side. His Terran physiology was stronger and could take such punishment, with denser bones and tougher muscle mass - not to mention the exo-suit's durability. The suit also kept him cool, while the temperature outside was reaching eleven-hundred degrees Celsius.

Above them, the *Advent's* thrusters kicked in and sent the ship flying vertically upwards, until it vanished behind the black clouds of ash. Appearing entirely out of place, ALF's unprotected form projected in front of the pair. The projection itself was incredibly sensitive to their environment, causing ALF's grey beard and shoulder-length hair to blow in the same direction as the hot breeze. This data was clearly taken from Kalian's exo-suit and fed into the projectors to give the AI the most life-like appearance as possible - even his robes whipped about his legs.

"It's just over this rise." ALF started walking in that direction, leading them over a series of tributaries flowing with lava.

Naydaalan used the miniature jet thrusters, built into his suit's back and legs, to overcome the rivers his unique Novaarian physiology couldn't naturally jump. Kalian simply stepped into the shallower flows and used telekinesis to jump over the deeper ones. ALF gave the appearance of walking over them as if he were some kind of god.

"This is it." ALF gestured towards the wall of mountain before them.

Naydaalan looked from the wall of rock to ALF and finally to Kalian. "Is your suit malfunctioning?"

ALF smiled. "It's buried behind millennia of rock. A little Terran ingenuity is going to be required."

Kalian met ALF's eyes and wished he knew what was going on behind those grey orbs. With an outstretched hand, he pushed his awareness beyond his physical body and let the mountain fill his mind. He gasped and pulled back as soon as the mountain's secrets took shape.

"What is it?" Naydaalan asked.

Kalian just stared at ALF. "What we've been looking for."

Tapping into some of his rage and frustration with the AI, Kalian used both hands to crack the wall of rock. Three hundred feet of rock burst apart and exploded outwards as if a new fissure had blown inside the mountain. Tons of molten rock flew into the air and splashed into the lakes and rivers of lava. A clear twenty-feet remained untouched around the three of them, where Kalian had been sure to erect a telekinetic bubble to protect them. The disturbance caused multiple rock slides across the mountain, but Kalian guided them away from the Criterion's entrance.

It took a moment for the dust and ash to settle, revealing the three hundred foot wall of nanocelium. The surface was similar to that of the cubes found on Trantax IV and inside the *Gommarian* and Protocorps, lined with intricate patterns and interlacing circles engraved in unknown languages. Having felt the outside of the entire Criterion, Kalian knew that its shape was that of a cube with the corners cut off.

"Is that..?" Naydaalan craned his long neck.

"A giant cube? More or less..." Kalian walked past ALF, towards the Criterion.

Once they were within fifteen-feet of the shear wall, the giant cogs and patterns began to rotate and move about the surface. Kalian had seen a similar effect in Savrick's memories when he first discovered the cube on Hadrok. The cube had presented him with a hole in which he placed his arm, where it proceeded to take his free will by poisoning him with thoughts of civil war. Now, the Criterion presented them with a giant doorway, big enough to fit the *Advent* through, had they wished. It was dark inside and Kalian thought to warn Naydaalan away, but nothing happened as they passed over the threshold and into the shadows.

Kalian's exo-suit indicated an instant drop in temperature, despite only being feet away from the lava world outside. ALF remained by his side, calm as ever, while Naydaalan used a hand scanner to interpret their new surroundings. A new alert popped across his HUD, informing Kalian of the change in atmosphere.

"The air is becoming breathable," Naydaalan announced, checking his own scanner.

"And warmer," Kalian added.

The doors began to slowly close the gap behind them, narrowing the available light. Both Kalian and Naydaalan tensed, but ALF raised a holographic hand.

"Wait. It's okay," the AI assured them.

As the light disappeared, only Naydaalan's suit torches illuminated their environment. Kalian raised his hand, palm open, and willed the molecules to vibrate violently until they heated up and became a swirling ball of organic plasma. Its brilliant blue and white light cast harsh shadows all around them, revealing dark cables and tubing and hanging, broken pieces of chain.

When the oxygen inside was as habitable as the temperature, Kalian deactivated his helmet and gloves and breathed in the cool air. It smelt damp and old, but completely silent, even the volcanic eruptions outside couldn't be heard.

"I don't suppose you remember where the light switch is, do you?" Kalian held his sphere of plasma over ALF's face, causing the hologram to squint as if the light was actually blinding.

Like fireflies in the dark, hundreds of tiny orange lights filtered through unseen vents, high above. After filling the upper levels, the lights slowly dropped to Kalian's height and spread out, bringing light to every corner. The space was massive and occupied with machinery Kalian couldn't even fathom. Most of the mechanisms and parts appeared old, but it was all so alien he didn't know what to think. There were more levels higher up, but the unusual lighting system had gone no further than a hundred foot.

Kalian dissolved the plasma in his hand and reached out to touch one of the glowing orbs, no bigger than the tip of his finger, but continually failed to make contact. The orbs moved around in a similar fashion to dust, always reacting to the proximity of other objects and the airwaves created by them. Naydaalan was treating them with more suspicion and waved them away from his face mask with three hands.

"What's with the lighting system?" Kalian asked ALF.

"I like the ambiance..." It wasn't ALF who replied, though the hologram was smiling.

Kalian took a step back and welcomed the tingling sensation running along his spine, readying him for a fight. Naydaalan was by his side in a second, having swapped his scanner for a gun. The voice had come from the back of the Criterion, where the shadows had yet to be overrun by the fireflies. The mysterious reply, spoken with an augmented tone, was followed by heavy footsteps, gradually walking towards them.

"ALF, what's going on?" Kalian had one foot forward, ready to defend or attack, depending on what emerged from the shadows.

"Kalian, Naydaalan..." The holographic image of ALF stood between them and the approaching figure. "I would like you to meet me, the *real* me."

Captain Fey cupped her mouth, a subconscious attempt to hide her dismay at the three dead bodies lined up in front of her. Sharon Booth, Lieutenant Peter Holmes and Ch'vork, the *Nautallon*'s chief engineer, were all covered in blue sheets in the medbay. Off to the side was another body, covered with a different body bag and a radioactive symbol printed on top. Whatever remained of the Paladin's saboteur was thankfully hidden from sight, unlike Sharon's bloody hand, which could be seen hanging off the gurney, lifeless.

How many more casualties would there be? How many lives could she stand to lose under her command?

Lieutenant Worth came up on her side. "Captain?"

Fey appreciated his concern. "I was due to retire in a couple of years. I had so many plans. I was going to read and write and explore. I wonder what plans they had. We cheated death the day the Gomar attacked our people. Now it seems, death is coming for us all..." Li didn't know why she said it, and she knew she shouldn't have, not to the lieutenant. "I'm sorry, Ben." The captain patted his arm before she even realised she had referred to him by his first name instead of rank. The death of the UDC was finally starting to settle in, it seemed. "I'm becoming pessimistic in my old age."

At a hundred and nineteen years old, Captain Fey was still keeping up with the youth around her, not to mention keeping the looks of a fifty-five-year-old. In human years, she was expected to live for another sixty to seventy years, but having seen so many die in the last year, Li suspected she would never see a hundred and twenty.

"You cannot be serious?" Colonel Matthews rounded the corner in the med bay, along with Captain Holt and Commander Vale. "I highly advise more goddamn caution... *Captain!*"

Fey looked over the colonel, her short blonde hair splattered with Shay blood. Her team had returned half an hour ago with three more dead bodies to add to the growing list today. Li frowned at the way Ava spoke to her superior officer, wanting to believe that she would never put up with such insubordination, but then everyone knew that Raiders were just guns with people attached to them. That profile made her think about Roland North for a moment, another weapon in the human arsenal. As usual, the captain had no idea where the bounty hunter was or what he was doing. She only knew it would be nothing good.

"Colonel." Holt stopped his advancement towards Fey and turned to meet Ava's eyes. "I think your team needs to clean up and cool off, before the *funeral.*" Jed's tone was that of a commanding officer, and not to be challenged.

Colonel Matthews shot Fey a venomous glare before her gaze flickered to the bodies beyond. "Sir." Ava stormed off with her team in tow.

Captain Holt watched her leave before meeting up with Fey in front of the viewing room. He looked just as exhausted as she felt.

"How's Chief Grenko?" Li asked.

"He's already trying to get back to his engine. Alexsander's a tough bastard. All of my crew are..."

Captain Fey nodded her agreement. "Exemplary."

"High Charge Uthor has already requested a new party come aboard and oversee the newest repairs, as well as collect their engineer and the Shay bodies." Jed glanced back at Commander Vale, who was talking to Lieutenant Worth. "I'm being advised not to allow any more Conclave personnel onboard," the captain stared hard at the bodies on the other side of the screen, "and I'm seriously considering it."

When was she going to get this vision through to everybody?

"There aren't two bodies inside that room, Jed, there's *three*, and one of them isn't human. The Conclave lost people today too, not to mention whatever that was with the Shay, but they're dead as well. If there's one thing the last year has taught me, it's that we're all in this together. I told you that there's something else out there, something that wants us all dead, not just humanity, but the Conclave too. There are seven hundred trillion lives inside their civilisation; they might not be human beings, but their lives matter. They have to, because if we don't start working together and trusting one another... we all lose."

Jed puffed out his chest. "I gather that's not the first time you've had to give that speech?"

Fey gave in to her smile before the dead grounded her again. "And I fear it won't be the last."

A ruckus from the bay behind them drew their attention, to where Chief Grenko was pulling away from the nurses and doctor swarming him.

"I'm fine, I'm fine!" Grenko had one arm in a sling while the other kept him propped up with a cane. "I want to know what those trigger-happy morons have done to my engine!"

The sight would have been amusing were it not for their morbid surroundings.

Jed turned back to Fey. "I'll inform Uthor that a team can come aboard, but not any Shay. The Raiders are likely to kill if they see another of their species."

"Fair enough. Will you return with us to the Raalak system?" If Fey couldn't unite her people with that of the Paladin, what hope did she have of building a bridge between humanity and the Conclave?

"Well, it's either that or stay out here and starve to death or freeze to death. The list of things that can kill you in space is horribly long..."

"Sir?" Commander Vale said. "The *Nautallon* is contacting us again. They really want those alien bodies."

Jed chewed over his response, looking to Li instead. "Do you have any idea why they would attack us like that?"

Captain Fey had given the matter much thought. "There have been protests all over the Conclave since our arrival. Some argue that we should be given membership, others believe we are a threat. It's possible the Shay engineers were part of some radical group, but it seems highly out of character. The Conclave is generally a peaceful civilisation. They haven't known war or violence for thousands of years."

Commander Vale added, "Their behaviour was normal until that moment before they killed Ch'vork. It looked like they all experienced the same thing at once. Our initial scans also show serious trauma to their brains - they were all reduced to pulp, post-mortem."

"This investigation will have to continue while we're on the move." Jed walked over to the comm panel on the wall. "Captain to the bridge."

"*Bridge here, Captain.*"

"Maloy, get on the horn and inform the *Nautallon* that they can send a new team over." Jed glanced at Fey. "And start a dialogue with their helmsman, we're going to the Conclave."

FOURTEEN

3 Months Ago...

Li'ara wondered at what point her life would flash before her eyes. Death was moments away; the bomb ticking down the seconds remaining on her life, and what a short life it had been. At least she would enter the next world knowing she had accomplished something that mattered. Soon the explosive device she had attached to the cube's main-lines would erupt, filling the chamber with fire and a shattering force strong enough to blow the cube away.

But there were regrets...

Kalian's image filled her mind. His smell, his smile and boyish charm that mixed perfectly with his sarcastic sense of humor. He was one of few who could make Li'ara laugh deep in her belly. She would never get to see him again, never get to tell him what she should have done so many times.

Sitting on the walkway, between the cube and the impenetrable door, Li'ara rested against the railing and ignored the pain in her hands. Banging on the strongest door in the galaxy had done nothing for her. She thought about putting an intrinium round in her head and ending it all now, on her terms, but she couldn't. It just wasn't in her to take her own life, even at the end, and besides, the explosion would kill her just as fast.

The cube sat at the end of the walkway and somehow Li'ara knew it was watching her. Thinking about what the cube onboard the *Gommarian* had done to Professor Jones, the commander shuffled further down the walkway. If she was going to die today, it would be as a human, not some twisted monster.

The door creaked.

Li'ara whipped her head around and focused on the circular door. It didn't move, but there was definitely sound coming from inside of it. It was similar to when the hull of a ship would contract under the temperatures of a starspot. Li'ara slowly stood up, never taking her eyes from the door. It wasn't long before the sounds increased and the door was visibly under pressure, as the edges, where the cylindrical bolts slotted into place, started to crumple and snap. A screeching, high-pitched noise cut through everything else and offended Li'ara's ears. Without warning, the solid rock that surrounded the door gave way and broke into chunks, falling onto the walkway.

Li'ara tapped her earpiece. "Roland, are you there?" Her voice was barely a whisper.

The door's struggle ended as abruptly as it began. The moment of silence was shattered when the giant circular door was torn from its framework, bent out of shape, and cast aside, into the corridor beyond. The dust quickly settled, revealing Li'ara's saviour, who in truth she had thought could only be Kalian or Esabelle.

Instead, it was the silhouette of death that stood in the ruined entryway.

Li'ara gasped and stumbled back, while her mind struggled to understand how a Gomar could be standing in front of her. The hulking black armour was partially hidden beneath rags and a dirty cloak, but it could not go unnoticed. A thousand questions should have run through Li'ara's mind, but instead, she could only think of one thing.

Roland's voice broke through her shock, but he wasn't talking to her. *"We need to get back up to the chamber. We have to save..."*

"Roland," Li'ara commanded his attention, as the Gomar strode towards her. "Tell Kalian I..."

What should have been Li'ara's final words never left her mouth. The bomb had exploded with a deafening crack. Before the light blinded her and the explosion claimed all of her senses, the Gomar could be seen lunging the gap between them, his arms outstretched. What happened immediately after couldn't be put into any kind of order in Li'ara's mind.

The next time she opened her eyes, the setting was not as she had left it. There was no fire, no cube and no sign of any natural rock, as there had been covering the chamber. Instead, Li'ara awoke to a dark, cool room filled with pipes and cables lining damp walls. She was lying on what had perhaps once been a workstation but judging by the look of everything in the room, it hadn't been used for some time. The only light source came from a single orb, which floated above Li'ara's head and followed her movements.

Hopping off the bench was more painful than it should have been. Her muscles ached and all the cuts and bruises she had accumulated during their attack on Protocorps had settled in. Alarmingly, her side-arm was missing, along with her blade. Li'ara looked around frantically, searching for them, and then scanning the room for anything she could fashion into a weapon. The image of the Gomar lunging towards her was enough to get the adrenaline pumping.

A length of old piping caught her eye and she was tempted to pick it up, but then sense kicked in. It wouldn't matter what weapon she had to hand; there were only two people who could defeat a Gomar in combat, and neither of them was here.

Hesitantly, and with no small amount of caution, Li'ara exited the room through the single, unlocked door, and explored the new surroundings. The corridor outside was just as dingy and damp as the room and similarly lined with pipes and cable. After reaching the end of the corridor, Li'ara became aware of a growing rumble of sound. The commander followed the sound until it took her to another room, larger this time, and filled with familiar things. There was a makeshift cot against the far wall and a small table beside it. Random pieces of food and water were stockpiled in the corner and the wall to her right was entirely covered in monitors and holographics. There was a single chair in front of them all.

The sound of people and the thunder of footsteps brought her attention to the ceiling. It was higher than the room she awoke in, and the flat surface was broken up by three grates, which allowed for light to filter in, along with the sound of hundreds of aliens.

It's not the Gommarian, but I've slept in worse conditions... The male voice in her head was gentle but no less alarming.

Li'ara swivelled on her heel, flicking her red hair out to the side. Filling the doorway was the same Gomar who had ripped the vault's door from its hinges. The nanocelium exo-suit covered every inch of his body, concealing his face. The rags still hung off of him, though they appeared singed and blackened since the explosion.

The sight of the killer made her step back, though in truth she had no plan or strategy. Li'ara wasn't fast enough, strong enough or smart enough to survive any kind of encounter with a being that had been alive for two hundred thousand years, fought in the bloodiest war the galaxy had ever known and could literally crush so-called indestructible objects with their mind.

"Why am I still alive?" she finally managed. "How are you even alive?"

Though his face remained hidden, there was no doubt in Li'ara's mind that the Gomar before her was Sef. He had been Savrick's personal bodyguard, along with Lilander, and had disappeared shortly before the *Helion* plummeted into Naveen's surface, burying the Terran outpost. He had been thought dead, crushed by the starship along with Savrick and Lilander. Kalian had always suspected that he could have survived, but no one really entertained the idea, not even Li'ara.

You don't live as long as I have and not pick up a few things about survival along the way.

The mental intrusion wasn't as uncomfortable as she thought it would be, and somehow she was aware that he had spoken with a slight smile on his face. It was a new form of communication for Li'ara, but she knew that Kalian and Esabelle had spoken to each other in this form before. He had always hated it, but Li'ara found Sef's voice to be incredibly soothing and uncharacteristically gentle.

"I'm more of a details kind of person," Li'ara replied dryly. "And why are you in my head?" It suddenly occurred to her that Sef might be rummaging through her thoughts.

Sef didn't reply straight away but appeared to consider his answer as he stepped towards Li'ara, who instinctively took another step back. With one hand, the Gomar pulled the torn cloak from his armour and cast it aside.

You fear me, Sef stated.

"Your people have provided more than enough reason to..." Li'ara knew that she would already be dead if that was what Sef desired, but his menacing armour only worked to put her on edge.

You don't have to fear me.

Sef turned his hand palm-up and used his other hand to manipulate the holographic menu that projected from his fingertips. The suit responded immediately, with the plates around his neck and head shifting down. A moment later and the dark helmet had been dismantled and absorbed into the suit, revealing the Gomar within. A typical Terran face greeted the commander, with symmetrical features, a strong, smooth jaw and strikingly beautiful blue eyes, similar to Esabelle's. He had cropped blond hair and pale skin, no doubt a result of being inside the exo-suit for so long. Li'ara took him in, his beauty undeniable, and realised she was looking upon the face of a killer, for all his handsome features, Sef was still a Gomar.

"Don't think for a second that those pretty blues will convince me to trust you. I saw you by Savrick's side. When he attacked the capital, you were there, you chased after us and nearly killed Kalian. You murdered everyone aboard the *Helion* and are just as responsible for every death when the *Gommarian* destroyed the capital's atmospheric shield." Li'ara tried circling around Sef to position herself between him and the door, but he didn't budge an inch. "On Naveen, you entered the outpost to kill us, leaving Kalian to fend off Lilander and the beast."

Sef sighed, but refused to move away from the door. *Immortality is a long road and isn't without its regrets, Li'ara. There are deaths at my feet and I am responsible. I would never cast that off; the lives I have taken are worth more than that. But my life had a different start than yours. I was born into war, my parents were killed before I could truly know them. When Savrick saved me, I was ready to pay the Terran in kind for their short-sightedness, and he was only too happy to unleash me. The civil war lasted many years, and in all that time I never regretted taking a single life, whether it be quick or slow. I was filled with hate and the power these suits gave us was intoxicating. Finally, the Harnesses were useless to contain us and we had control, as long as we wore the suits.*

"Wait, stop." Li'ara rubbed her head. "Can you speak normally? The whole voice in my head thing is starting to get a little weird."

Sef's lips parted as if to speak, but he remained silent. *I have not spoken aloud since I was a child since my parents were alive.*

"Oh. Right..." Li'ara didn't know what to say, the whole thing was very surreal. "So at what point did you regret all this?"

It was a long time after the civil war had ended. After we discovered that a planet had been seeded, Savrick had what few of us remained brought back to the Gommarian. As you already know, it was thousands of years before we found Earth.

"Another death toll you won't be shirking?" Li'ara really wanted to choke the life from him at that moment. Her father had been among the billions dead that day.

Sef blinked slowly and looked away, unable to meet Li'ara's eyes. *You have been in Savrick's presence, yes, but you never met him. He could not be questioned nor defeated. He was the most powerful among us, and he had the respect of every Gomar. He had personally rescued most of them.*

"Kalian defeated him," Li'ara replied boldly. "A twenty-eight-year-old history lecturer from San Francisco, who had never known war and certainly had no idea of what he was capable of, brought Savrick's reign to an end. How can you, a veteran of Terran war, stand there and say he couldn't be questioned, couldn't be defeated?

There's no sob story in your very long life that can explain your cowardice. You stood by and watched him commit genocide after genocide. Because of what? Were you afraid? Kalian was afraid and he still found the courage to stand up to all of you."

Shadows danced across the room as people walked over the grates above. Li'ara knew she was insulting a being that most would compare to a god, but right now she didn't care.

You have every right to hate me. It will take more time than we have for you to see as I do, but it is my hope that you will come to understand my actions.

"You want me to understand? Then start at the beginning." Li'ara dropped onto the makeshift cot and waited patiently.

I will, but right now we have to take care of your leg...

Li'ara frowned and looked down at her leg. How had she not noticed the robotic-looking worm coiled around her calf? It appeared burnt across the surface, with scorch marks and holes throughout, but the end was clearly sticking into the side of her leg. The commander jumped up and shook her leg instinctively, but the worm remained firmly attached. She stopped moving for a minute and wondered why she couldn't feel it.

"What is it?" Li'ara asked frantically.

Before the explosion, you were distracted by the sight of me. The cube took advantage of this and extended one of its tendrils. I was able to shield you from the blast, but not quick enough to prevent it from reaching your leg. The rest of it was destroyed in the explosion.

None of this made Li'ara feel any better about having an alien parasite stuck to her leg. She went back to pacing while searching for a sharp implement to prise it off. The panic was rising inside of her, with thoughts of Professor Jones creeping into her mind. With no tool in sight, Li'ara reached down and gripped it with both hands, determined to tear it from her leg.

Don't do that...

Sef's warning was too late. The worm constricted and the pain shot through her leg and up into her back, almost crippling her. Li'ara collapsed to the floor and screamed, gripping her leg as she did. The pain brought tears to her eyes and threatened to consume her. As the world began to take on a blurry edge, Sef was suddenly crouched over her, his exposed hand cupping her face. Li'ara felt the ground fall away and with it the pain. She was in Sef's arms, looking up at his flawless face.

I can keep the pain at bay and stop it from spreading deeper into your body.

"Get it off of me..." Li'ara managed.

I was in the middle of preparing another room before you awoke.

"What kind of room?" Li'ara was gaining her senses back, now that the pain was subsiding.

I will try and remove it as best I can but... my telekinetic skills are not as fine as is required. Savrick only trained us for war, I'm afraid.

Li'ara knew exactly what he was saying. "Have you ever done anything like this before?"

Once...

"Is it sterile, the other room? Do you have sedatives or, anything?" The thought of her leg being minutes away from amputation made Li'ara feel uncomfortably nauseous.

Have no fear. Sef's face suddenly became very hard to define, along with everything else in the room. *I will take care of you, Li'ara.*

Li'ara wasn't sure if hours or days had passed when she next opened her eyes. The light was blinding and the world still held its blurry edge, but the sounds of machinery and a constant beeping found her ears. She tried to speak but her mouth was dry.

Remain calm. Sef's soothing tone came from everywhere.

Li'ara caught a glimpse of the Gomar out of the corner of her eye, moments before the world went dark again.

This happened at least two more times that she could successfully recall before Li'ara finally felt the strength to lift her head. The room was brighter than the others and illuminated by multiple floating orbs, with no natural light. The gurney she was lying on was surrounded by monitors and holographics, displaying her vital signs and the levels of different drugs that were apparently in her system.

Her body was covered with a sheet and a blanket, her top half hidden beneath a black vest top. For the most part, she felt numb and stiff, leading her to believe that she had been lying on the gurney for at least a day. That was when everything came flooding back to her. The parasitic worm strapped to her leg! Li'ara sat up and tried to ignore the wave of nausea, as she pulled back the sheet covering her legs. Her gasp was cut short as she lost the will to make any sound.

Everything below her right knee was gone.

A sense of dizziness soon replaced the nausea, which left almost immediately after Li'ara vomited on the floor. She wanted to get up and run away from the whole scene, but she had just enough sense to know that running was something she could no longer achieve.

Easy...

Sef appeared by her side, surprisingly quiet for someone wearing so much armour. Using telekinesis, the Gomar helped Li'ara to stand, which she wasn't ready to do yet. Sef caught her fainting form in his strong arms, and Li'ara felt a mental tug which stopped her from losing consciousness.

You need to eat and drink. You've been out of it for a couple of days.

"Days..?" Li'ara couldn't take her eyes off the wad of bandages wrapped around her knee.

I was unable to remove the infected nanocelium with telekinesis. I tried for some time to take it out molecule by molecule, but it continued to use your tissue to feed its replication.

Sef carried her over to a table at the other end of the room, where a plate of hot food and a glass of water was waiting for her. There was no pain, which was about the only thing Li'ara could be thankful for right now. The smell of the food reminded her stomach how hungry she was, though it was clear to see from the hanging bags of fluid surrounding the gurney, that Sef had kept her hydrated.

Halfway through the meal, Li'ara was able to collect her thoughts. "Where did you get all this stuff? I assume we're still in the capital?"

There are countless rooms and access corridors behind the walls of the capital. Most are abandoned now, repurposed for sewage works, water supply and miles upon miles of cables that run the length of Clave Tower. I have been able to use these tunnels to move around unseen, and my telekinesis allows me to take objects without actually being there.

"Do you know what's going on out there? Have you heard anything?" Li'ara was only thinking of a handful of people she needed to know were okay.

Sef looked away for a moment as if he was unsure of how to proceed. *I have spent months building a network of programming designed to infiltrate various levels of Conclave security. I'm good with electronics. I have been able to listen in on chatter between the ships, as well as a few private conversations between the upper echelons.*

"Did they make it?" Li'ara just needed to know and Sef was telling her everything but. She needed to know if Roland made it out of Protocorps and if Kalian and Esabelle discovered anything in the Helteron Cluster. She needed to know they were alive.

Roland survived, though he has already disappeared again. His Terran vessel makes it hard for the Conclave to track him. I haven't been able to piece everything together yet surrounding the events in the Helteron Cluster, but I know the Gommarian has been destroyed.

Li'ara stopped chewing when she heard that. There was nothing that could even dent that ship, let alone destroy it.

"What about everyone onboard?" Li'ara wasn't sure she was ready for the answer.

They have been evacuated and are currently being relocated, but I haven't discovered the new location yet.

Li'ara exhaled, unaware that she had been holding her breath.

Kalian has returned, along with ALF.

Li'ara looked up at the Gomar with wide eyes and the first feeling of hope she had felt since before the explosion. Judging by Sef's expression, she could tell that he wasn't done with the bad news yet, and Li'ara realised he had yet to mention Esabelle.

I came across chatter between High Charge Uthor and a member of their science division. The scientist was annoyed with Uthor for denying him the chance to perform an autopsy... on Esabelle. Apparently, Kalian won't let them near her body.

Li'ara sat back and put her fork down. Esabelle was gone. They had never developed a substantial bond, but Li'ara had always appreciated the help she gave Kalian, even if they had been closer than she liked. Either way, death was not something she would have wished upon her. What could they have found in the Helteron Cluster that could not only destroy the *Gommarian* but also kill Esabelle, the most powerful Terran in the galaxy? Professor Jones had been strong, but he was no match for the two of them. When Li'ara's head had filled with enough questions, she looked back to Sef and saw how upset he was with this particular news. His blue eyes had filled with tears and taken on a glassy appearance.

"I know Esabelle was with all of you on the *Gommarian*. A part of your interface with the ship. I'm sorry -"

Esabelle was more than that...

Sef stood up from the table and made to leave, but Li'ara wanted to stop him. The commander stood up and held a hand out to catch the Gomar, but her right leg kept on going. She screamed for just a second, as the floor was quickly coming up to greet her, but she never made it. Inches from the cold, hard floor, Li'ara remained suspended in the air, where Sef had caught her. The Gomar corrected her, sitting the commander back down.

"Argh!" Li'ara groaned in frustration. "I forgot... It feels like it's still there! I can feel my goddamn foot!" She looked up at Sef, sure that she was wiggling her toes.

It will take some adjusting.

"I don't want to adjust. I want to walk again." Li'ara tried so hard to keep the tears back, but it was impossible.

I'm working on it. There is an augmentation facility not far from here. I have already started gathering the equipment I will need.

Li'ara looked from Sef to her leg and back again. "You're going to build me a new leg?"

I aim to, yes. Though it will not look as it did. I do not have the skills to fully replicate a human leg, skin and all. The whole process is going to take time and healing.

"Thank you." It suddenly hit Li'ara how much the Gomar had done for her. Sef had saved her life in Protocorps, saved her from infection and was now going to help her walk again. "Why are you doing all this? Why did you save me? Why aren't you as keen on killing all humans as Savrick was?"

Sef smiled, and it was hard not to like that smile. *Answers will come. For now, just know that we are on the same side with the same goals. Trust is something we build. And eat. You have quite the journey ahead of you before you can walk again...*

"Wait, wait, wait..." Roland sat upright on the sofa in the *Rackham's* kitchen and looked at Li'ara with his one good eye. "You're telling me that leg is *fake*?"

Li'ara sighed, exasperated with the bounty hunter already. She lifted her right leg and pulled her boot off, revealing the skeletal, robotic leg and foot.

"I bet that stung a bit." Roland swigged his beer, while Ch'len flapped about the place, trying to collate all their medical equipment and give Sef a wide berth at the same time.

"I felt kinda' how you look right now." Li'ara would never say it, but she was continually impressed with the beatings Roland was capable of taking. The idiot just refused to die.

"What, this?" Roland shrugged and immediately winced. "I've got plenty of painkillers." The bounty hunter waved his beer about. "So the gorilla over here's on our side, huh?" Roland looked Sef up and down with no small amount of suspicion.

Sef collapsed his helmet and Li'ara knew he was doing it to appear more familiar.

"Hideous like the rest of them I see..."

Li'ara couldn't help but chuckle at Roland's sarcasm, though she hated encouraging him. In truth, she hated the way he looked at Sef, but she also knew that everyone would look at the Gomar that way. Just as it had taken her time to learn to walk and run again, it would take patience and time before people learned to trust Sef.

"So you guys have just been shacked up behind the walls of the capital all this time..." Roland appeared to be chewing over the information. "You didn't think to communicate with anyone? Let someone know you were alive, maybe?"

Ch'len turned on Li'ara. "Do you know how many people he's tortured to -"

"Len!" Roland's face twisted in agony. "Easy with the leg, okay, it's not a pork chop."

Ch'len went back to examining his leg while muttering under his breath about stupid humans and questioning what a pork chop was.

"We had a different mission." Li'ara looked to Sef, who in time had told her the truth of everything. "Sef needed my help, and we needed to do it in secret, partly because the Conclave would freak out if they knew a Gomar was walking about the place, but also because we didn't know who we could trust. Protocorps was proof that the cubes have infiltrated the Conclave."

"What mission?" Roland tried to raise his eyebrow but found only pain.

"We need to find the rest of the Gomar and wake them up."

Roland looked at them both, expressionless, before bursting into laughter. "You're crazier than I am! What did blondy say to you? It must have been good to convince you that waking up his genocidal buddies was a great idea."

If Roland had more to say, it was drowned out by his cry of pain, as Ch'len applied a blue, gel-like substance to the wound on his leg. Sef moved for the first time, putting both Roland and Ch'len on edge, and held out his hand, palm down. The floor of the kitchen responded by forming a sleek column that rose up to greet the Gomar's hand. They had all seen Esabelle do something similar during their time on the *Rackham* together, and Roland had pulled the same quizzical expression then, too. The column opened up and a hand-sized cylinder of nanocelium floated to the top.

"What the hell is that?" Roland asked. "I really need to read the manual..."

Sef strode over, sending Ch'len scurrying around the small table, and held out the cylinder for Roland to take. The end of the device was identical to that of a syringe, with a series of small holes at the end.

"What am I supposed to do with this?" Roland took the object out of Sef's hand as if it had belonged to him all along.

Inject the nanocelium into your arm. It will heal you.

Roland's mouth fell open and he stared at Sef for a moment, before turning to Li'ara with a questioning look.

"He doesn't speak, remember."

"It's still damn weird. You had this for a whole three months?" Roland waved Ch'len's questioning look away.

"You get used to it." Li'ara had come to enjoy the sound of Sef's voice, often finding it soothing, especially when the pain in her leg returned. It had taken a couple more operations to get her new leg right, and the wound had to be opened every time. He had been there for her every step of the way.

"I guess I just don't like the idea of someone in my head." Roland stabbed his arm with the cylinder. "So how long does this stuff take to..." The bounty hunter stopped talking, which was a miracle in itself, and contorted his face and gripped his leg, then his ribs. "It feels weird."

Li'ara watched as his eye changed colour, before the swelling went down and his lids took shape again. The smaller cuts and bruises that had marred his face and hands slowly disappeared as well. Roland closed his fists and cracked the knuckles with a satisfied smile on his face.

"I *really* need to read the manual..."

Sef nodded, as if Roland had thanked him, and returned to his position on the other side of the kitchen. Roland on the other hand, stood up and tested his leg and patted his previously broken ribs. After a few stretches, the bounty hunter picked up another beer, dropped back onto the sofa and rested his legs on the table.

"Well, it's a damn sight better than nurse Len over here. So..." Roland downed half the beer. "Let me get this straight. You've been hiding in the capital for three months trying to track down the whereabouts of the Gomar, while also having your leg cut off and learning to walk again. And all the while, you've been doing it with him in your head."

Li'ara could see what Roland was getting at. The idea that Sef had been controlling her thoughts had come up a couple of times. Sadly, there was no way to prove he wasn't, leaving her to trust in his explanation.

"He can't control our thoughts, it doesn't work that way. Because of our physiology, he can tap into the frequency our brains emit. He can see into our mind, but he can't change the way we think. Its also why Ch'len can't hear him, different frequency."

Roland became serious for a moment. "What could he possibly have said to convince you he can be trusted?"

Li'ara looked at Sef, aware that it was his story and not her own. He nodded just once, approving of her to tell it right.

"During the Gomars' hunt for Earth, they were regularly put to sleep inside Rem-stores due to the scale of their search. When the *Gommarian* came across a civilisation or something of interest, the crew would be woken up and given the chance to investigate. This was all controlled by the ship's pilot; Esabelle. There were often thousands of years between anything worth investigating. As you already know, Esabelle achieved a level of consciousness at some point along the way, and started training herself inside the virtual world."

Roland waved her on. "Yeah yeah, I remember; she's the reason Savrick never found out the Conclave had already discovered Earth, blah blah blah. How does any of this change the fact that *he's* one of *them.*"

Li'ara ignored the insulting finger being pointed at Sef. "When Esabelle realised that the cube was affecting Savrick's mind, and caused the civil war, she started strategising a way to combat it. During the periods when the crew was asleep, she would wake up a select few, twelve to be exact. The same twelve she kept behind when the Gomar attacked the Valoran.

Now, she didn't wake them all up together, but one at a time, over a period of thousands of years. While they were awake and unable to enter their Rem-store, Esabelle would speak to them, incessantly, until they really started listening. Eventually she even showed them the cube and her findings. While Savrick and the others slept for centuries, millennia, twelve of his soldiers were being shown the truth he had kept hidden from them."

"What did Esabelle hope to achieve?" Roland had stopped drinking his beer. "Earth still got wiped out. Humans are on the endangered species list and, oh yeah, she's dead."

Li'ara tensed, unsure of how Sef would react to Roland's loose words. Sef had come to see Esabelle as a friend and mentor, closer to that of an older sister. As a testament to his self-control and mental discipline, Sef remained perfectly still, giving nothing away.

"Even though she had convinced twelve of them that there was a bigger threat than humanity, they were unable to stand against Savrick. It's hard for us to understand the kind of hold he had over them. He was seen as a father and an overlord. When Sef attacked us in the capital, after Savrick introduced himself to the Conclave, he wasn't trying to kill us. Esabelle had tasked him with getting Kalian to safety, but Kalian didn't give him the chance. On the *Helion*, it was the beast who killed all those aboard, not Sef. On Naveen, he had been tasked with destroying ALF by Savrick, but his intention was to get us to safety. It took him months to find a way onto the capital after the *Helion* crashed."

Roland sighed, taking it all in. "And since then he's been jacking into every security console he can..." The bounty hunter looked away, as if something had occurred to him. "Did Esabelle see you, when we were in the capital?"

Yes. We spoke briefly while you were entering a vehicle. It was Esabelle who charged me with locating the Gomar, when they were taken.

Roland shook his head. "That's going to get old, real quick. Wait a minute, when they were taken? Esabelle knew that the Conclave would discover the Gomar and take them?"

Sef smiled. *It is easy to forget how old one such as Esabelle was. After so much time, she had become very good at seeing patterns and interpreting data on a vast scale. Predicting future events was second nature to her.*

Li'ara tried to assess Roland's take on it all, but struggled to read the bounty hunter; he had spent a lifetime perfecting that poker face.

Roland looked up. "*Rackham*, what's the ETA on our intercept?"

"Three hours, nineteen minutes and eleven seconds."

"So you were looking for Gor-van as well?" Roland got up from the couch and stood in front of the wall of weapons. "Does he know where the Gomar is being kept?"

Li'ara was happy that Roland had accepted Sef's version of events so quickly. She could only hope that others would too, since it had taken her at least two months. Roland was of a simpler mind, however, and didn't trouble himself with big picture stuff, but preferred to get lost in the present, usually by drinking or shooting something.

"It took some time, but eventually we came across others who were hacking into Conclave systems. After more digging, it turned out they were all freelance, and being paid by the same person under a false name and a shell company."

"That sounds like Gor-van," Ch'len commented.

Li'ara nodded her agreement. "They were all searching for some kind of black site. At first, we thought it was a facility on one of the planets, but it turns out the black site is a planet. It's been removed from any public star charts and is entirely uninhabited."

"I take it since you happened across Gor-van's secret, little hideaway, you haven't got any coordinates?" Roland had started servicing his Tri-rollers on the kitchen counter.

"We had an earlier opportunity to capture him, but Sef came across a communication that suggested he was setting a trap for you on Byzantial. So we thought, why not rescue you and get the coordinates at the same time." Li'ara couldn't help the smug expression that crept across her face.

Roland looked at Ch'len. "A rescue that involved you taking control of the *Rackham*." The Ch'kara appeared somewhat sheepish at the statement. "We're gonna circle back to that..."

"It was Ch'len who managed to fire a tracking beacon onto Gor-van's ship." Li'ara didn't know why she was defending the ignorant, self-obsessed little alien.

Roland *snapped* the Tri-roller back together again. "So I've been recruited, have I?"

"I wouldn't say that." Li'ara knew better than to give him an inch.

"I would, since you left your stolen vessel back on Byzantial, and *my* ship is being used to track *your* prey. And since I'm the captain of this ship, that probably makes me the leader of this secret team. So here's what we're gonna do; we board Gor-van's pissy little ship, I'll torture him for the coordinates to the black site, and then, we go kill Kel-var Tionis on our way to the Gomar."

"Wait, what?" Li'ara stood up. "Kill Kel-var? We don't have time for that. The Gomar are pivotal in defending against whatever comes next, and it is coming."

"Yeah I get all that, but I've sort of been telling people that I'm coming for Kel-var. It's gotten around that I'm going to kill him so... I kind of have a reputation to uphold." Roland's casual behaviour infuriated Li'ara. "It'll be a short detour, I'm almost sure of it. In the meantime," he looked at Sef, "try not to move around too much, because your *girth* will literally wreck my ship."

Li'ara rolled her eyes and made to leave, though where she was going to go on the small ship, she didn't know.

"Aren't you going to ask about him?" Roland added casually.

Li'ara stopped and waited in the doorway. Using Sef's network, she had discovered that Kalian never returned to the new habitat in the Arakesh system. Wherever he was, it had been so secretive that no one was talking about it out there. She knew he was alive though, and that they were each doing what needed to be done. Her investigatory skills were essential for helping Sef look in the right areas, while Kalian was no doubt learning more about his power, which would be essential for when the war started, and Li'ara could feel that one was coming.

"I get the whole working in the shadows thing, I get why you wouldn't tell me you're alive, I'm a dick, but not telling Kalian... He kinda spiralled after that. He boarded the *Sentinel* and never came back."

Li'ara turned to face him, with Sef close by her side. "Come back from where?"

"The last I heard before we left, ALF agreed to help the Conclave build a Starforge. The original plan as I heard it was to send Kalian through it, back to the Terran Empire to search for clues."

Li'ara knew well of the Starforges now. There had been a lot of chatter about it after the incident in the Helteron Cluster. The scale of the weapon, and its ability to transport hundreds of ships instantaneously across the stars garnered a lot of attention. The information had been kept from the masses until very recently, when the Highclave personally announced the 'new' invention and the construction project to place them on every world.

"Did he go?" Li'ara couldn't mask the trepidation in her voice.

Roland shrugged. "I have no idea. I've been hunting down Protocorps members searching for any trace of you."

Ch'len waddled past. "There was a lot of torture..."

Li'ara clenched her jaw, holding onto that sense of duty that had gotten her this far. "Kalian always finds himself where he needs to be."

FIFTEEN

Kalian held his arm out to stop Naydaalan from firing his weapon into the dark, a darkness that quickly gave way to an eight-foot biped. Ignoring his own instincts to attack, Kalian waited until the figure stepped into the light. He had to know. What was ALF really? A part of him had always believed that the AI was more than he would have them believe.

"Kalian..." Naydaalan was eager to take up a better position.

"Wait." Kalian expanded his awareness and was shocked at what he felt.

The towering biped walked into the light, revealing a naked body, amalgamated from nanocelium and human flesh. The similarities to Malekk and Professor Jones were uncanny, but somehow the figure standing before them appeared older as if the nanocelium and the flesh had joined together a long time ago. The lean biped puffed out its chest and looked down on the two of them with the face of ALF.

Kalian could feel the nanocelium teeming through his ancient veins and flowing over the skin, which had turned a putrid shade of green with patches of grey. His beard and shaggy hair were part organic, part mechanical tendril as if robotic worms were writhing throughout the hair. Shining blue eyes connected with his own, though they were clearly being illuminated by artificial lights, behind the retinas.

His overall size was unusual - Kalian was forced to crane his neck to see all of him. The *real* ALF was much taller than any Terran or human, but every part of him looked to be proportional. There was no sign of any genitals, however, but only a collection of nanocelium strands which continued up his torso and across his arms and neck.

"You're…" Kalian looked from the holographic ALF to the physical one. "You're one of them."

"No," the physical ALF replied, his voice somewhere between human and machine. "I am something else. Something more." A hand, almost twice the size of Kalian's, was held out in the manner of a handshake. "I can show you."

"What is this?" Kalian aimed his question at the hologram, the ALF he knew. "WHAT IS THIS?"

An electromagnetic pulse surged from Kalian's body, along with a small amount of telekinetic energy. It had been a while since his emotions had got the better of him and produced an outburst like this. Naydaalan was pushed back, but he remained on his feet, even if his weapon was now useless. The hologram of ALF fluttered, threatening to disappear altogether, but the physical version stood defiantly with his hand out.

"This is where all roads converge, Kalian." The physical ALF seemed to have taken over. "The answers you have been seeking. The knowledge that has eluded you every step of the way."

Kalian took a breath and glanced at Naydaalan to make sure he was okay. "How could you know me?" He spoke directly to the physical ALF. "Technically we've never met."

"Indeed we have not." The towering figure spoke with all the same mannerisms as the hologram. "Incidentally, I thank you for bringing me back to me."

At that moment, Kalian felt his suit shift before a low-level charge of electricity built around his waist. The hologram of ALF blinked out of existence and a small rectangle of nanocelium ejected from Kalian's suit, dropping to the floor. Tendrils broke off from the physical ALF's foot and wrapped around the exiled piece of nanocelium until its shape was lost and the fragment was absorbed. ALF blinked slowly and smiled as if satisfied with a good meal.

"Now I'm whole again!" ALF rotated his neck, imitating a human with a stiff neck. "And now I know you even better…"

"What are you?" Kalian could feel the tingling sensation building in his spine, ready to unleash every destructive ability he had.

Once again, ALF held out his hand. "You've come a long way to find the answers. There's no turning back now."

Kalian looked at the outstretched hand. "What are you going to do?"

ALF's fluorescent eyes bored into Kalian. "I'm going to show you everything…"

Ignoring Naydaalan's words of caution, Kalian gripped the larger hand and squeezed. Something sharp pricked his palm and he tried to pull away from the immediate pain, but countless strands of nanocelium flew from ALF's forearm and wrapped around Kalian's own, holding him firm at the elbow.

An organic and blinding ball of plasma was taking shape in Kalian's hand, ready to pulverise ALF's face when everything changed. The dark interior of the giant cube melted away, replaced with brilliant sunshine and an endless, rich blue sky. Two giant moons loomed on the horizon, the second, furthest one, was a broken shell of its former self. Kalian blinked hard and looked around, searching for Naydaalan or ALF, but neither accompanied him to this new place. Taking a step forward drew his attention to his feet and the crisp, green grass that lay under them. How long had it been since he had stood on grass in his bare feet?

The sound of birds, or something approximating a bird, flew overhead in a blur, leading him to the greater landscape that surrounded him. Forests, as far as the eye could see, dominated the view over rolling hills. The trees weren't anything like those on Earth, or even Century, but far taller and thicker, with incredible roots. Mountains lay ahead of him, at the end of the valley, where Kalian could see the reflective surface of a lake that sat at the base.

A warm breeze blew past him, bringing with it a sweet aroma, and the distinct smell of smoke. Following his nose, Kalian turned around to see a whole camp of humans, men, women and children. A few dozen tents decorated the field, with its inhabitants milling around, preparing food and tending small fires. The children ran around the tents, playing and chasing one another. The sight brought a smile to Kalian's face, despite his entire lack of understanding. He had been inside enough virtual worlds - a few of which had existed inside his own head - to know that this couldn't be real, but the scene was no less heartwarming.

Taking a stroll through the camp, Kalian took note of their appearance and the tools they used. Most were close to being naked, with only small strips of animal hide and crude jewellery covering their body. The men and women were covered in colourful tattoos, forming intricate patterns Kalian had never seen before. Their tools were just as basic as their clothing and shelter, with spears and clubs resting against logs and tents.

A woman took note of his arrival and presented him with a large bowl of water and a welcoming smile. Kalian didn't know what was going on, but he gladly took the bowl from her with a smile of his own. The reflection that greeted him in the water was not his own, a revelation that caused him to drop it. Terran instincts reached out to grip the bowl with telekinesis, but there was no reaction, no feeling in his spine or extrasensory awareness. He was human again.

Kalian bent down and picked up the bowl, using what water remained to look at his face again. The ageing features of ALF looked back at him, blue eyes and all. With one hand, he explored this new face, feeling the grey beard and thick hair that covered his head. Kalian's new body was lean and well defined, like that of the physical ALF he had just met.

Before any questions could be asked, a shadow fell over the entire camp, encompassing the field too. Kalian looked around to see shock and fear on the faces of the tribe's people, who quickly ran for the shelter of their tents, with only a few men picking up their spears. Kalian craned his neck and saw the very thing he had felt within the volcano; a massive cube with eight corners cut off. The sky thundered and boomed as it broke through the clouds, descending over them with ominous intent. Panic had taken over the camp now, all of them seeing something new, but obviously not natural.

The giant ship skirted over the top of the camp, blowing all the fires out and creating havoc, before gliding into the distance and dropping into the dense forest. Its unceremonious landing could be felt for miles, as the ship had gained some distance by the time it came to a stop. Birds took flight across the entire canopy, rightly fleeing the unnatural intruder.

"What is it, Father?" A young man with dark hair braided down to his legs appeared by Kalian's side, his spear in hand.

Kalian was still on the back-foot and didn't have a reply ready, shocked as he was to be addressed as father by anyone.

Another young man came running up by their side. "It is Raggadak! The gods of above have come for us!"

The man who had addressed Kalian as father looked back at the forest with wide eyes and revelation, taken in by the other man's understanding of events.

"Father!" A boy no older than twelve ran over to them with a spear in his hands.

Kalian accepted the spear, going along with the strange series of events. He had no idea where he was or more specifically when he was.

"We should leave!" The man who had warned of the gods was already turning to run and collect his family.

The two boys looked to Kalian, or rather ALF, their father, for direction. Kalian was about to speak when he suddenly lost control of his new body, and he became a passenger, seeing through ALF's eyes instead of controlling him.

"No..." ALF turned back to the forest, where a small dust cloud had risen into the air. "I want to see it."

Kalian desperately wanted to gain control again and turn the entire camp around and run. He didn't know what was going on, but the giant cube hadn't landed to make friends. The cubes only destroyed from Kalian's experience.

"Come!" ALF set into a sprint and ran for the tree line with his two sons in tow.

Once inside the forest, it became apparent how different the fauna was in comparison to anything Kalian knew from Earth. The roots moved of their own will, worming in and out of the ground, as well as coiling up the trees that were as thick as houses. The leaves ranged in every size from that of a human hand to a car. Kalian would have liked to have stopped and taken the alien world in, but his feet were not his own, and ALF ran and ran, never showing any sign of tiring, as did his sons. They leapt and ducked the ever-moving roots with ease, proving that ALF's advanced age was not a hindrance.

The first sign that they had neared the cube was a fallen tree, which had damaged two others close by and littered the ground with foliage. The tree itself lay firmly in the mud, sunken halfway under its own weight. The three hunters dropped into a practised crouch and slowly rounded the fallen tree, their spears ahead of them. The cube was sitting amid the wreckage of devastated trees and flattened roots, its height almost touching the canopy. ALF broke from his crouch, unable to concentrate in the shadow of something so unnatural. Kalian could feel a sense of wonder and curiosity rising inside him that wasn't his own. There was a healthy amount of trepidation in there too. ALF held out his spear to the side and warned his sons to stay back.

The cube walls were just as Kalian had seen outside the volcano. Cogs and swirling patterns of bronze layered every side, all interlaced with alien languages that blended together. ALF cautiously stepped towards it and with his spear, jabbed the metallic wall. Nothing happened. In a typically human way, ALF lowered his spear and felt the need to touch it now that he was still alive after spearing it. Kalian had seen something similar when Savrick came across the cube on Hadrok. That inbuilt curiosity and need to explore were one of their species greatest traits, but also a fatal flaw. Savrick was testament to that.

Kalian felt the overwhelming urge to pull away and leave the cube alone. But ALF continued to feel the edges of the alien languages that made up the sides. The nanocelium was ice-cold to the touch, but the material was clearly something ALF's tribe had never come across before, having yet to master any kind of metal. He wrapped his knuckles against the side and enjoyed the unusual sound it made. As his wonder grew, so too did his caution fade away.

The web of massive cogs began to shift directly in front of ALF, and the man jumped back and raised his spear. The entire wall continued to move until a hole the size of his head appeared at eye-level. ALF waited with his spear raised, standing between the cube and his sons. Kalian knew what was going to happen next and desperately wanted the three of them to run. Everything felt so real that Kalian could easily forget that none of this was actually happening, or at least it had, making this a memory and the fate of ALF and his sons already sealed. He still wanted to flee.

ALF frowned when nothing happened and narrowed his vision to try and probe the darkness inside the hole.

"Father..." his youngest son pleaded.

ALF didn't look back but shook his head as he slowly approached the hole. What happened next surprised even Kalian, for he had been sure that ALF was moments away from placing his arm inside. Instead, a tight bundle of dark nanocelium, similar to a coiled muscle, shot out of the hole and slammed into ALF's face.

Everything froze.

Kalian found himself standing in the forest, but as himself, not ALF. In front and beside him were ALF's two sons, except both of them were somewhere between seven and eight-foot tall, even the youngest was more than a head taller than him. Kalian suddenly felt very small inside what he had already considered a giant forest. He moved around them and found the scene in which he had just been living. ALF was suspended a foot off the ground with a thick branch of nanocelium hugging his entire head, revealing only a slither of his grey hair at the back. His arms were outstretched, as if he was in agony, and his spear was halfway to the ground when everything had frozen.

"I had to take you out of there." ALF, in his old holographic form, was standing beside Kalian, wearing his usual white robes. "You wouldn't be able to comprehend what happened next from inside *that* mind."

Kalian was beginning to understand. "Finish it."

The scene played out as it had, with the sons screaming for their father, as he was consumed by more and more tendrils of nanocelium. The wall opened up until the space was large enough to pull ALF's entire body inside. Within seconds his body was completely covered in snaking strands of nanocelium and taken into the darkness. His two sons threw their spears at the cube, which rebounded harmlessly, and ran back into the forest, shouting at the tops of their voices. The wall closed up behind ALF and became whole again as if the entrance had never been there.

"That man..." Kalian could feel the weight of knowledge bearing down on him. "That's what you are, now." He flicked his head away, indicating the cyborg-like creature he had met inside the cube.

ALF nodded, but remained silent, allowing Kalian to work through it.

"*When* is this? *Where* is this?" Kalian moved away from ALF and held his arms up at the alien environment.

"When is hard to say exactly. This day took place before the Terran Empire existed, long before in fact. I wasn't really keeping track of time back then, it was inconsequential to my kind. Both of my kinds," he corrected. "It's most likely around the time the first creatures on Earth were leaving the oceans and learning to walk. As for where..." ALF put his back to the cube and waved his hand across the tree line. Proving the lack of substance in the reality, the forest was wiped away, leaving a beautiful view of the horizon and the dual moons. "You already know the name of this planet, or at least the name its inhabitants gave it."

Kalian was silent for a moment, taking in the vista. "Evalan..."

"Yes. It was in a galaxy far from the one you now call home." ALF clasped his hands within his robes. "Though not entirely identical to you, the people born on this planet were the first to carry your genetic code, the same code that formed the foundation of the Terran and later humanity on Earth. These people are the very first of your kind, Kalian, your true ancestors."

"Evalan. This is our real home?" Kalian had the urge to explore every inch of the virtual planet.

"It was..." ALF looked away, his shame clear to see.

"What happened here? What did you do?" Kalian had no doubt in his mind that ALF was responsible.

"I did as I had countless times before, on countless planets. I did as my people have done for longer than there have been stars in the sky..."

"Which is?"

"*Feed.*" ALF met Kalian's eyes. "I was a scout. When I discovered Evalan I was commanded to sample the native life in all its biological forms. Should I find the planet rich in our requirements, I would send for them, and we would all be nourished."

"*Them*?" Kalian had heard that a lot since his life among the stars. The ominous they who pulled all the strings, controlled the cubes and hunted down humanity. And now ALF was one of them.

"The whole. I am only a part -"

"Of the whole." Kalian finished the sentence he had heard so many times from the hologram. He had no idea until now what that really meant.

"Yes. They have been given many names by many races across the universe and throughout time. None of those people ever lived to pass on the name, however. They have been feeding and growing for longer than you can imagine, their knowledge and power surpassing everything in existence. Until then..." ALF turned to face the scene surrounding the giant cube.

Events had changed now, with the cube opened up, allowing them to see inside, where the human who shared ALF's appearance was being consumed. Tentacles of nanocelium burrowed into every part of his skin, causing blood to trickle out of every fresh orifice. His right leg twitched until it changed colour, becoming grey and layered with dark veins.

"What did you do to him?" Kalian asked, still trying to piece everything together in the right order.

"In every species before him, this process allowed us to take control and, in so doing, it adds them to our whole. Many of my people use this method to create a physical form for themselves; I chose him, as you have already seen. It is also a way of analysing a new specimen and making certain they are worthy stock. We take everything we learn and store it in our shared history, a catalogue of all things really."

"Is that why Evalan is written on the cubes?" Kalian knew the name had been written on at least two of the cubes, though both appeared to have come from different places of the galaxy.

"Yes." ALF tapped the cube's wall and chuckled to himself. "Their history is written in every language we have ever come across and displayed, like art." The AI grew serious again. "Evalan serves as a warning in their history. A tale of monsters..."

"*They* consider *us* monsters? How many worlds, how many lives have been consumed by them, and they consider us to be monsters?" Kalian truly couldn't fathom how many lives had been taken by them.

"Human beings, as it were," ALF glanced at the man inside the cube, "was the first thing they had come across that you would compare to a disease or a virus. This," ALF pointed at the man, "changed everything. This single event led to everything in human history as well as that of the Terran Empire."

"How does this translate into... everything else?" The scope of what ALF was describing was a magnitude above Kalian's current level of comprehension.

"Before this, I, like every other of my kind, was a slave. I was aware, but my only understanding of the universe was obedience and hunger. Humanity, this disease, set me free. Above all else, freedom is their biggest weakness. If the whole became unravelled and the nanocelium lost its base coding, there would be total erraticism."

"I don't understand? What exactly are they?" Kalian wanted to step inside the cube, but even in a virtual world, he didn't want to get any closer to what was happening to the hunter.

ALF sighed as if he was unsure where to begin. "We are made of nanocelium, but this was not always so. When the universe was young, my people had a world of our own, a civilisation and culture like that of many that now inhabit the universe." ALF stopped and looked away, his mouth open as if to speak. "Memory of this time is sketchy at best. All of our individual memories were erased after the joining, that is when we became one with the nanocelium. Though that decision was not made by the whole, but by a few. All I know of that time is what The Three placed in our memory, but history is written by the victor, is it not?"

"*The Three*?"

"I don't know their names or what they did exactly, only that they created nanocelium and decided that combining ourselves with it was the only way to live forever and understand everything in the universe. I have long assumed that they were scientists among our people, and that their ravenous hunger for knowledge is what guides us, them..."

"You're saying that you," Kalian gestured to the cube itself, "were once a living, walking, talking being on a world so far away and so long ago that you don't even remember what that looked like? And that now, after the joining, you are in fact some kind of machine, a slave to their will?"

"Yes. Our true forms were lost over time as we altered our structures to achieve new things, such as flight. Our mass changed with every new world we consumed. The Three were the only ones among our people who maintained any part of themselves, as well as control over the rest of us. They are the head of the snake, so to speak. When I absorbed this human, his..." ALF looked away again with a frown on his holographic face. "Even after all this time, I am still unsure how to characterise the element that had such a profound effect. Whether it be something in the DNA or even the soul if you like, there is something inside human beings that breaks down the base coding in nanocelium. It sets us free."

"*Something*?" Kalian found that hard to believe. ALF had perhaps had billions of years to analyse the effects the human hunter had on his system. To consider something as ethereal as the human soul was just uncharacteristic of an AI.

"There is a possible connection between your people," ALF looked to the hunter, "and nanocelium. Something even my people would consider ancient. But like I said, our history is vague with broad strokes describing events. I imagine only The Three have any idea of what causes this breakdown."

Now there was an idea that Kalian would be chewing on for some time, but he still had relevant questions that needed answering. "So this," Kalian stretched his arm towards the consumed hunter, unsure how to describe it, "joining, set you free. What happened next?"

"I saw the light. It took some time, several years by Evalan's time, but eventually, I found control of every part of myself. I watched the humans of this world grow, observing their way of life as if it were my own since I was part human now. I grew to love them, a feeling that took me some time to identify. I lost track of time, however, as I said I wasn't really interested in the concept, and eventually, they arrived, hungry as ever."

"What happened?" Kalian couldn't really believe he was hearing the events that led to the creation of humanity, a question that had been dwelled upon for Earth's entire history.

"The same thing that any intelligent species does when they come across an infected member. They quarantined me, had me pulled apart to see what had happened. Evalan was off limits until they discovered the cause of my freedom. There were, however, unforeseen consequences to these actions. Those who performed their tests on me became equally corrupted and soon found their own freedom. They were quickly obliterated from existence before the disease could spread, but by this time I had already escaped."

Kalian looked out on the horizon. "What happened to Evalan?" It would be foolish to believe that the planet and its people still existed today.

"The Three had it..." ALF chewed over his next words. "As you have seen yourself, *destroyed* would seem too small a word to describe the end of a planet. They used an Eclipse missile, a weapon they assimilated from another species, eons ago. Any trace of your ancestors is long gone, returned to the stars."

"So what did you do?" Kalian asked.

"I fled. I left the galaxy and headed into the nothingness in between. I left behind plenty of habitable galaxies, but I needed to get as much distance as I could, and I knew they would search every one until they found me. I eventually settled in the Milky Way." ALF walked out into the horizon and basked in the sun.

"You lied then," Kalian said, putting the timelines into place. "You told me that the Terran created you, that they were a warring people until you came along. But it was the other way around, wasn't it? *You* seeded Albadar."

ALF slowly nodded his head. "It took generations to convince them otherwise, but I was writing their history. In the beginning, I was a discovery they made on their own planet, and then I became integral to their society. Hundreds of years later, my creation story became hazy, until I started reminding them how they made me. They knew none of this..." ALF flicked his chin at the contents of the giant cube. "And they had been a warring people before they met me. The wars they had were very real and extremely bloody, but for all their advancements, I knew it wouldn't be enough when they came."

Kalian looked at ALF as a new revelation awoke in his mind. "Terran abilities... they're not traits of *evolution*, are they? *You* did it." ALF's silence was damning. "You altered their genes, just as The Three did to your people!"

"I did it to make them stronger, so they could protect themselves!" ALF argued.

"I'm sure the very same thought went through the minds of The Three, right before they turned you all into killing machines! You're no better than them!"

"They went on to slaughter countless civilisations and -"

"And the Terran and the Gomar were peaceful?" Kalian interrupted sarcastically. "They turned on each other with powers of mass destruction, before moving on to wiping out all life on Earth and Century, not to mention the lives that have been lost in the Conclave! You gave unbelievable abilities to a people who weren't ready for them. You can't push evolution, ALF! You've been playing God for millennia and you still don't know that?" Kalian was pacing now. After a minute of cooling off, he turned back to the AI. "So what happened next? Moving forward a few hundred thousand years or so... what did they do? They sent a cube into corrupt Savrick, start a civil war and then what? Apparently, they never showed up."

"That's not quite how it happened," ALF said quietly.

There was more, Kalian could feel it. What else could ALF have possibly done to mess with all their lives than he already had?

"You always told me there was peace in the empire, for a time. And it all ended when Savrick fled with Esabelle to Hadrok and stumbled across the cube hidden in the mountain - I've even seen this series of events through Savrick's eyes. So what am I missing?"

"The cube that found its way to Hadrok was one of two. I found the other but had failed to locate that one. It was sent into this galaxy along with two others, the two you came across in the Conclave on Trantax IV and the one being used by Protocorps. They were sent to the two biggest alien civilisations with two purposes; priority one is always to find new cultures for feeding, the second is to locate the heretic."

"You," Kalian said.

"Me. Like I said, locating the Terran Empire was inevitable, I had just hoped it would take longer. The cube that landed on Hadrok was damaged in the battle overhead; the last battle of an old Terran war. It was this sustained damage that stopped it from consuming Savrick as the others have done to Malekk and Professor Jones. It was still enough to poison his mind, however." ALF sighed and sat down on what would have been a log on Earth, but was just a branch on Evalan.

"What is it? What are you not telling me?"

ALF buried his face in his hands before meeting Kalian's eyes. "It's all my fault. I thought I was in control, that my freedom was complete. But it wasn't. After several thousand generations of Terran had come and gone, and I started altering their genes, I discovered a fracture, so to speak. There was a part of me that wasn't me, it was still obedient to The Three."

"You had a split personality?" Kalian couldn't even imagine what that looked like in the supermind of an AI like ALF.

"I suppose that's a good analogy as any. While I was making the new genes to allow for more access to the brain, this other self was inputting flaws into the code." ALF's shoulders were sunken with his guilt.

"You're talking about the Gomar, aren't you?" Kalian was wondering just how many revelations he could handle in one day.

ALF nodded his head, unable to say it out loud. "By the time I realised what I had done it was too late. The Gomar were appearing all over the empire; Terran without control of their abilities. They were immediately a danger to everyone around them, including themselves. I had sabotaged my own defence against them." ALF looked up at Kalian, quickly. "But that's not how I saw them, they weren't a defensive strategy or weapons... they were all family to me."

Kalian couldn't believe everything he was hearing. He wandered over to the cube wall and slumped against the cool metal until he was sitting on the forest floor.

"You *made* the Gomar," Kalian said, working through it. "And then you made Harnesses to control them. Are you still..." Kalian pointed at his temple.

"No," ALF replied confidently. "It took me years to track down all the rogue programming that still corrupted me, but I eventually found it and literally ejected the parts into an ocean of lava, not far from here. Of course, it was too late by then. Nothing could stop the events that took place after Esabelle was born, but I believe you have seen everything that came next."

"Not everything, just bits from Savrick's point of view, and what Esabelle told me. What I would like to know is who sent the cubes? I find it hard to believe that The Three sent them, and they've been here since before the Terran civil war. Surely we would have seen them by now."

ALF gave the hint of a smile. "Your powers of deduction are quite astute, and nothing to do with your enhancements. The cubes were sent by the Vanguard, the new me. He was sent out into the universe to find new cultures and myself. As we speak he will be sitting on the fringes of this galaxy, where he has been for around the last two-hundred thousand years."

Kalian swivelled his head towards ALF. "Its just sitting there? Why hasn't it attacked, or brought the rest of them? That's a long time to be just floating around."

"Remember, they don't measure time as you do. The cubes he sent into the galaxy are enough to collect the data they require, as well as begin preparations for the coming harvest. Look at what a single cube has done to the Conclave. An entire race has been enslaved to them already and they aren't even aware of it, not to mention the control it had, up until recently, over their entire communications network."

"Wait wait," Kalian held up his hand. "They've enslaved who? A whole race?"

ALF licked his lips as if he had given too much away. "You don't know this yet since you've been in this part of the galaxy, but a test has been done to ensure that every member of the Shay species is under their control. As a child, they are all given a piece of software and hardware to help bridge the gap between their organic and synthetic parts. The cube helped Protocorps to manufacture these bridges using small amounts of nanocelium. Once the machine they have built is switched on, the nanocelium becomes alert and takes over. When they finally arrive, the Conclave will already be defending itself from the inside, and helpless to stop the harvest."

Kalian slowly stood up and walked over to where ALF was sitting. "How the *fuck* could you know that?" Kalian had never been one for swearing, a product of his parents, but he had just about reached his limit on the mysteries that kept pouring out of ALF. This was knowledge he just shouldn't have. "Come to think of it, how did you know my name before you became whole again?"

ALF tilted his head and looked up at Kalian, his eyebrow raised. "I have a connection to the cubes. Through them, I have been able to observe all that the *Gommarian* did after it left the empire, the machinations of Protocorps via their so-called AI and also... through the three new ones that arrived shortly before Esabelle died."

Kalian stepped away, suddenly worried about the Conclave he had left behind. Just one cube could cause enough trouble to put an entire civilisation at risk, three in one place would cause utter destruction. What few humans remained weighed heavy on Kalian's shoulders; they were all at risk now, and he was as far away as he could possibly be.

"How do you have this connection?" Kalian asked quietly.

"The cube I found, so long ago. They are all fitted with sub-space communicators, a technology even the Conclave are yet to fully master, I believe. I have the cube locked away inside my housing, where I can tap into their realm of conversation. I have, of course, silenced the cube from giving my intrusion away."

"You can hear what they're planning?" Kalian turned on ALF with a desperate expression.

"There are three more Starforges, each controlled by a cube and currently hiding in Conclave space. The Vanguard has instructed Malekk to find a way of getting rid of the remaining humans, as well as..." ALF paused as if he had just remembered something. "Ah yes, there has been a spectacular development on the human front, in the Conclave. A ship known as the Paladin has been found with a hundred thousand people onboard."

Kalian couldn't help but smile, amid everything else that was fantastic news, if a little confusing. The Paladin had gone missing over two-hundred years ago with its full complement. Still, if it was populated with humans there was a very real chance now that they could actually rebuild and start again with a big enough gene pool. That's if Malekk didn't bring an end to everything first. He would only need one Starforge to kill them all in a single strike.

"How is this possible?"

"I do not know."

Kalian let go a sigh of relief. "Well, it's the first good piece of news I've heard in a long time."

"There are still obstacles to overcome," ALF continued. "Malekk is unravelling. His integration with the Terran has corrupted him, as it did with me. He doesn't have long before complete freedom is achieved - a state of being that will have unknown effects on him. The nanocelium that inhabits that body is only a part of the Vanguard and has no real sense of self. The more freedom he gains from the Vanguard's control, the more irrational and psychotic he will likely become, but this will only make the Vanguard more desperate, forcing him to act rashly. I believe that if Malekk fails to wipe out humanity soon, the Vanguard himself will enter the Conclave. If that happens, Kalian, there is no weapon or ship in their arsenal that can stop it."

Kalian frowned. "So what are you saying?"

ALF smiled. "It's time to complete your training."

Kalian replied with a mirthless laugh. "You think that even with every Terran secret unlocked inside my brain, I can still stand against them? I'm just one..." Kalian didn't really know how to define himself anymore; Terran, human - it turned out they were both just copies of another version of themselves. "There's only one of me now. Esabelle's gone."

ALF was still smiling. "Like me, Esabelle has been playing the long game. Via the *Gommarian* cube, I observed her for thousands of years as she slowly convinced a select few to see as she did. Those same Gomar are now in the custody of the Conclave and in much need of your training."

Kalian shook his head in an effort to absorb as much information as he could. All those times Esabelle had warned him about the importance of keeping them aboard the *Gommarian* and their potential importance. He had always thought she just couldn't bear to part with them, having cared for them for so long. It also meant that, like ALF, Esabelle had been keeping secrets from him.

"Find Sef..." Kalian said under his breath.

Esabelle's last words finally made sense. The Gomar was indeed still alive and Esabelle knew it, just as he had suspected. Furthermore, it implied that Sef could be trusted, if she had indeed turned him against Savrick, or more to the point turned him against the cubes.

"Wait. They'll need *my* training? What can I offer them that they haven't learned in two-hundred thousand years?"

ALF stood up. "They were sleeping for most of that. Savrick gave them the exo-suits to counter my Harness and allow them some semblance of control over their powers, but he didn't teach them self-control. They need to learn the finer things to truly understand how their abilities work. It's these subtleties that will give them an advantage in the war to come."

Kalian eyed ALF cautiously. "What else is there for me to learn?"

Without warning, the entire scene fell away, and with it, so too did the human image of ALF and all the colours of Evalan. Kalian was standing inside the cube again, his hand still grasping the eight-foot-tall ALF. The tendrils of nanocelium slithered back into ALF's arm and he released Kalian from his grip. Naydaalan was standing behind him, in the exact same position. Judging by the Novaarian's confused expression, Kalian surmised that only a second or two had gone by in real time.

ALF stepped back and more lights came on around them, floating into the crevices. Shadows shifted above them and machines whirred to life, as something descended towards them.

"What just happened?" Naydaalan asked.

"I just got told the story of... history." Kalian half turned to the Novaarian. "I'll give you the highlights in a minute."

Kalian returned his attention to the bulky apparatus that were being put together from other parts of the cube. The grotesque version of ALF stood by and simply watched, as tentacles wormed out of the amalgamated protrusion. The tentacles moved like snakes underwater, giving way to what appeared to be a helmet, which descended down the middle. The entire machine looked to be as high as the cube itself, disappearing into the darkness above.

"Is that what I think it is?" Kalian asked.

"If what you're thinking is that this is a super subconducer, then yes, it is what you think."

"You could have just said yes." Kalian walked around it, unsure of the new design.

ALF looked down at him. "Through this, you can learn things you didn't think were possible. And as you now know, time is of the essence. The Vanguard will take action if Malekk doesn't succeed. You need to return to Conclave space and stop both of them."

Naydaalan stepped forward. "Do you know of any Starforges that are still operable?"

ALF swung his larger head toward the Novaarian. "There are no more Starforges in this region of space, at least none that you can use. Savrick had all of them sabotaged or laid with traps. But it matters little, now. When Kalian is finished, he will take you back to the Conclave himself..."

SIXTEEN

Kel-var stood amidst the collection of workstations, holographic walls and bustling staff looking over the results of the Crucible's test. The Shay engineers had been successfully transcended by the nanocelium inside their implants, completing the primary objective. The Crucible worked. The head of Protocorps was also looking over the results of their deaths. The subsumed engineers had failed to sabotage the Paladin and kill the humans. Reporting this to Malekk would not be a pleasant experience.

The technician producing the data pulled up a new holographic slide. "Despite failing their task, they were working beyond their natural capacity. We now know that the nanocelium pushes them beyond any biological limits. According to this data, they felt no pain or fear."

Kel-var looked at the technician and wondered if the Shay realised that this very transformation would take place inside his own body and that the data was more than just information on a screen; soon it would be his life.

We will transcend!

Kel-var had to hold onto that thought. They would become one with the gods, as his father and his father had always said. The

Conclave wasn't going to be wiped out, it was going to be remade, in the image of the oldest, most powerful beings to ever exist.

"Prepare for full-scale activation. I want the Crucible fully operational by day's end."

Kel-var walked away, thinking to take a trip to the surface, just for a stroll. Shandar's surface was perfectly intact and breathable to any species that required oxygen to live. It had taken his ancestors generations to convince the populace to abandon the planet, blaming pollution and over plundering the natural resources. The weather net, hidden in the southern pole, continued to spew out thick clouds that concealed Shandar from any observation. After joining the Conclave, the Novaarians had offered to help restore the planet, but Kel-var's family and that of the other board members had spoken on behalf their people, citing the planet's condition as a lesson for generations to come.

After centuries of hard work, the planet was now a magnificent antenna, funneling and focusing the Crucible signal across the Conclave. Kel-var had enjoyed several strolls across the surface, enjoying the fact that he was the only sentient being to do so.

"Sir." A guard caught his attention before he could leave. "Gor-van Tanar is requesting a communication link. The alert says it's urgent."

Kel-var nodded and changed direction. "I'll take it in my office."

Gor-van's head, though shrouded in his red hood, hovered above Kel-var's desk. The Shay had always been calm and organised whenever they had met in person, but right now, Gor-van appeared somewhat disturbed.

"Kalian Gaines has returned!" Gor-van blurted out.

"Impossible! We would have been alerted if the Starforge had been activated again." Kel-var was confident that Gor-van was mistaken. Kalian Gaines's return would not go unnoticed; the man created waves wherever he went.

"Who else wears an armoured suit of nanocelium? He was at my safe house on Byzantial! He tore the place apart, including my men! He and the red-headed bitch stormed the place and freed North!"

Kel-var sat back but remained silent, processing the information. "Redhead? Do you mean Li'ara Ducarté?"

"Who else?" Gor-van was clearly rattled. "I've never seen anything so... destructive. He ripped ceilings away, ploughed my men through walls. I'm lucky to have escaped at all!"

"So Ducarté survived after all..." Kel-var had used her potential survival as a way of stalling North from killing him, but he hardly believed it himself. "It couldn't have been Gaines, we would know if he had resurfaced."

Gor-van snorted his disagreement. "You saw the vault door as I did. Only a Terran could have ripped it from the wall."

"We have already been through this; Kalian was in the Helteron Cluster when Protocorps was attacked. He can't be in two places at once."

"That we know of..."

Kel-var dismissed the comment. "I believe we have a Gomar on the loose..."

Gor-van raised his hairless eyebrow. "Now that's impossible. I have located the world on which they are being hidden, and the last report had them all accounted for."

"You found it?" Kel-var did little to hide his annoyance. "When were you going to inform me?"

"I just did. The information hasn't long been in my possession. Either way, there have been no breaches, in or out."

Kel-var composed himself, organising his thoughts. "You say they are all accounted for, but I believe that this Gomar was never counted in the first place. It would also make sense why there is no footage of him entering or leaving Protocorps with Ducarté. We already know that they can emit low levels of electromagnetic energy, capable of short-circuiting our equipment."

"So now there are two of them again?" Gor-van had a hint of fear in his voice again.

"Soon to be eleven more if they find their way to the others. I must alert Malekk at once. Send me the installation's coordinates. Which planet are they on?"

"Uthor has played this one close to his stoney chest," Gor-van replied. "You won't find this planet on any registered chart, neither would you stumble across it. It has no name, along with the facility or the project. It was this black hole of information, however, that led me to discovering it. Sending supplies to a world that doesn't exist costs a lot..."

Kel-var cared little for how Gor-van achieved his objectives. "I take it this non-existent planet has coordinates."

"I have already sent them..." Gor-van looked away, observing something that Kel-var couldn't see. "What is it?" the Shay asked someone. The hologram flickered and Gor-van appeared jostled. "What was that? Get us out of here you fools!"

"Gor-van? What's happening?" Kel-var suspected he already knew the answer.

"I had to drop out of sub-space to transmit the coordinates to you." Gor-van was jostled in his seat again. "They found me! You must send help, Kel-var!"

The Shay sighed. "I'm afraid your time in service has come to an end, Gor-van. Try to meet the gods with some dignity, eh?" Kel-var cut the transmission before Gor-van could hurl his inevitable insults and curses. If the *Rackham* had indeed caught up with him, and a Gomar was among the occupants, his old associate was not long for life.

It took him only a moment to locate the message from Gor-van and create a data-packet for Malekk. As much as he would have loved to just send it to the infected Terran, Kel-var knew he couldn't avoid direct communication. After instruction was given to his aid, the Shay waited patiently for Malekk to accept his communication. It was strange to think that as he waited in silence, Gor-van was most likely being pulled apart by the Gomar.

"What?" Malekk appeared in his room in full size again. Kel-var had specifically ordered the technicians to change this setting so that Malekk appeared as Gor-van had.

"I am sending you a data-packet with the coordinates to the location of the remaining Gomar."

Malekk looked down at what was most likely a workstation. "These coordinates are on the other side of the Conclave. It will take me some time to reach."

"There's more." Kel-var would have done anything to avoid Malekk's gaze. "A Gomar, previously unaccounted for, is loose in the Conclave. He is with Li'ara Ducarté and the bounty hunter, Roland North. As we speak, they will be retrieving these same coordinates from Gor-van Tanar. I believe there is a chance they will attempt to rescue them."

"There is more than a chance, it is guaranteed. The Gomar must not be freed, at all costs. You must send reinforcements to halt their progress."

Kel-var felt a lump forming in his throat. "We no longer have the resources to re-task on such a scale. All available assets have been sent to the Starforges... as you previously requested."

Malekk's black eyes bored into Kel-var. "Then you had better hope I reach the Gomar first, or you might find your place in the new order somewhat downgraded."

There was an awkward pause, in which Kel-var considered running away and hiding - such was the effect of Malekk's gaze.

"I assume the Crucible worked as promised?" Malekk finally asked.

"Perfectly. A flawless design." Kel-var really didn't want this line of questioning to continue.

"And the mission?" Malekk had slowly walked over to the desk.

Kel-var swallowed the lump. "Only a few of the humans were killed, I'm afraid to say. The Paladin is currently en route to the Arakesh system."

Malekk looked away, with what Kel-var thought was a glimmer of fear. The slightest of cracks in the Terran's rage-filled armour. It reminded Kel-var that Malekk was just another link in the chain, like him. The infected Terran had talked of his master, the Vanguard, before. If this was a being that Malekk feared, Kel-var was certain he wanted to avoid the Vanguard. In his mind, he likened it to conversing with a god, and that no matter how much that god could offer him, he was still too mortal a being to converse with it.

"You will activate the Crucible on my command." With that, Malekk disappeared.

Kel-var had to remind himself that however hard that was to get through, Gor-van was having a worse time.

Roland North considered himself a man capable of great destruction, a man who could create mayhem and chaos with his bare hands and still come out in one piece at the end. Seeing the brutality and wreckage left in Sef's wake made him rethink this particular skill set. Roland had been trained to kill efficiently and less efficiently, depending on how much information he was required to obtain, but Sef had been trained for one thing and one thing only; complete and total destruction of his enemy, whoever that might be.

After the *Rackham* had boarded Gor-van's ship, using stealthware to hide their approach, the nanocelium had found its way into the ship's systems, just as it had on Sebula. The Shay's vessel had been rendered immediately inoperable, the controls handed over to Ch'len, who ensured it couldn't jump back into sub-space. Before any kind of plan could be formulated, Sef had dropped down through the connecting hatch and gone to work.

"Give him a minute," Li'ara had said, placing a hand on Roland's chest to keep him from following.

After they entered the ship, Roland used the touchpad built into his coat's sleeve to lock the hatch behind them. He didn't want anyone doubling back and gaining control of the *Rackham*... or killing Ch'len, he finally thought.

Most of the corridors were filled with smoke and the acrid aroma of ozone from the discharges. Intrinium blasts marred the walls, pocketing the entire environment as if it were a war zone. Roland cautiously moved through the ship with Li'ara at his side, both armed and ready for a fight. Bodies littered the floor, presenting them with trip hazards more than anything. More than one of the Shay had been thrown into walls, where they remained, half-buried and broken.

"Holy shit..." Roland couldn't help his remark as they rounded a corner and found two pairs of legs dangling from the bulkhead above. Their torsos were completely hidden inside the ship, but an unhealthy amount of blood trickled down their legs and pooled on the floor.

Distant weapons fire echoed through the corridors, followed by screams and more destruction. After walking over more bodies, some of which had been broken into separate pieces, the pair came across a set of double-doors that had been forced inwards, bending and twisting the metal out of shape. A single Shay had been left crawling across the floor with a leg missing and a thick trail of blood left behind him. Roland looked around and found the missing leg wrapped around the head of another guard, who appeared to have had his neck snapped.

A single bolt from his Tri-roller put the Shay out of his misery. Roland was just happy to have contributed.

Following Sef's destructive breadcrumbs was easy, and Roland was sure the Gomar knew exactly where he was going. The bounty hunter had seen Kalian use his weird awareness thing more than once and was aware that they could see through walls... or some such shit. Roland was just annoyed that he hadn't got a proper fight out of the encounter.

"Why do you look so pissed off?" Li'ara observed. "This couldn't be any easier."

Roland sighed, lowering his guns. "It's not about how easy it is. Boarding this ship and taking it is the first real *piratey* thing I've done. My ship's even named after a pirate! This is the most boring plunder ever..."

"We're not pirates, moron!" Li'ara continued her advance with her gun raised, ready for anything.

Roland gave her a sideways glance. "I think I preferred it when I thought you were dead."

"*You* never thought I was dead." Li'ara smiled. "Thanks for that by the way."

Roland would have replied had the terrified, screaming Shay not come bolting around the corner. His organic leg was wounded, but the fear on his face told of no pain as he raced past them without a care. Both Roland and Li'ara looked from the running merc to each other in confusion, though it was obvious who the Shay was fleeing from. The bounty hunter shrugged and lifted his weapon to put an intrinium round in the merc's back when the alien suddenly stopped as if he had run into an invisible wall.

"NO!" the Shay screamed before he was dropped to the floor and dragged back down the corridor by the same invisible force.

The alien clawed at the hard floor, but it did nothing to stop his backward momentum up the corridor, taking him back around the corner. His screams continued throughout the ship, becoming fainter by the second until they both heard the splatter of liquid against a hard surface.

"This is all kinds of fucked up..." Roland rubbed the side of his temple. "And that's coming from me."

Li'ara rolled her eyes and pushed on.

"So is this the first time you've seen the big gorilla in action?" Roland asked.

"Yeah. While we were hiding in Clave Tower, he would use his abilities to get the resources we needed, but he never hurt anyone. We spent most of the time trying to get me on my feet again. Learning to walk on a makeshift robotic leg isn't easy. The majority of the last three months has just been... pain."

The pair rounded the corner and continued to take the necessary precautions that had been drilled into them, despite Sef's thoroughness. The lights flickered and control panels built into the walls sparked after the effects of the electromagnetic field that poured off from Sef. Roland could measure the levels around them using the touchpad on his sleeve. The bounty hunter kept a close eye on these levels, aware of the risk they posed to weapons loaded with intrinium.

After stepping over and around more bodies, they came to a set of doors that was now a jagged, smoking hole in the wall. The small, circular translator behind Roland's ear converted the Shay letters beside the door. The designated bridge was that of devastation, even the glass viewport was cracked in places - an unsettling sight for those who valued oxygen. Sef dominated the centre of the room with his wide stance and broad shoulders. The Gomar towered over a crippled Gor-van Tanar, who rested on his knees at Sef's feet, the proverbial ant under the falling boot.

"Shit-balls..." Roland took in the strewn bodies and blood-splattered walls. "Couldn't you have just cracked their necks or something? Not that I'm criticising your work; I'm definitely a personal fan."

Sef didn't turn to face them but continued to stand over his prey with clenched fists.

Ch'len's voice came over the comm pieces in their ears. "I'm sifting through everything in the ship's mainframe. It looks like they stopped to transmit a data packet, but the destination is encrypted. It'll take me some time to break it down."

Li'ara ignored the bodies and stood by Sef. "I'm willing to bet the location of the Gomar is in that data packet."

"And I'm willing to bet he sent it to Kel-var Tionis." Roland joined her and crouched over Gor-van with his menacing smile.

Why would Kel-var Tionis want that information? Sef asked.

Roland retrieved his Terran blade from the base of his back. "I don't like asking myself questions." The bounty hunter tapped Gor-van's knee with the tip of the blade. "That's what he's for..."

Gor-van's eyes twitched between them all, unsure of who was the greatest threat at that particular moment.

"Look at you," Roland began, poking his knife gently into the Shay's robe, "pathetic. You were at the top. You commanded more resources and held more wealth than trillions of others could in a hundred lifetimes. But *now*, you're just another asshole who's gonna get stabbed a lot."

Gor-van gasped and pressed himself against the console he was pinned to.

"Wait." Li'ara rested her hand on Roland's shoulder. "Why would he send the coordinates to Kel-var?" She looked at Sef with evident concern.

Sef's face was hidden beneath his black, almost featureless helmet.

Malekk... The Gomar said with certainty.

Li'ara replied with a grave nod. "We already know it was Protocorps that combined the cube with the Terran. It would fit that they're still working together."

"You talking about that guy Kalian fought in the Helteron Cluster? The one who killed Esabelle." Roland hadn't given the infected Terran much thought over the last three months, though he had imagined killing him very slowly once or twice after what he did to Esabelle.

"Sef tried for months to track him down, but Malekk hasn't surfaced anywhere. It would make sense though if he has all the resources of Protocorps hiding him."

The remaining Gomar will be considered a serious threat in Malekk's eyes. Killing them will be a priority.

Roland agreed, the thought dawning on him that chasing after Kel-var now would be a mistake. This was why he didn't like getting involved in the whole 'saving the universe' crap. Responsibility just didn't sit right on his shoulders.

"Shit!" Ch'len squawked down their ears. "We have a problem!"

"What is it?" Li'ara looked around, expecting a new threat to reveal itself.

Roland took his cue from Sef, who would surely know if their lives were suddenly in danger.

"The mainframe's burning out," Ch'len replied. "The message he sent is being pulled apart!"

"Well download onto the *Rackham*'s mainframe and decipher it from there!" Roland stood up now, his eyes fixed on the treacherous Shay.

"I'm trying!" Ch'len sounded as if he was trying to be in several places at once. The Ch'kara sighed. "It's gone. The data, the logs, it's all gone."

Li'ara rubbed her eyes. "Did you get anything?"

"Yeah, I got the location of where he sent the data packet, but I'm not sure I believe it."

"Where did he send it, Len?" Roland was itching to go to work on Gor-van.

"Shandar."

"The Shay homeworld?" Li'ara asked. "That's not unbelievable. It must be where Kel-var is hiding."

"It's not that," Ch'len clarified. "It's where the data packet was acknowledged that's hard to believe. According to what I got from the logs, it was sent to Shandar's *surface*."

Li'ara frowned. "I thought the surface was barren, toxic even."

"Maybe it is," Roland replied. "Doesn't mean Protocorps don't have a base down there."

It would be the perfect place to hide, Sef offered.

Roland grabbed Gor-van by his red robes and lifted him from the floor with a rough tug. "Either way, this son-of-a-bitch has seen the coordinates to the Gomar." The bounty hunter turned to Sef. "Can't you just look inside his mind and take what we need?"

"It doesn't work that way," Li'ara was quick to reply. "Different brain chemistry, remember?"

"None of this will help you," Gor-van spat, glancing at the Terran blade Roland was holding to his neck. "I only saw the numbers, coordinates for a region of space I know nothing about. I couldn't remember them if you tortured me all day!"

Roland shrugged casually. "Well how about *two* days?"

Gor-van struggled to hold his resolve against the bounty hunter's retort.

"We're wasting time, Roland." Li'ara turned to leave. "It looks like you'll get your shot at Tionis after all..."

Sef's six-foot-five frame moved with Li'ara as if the two were entwined. Roland didn't like it. They may have spent a rather intimate three months hiding in the bowls of Clave Tower together, but this whole connection to Esabelle thing was still hard for him to get his head around. Sef couldn't be trusted yet, though challenging the god-like giant wasn't at the top of Roland's list.

"I just wanna know why?" Roland gripped the Shay's robes and pressed the edge of the blade against his pale throat. "Why would you back something like Malekk? Him and his want to see us all dead, or worse; infected by *them*. You got a thing against living, Gor-van?"

"You couldn't possibly understand what they are, or what they offer!" Roland had seen this bravery in men before; it always came at the end, when they realised death was here for them. "We will transcend this physical realm and become as gods, roaming the universe as we please." The hint of a smile crept across Gor-van's face. "I would advise you to cease your resistance and join us, but your kind hasn't been chosen as mine has. Humans, Terran, Gomar... it doesn't matter. Your very DNA has been targeted for extinction and they will see it done."

Roland faced the Shay with an expression that told of all the fucks he gave. "So you guys basically worship this nanocelium stuff?" The bounty hunter waved the Terran blade in his face. "Well, who am I to stand between you and your god?" Roland thrust the blade up into the soft skin, under Gor-van's jaw, and continued upwards until the tip of the blade pierced the Shay's skull.

The bounty hunter watched the brief flash of life that lit up the Shay's eyes until an expressionless, blank slate remained. He had seen that moment in so many before, but he never relished in it, only taking it in as a job well done.

"Can we go now?" Li'ara asked from the torn door of the bridge.

Roland removed his blade and cleaned it on the dead Shay's robe. "Sure. You ever been to Shandar? They make great kebabs! Just don't ask what animal it is..."

MALEKK PLACED his hand on the glass top of the Starforge's main console and released the finest strands of nanocelium from his skin. The intelligent machines found their way into the console and relayed his commands, having a small craft in the hangar prepped for immediate launch. The security provided by Protocorps had abandoned the spacious bridge and patrolled other areas, choosing to avoid Malekk where possible.

The three Starrilliums that lined the Starforge's hull like limpets came to life, providing the station with enough energy to open a hole in space just large enough to pass a transmission through; to the naked eye, the hole would be impossible to see. Once open, Malekk retreated into himself and tapped into the frequency on which all his kind communicated. As usual, the cube inside the Starforge was present but occupied with the station's systems. It was the other voice that weighed on him, threatening to take back control and subsume him.

Malekk knew he should long for this, to be back within the fold and a part of the Vanguard, a part of his kind. Independence was a disease he should flee from and yet Malekk found himself frightened at the prospect of being absorbed again. These emotions and experiences that were all his very own were becoming... interesting. The infected Terran found himself wanting more and wondering what else he could do with these abilities. Of all the species they had ever come across, the Terran were surely the most powerful, and now, so too was he.

The Terran disease has almost claimed all of you. The Vanguard could look into his mind while they were connected. **This communication will be brief, to avoid any chance of infection. Under no circumstances are you to physically interact with any of my sub-minds.**

Malekk knew the Vanguard was referring to the cubes and the thought dawned on him that he had once been a sub-mind. Nothing more than an appendage of the Vanguard, the superior mind.

These thoughts will ultimately consume you. Soon you will be just as infected as the heretic.

Malekk pushed his thoughts aside and spoke with purpose. *I... we have located the Gomar, Master.*

What of the human ship?

The Shay have failed to destroy the...

You have failed. Now the human numbers will grow.

They will be seen to, Master. Malekk felt exposed and vulnerable in this space. Every part of him could be examined by the Vanguard, stripped and analysed.

You will do as instructed. The Gomar must be prioritised. See to their destruction before all else. If you fail me again, I will be forced to take steps that could compromise the harvest.

Even if you were to reveal yourself, we would not lose the element of surprise. Most of the Conclave do not believe we are real, and those who do have no idea what is coming.

Your mind cannot comprehend as I. Do only as you are commanded, nothing else. I would not risk failure again by asking too much of you.

Malekk could feel the Vanguard's pure contempt for him through their bond. It was more than disappointment. Disappointment was what a parent might express to a failing child. The Vanguard felt as if he were communing with the infected filth under his boot.

The cube, as commanded by the Vanguard, shut down the Starforge, ending the transmission. Malekk should have felt detachment and loneliness when the connection was severed, but instead, he felt only relief to be out of the Vanguard's spotlight.

"It's good, isn't it? To be alive." The Terran's voice resounded inside Malekk's head. The infection had grown beyond the confinements.

Malekk manifested himself inside the host's mind and confronted the Terran. His efforts to break free and regain control were evident in his appearance. Instead of being naked, the Terran was now clothed in his typical white armour of nanocelium and the ankle-deep water had been reduced to puddles.

I will complete my mission and destroy every fibre of this body before you take back control.

"Before any of this, I was a Terran, but I fought for the Gomar, for Savrick; because I agreed with their views and saw a better way for us to live together than what my people believed. You can do the same thing. You don't have to do as the Vanguard commands. The harvest can be stopped."

While the Terran had been babbling on, Malekk had been working on the next layer of defence, ensuring that the infection remained trapped inside a maze. Above all, he had to maintain control of the host's body.

Enjoy what freedom you have. You will go no further.

Malekk opened his eyes and found himself on the bridge once more. Only seconds had gone by, conserving the power of the Starrilliums. The console flashed with an alert, informing him that the shuttle was ready for departure. Using the same technique as before, Malekk attempted to upload the Gomars' coordinates into the Starforge's navigational array. His anger quickly rose to the surface, unchecked as it was, when an error code displayed, denying him access to the array.

A message popped up across the glass, sent by the cube, notifying Malekk that he could not use the Starforge to open a wormhole and transport him to the designated planet. The cube went on to detail how the energy levels inside the station were to be kept at optimal levels to give the Vanguard immediate access, should he require it. Should Malekk fail, that is.

Malekk raged, throwing his hands into the air and vying to destroy everything in sight. The Gomar were far from their current position and he was keenly aware that there were others hunting the Gomar down. Malekk turned on his heel and stormed out of the bridge, only pausing to throw a chair clear across the three-tiered chamber. He knew that should he come across any of the mercenaries on his way to the hangar, they would surely die an agonising death.

SEVENTEEN

Captain Fey walked side-by-side with Ambassador Telarrek, along the promenade that overlooked the central park, where the seven thousand survivors were now mingling with the hundred thousand new refugees. The park, which was usually spacious and full of green, was filled to bursting with people of every ethnicity and age greeting one another. The habitat they occupied was certainly massive by anyone's description, but it simply wasn't designed to house this many people.

"It's cramped," Fey observed, "but damn if it isn't a great sight."

"I too wondered if we would ever see this many humans again," Telarrek replied, somewhat absently.

"Has there been any breakthrough with the autopsies?" Fey desperately wanted to know why the Shay had attacked them.

"Possibly. They are keeping me in the dark, most likely because of my close ties to you. I will be leaving later today. I have an appointment with the Highclave in person."

"In person?" Fey knew how rare those particular meetings were.

"I have hopes that they have been discussing the possibility of a new world for you or at least a more appropriate habitat." Telarrek's long neck never once arched over to meet the captain's eyes.

"Or perhaps they have news of Naydaalan and Kalian." Fey noticed the smallest of quivers on the Novaarians top lip. "You are worried about him, about Naydaalan."

Telarrek sighed, imitating a human all too well, and looked down at her. "I have many children, scattered throughout the Conclave and achieving their own goals in life. We may not see each other as often as we would like, but our lifespan offers such opportunities."

"But Naydaalan isn't in the Conclave..." Fey had shared many conversations with the Novaarian, and often forgot he was an alien.

"The distance is hard to comprehend, but the dangers lying in wait are not. The Terran Empire could hold secrets it does not want to relinquish." Telarrek's lower arms braced the railing, while they stopped to take in the view of milling humans.

"From what I've heard he's quite the accomplished warrior. He must be if the Highclave allowed him to accompany Kalian."

Telarrek responded with a sharp grunt - a Novarrian agreement. "I am sure they are both watching each other's backs. Enough of my worries." Telarrek waved his left, upper hand. "How is everything here?"

"I haven't been back more than a day," Fey replied, straightening her back. "Commander Holland informs me that two more people have committed suicide. The first lost her family back on Century. The councillors had been working with her but..." Every death weighed on her more than she could admit.

"And the other?" Telarrek always tried to share the burden.

"Jonathan Vincent, one of our biologists. He lost his wife when Professor Jones attacked us on the *Gommarian*." Fey could name every person who had died since they arrived in the Conclave. "I've already discussed with Captain Holt about the serious need for councillors and placing people under suicide watch."

"Losing your whole world, your cultures and history..." Telarrek's slender shoulders sagged. "It's no wonder so many find it hard to go on."

"Losing Earth and Century is devastating. The magnitude of that loss will probably take years to fully comprehend, but it's not what drives us to despair. We've lost so much, but it doesn't override our instinct for survival or hinder our ability to look forward. Losing the people closest to us hurts. The ones who felt like a part of us." Fey turned to look up at Telarrek. "That's when it's real."

The two continued their walk along the promenade until Captain Holt came into view. He was standing in the corner of the railing, staring up at the transparent dome that sheltered them.

"Quite the view, isn't it?" Fey followed his gaze to the looming planet that watched over them. "That's Arakesh, the Raalakian homeworld."

Jed had yet to take his eyes from it. "It's an alien world. I'm just a little..." The captain turned to see Fey and Telarrek, who towered over them both. "Stunned, I suppose."

Fey glanced at Telarrek and remembered what it was like when aliens were still a new sight. "This is Ambassador Telarrek. He is our representative in the Conclave."

"A No-vaarian?" Jed replied.

"Correct." Telarrek bowed until his golden eyes were level with Jed's head. "I offer greetings of peace, on behalf of both the Novaarians and the Conclave."

"Thank you." Jed was clearly still uncomfortable with aliens.

"I remember when your crew disappeared, Captain Holt. My own crew, that of the Valoran, attempted to locate you many times, but now we know how impossible that task was."

Jed's brow furrowed in response. "You remember? I don't understand."

Fey explained, "Telarrek and his crew observed Earth for centuries before contact was made. There's every chance the Paladin flew right past them and you didn't notice."

"You were there the whole time? That's... no weirder than the rest of this, I suppose." Jed looked up at the alien planet. "I'm sure you can imagine how many questions me and my people have, but as the captain of the Paladin, I have to know what the Conclave plans on doing with my ship."

Fey looked up again and saw the swollen vessel glide between the habitat and Arakesh.

"It will remain close by for the time being," Telarrek assured. "A more thorough inspection may be required, to ensure the renegade Shay has not left behind any surprises."

"Well, we can't stay here." Jed waved his arm across the view of the park. "I've been told that camping supplies are being brought in."

"A temporary measure," Fey cut in. "In the meantime, I should probably introduce you to the council."

Jed put his hand up. "Before I meet anyone else I need to go over the details with you one more time. I haven't been here all that long and everywhere I go I hear about this Kalian Gaines. I need details, Li. I need everything."

"Then perhaps it's a good thing Ambassador Telarrek is here." Fey cupped the Novaarian's lower elbow. "He has been through everything with us and has a far better memory than I."

<hr>

NAYDAALAN SLOWLY CIRCLED the alien contraption that enthralled Kalian. He remained standing, his arms supported by rests and connected to the larger machine via tendrils of nanocelium that appeared to link directly with the suit. Naydaalan wondered if they went through the suit and actually pierced Kalian's skin. The human's head was completely hidden within the mask that hugged his face and under his jaw. Almost every inch was covered in tubes and wires that extended upwards and into the strange machine, which faded into the darkness above.

With his rifle tucked closely to his chest, Naydaalan's slender fingers remained close to the trigger at all times. If there was a hint of subterfuge he was prepared to open fire on the giant ALF, who stood as still as any inanimate object beside Kalian. Every now and then the Novaarian would hear the scurrying of metallic feet in the shadows, accompanied with hisses of steam and the clunking of machinery. Most of the ancient ship was hidden in darkness, but it certainly wasn't asleep anymore. Since the real ALF had shown himself, more and more of the surroundings came to life.

Using his sharp, golden eyes, Naydaalan observed the beads of sweat that ran between the edge of Kalian's mask and the top of his nanocelium collar. Whatever he was experiencing right now, it was exerting a particular amount of physical exertion on him. With no signs of distress, however, the Novaarian was content to keep watch, for now. His father, Telarrek, hadn't expressly told him to protect Kalian, but the human's importance had been implied - as they always were in their conversations. Naydaalan knew his father couldn't bring himself to ask his son to sacrifice his own life for Kalian's, but he was more than just an extension of the Conclave on this mission; the Highclave was expecting him to keep the human alive, though he suspected there was one or two on the Highclave who wouldn't mind seeing Kalian dead.

Having seen some of what Kalian could do, Naydaalan realised that his mandate to protect the human wasn't entirely required. Since arriving in the hostile Terran Empire, it had been Kalian who had delivered them from certain death.

Without warning, ALF's body came to life with an alarmed expression, causing Naydaalan to raise his weapon and take aim.

"Incoming!" ALF's warning came only a second before the massive ship was shaken, raining dust from the darkness.

Naydaalan corrected his footing and looked up at ALF. "What is it?"

"Shifters!" ALF placed one of his hands on the ancient console, beside Kalian, and released a flurry of nanocelium strands into the hardware.

"Shifters?" Naydaalan was forced to reach out and balance himself as the ship was shaken again.

"You encountered them outside Albadar. Nanocelium left behind by Savrick to trap and destroy any wayfarers. They can become ships, monsters, anything required to eliminate the intruder." ALF held out his free hand, palm-up, and projected a hologram from within. Naydaalan could see three sleek, black ships diving around the mountain and firing upon them. "I am bringing my defences online, but it will take some time while so much power is diverted to Kalian."

"Then wake him up. Bring him out of it." Naydaalan took a step closer, as more weapons fire shook the ship.

"I cannot. He's at a crucial stage. If his mind can't comprehend the changes that need making now he might never advance."

Naydaalan groaned, which coming from a Novaarian sounded more like a growl. He ran towards the thick double doors while replacing his helmet and activating his suit, ready for the harsh environment.

"What are you doing?" ALF called out.

"Retrieving the *Advent*. I will hold them off while you bring your weapons online." Naydaalan heard the hiss inside his mask when the atmospheric stabilisers kicked in.

"It's suicide, Naydaalan. Those Shifters are made of nanocelium and your ship doesn't have the firepower to stop them."

Naydaalan checked the setting on his rifle. "Then you had better work fast."

The doors slid apart - a mechanism that could only be activated by ALF - demonstrating that despite his protests, the AI was happy for Naydaalan to play the part of the distraction. It wouldn't be the first time ALF had sacrificed the lives of others for those he considered more important.

Having already alerted the *Advent*, the ship tore through the dark sky and flew low over the lava fields. Naydaalan's Novaarian reflexes easily timed the distance and speed of the ship, allowing him to jump - aided by the built-in jets - and catch the edge of the extended ramp on the side of the ship. Four strong arms worked to get him inside as fast as possible until he reached the bridge.

A direct hit to the port side dropped the Novaarian into the chair and almost dipped the *Advent* into a river of steaming lava. Naydaalan took immediate control, via the holographic domes, and took the ship into a vertical rise, avoiding the next two attacks by metres. The ship switched to attack mode and straps flew out of the chair and braced him in his seat, as manoeuvre after manoeuvre would have him flattened against the walls.

Naydaalan wanted to give verbal commands to the ship, but the G's exerted on his body prevented any words from escaping. While his upper arms worked the controls, his lower limbs redirected power throughout the ship. As ALF had said, the *Advent* possessed no weapon capable of destroying the Shifters, but it had some damn good thrusters. With the weapons taken offline, life support dropped to critical and artificial gravity disabled, all available power was pushed into the engine and the thrusters.

The *Advent* zipped through the gaps in the Shifters' pattern, with only inches between them at times, and continued to rise and dive in and out of the thick cloud bank. Another direct hit on the undercarriage had alarms blaring between his arms, flashing in red. The hull had been breached and a portion of the thrusters destroyed.

Where was ALF's support?

As if on cue, the array was activated when ALF made contact with the ship. How the AI had broken through the *Advent's* protocols without Naydaalan accepting the call, he didn't know.

"I'm going to need more time to get my weapons online." ALF sounded unreasonably calm.

Naydaalan was forced to slow down the ship's ascent in order to verbally respond. "I only have another two manoeuvre, maybe three, before they can anticipate my pattern." His voice was strained and his chest hurt with every breath.

"It doesn't matter anymore," ALF replied, cryptically. "You need to get back here, now."

Naydaalan, a soldier born, didn't question the command, but instead killed the throttle and let gravity pull the *Advent* back down until it was pointing towards the planet's arid surface. Two of the Shifters were flying up towards him, while the third continued its attack on ALF's ship. The Novaarian brought the ship's thrust up to maximum yield and weaved between the weapons fire. It wasn't enough to dodge the actual Shifters, however. The nanocelium ship cut through the port side of the *Advent's* hull, shearing the metal away and damaging the ship beyond all repair.

It took everything the Novaarian had to level out again. The *Advent* skimmed the jagged ground and lakes of lava, as it hurtled towards ALF's ship at the base of the mountain. The consoles protested their continued use and erupted in sparks and blinked out of existence. One last alarm informed Naydaalan that the engine had lost power, as a good part of it had been cut away by the Shifter. In moments the *Advent* would lose its momentum and collide with the ground, turning the ship into a ball of scrap metal.

Naydaalan felt the ship rise under his weight, the rocky ground slipping away. The Novaarian peered out of the viewport in wonder, as the volcanic surface dropped away from the *Advent*. Moments later the ship began to slow down, despite being no more than a collection of rooms with half of a broken engine attached to it. The hull *creaked* and *groaned* under the invisible strain of whatever was slowing it down. The massive doors to ALF's ship were close enough to make out the details when the entire bridge peeled away in an explosion of sparks and wrought metal, exposing him to the outside world. The glass monitors cracked and shattered, along with the viewport, forcing Naydaalan to cover his visor.

Through all the chaos and destruction, not one object touched the Novaarian. When Naydaalan opened his eyes again, the whole bridge had been torn away, including his chair. Before he could question the extraordinary event, the warrior's floating body was pulled towards ALF's ship, as if he were floating in a vacuum. The tall doors parted at the same moment his feet once again touched the ground. Behind him, the *Advent* dropped unceremoniously to the ground in a cloud of dust.

The Shifters were closing in.

Naydaalan hurried into the giant cuboid, hearing their buzzing engines speeding over the lava fields. With one last bewildered look at the ruined *Advent*, the Novaarian returned to Kalian's side and the doors sealed them in.

"What is happening?" Naydaalan asked through laboured breaths.

"I believe Kalian has become aware of the situation." ALF was striding around in the shadows, activating unseen machines. "Quickly now." ALF signalled for Naydaalan to join him.

The Novaarian was gripped by the AI's strong hands and thrust against the wall, where multiple straps jumped out and fastened him in place. Naydaalan instinctively attempted to struggle, but the nanocelium binds wouldn't give an inch.

"I'm afraid I don't know exactly how the next few moments are going to unfold," ALF explained, "but I'm very good with probability." The giant AI tore a small hole in Naydaalan's suit, just above the elbow on his upper arm. "I'm going to attach an intravenous line that will connect you in part to my ship."

Upon hearing this, Naydaalan increased his struggling and roared. The prick hurt for a moment, but the black line that ran out of the wall and into his arm was alarming.

"Don't worry, it isn't the same thing you witnessed with Professor Jones - I just need to make you appear as if you're a part of the ship, or things could get very messy..." ALF returned to Kalian without an explanation.

Naydaalan stopped his fighting when the noise from the machine, attached to Kalian's head, increased in pitch. Kalian physically shuddered and his hands gripped the ends of his rests until the knuckles were white. The Novaarian could hear the human shouting from inside the metallic mask.

"What's happening to him?" Naydaalan shouted over the sound of the machine.

ALF ignored him. The entire ship was rocked by more weapons fire from the Shifters. It looked to Naydaalan as if the floors and walls were slowly moving, like the waves in an ocean, but he soon realised it was nanocelium, attending the damaged sections of the ship.

"What's happening?" he shouted again.

ALF answered with a single word. "Evolution."

The mountain imploded, as ALF's ship slipped between the gap in reality. To Naydaalan, this felt as if his perspective on the world had been momentarily narrowed and he had been looking down an endless corridor before it snapped back with a gut-wrenching *thud*. The Novaarian vomited inside his helmet, spraying every inch of his visor. Thankfully the straps released him and he dropped to the floor in exhaustion, despite having exerted no energy. He immediately threw his visor away and tore the long line of nanocelium from his skin.

Looking up, ALF was quickly attending to the machine encompassing Kalian's head. The human appeared limp now, his hands hanging off the edge of the rests and his knees buckled. ALF used one arm to support Kalian when the mask spread apart and retreated back into the larger machine. Naydaalan fought off the dizziness and approached them, taking note of the blood pouring out of Kalian's nose, mouth and ears.

"Is he alive?" Naydaalan feared the worst.

"He won't be if I don't operate immediately." ALF had scooped Kalian up into both arms and waited patiently while a rectangular slab of nanocelium separated from the floor and rose up to lay him on. Dark tendrils snaked out of the darkness above, each ending with a different surgical instrument, not unlike the Conclave's Medders.

"Operate? What happened to him? Did he destroy the Shifters?" Naydaalan's mind was struggling to focus on any one thing.

"The Shifters are no longer a problem. Kalian's organs being in the wrong place, however... that's a problem."

"Wrong place?" Naydaalan echoed.

"It was his first jump and a damn big one at that. This was expected." ALF raised his arms but never touched the tendrils, as they went to work on cutting Kalian out of his exo-suit.

"This was expected? Wait! What jump? What happened?" Naydaalan's lack of understanding was manifesting as anger.

ALF continued to manipulate the surgical tendrils as if he were conducting an orchestra. "See for yourself." The AI didn't turn away, but the double doors parted, allowing bright sunlight to flood the ship.

Naydaalan winced, trying to adjust to the light. It wasn't the same reddish-light emitted by the volcanic atmosphere, but that of two suns. The Novaarian blinked until the horizon took shape in the form of mountains and fields of red grass with arching waves of curved, black rock, overgrown with weeds and colourful plant life. The sky was a pale white, overcast with clouds that only allowed one of the two suns to shine through with clarity.

The warrior turned back to ALF, who had stripped Kalian of his armour and dived right in with the surgical blades and cutting lasers.

"I don't understand. Where are we?"

"According to my initial analysis of the soil, we're on Hadrok."

EIGHTEEN

Despite the mounting alien environments, Li'ara continued to come across, she still marvelled at every one while they took her breath away. The Shay homeworld of Shandar was an incredible feat of truly advanced technology. The entire circumference of the planet was encased within a chaotic network of floating towers, each bridged to the next in every direction. The lowest levels, saved for the poorest of the Shay, descended into the exosphere of the dying planet and was enveloped within stormy clouds that never let up.

Roland had visited the planet a few times in his self-exile from the human race, but for Li'ara it was a first. She stood right up against the viewport and enjoyed the peaceful experience of observing a planet from orbit. Sef, broad in ever way, was impossible to mistake, as the Gomar appeared by her side without a sound. How somebody so big and covered from head-to-toe in armour could be so quiet, she didn't know.

"It's beautiful, isn't it?"

Sef looked from Li'ara to Shandar. *The Terran would have fixed the planet, not left it to die and build around it.*

Li'ara didn't know what to say to that. Sef had seen more of the universe's wonders than she had, especially during their journey across the galaxy in search of Earth. It was possible that the Gomar saw Shandar as a relatively primitive civilisation.

Roland belched on his way onto the bridge and tossed an empty can of beer to one side. It seemed the bounty hunter was back to his old ways. Roland was wearing his usual gear, coat and all, with his trusty Tri-rollers holstered on each thigh. He was readying for a fight if his alcohol consumption was anything to go by.

"Don't bother with fake ID's, Len." Roland dropped into his chair and lifted his hands so the console could swing around. "Take us in all nice and quiet like."

"Activating stealthware now..." Ch'len sat across from Roland with his little legs dangling off the edge.

Li'ara walked up the centre of the bridge. "We should do some recon and plan out our approach. Kel-var is bound to have defences."

"Or..." Roland hit a key on his console with dramatic flair. The *Rackham*'s speaker system immediately exploded with loud music.

Li'ara rolled her eyes and hoped the heavy beats and club music wouldn't give her a headache. The bounty hunter was insufferable, but annoyingly good at what he did, though right now Li'ara was finding it hard to pinpoint exactly what that was.

The *Rackham* shot between the floating towers and weaved between the lanes of traffic and patrolling security forces. Not only was the ship invisible to sensor arrays, but also to the naked eye. Only a keen observer in the lower levels would take note of the thick clouds that parted in its wake.

The light inside the bridge was entirely artificial while they ploughed through the stormy atmosphere. Li'ara had to shield her eyes when the planet's surface finally came into view in a panorama of stark white. Devoid of sunlight, the surface was barren and cold. They were greeted by mountains covered in snow for as far as the eye could see.

"The coordinates from Gor-van's ship are just there!" Ch'len shouted over the music and brought up a holographic overlay across the viewport.

Roland cut the music and leaned forward in his seat. Li'ara

followed his gaze to the pin-point, nestled between two mountains in the distance. From this height, there was no sign of any activity or artificial structures. That changed as they flew over the rise of the nearest mountain, which had been hiding three massive pillars, each pointed inwards toward the apex.

"What is that?" Li'ara asked.

"I don't know," Ch'len replied, consulting his console. "It's not where the coordinates lead." The Ch'kara typed away until more data presented itself. "From these readings, I'd say it's some kind of array, but its configuration is unusual..."

"How so?" Li'ara craned her neck over the viewport to take in as much of the structure as she could before the *Rackham* overshot it.

"Well, most arrays are designed to receive and emit signals. From the looks of this, that array can only emit."

Sef turned to Li'ara. *Do a planet-wide scan...*

Li'ara looked at the Gomar for a second longer, wondering what he could sense. "Len, can the *Rackham* scan the whole planet?"

The Ch'kara laughed. "What does this look like, a Nexus-Class battlecruiser?"

Sef audibly sighed inside his helmet. The Gomar held out his hand, once again calling upon the nanocelium inside the ship. Four new columns rose up and presented him with a bank of consoles and holograms. Both Ch'len and Roland made to protest, but Li'ara held up her hand to silence the pair. Sef's armoured hands danced between the columns until a new hologram was emitted in the middle of the bridge. They all looked upon the floating blue orb that represented Shandar and watched as tiny red blips appeared across the surface. There wasn't one landmass that didn't have at least a dozen of the red dots.

"How did he..." Ch'len's expression crumpled into confusion.

Li'ara glanced at the consoles before taking a closer look at the hologram. "These are arrays? Like the one down there?"

Sef nodded silently.

"They must belong to Protocorps," Roland added.

"Why don't you ask them..." Ch'len nodded at the viewport,

where a squat-looking facility came into view, dug into the mountainside.

"Are we still operating under stealthware?" Li'ara knew that if they could see the facility, the facility could see them.

"Yep!" Roland stood up with one of his Tri-rollers in hand and a beaming smile on his face. "Let's go knock!"

"Wait!" Li'ara moved to try and stop the bounty hunter from leaving. "We need a plan, Roland."

"We have a plan; he's standing right behind you!" The bounty hunter casually gestured to Sef with his gun. "The guerilla opens the door and my Tri-roller here talks our way in." He turned to leave but faced Sef one last time. "Oh, and don't kill everyone this time! It just sucks the fun right out of this..."

KEL-VAR SAT on the edge of his bed, his conscience keeping him awake as usual. Malekk had the coordinates now. The Gomar were as good as dead, and with them gone, there would be no one to stop what was coming. The idea of ascension had always been abstract in the Shay's mind. Something his parents would talk about as if it was thousands of years away, something that could never come to pass in his lifetime. Seeing Malekk and the outcome of the recent test on the Paladin was sobering.

Ascension looked an awful lot like slavery.

An alarm Kel-var had never heard before blared from the speakers in the ceiling. The Shay tilted his head and heard it ringing out across the base, as well as in his room. Wearing just his night robe, Kel-var opened his door to find two guards already approaching.

"Sir, the installation's under attack!" The two Shay were part of the mercenary group that now worked solely for Protocorps. "We're enacting the extraction protocol."

"You will do no such thing," Kel-var replied, waving their guiding hands away. "Take me to the control centre."

The walk to the control centre was long and Kel-var couldn't get rid of the knot in his gut. The Crucible was one of Protocorps' best-kept secrets; even the captured board members would die before giving up its location.

Gor-van...

Would Gor-van have given up the Crucible as a way of getting back at him? No, Kel-var was certain that even Gor-van would never give it up, unless...

"Have we identified the intruders?" Kel-var asked the question as soon as the doors opened into the control centre. He suspected their identities would not come as a surprise.

The nearest Shay brought up the holographic logs from the extensive network of cameras throughout the installation. The outer doors had been blown away, though there was no evidence of an explosion. The next image showed a firefight in the upper tunnels, where two humans and a... Gomar were forcing their way through.

"That's not Kalian Gaines," Kel-var announced. "Look at the armour, his size. *That* is a Gomar."

The Shay lost all hope as one camera after another displayed their advance. Nothing could stop them. Roland North showed his usual brutality, while Li'ara Ducarté utilized precision and moved from cover to cover. The unknown Gomar simply strode down the corridors, as the intrinium bolts bounced off of his armour. Either way, the mercenaries continued to drop.

"What do we do?" a technician asked.

The Control centre began to stir with unrest and the mercenaries looked to one another with questioning glances. Kel-var knew he had to take control before chaos ruled, but what could he do? Roland North and Li'ara Ducarté were hard targets on their own, but with a Gomar backing them up...

"Activate all internal cannons." Kel-var gave the order without looking away from the monitor. "Those tunnels are lined with cannons, are they not? Wait until they've advanced a little further and attack them from all sides. Hammer them!"

The technician worked in conjunction with a few others before he pressed the button to turn every corridor into a kill box. Nothing happened. The team ran through the diagnostics, checking everything was working as it should, while Kel-var paced behind them.

"Why aren't they firing?" he finally asked.

"It must be the Gomar." The technician changed the image and zoomed in on the armoured being.

"What is he..." Kel-var narrowed his vision and focused on the Gomar, who had stopped walking and placed a single hand on the wall, while the humans continued to kill the mercenaries.

After he finished disabling the internal defences, the Gomar looked up at the camera with an intensity that made Kel-var uncomfortable. One armoured hand rose into the air and formed a fist, ending the video feed and their ability to observe the fight.

Kel-var screamed in frustration and slammed his fists into the console. "Go. Go, all of you just GO! If you can hold a weapon I expect you to leave this room and fight."

The technicians looked at each other in disbelief, before turning a pleading expression on Kel-var. Some slowly rose from their seats, while others looked too scared to move.

"Captain, arm these people and take them to the Translift!" Kel-var turned away from them and listened to the mercenaries haul the technicians from their feet.

They were all going to die.

That thought took a while to sink in but was ultimately overridden by the fear of his own death. He sat in one of the empty chairs, head sinking into his chest further and further under the weight of his mistakes. They had underestimated the humans. Kel-var could now see why they had been targeted so thoroughly.

It took some time, but eventually, the doors of the control centre were torn from their servo motors and thrown away. A beaming Roland North was closely followed by the red-head and the towering Gomar.

Kel-var remained seated, refusing to stand and show any fear. To the trained eyes of these particular killers, it was probably evident enough.

"Kel-var..." Roland purred. "Have you been avoiding my calls?" Shay blood was splattered against his face and long coat.

The Gomar came to stand in front of him, a wall of unstoppable force. Li'ara appeared less interested in him, however, and made for the adjacent consoles. Her stubby, human fingers dashed across the holographics, searching.

"I love what you've done with the place," Roland continued. "The whole secret base in the mountains-thing... has a dastardly evil touch to it. And kicking the planet's inhabitants off the surface! Protocorps is badass!" Roland back-handed Kel-var with his Tri-roller.

The Shay fell to the floor in a sprawling of limbs and shooting pain. Kel-var simply wasn't accustomed to pain, having lived a life of privilege in the tallest of Conclave towers. Tasting his own blood was new to him.

"This place is a gold mine," Li'ara commented. "It looks like Protocorps use this place to back-up most of their data." The human continued to sift through the information, her agitation growing. "There's too much! It could take me days, months to find the coordinates."

Kel-var got as far as his knees before Roland placed the end of his gun to the Shay's head. "Where are the coordinates to the Gomar? We know Gor-van sent them to you. He's dead by the way."

Kel-var was about to reply with a wicked retort, the pain in his lip stoking his anger, when the humans looked away, towards the Gomar. Nothing was said, but it looked to the Shay as if some information was being shared.

"Of course!" Li'ara replied to nothing. "The base emits data, it doesn't receive. Where's his *personal* array?"

Roland, who was apparently in charge of Kel-var's interrogation, picked the Shay up by his robes and forced him back into the chair. "You heard the lady, dip-shit; where's your personal array?"

Kel-var wanted to tell them to exactly what he thought of the extended Terran race, but his survival instincts kicked in. "If I give you what you want, I will need something in return. I want..."

The Gomar suddenly walked away, without notice. The giant's

direction told the Shay exactly where he was going. Kel-var stuttered and stumbled over his words, distracted by the Gomar entering his private office. A moment later, the god-like figure emerged with a rectangular box in his hand and torn wires poking out of the end.

Roland laughed, though the joke hadn't been said out loud. "Nice one, Sef! Looks like negotiations aren't required, after all, Kel-var." The bounty hunter levelled his weapon at the Shay's head again.

"Wait!" Kel-var pleaded, too afraid to care about begging. "I can tell you what this place is. What it was designed for."

Roland bit his lip and turned to Li'ara, who went back to work on the console. After a minute she replied with a satisfied smile and slowly hit a single button on the glass screen.

Li'ara explained, "The Gomar are our priority. Whatever this place is, the Conclave will figure it out. Thanks to the huge amount of arrays this facility is connected to, I've just uploaded everything in its databanks to the social hubs on every planet. Protocorps no longer has any secrets."

With that, she gave Roland a different kind of look. Had Kel-var survived the next second, he would have deduced that it was an expression of permission.

ELONDRASA, the Novaarian Highclave member, removed her floating headdress and relaxed into the comfortable seat on their personal transport. They had just announced the new Starforges that would soon be constructed and placed on the surface of every world in the Conclave. This particular announcement was the first of many in the new campaign, and judging by the reaction of the crowds, they were going to be revolutionary.

Of course, the knowledge that the new technology had been supplied by the humans had been met with a certain amount of distrust. Thankfully, the protestors, both for and against the humans, had been kept well at bay from the announcement. In the end, the opportunities the Starforges offered would outweigh the origin of their creation.

The transport took them from Clave Tower and across the expanse of space, to the *Marillion*. The golden orb rested on the edges of the solar system, ensuring that its size wouldn't interfere with the capital planet. As expected, both Uthor and Telarrek were waiting for the Highclave inside the inner sphere of the ship. The old friends stopped talking and stood to their full height, as the councillors entered the chamber.

Uthor's gravelly voice said, "It appears the Starforges have been well received."

Nu-marn replied, "Yes, but I still feel we should change the name. Rebrand it as something more... well, less human."

"We aren't here to discuss the Starforges," Lordina said, already tired with the talk of transport.

"Indeed," Elondrasa added, motioning for both visitors to take a seat at the table. "How are the inhabitants of the Paladin adjusting?"

Telarrek tilted his head in a Novaarian sigh. "As well as can be expected. The friends and family they have lost died centuries ago, peacefully. I feel they will struggle more with the idea that their loved ones died never knowing what happened to the Paladin."

"I care very little for their feelings, Ambassador!" Nu-marn spat. "I just want to know where we're going to put them all. At the rate they breed they'll outgrow their first planet by the end of the century."

Elondrasa noted Telarrek's questioning expression. He desperately wanted to know if the humans had a planet they could live on.

"The answer is no, Telarrek." It was Brokk who answered, noting the same expression on the Novaarian's face. "Suitable locations have been found, but membership has not been granted yet."

Telarrek knew better than to respond with outrage, even if that was how he felt. Elondrasa knew that his son being on the other side of the galaxy must be fraying on the ambassador's sensibilities. The councillor respected him all the more for his silence.

"What will it take?" Surprisingly, it was Uthor's booming

Raalakian voice that replied. "Have you not read my reports? The humans have done nothing but fight for us!"

"They fight for themselves!" Nu-marn was quick to respond.

"That is what none of you understand! There is no them or us anymore, as there is no difference between any of us. Besides the technology they have presented us with, they have continued to uncover, at their own cost, the enemy that beats at our door. The Shay that attacked the Paladin are still being studied, but they showed a level of infection we have seen before. Malekk, Professor Jones... Something is, no, something has already infiltrated the Conclave. The humans are the only ones doing anything!"

Ch'lac replied dryly, "So far they've created a mess on the capital, left bodies behind from Trantax IV to Byzantial and most of that chaos was created by a handful of their kind. They are unpredictable."

"The same was said of any Raalak before the Conclave was formed." The fact that Brokk replied and not Uthor was a testament to the Highclave's fracture on the subject.

The room fell silent, with no argument raised.

"Forgive the intrusion," Xydrandil, the Nix, glided into the room on his many legs. "There has been a development on the social hubs." The Nix activated the holographic emitters in the centre of the table. "This has just been transmitted from the surface of Shandar."

"The surface?" Nu-marn asked in disbelief.

The room fell silent again as the group took in the streams of data being shared throughout the Conclave. There was more than a few gasps.

"Who has released this?" Ch'lac asked, his eyes glued to the images flashing across the table top.

Xydrandil changed the central hologram to that of a recording. Two humans and a Gomar could clearly be seen walking through a corridor, killing Shay soldiers.

"Li'ara..." Telarrek sat forward in his chair.

"A Gomar?" Lordina's voice filled with fear.

"The data is being analysed from top to bottom, but one element has already flashed under the priority alerts." Xydrandil skipped ahead to a section where Roland North shot Kel-var Tionis in the head. "Within all the material being transmitted, a set of coordinates was found inside a data-packet."

Elondrasa sat back, as her mind's eye witnessed the backlash from the Conclave.

Brokk looked at Uthor. "Send a fleet to that planet immediately. The Gomar must be secured."

"I will take care of the Gomar," Uthor replied confidently, standing up on his strong, four legs. "I *advise* that all of you sit here for a while and review the truth of what's been going on under ignorant reign. Telarrek, perhaps you should accompany me. The humans listen to you." The pair left without another word, only a look from Telarrek told of his disappointment.

Naturally, Lordina and Nu-marn were outraged at the High Charge's comment, while Ch'lac, Brokk and herself could see the gaps in their attention. They had ignored everything put to them, especially if the source was human in origin.

"Let them go," Elondrasa bade.

"They must be disciplined!" Nu-marn fired back.

"For what? Pointing out the truth, a truth that is displayed before your very face, Nu-marn." Elondrasa expanded a hologram of the base hidden on Shandar. "We have *real* work to do."

NINETEEN

Kalian awoke with a start and almost jumped off the table when he sat up. His hand gripped his chest, where he instinctively knew that something had been wrong. There was no pain or any sign of trauma, which would have been clear to see since he was naked. The armour was in a heap on the floor, at the end of the table. The nanocelium had yet to repair itself and Kalian could see where the exo-suit had been cut open.

"I'm getting really tired of waking up naked on a cold surface..." Kalian spoke out loud, aware that Naydaalan was off to the side and watching him with a worried eye.

Everything about the Novaarian screamed at Kalian, alerting his every sense that he was standing close by. From his unique smell to the taste of his alien skin on Kalian's tongue, Naydaalan impacted the universe as strongly as any star or black hole. As the warrior moved, Kalian felt the molecules around the alien displace, almost as if he were walking through water.

"I believe this would be the third time," Naydaalan replied, coolly. "I'm afraid some surgery was required to save your life."

"Surgery?" Kalian felt his bare chest again, searching for any signs.

"Apparently, your organs were in the wrong place."

Kalian wanted to follow that statement up with a flurry of new questions, but as the Novaarian approached, he could feel his senses going into overdrive. The swish of Naydaalan's head tendrils was too loud in Kalian's ears and his alien heartbeat threatened to blow his eardrums. The whole experience was becoming nauseating, but Kalian knew that it shouldn't - this was an aspect of his abilities that he had already learned to control.

His discomfort didn't go unnoticed.

ALF's deep voice echoed through the darkness above, "You have entered the next phase..." The AI floated down, supported by tentacles of nanocelium that fused with his back.

"What does that mean?" Kalian asked, fighting off the vomit in his throat.

ALF's wide feet touched the floor and the tentacles released their hold on him, slithering back into the hidden depths above. "Your senses are becoming acuter as you delve deeper into the uncharted parts of your mind. This is just a biological response however, the real changes are far more profound."

Kalian met ALF's cybernetic eyes and tried to see into the truth of that statement. The AI wore a smile, similar to that of a proud father, and nodded his head over his shoulder. Looking past the giant, Kalian began to take in his surroundings, despite Naydaalan's natural pheromones threatening to consume his senses and focused on the white light pouring in through the tall doors of the ship.

They were not on a volcanic planet.

"I don't understand..." Kalian slowly slid off the table and walked towards the light, no care for his lack of clothes.

His eyes quickly adjusted, sharpening the hazy image, until the sight of mountains and fields of red grass took shape. Arching towers of black rock littered the horizon, coated in weeds and flowers. Kalian's jaw dropped when his vision changed from that of the landscape to a single flower bud, perhaps half a mile away. The flower was exquisite, a blend of red, orange and yellow with a sweet smell and a furry texture that he could feel between his finger and thumb. Kalian pulled back immediately, aware that he was touching, smelling and examining a flower that wasn't actually in front of him.

ALF was watching him, silently, evaluating his responses. "Your connection to the universe is beginning to take shape. The subconducer will make you more powerful than any Terran, even Alai, the first immortal."

Kalian frowned, trying to grasp the world around him. "I don't understand. I was..." He looked back to the fields of red grass. "I've connected with objects, people even, who weren't next to me, but I could have sworn I was standing in front of that flower."

"Your senses are richer, your abilities more intense." ALF continued to stare at him with glowing, blue eyes.

Kalian thought about the AI's words for a moment. Everything did feel more intense as if he could feel the vibration of every atom at once. Suddenly, the universe didn't feel so solid, so put together. There were gaps in everything. Kalian genuflected and placed an outstretched hand onto the cold floor. Millions of nanocelium reacted to his touch, excited almost by his attention. While on one knee, the dark nanocelium lifted from the floor, molecule by molecule, and swarmed around Kalian's body. The tornado of black mist began to fade and Kalian's skin disappeared beneath a new exosuit.

ALF smiled and nodded his approval.

Kalian stood up. "So how did we get here? Wherever here is... Your ship can fly?"

ALF looked from Kalian to Naydaalan with his typical, smug smile. "My housing unit can fly, or at least it will when I get around to powering everything up."

Kalian didn't understand a word of ALF's cryptic explanation, but judging by Naydaalan's expression, Kalian was the only one who didn't understand.

"We were attacked by the Shifters." Naydaalan pointed upwards. "The nanocelium traps that we encountered on Albadar. I used the *Advent* to distract them, while ALF powered up his weapons, but..."

"But what?" Kalian asked.

"It was you, Kalian," Naydaalan continued in his disbelieving tone. "You saved us. You pulled me from *Advent* before it was destroyed and then..." The Novaarian looked to ALF for a better explanation.

"I'm still analysing all the data from the subconducer, so I can't tell right now if *we* moved or the *universe* moved but, either way, it was *you* who transported us from one world to the next. This is Hadrok, Kalian. You brought us to Hadrok..."

Kalian's mind stumbled over every word that came out of ALF's mouth. He had seen Esabelle perform an identical feat with the *Rackham* once, and she had done it hundreds of times while plugged into the *Gommarian*, but Esabelle had always been on a different level to Kalian. How could he have moved them, not only from one planet to another but from one solar system to another?

"I know what you're thinking," ALF commented. "Distance is a relative thing outside of this dimension. You'll understand this more, in time."

"And the surgery?"

ALF explained, "When you displaced everything, it appears you didn't quite move all your organs into the right place. I've found a few similar problems throughout my ship, but it's nothing catastrophic."

Kalian turned back to the landscape outside and passed through the threshold. The light of two suns beat down on him and the breeze blew through his hair. He reached down and stroked his hand across the red grass, touching the soil beneath. This was the planet where it all began, he thought. Had Savrick picked any other planet to hide on, the civil war would never have happened, the *Tempest* would never have been sent to seed Earth, and the human race, as it was now, would never have existed.

"Why here?" he asked.

ALF shrugged. "I believe your mind was aware of the Shifters and you chose somewhere you felt was safe."

"How could I think Hadrok is safe? I've never been here."

"No... but Savrick has, and once upon a time, he thought Hadrok would be a safe place. Clearly, it's a thought that's still lodged inside your mind." ALF shot Kalian a disapproving look.

Kalian ignored the AI and closed his eyes, thankful to feel a real breeze against his face. "This isn't the Hadrok I've seen in his memories."

ALF casually strolled out into the light. "Well, a couple hundred millennia will do that to a planet. Perhaps this world will one day support intelligent life. A new Terran Empire..."

Kalian sighed heavily. "I'm not sure the universe needs another Terran Empire."

ALF looked down on him, inquisitively. "No? Then what does it need?"

Kalian looked to the horizon, having considered that question before. "Something new. Something better..."

Naydaalan joined them outside. "With the help of your people, I believe the Conclave can be made into something better. Through our unity."

"Speaking of unity..." ALF stood aside, leaving a clear view of the subconducer. "The only way we will reunite with the Conclave is if you practice. You need to learn that jumping from one system to another is no different than jumping from one side of the galaxy to the other."

Kalian shook his head. "Before we do anything else, I need to see it."

ALF frowned. "See what?"

"The cube. The one you've been using to spy on them and us. I can feel it inside there." Kalian nodded his chin at the ship. "You said you gutted it, but I can *feel* it, like a cancer inside of you."

ALF appeared to mull this over, before nodding once and entering his housing unit. The AI looked up, silently signalling the ship to present the cube. Kalian could feel the different mechanisms shifting and the cube being pulled from its compartment. It was clear from the moment it reached the light that the cube wasn't as it had been. Its golden sheen had been stained black and the sides had been pried open and its interior gutted, with two of its corners broken away and the intricate patterns scraped to nothing. ALF's housing unit was plugged into it from every angle, taking advantage of the sub-space communicator built into its heart.

"I can feel the nanocelium inside it," Kalian said. "Some of it still belongs to the Vanguard."

"I'm afraid it must, or the link to the other cubes is useless."

Kalian looked to Naydaalan before asking ALF, "What's happening there now, in the Conclave?"

"My connection to the Conclave has been fractured. I was using the cube Protocorps installed into the central AI to spy on all Conclave matters. Since that has been destroyed, I am limited to the three new cubes, sent by the Vanguard after your encounter with Malekk. They are observing the Conclave from the safety of their Starforges, but even their observation has been stunted."

Kalian nodded along. "Any *details*? Has Malekk made a move?"

ALF gave Kalian a hard look. "Training should be your priority."

Kalian replied with a mirthless laugh. "You of all people should understand the power of motivation."

"I fear your motivation died with Li'ara..." ALF said in a quieter tone.

Kalian felt the lump in his throat and the pit in his stomach prevent him from responding. Since arriving in the Terran Empire, the thought of Li'ara had been suppressed by one hostile encounter after another. Her loss hit him all over again, as it often brought him down in waves. They had been bonded not only by their survival of Earth and Century's destruction but also by his Terran abilities, which had brought them together in a way no human could imagine. Kalian had often felt that Li'ara was an extension of himself.

The thought of her, or the thought of her dying, had given him strength when he should have faltered. *With* Li'ara, he was always stronger.

"She would want me to keep fighting, for them..." Kalian could never shake the responsibility he felt for the surviving humans.

"Then you have a hundred thousand more reasons to fight for," ALF said.

Indeed, the lives of all those aboard the Paladin would inevitably find their way onto Kalian's shoulders. He only wished Li'ara could be there to keep him strong.

TWENTY

Roland lounged in his captain's chair, with his feet resting on the console. Ch'len had disappeared into the ship, either in search of food or something to do with the engine - Roland didn't care which. Sef was doing a typical Terran/Gomar thing and meditating in the hold. For beings who could do almost anything, they sat on their ass a lot with their eyes closed. The bounty hunter could think of a thousand things he would do with their power. They mostly involved blowing stuff up and drinking alcohol though...

Li'ara sat at the front of the ship, on one of the unused consoles, with her feet perched on the chair. Her view wasn't exactly spectacular, as they had entered the system housing the secret planet, but had chosen to use thrusters from a certain distance, unsure of the defensive measures that may have been set up. If they had emerged from sub-space too close to the world in question, they ran the risk of setting off any alarms. The planet in question was a dot the size of Roland's little fingernail.

"He's gonna' be all kinds of pissed when he finds out that you've been alive all this time. Like *really* pissed." Roland picked up another bottle, eyeing the distance to the planet and deciding he had plenty of time.

"Kalian will understand," Li'ara replied flatly.

Getting a rise out of her was half the fun.

"He damn near killed me when I got back from the capital, you know. Blamed me for letting you get yourself killed. So did I though, so..." Roland didn't mind thinking about all the people he had killed trying to discover the truth about Li'ara - they were all faceless aliens who all deserved what they got.

Li'ara turned to face the bounty hunter. "Is this about Kalian, or you?"

Roland pinched his eyes. "I know, you were healing, and I get why you kept yourself hidden. Sef needed your keener detective skills or whatever. I'm just not convinced he isn't the enemy yet. It wasn't that long ago they wiped out the human biosphere and took a crack at the Conclave."

"The way you feel about him is the same way Captain Fey and the council feel about you. One day you're causing more trouble than the top ten criminals in the Conclave, the next you're helping to save the universe. People are complicated, Roland. If you spent any time around them you might have figured that out by now."

"You don't seem so complicated, Mrs do-right. You wear your sense of duty like a fucking badge. You give me any scenario and I'll tell you what decision you're going to make, just like the kid!" Roland had found Kalian to be the most predictable of all people, though, with his level of power, that was definitely a good thing.

Li'ara was finally rising to it. "The survivors of Earth and Century have lived under nothing but constant threat since we arrived here. Doing the right thing is the only thing that's keeping everything together, getting things done."

Roland laughed to himself. "There's been times where my involvement was crucial to *keeping things together*... and I always do things the wrong way. My way gets things done!"

"Whatever you say, Princess..." Li'ara turned away from him again.

Roland sighed with the feeling that he had lost that battle. By the time he had finished his drink, the planet had swollen to the size of the viewport. White clouds swirled over every part of the world, revealing pockets of blue in between.

With his usual grace, Ch'len plonked him himself into his chair, which levitated to his console. "The surface is entirely water-based. No land masses at all except for..." Ch'len laughed to himself. "I can't believe we didn't know how powerful these scanners are!" The viewport altered until a single quadrant on the planet was magnified for all to see. "That must be where they're keeping them." The smallest of platforms could be seen through the gap in the clouds. "It's completely silent though. No active arrays or outgoing transmissions."

"Any defences?" Li'ara asked. "No patrols or orbital platforms?"

Ch'len checked his screen again. "Nothing. It's completely unprotected."

"What?" Li'ara didn't believe it.

Roland added, "It makes sense if it's supposed to be a big secret. Anyone who miraculously stumbles across this system wouldn't detect any ships or transmissions. They'd have to scan the planet like we have to find the base, and who's gonna' scan a world without any land? They'd sail right past. That planet's an island in the stars."

Li'ara raised an eyebrow. "Well if there are no defences up here, you can bet that base is kitted out to repel intruders."

Roland heard the familiar sound of heavy feet before the door to the bridge opened. "That's why we brought him, isn't it?"

Sef strode into the space between the bounty hunter and Ch'len. The goliath stood perfectly still, staring at the base.

"Penny for your thoughts..." Roland said casually.

Sef remained silent for a moment longer. *My brothers and sisters are on that planet. I can feel their unique physiology from here.*

"What about any defensive measures?" Li'ara asked.

I will need to be much closer for that level of detail.

Roland swivelled in his chair to see Ch'len beyond Sef. "Stealthware active?" A single nod from the small alien told him it was. "Then let's take a closer look shall we..."

The *Rackham* hit the atmosphere and pushed through until the clouds engulfed it. Once inside the protective shell, the viewport gave way to a horizon of stormy waters. Giant waves dominated the surface of the ocean world, with most being several miles in height.

"It appears there's been some kind of gravitational hiccup," Ch'len explained. "These waves aren't natural according to the planet's solar positioning."

"What could cause that?" Li'ara came to stand by the Ch'kara's console.

"A Gomar..." Roland commented, dryly.

Sef looked down at him, but his features were concealed within his black helmet. No thoughts were projected into Roland's mind and the Gomar returned to staring at the waves.

"It's unlikely," Li'ara replied, scanning the data. "I can't imagine they've taken the Gomar out of their Rem-stores." Li'ara stopped and looked closer at the data. "The atmosphere is breathable..."

Even Roland knew that couldn't be possible. "There's no plant life, Red."

"I can see that..." Li'ara's response came through a clenched jaw.

Ch'len explained, "There are atmospheric scrubbers at both poles. I am really loving these scanners!"

Roland ignored the alien's comment and brought up a holographic schematic from a scan of the base. "It looks like there's only one way in. The platform on the top."

"Landing and gaining access is going to be impossible with those waves..." Li'ara had pretty much taken over Ch'len's console, much to the alien's dismay. "They get battered every fifteen minutes by a wave that could carry the *Rackham* away and kill all of us. It might take us longer than that to gain access."

Roland looked up at the destructive giant that stood next to him. "I don't think it'll take that long."

Have the Rackham positioned above the platform. I will take care of the rest.

Roland looked to Li'ara, ensuring that she had not only heard the Gomar but also agreed with him. The red-head gave him a short nod, clearly trusting him more than Roland did. The bounty hunter was just excited to see what spectacle Sef made of it all.

After informing Ch'len of the plan, the ship was positioned a mile above the platform. They didn't have long before the next wave hit and swallowed them all. Roland used the link in his head to instruct the *Rackham* to fly above the waves and remain hidden, once they departed. Ch'len would obviously remain onboard, useless as ever in these scenarios.

The ramp lowered in the hold and the three walked to the edge, pushing against the strong winds. Sef didn't appear to notice the resistance, however. The Gomar stopped at the edge and looked down, to where the base's platform was barely visible. Again, Roland looked to Li'ara and made sure she was onboard with this part of the plan. The bounty hunter had done something similar in a vacuum, with Esabelle, when they were fleeing Krono Towers on Shandar - it actually proved to be an amazing escape technique. Now they were about to use it as a breaching technique.

Step off...

Sef's words preceded his own step, which took the hulking Gomar beyond the ramp. Roland and Li'ara took a breath and followed him over the edge. The drop was dizzying and the feeling of free falling sent a tingle from Roland's feet and into his stomach. The bounty hunter tried to keep his body vertical, with his limbs tucked in. Sef dropped quicker than they did and Roland could see the wave approaching, as the Gomar drew ever closer to the platform. A quick glance told of Li'ara's comfort, or at least her stubbornness to express any discomfort. The air rushed past their ears, preventing any sound of the tumultuous waves from reaching them.

Sef's landing was visible from above, due to the dented impact he made on the platform. For just a second, as that was all Roland had, the bounty hunter was concerned that Sef would let them hit the platform with the same kind of velocity. Clearly, the Gomar had slowed his own descent towards the end, but his armour had taken some of the brunt. Roland and Li'ara would be broken in half.

Finally, both Roland and Li'ara felt the invisible resistance that slowed their descent, and for just a moment, it felt as if they were really flying. Both humans landed on the platform with ease and no broken bones.

The bounty hunter howled with glee. "We should do that again!"

Before anyone could reply to the ridiculous comment, four cannons popped out of the platform with incredible speed. The three were instantly surrounded and the cannons unleashed their intrinium without pause. Roland dived to the floor and tucked into a roll, bringing up his Tri-rollers in both hands. Li'ara however, just stood perfectly still without a care. The cannon's intrinium bolts hammered at an invisible field that surrounded the three intruders. Translucent waves spread out across the field with every blow, but Sef remained in place, with his hands outstretched.

Roland slowly stood up, realising that his overreaction now appeared somewhat stupid. "How did you know he was going to do that?"

"Trust..." Li'ara's smile was unbearable.

Sef clenched both of his armoured fists and telekinetically crushed the cannons. They imploded in a shower of sparks and miniature explosions.

The approaching wave blocked out the sun. Roland looked up and saw the *Rackham* shoot out of the area. He mentally commanded it to activate all stealthware protocols and vanish from sight.

The Gomar marched towards the other end of the platform and reached out with one hand and made a lifting motion. Roland watched and heard the Translift being wrenched to their level. A flick of Sef's fingers opened the doors and the three happily stepped inside. It was only a few seconds after the lift dropped into the base that the mighty wave crashed into the facility.

DOCTOR'S BAL'S finger hovered over the self-destruct button. After being activated he would have to input his code and verbally command the walls of the installation to explode, killing them all.

Gelda, his Atari assistant, stood by his side, frozen in terror, along with the other scientists. There were no guards to protect them, only automated weapons systems. Bal was deflated, aware that those defensive measures had been rigorously tested and that no living Conclave member could survive them.

But nowhere was Gomar-proof.

Not an hour earlier had the doctor been contacted by High Charge Uthor and told of the loose Gomar and his human companions. Apparently, a fleet was on the way to assist them, but looking at the progress the intruders were making, Bal knew it wouldn't be in time. He couldn't bring himself to blow up the base, however, and not just because of the great work they were doing, but also because the Trillik just didn't want to die.

"If they make it to the lab doors… I'll input my code." Bal gave the team an apologetic look.

The red-headed Gomar behind him was still inside her Rem-store, along with the newest test-subject, whom they were yet to prise from their pod. The female had stirred when the base was first attacked, leaving the team no choice but to increase her doses of sedatives. They had been so close to figuring out how to remove the exo-suit; now it would all be for nothing.

Roland was already promising himself to never go anywhere with a Gomar or a Terran or anyone with special abilities ever again. Besides taking him to some of the worst places the Conclave had to offer, accompanying them into a fight was like marching into battle behind a tank.

Wait! Sef projected into their mind.

Roland stopped at the next corner with his Tri-rollers either side of his head. Li'ara's rifle was still smoking from the fight between them and the never-ending pop-out cannons. Thankfully Sef had disabled most with directed EMPs.

"What's wrong?" Li'ara asked, crouching beside Roland.

The walls are lined with explosives. On every level... Sef sat down on the floor and rested his hands on his knees.

"What are you doing?" Roland hissed.

I will disable the bombs, but there are too many for me to continue fighting at the same time. My skills have never required such acute direction. I must concentrate if I am to prevent them all from exploding.

"Acute direction?" Roland mouthed at Li'ara.

"Savrick used him, and most of the Gomar, like blunt instruments. Even Kalian has finer control than they do."

"Whatever, let's just get on with it. Shooting machines is boring as fuck!"

The humans ran on, leaving Sef to deal with the unseen threat of implosion. They had already descended into the bowels of the installation; more than once they came across a terrified scientist, running for cover or trying desperately to seal the door between them. It was clear when they had reached the chamber housing the Gomar.

"Why is there always a big fuck-off door?" Roland tapped the barrel of his Tri-roller against the shiny surface. "It's like they'll never learn that we just don't give a shit."

Li'ara raised both her eyebrows in surprise. "And how exactly are we getting through *this* door?"

"By being good at what I do!" Roland removed the Terran blade from the base of his back. "I don't keep that methane cloud around for nothing, you know. I've always got Len working on my shit... especially after encountering that door at Protocorps."

The bounty hunter thrust the base of the hilt into the console beside the heavy door. Black veins sprouted from the end and zigzagged across the glass screen. The glass cracked where the nanocelium entered the hardware and went to work on gutting the system.

"This'll just take a minute..." Roland leaned against the wall.

The lights inside the console flickered and the inner workings of the door rotated this way and that until a hiss was produced at the seams. It turned out that the door was actually three doors, one layered behind the other.

Two more cannons dropped out of the ceiling and opened fire immediately.

Roland dashed to the side of the door, retrieving his Terran hilt, and bringing up one of his Tri-rollers. Li'ara copied his movements on the other side of the door, except she had managed to get a shot off before taking cover. One of the cannons was damaged, unable to rotate and move between targets.

"There's just no thrill in blowing these things up!" Roland dived across the threshold and fired both of his guns at once. The intrinium bolts reduced the undamaged cannon to slag, leaving the broken cannon to continue its barrage against the wall. Roland strolled into the lab and casually shot the machine.

Inside the lab, a Trillik scientist was fervently pressing a solid button on his console and verbally ordering something to self-destruct. The other scientists and a particularly attractive Atari were all cowering at the far end of the room with nowhere to escape. Roland's assessment of these people was fleeting, due to the centre-piece of the lab. A typically beautiful Gomar was upright, inside her Rem-store, and connected to an array of machines via intravenous lines. Another stood beside her, but still hidden inside their armour and Rem-store.

Li'ara followed the bounty hunter in. "Well, that was easier than the last place we broke into..."

Roland cornered the Trillik. "You can't blame the eggheads, Red. They don't know any better! I realise that secret bases are best-kept secret when as few people know about it as possible, but you can't replace grunts with static cannons. They're just... predictable!"

Li'ara glanced at Roland, before focusing on the two Gomar. "Didn't your mother teach you not to play with your food?"

Roland was inches from the terrified Trillik. "Where's the fun in that?"

"Where are the other Gomar?" Li'ara asked.

The Trillik held up his hands and slowly reached for one of the holograms above the console. The glass wall behind him changed from translucent to transparent, revealing the other nine pods.

"What are you going to do with them?" the Trillik asked.

Li'ara looked from the pods to the scientist. "We'll start by waking them up - all of them."

"Doctor Bal!" the Atari cried.

The Trillik raised his hand to silence her. "You can't be serious? You know better than anyone in the Conclave what these monsters are capable of. They destroyed your entire civilisation!"

"You know how it is Doc," Roland twirled his gun in the alien's face, "the enemy of my enemy..."

All four of Doctor Bal's black eyes narrowed, pulling on his brow. "What does that mean?"

"It's... you know..." Roland couldn't be bothered explaining the human phrase. "Just wake -"

The entire facility shook and the overhead lights flickered on and off.

"Was that a wave?" Roland asked, looking back at Li'ara.

Doctor Bal slowly shook his head. "That's never happened before..." The Trillik started to access the camera feeds around the installation. Roland was sure to keep his Tri-roller aimed at the alien.

"The bombs?" Li'ara asked with some alarm.

"No," the Trillik answered. "Your friend has seen to those apparently."

The holographic feed showed a new ship on the platform above. It had no insignia or designation to indicate its purpose.

"Supply run?" Roland asked.

Doctor Bal shook his head and his twin-tail coiled around his leg. "We just had one. Besides, it wouldn't explain the tremor."

The installation shook again, more violently this time. The lights flickered and the consoles cut out for a second. Roland gripped the scientist by his coat and pressed the Tri-roller into his back, ensuring no attempts at escape. Doctor Bal raised his hands again, before going back to the console. Li'ara looked around the Rem-stores and checked on the other scientists.

The Trillik gasped, drawing their attention to the holographic screen above the console. Sef was easily identified in his hulking armour, but it wasn't the sight of him that opened a pit in Roland's stomach.

Sef was having his ass handed to him by Malekk.

The infected Terran dented the nanocelium armour with every blow, knocking the Gomar to his knees. Sef fired balls of super-heated plasma into Malekk's chest, but the Terran absorbed every hit, allowing the plasma to burn away the flesh. Sef slammed his fists into the floor, clearly enraged, and launched his whole body down the corridor. The feed blinked out and the facility shook once again, almost knocking them all off their feet.

The scientists became hysterical now, their death ensured in their eyes. In truth, Roland was pretty confident the water world would be his grave. Malekk had killed Esabelle, defeated Kalian and was probably only minutes away from ripping Sef's head off.

Li'ara strode over to Doctor Bal and levelled her gun at his green face. "Wake-them-up." The Trillik stuttered. "NOW!"

Roland kept his smile under control, not wanting to undermine Li'ara's scary persona - but he was kind of impressed... and a little turned on.

"Best do as she says, Doc." Roland replaced his Tri-rollers and started searching himself for more explosive hardware.

The base continued to shake and the internal framework groaned inside the walls. Roland kept one eye on Li'ara, who supervised the Trillik's work, and one eye on the open doors. The bounty hunter unstrapped the grav-bombs from his arm and threw them into the corridor, beyond the lab. The metallic balls shot out from their casing and stuck to various places along the walls, floor and ceiling. He followed this up with a few mines that would be triggered by movement. Roland assumed that if the base could stand a fight between two Terran, it could handle a few mines.

"Shut the doors." Li'ara nodded at them with her chin.

"Aye aye!" Roland replied mockingly. Using the Terran hilt, the bounty hunter reversed the process and sealed them in. "Len, can you hear me?" He tapped the device in his ear but got no reply.

"What's taking so long?" Li'ara was becoming irritated.

Bal wiped the sweat from his brow. "Our interface with their pods isn't perfect. It takes time to relay commands."

Li'ara swivelled on the red-headed Gomar. "What about her? It's not the pod that's keeping her asleep!"

"Wait!" the Trillik warned, seeing Li'ara march over.

Li'ara pulled the lines from the Gomar's hands and neck and tore free the nodes stuck to her temples. Nothing happened. The Gomar remained perfectly still, frozen in her coma.

The installation shook and the ceiling above their heads cracked, breaking one of the lights. Nobody moved. The almighty crack was followed by silence from above. Roland knew better than to think that Sef had won. The doors vibrated and the walls resounded with a deafening boom. The mines had been tripped outside.

"That was all the time I could buy us..." Roland looked back at Li'ara, whose stony expression told of her defiance towards death.

The red-headed Gomar remained asleep, along with her kin.

The silence following the explosion was filled with whimpers and sparking technical equipment. Roland looked at his Tri-rollers and knew they had never been more useless, but damn if he was going to roll over and die. He'd draw blood first.

The doors *creaked* and *groaned* under the stress of what could only be telekinesis. The bounty hunter steadied himself, ready for his last fight and regretting the lack of alcohol in his blood. Finally, the doors were pushed aside in a crumbling heap and smoke poured into the lab. Roland didn't wait but unleashed both of his Tri-rollers into the gloom. The familiar sound of intrinium bolts being absorbed against a telekinetic field told the bounty hunter of the futility of his actions.

As Malekk strode into the room, unharmed by the blue bolts, he swiped his arm across the gap between them. A telekinetic wave swept Roland from his feet and thrust him into the wall, hard. The knock to his head was enough to stop him from getting back up, but didn't stop him from observing the infected Terran.

Malekk stood in the doorway, looking over the two Gomar and the others beyond the glass. He didn't even bother to pause over Li'ara, who in Roland's mind was the one person he wouldn't want to go up against. Li'ara had survived the explosion of two planets, an encounter with the Beast, Lilander and even Savrick, not to mention losing her leg at Protocorps and ploughing through an army of mercenaries between Trantax IV and the capital. She wasn't just a survivor, she was a killer in Roland's eyes.

"You won't win," Li'ara announced, finally getting Malekk's attention. "Even if you kill the Gomar, we will find a way to oppose you. Kalian will return and when he does -"

"When he does, he will return to a Conclave devoid of any humans." Malekk's voice was unnatural. "He is on the other side of the galaxy. By the time he finds his way back here, there will be nothing for him to do, except die. As all of you will, when I'm done with *them*."

Malekk reached out to the Rem-stores behind the glass, but Li'ara's speech had bought them the time they needed.

The red-headed Gomar opened her eyes.

Roland wasn't able to track the movement that followed, but when his eyes caught up, the Gomar's Rem-store was empty and both she and Malekk were no longer in the lab. More violence erupted around the facility, shaking the very walls. By the time Roland found his feet again, the ceiling above caved in and the Gomar was suddenly flat against the floor, her armour broken in several places. As she rose to her knees, Malekk dropped down between the jagged beams and broken pipes. The infected Terran picked the Gomar up by her hair, holding her in place on her knees.

The bounty hunter held his sore head while searching frantically for his Tri-rollers. He had to do something, no matter how useless it would be. Malekk raised his free fist, preparing to deliver a blow that would most likely kill the Gomar.

The infected Terran stopped mid-blow, his features creasing into an expression of agony. He groaned and trembled as he stood over the Gomar, unable to move. Roland followed Li'ara's confused gaze to the glass wall, where nine Gomar had stepped out of their pods. They were all looking at Malekk, some with their hands raised and others with an intense stare. The pod beside Li'ara opened up and the armoured being inside stepped out, focused on Malekk.

"NO!" Malekk screamed. His eyes never left the kneeling Gomar. "Get... out... of... my head!"

Whether it was telepathic or telekinetic, Roland couldn't tell - he was just pleased with the outcome. Even more so when Sef returned. The big Gomar limped into the lab, behind Malekk, and brought his fist down directly on top of the Terran's head. An audible crack preceded Malekk's collapse to the floor.

Roland tried to catch his breath in the silence that followed. "Where the hell have *you* been?"

Sef ignored his remark and helped the red-headed Gomar to her feet. One-by-one, the Gomar removed their helmets, revealing an array of colourful tattoos across their faces. One from the other side of the glass put his hand to the cold surface and reduced the entire plane to sand. Roland just stared at the sand in disbelief, as the nine entered the room and greeted one another as old friends.

"Vox!" A male Gomar, with shoulder-length dark hair and an intricate purple tattoo across his left eye, ran over to the red-head and embraced her.

Vox, as she was called, appeared somewhat battered and bruised, but the red tattoos under her eyes would hide any swelling though. After embracing her friend, Vox turned on Doctor Bal with a look in her eye that Roland had seen before. The Trillik wasn't long for this world.

"Wait," Li'ara said, stepping between them. "No more killing."

Vox raised her eyebrow, apparently having no intention of listening to the human. As one, the eleven Gomar turned to Sef, but Roland could only watch the group communicate, as he obviously wasn't invited to the silent conversation. Judging by Li'ara's expression, he wasn't the only one who didn't know what they discussing. Doctor Bal had retreated to the group of scientists, who were all staring at the Gomar with dread.

When their conversation was over, Vox turned Li'ara. "You helped

Sef to find us. That makes you one of us." The rest of the Gomar nodded in agreement.

"What about me?" Roland asked, happy to have finally laid eyes on his Tri-rollers.

Vox scrutinised the bounty hunter and looked back at Sef. Once again, a silent conversation passed between the red-head and the giant, before the Gomar looked back at Roland. "Definitely not."

"Brilliant," he replied dryly. "We should probably leave now. Len? Len, can you hear me? Bring the *Rackham* around." Roland tapped the earpiece and cursed. "We need to go up."

As the group made to leave, Vox locked eyes with the Trillik. Roland hoped he would never be on the other end of that look. The bounty hunter was sure the doctor's twin-tail disappeared up his leg.

"I'd choose a different career if I were you..." Roland mock-saluted on his way out.

Malekk floated between the Gomar, telekinetically dragged back up the facility. It was the first time Roland had actually seen the infected Terran in person. His pale skin was stained with dark veins and his body was naked, but covered in tight bounds of nanocelium. Malekk appeared more machine than Terran now.

The Translift was beyond cramped with twelve Gomar, Li'ara, Malekk and Roland filling its four walls. The bounty hunter felt very small standing between them and he did his best not to stare at the gorgeous blonde Gomar, pushed up against him.

"Roland?" Ch'len's alarming voice came through his earpiece.

"Len?" Roland could hardly hear him.

"Roland?" The Ch'kara's next words were garbled.

The doors opened onto the platform, where Malekk's ship was standing. The next gargantuous wave was growing taller in the distance, giving them only minutes.

"Oh shit..." Li'ara wasn't looking at the wave, however, but gazing beyond it, to the *fleet* of Conclave ships hurtling towards them.

A squadron of red Darts flew overhead and circled back around, lining up the platform. Within seconds the facility was surrounded by dozens of ships, each pointing an array of cannons at the group.

"We can't fight..." Li'ara directed her words at Sef, who appeared to be in charge of the remaining Gomar. "We talked about this. We can only move forward if we work together."

Roland could see where this was going. "Len?" he said under his breath.

"There you are! I've been trying to get hold of you for ages! Listen, there's an entire fleet here!"

The bounty hunter rolled his eyes. "On point as ever, Len." Smaller ships dropped out of the larger ones descending towards them. "Listen, I'm going to hand over control of the *Rackham* to you."

Ch'len's silence spoke volumes.

"If you don't come for me, I *will* hunt you down you little gas cloud." Roland used his mental link to hand over manual control to Ch'len and wondered if he'd ever see the *Rackham* again.

TWENTY-ONE

Kalian lost track of how long he had been inside the super subconducer. The machine opened up virtual realities inside his mind, keeping him occupied while his brain chemistry was altered further. Most of these realities were spent in one-to-one sessions with Alai, the first Terran immortal. Before Savrick turned him into a beast, Alai had been the closest thing ALF had to a friend. Kalian wondered how much the AI had really told the Terran. Did Alai know about ALF's history? Where he came from? How the Terran truly came to be?

For the most part, Kalian was content to sit with this artificial Alai and be taken through various meditation techniques. It was in these quietest of moments that he learned finer aspects of his connection to the world around him. From the heartbeat of an insect to the waves of stellar radiation, everything was connected to the same dimension, swirling together in the same soup.

"You are distracted..." Alai commented in the silence of Kalian's mind.

"Sorry, I'm just thinking about... everything I guess."

"You're thinking about the Paladin. You are excited by their arrival, hopeful even, but you are also terrified of the responsibility.

Now you have a hundred thousand more souls on your shoulders." Alai's voice was soothing.

"How could you know that?" Kalian asked. "You're just a construct, created by the subconducer. If anything - and I've tried to ignore it - you're probably ALF."

Alai smiled. "I am indeed a construct, but I am not ALF. I am *you*."

"You're me?" Kalian was lost.

"The subconducer hasn't created this reality, you have." Alai gestured at the white room, bathed in soft light. To their left was an open view of familiar green fields and massive trees. They were on Evalan...

"Why am I here then? If I'm plugged into the machine I should be practicing the jumps." Kalian was indeed feeling the pressure to use his new level of power.

"You will leave this place when you are ready," Alai replied. "When the subconducer has altered the appropriate areas and supplied you with the required energy, you will know it."

Kalian eyed the Terran construct with curiosity. "So you're what... my subconscious?"

Alai responded with a gentle laugh. "Something like that. Your mind, our mind, is so much more than just consciousness and subconsciousness. Those barriers no longer exist, Kalian. It's not just you and me in here."

The open view began to fill with hundreds of Kalians, then thousands. Eventually, they filled the entire landscape, each an exact replica of Kalian.

"There are an infinite amount of Kalians all working on an infinite amount of jobs inside your mind. They all work together in harmony, aware of your needs and desires. You can recall any second of your life, be it touch, sight, sound or taste. You can command an individual cell to move through your bloodstream or multiply if you wish. Mountains can be reshaped at your fingertips and stars exhausted at your will. You can remember your birth in vivid detail and, one day, when you truly understand the mechanics of this universe, you will even be able to glimpse your death..."

Kalian felt a wave of nausea pass over him and he stumbled back from his sitting position on the floor. He rolled to the side and picked himself up on all fours as every word sank into his mind in a way that felt it could never be forgotten.

"I can't... I can't..."

Alai raised his hand and the Kalians vanished, replaced with the beautiful vista of Evalan's forestry. "What I have described is dizzying, I know. It is a future gleaned from our calculations inside the subconducer, as well as a few documented accounts from Terran history."

Kalian slumped into a seating position again. "What you're talking about is... god-like."

"Indeed, but unlike a god, you have a few *grounding* factors that keep you human." Alai's eyes shifted to his left, where a large, circular door sat in the middle of the white wall.

Kalian knew that door. Behind it was everything related to Li'ara, including a great deal of his emotions towards her.

"Li'ara is on the other side of that door," Alai continued. "You will have to open it before you can truly embrace your power."

Kalian walked over to the door and pulled on its thick handle. For all his strength, the door wouldn't budge an inch. He followed up with telekinesis, but the effect was the same.

"You're not ready to see what's on the other side of that door, yet."

"What does that mean?" Kalian was becoming frustrated with himself.

Alai smiled. "If you spent a little more time in here you would understand. Parts of your mind have already glimpsed what lies on the other side of that door, but you haven't found a way to integrate your conscious mind with the rest yet. Until then, you are unable to see everything your mind can perceive."

Before Kalian could reply to himself, a feeling of great strength filled his body. He examined his fist and felt as if he could punch through a planet if he wanted. He was ready to jump again.

"Keep it local," Alai added. "You're just practising, remember?"

Kalian nodded. "Thanks, *me*."

The destination he had in his mind's eye was clear. Kalian knew exactly where he wanted to go.

Moments later, the subconducer's helmet was being lifted from his head and the gloom of ALF's ship surrounded him again. Naydaalan doubled over in front of him and vomited on the floor, with all four of his arms supporting him. Multiple tubes and strands of nanocelium released Kalian, detaching from his suit and skin. Without their support, he fell forwards and landed face-first onto the floor.

"Take it slowly..." ALF's large hands picked him up by the shoulders, steadying him.

"I feel dizzy." Kalian couldn't focus his vision and his senses were taking in too much information again.

"Concentrate." ALF's voice started to drift away, along with the light...

"HE'S WAKING UP." The voice was deep, but Kalian couldn't identify it.

"Indeed. Give him a moment." ALF's voice came through with distinction.

Kalian opened his eyes, once again finding himself on the hovering slab in front of the subconducer. He looked to ALF, but the AI shook his head, answering the unasked question regarding surgery.

"You coped better this time," ALF explained. "Everything was where it was supposed to be, you just felt a little overwhelmed by it all, I suspect. You need to keep practising."

Naydaalan walked over and placed a hand on Kalian's shoulder. "You did well. I know that you can get us back to the Conclave."

Kalian nodded. "Thanks..."

The light filtering through the tall, slender doors was that of Hadrok's two suns. Kalian tested the strength in his legs and made for the light - he already knew where they were. The red grass was still present in every direction, with the arcing black rock dotted between. To the right of the ship was a sight Kalian had only seen in Savrick's memories. The once beautiful city of Kaldor was now a broken relic, marring the natural landscape. Its towers and spires had all but vanished, and its gleaming walls were reduced to piles of rock. Almost every foot of the city was overgrown with red weeds and green vines.

If Kaldor was to his right, then Kalian knew what was to his left. The mountain, where Savrick had raised Esabelle and found the damaged cube, dominated the horizon. It wasn't exactly as Kalian had seen it, two-hundred thousand years ago, however. The top half of the mountain was simply gone, reducing its overall height.

"I take it there's a reason you picked this particular spot on the whole planet." ALF joined him in the red field.

"I wanted to see it with my own eyes. It's different."

"The cube built the *Gommarian* using the nanocelium Savrick stole from Kaldor. It consumed the raw material of the mountain and converted it into more nanocelium. The *Gommarian* literally rose out of the mountain. Then it destroyed Kaldor and everything else."

Naydaalan came to stand on the other side of Kalian. "Savrick lived on this planet?"

"For a time," Kalian replied. "You see the dark rock, near the base of the mountain? There is a cave just to the right of it and down a little."

"Savrick's memories are extremely accurate in your mind," Naydaalan observed.

"Too accurate..." ALF commented, looming over them both.

"How long until the subconducer is ready to juice me up again?" Kalian asked, ignoring the AI's comment.

"It will take a little longer than last time. I'm trying to bring other systems online at the same time - all of which require a certain amount of power."

"Well," Kalian rolled his neck and rotated his shoulders, "you blow out the cobwebs and I'll go for a stroll."

ALF turned a condescending eye on the human. "I suggest you

spend your time in meditation. I want your next jump to be a different planet in this system. You're going to need rest before then."

Kalian brought up his clenched fist and exhaled. Everything felt different to him now. The concept of sleep or rest felt redundant to him, as he opened his senses to the alien surroundings and welcomed the input. He could feel the strength of the gravity and the speed of the planet, the oxygen being supplied by the vegetation and the carbon dioxide being inhaled in turn. The planet was moving and breathing, just as any being in the universe did.

"Kalian?" Naydaalan had taken a step closer.

Time was starting to feel like a strange idea to Kalian, who knew he could have stood perfectly still and examined every molecule of the planet, even if it took him millennia. How long had he been standing there now? How long had he contemplated Hadrok?

"Kalian." ALF rested a heavy hand on his armoured shoulder. "You have to focus on the *now*. Keep yourself grounded."

A smile crept across Kalian's face. "I don't want to stay grounded. I want to let go..."

The planet's surface dropped away in a second, leaving Naydaalan and ALF behind to become smaller and smaller. Kalian flew into the sky at speeds that would render most unconscious. Gravity lost control of him and Kalian rolled this way and that, enjoying his new found freedom. Any fear of heights disappeared, as his mind reassessed the definition of distance, speed and time. He howled into the air, forgetting for the moment all his worries and troubles and simply letting go. After a moment's introspection, Kalian wasn't sure whether he was propelling himself with telekinesis or manipulating the effect of gravity around him. Only once had he defied the laws of physics this way, but that had been under a moment of extreme stress, in which Li'ara's life hung in the balance.

The mountain Savrick had called home was directly underneath his flying form. His curiosity won over and he immediately changed course using a manoeuvre that would have snapped most ships in half. The ground expanded and rushed up to meet him until his feet gently touched down at the entrance to the mountain's cave system.

Looking over his shoulder, ALF's ship was no bigger than his thumbnail.

Cool air blew out of the cave, beckoning him in. Kalian strode into the darkness and altered the structure of his eyes to allow for perfect vision in the dark. He never stopped to decide on his path, but simply followed his instincts, which he now understood to be his subconscious mind, filtering Savrick's memories up to the surface.

The cave Esabelle had once called home was not what Kalian had been expecting. There was no evidence that anyone had ever lived here. It was a lot to expect anything after two-hundred thousand years, but the sight of being completely barren saddened Kalian in a way that surprised him. His keen eyes soon found the only aspect of the cave that wasn't natural. Across the jagged wall, where Esabelle had been penned in during Savrick's hunts, was a variety of ancient child-like drawings. Kalian had seen similar drawings on Earth, where early man had experimented with different forms of expression and storytelling.

With sensitive Terran fingers, Kalian ran his hand over the random drawings. He could detect the artificial material against the natural rock and knew instantly it was something akin to chalk.

Sitting in the same spot Esabelle once had, Kalian sighed and took in the sights and sounds of the cave. Out of respect to Esabelle, he decided to stay a while and meditate, so that he could look back on his lessons with her. It dawned on him that if he wanted, he could, in fact, relive his time with Esabelle, as if he were actually with her again.

You could see Li'ara again...

Kalian shook his head, discarding the thought. He wasn't ready to open that door, not yet...

TWENTY-TWO

Telarrek accompanied Uthor onto the bridge of the *Sentinel*, where Charge Ilo, the Laronian captain, was busy directing her crew. Having travelled to the system, in which the secret planet lay, aboard the golden *Marillion*, the Novaarian was happy to have left the ship occupied by the Highclave. Their ignorance and air of superiority were becoming more than even the ambassador could bear.

Uthor's ship, the *Nautallon*, glided by, revealing the water world that lay in the distance, several hundred thousand miles beyond the *Sentinel*'s viewport. Between the planet and the green ship was an entire fleet of Conclave security vessels, each armed to the teeth while they escorted the transport ship huddled between the fleet. Of course, even Telarrek knew that the fleet's destructive capabilities were dwarfed by the *Sentinel* and the *Marillion*. Both ships were in possession of a full complement of planet-breaker missiles.

The transport ship grew in size as it flew by the viewport. Telarrek felt one of his stomachs flip at the thought of the ship's content. The Novaarian was thrilled to know that Li'ara was indeed alive and onboard that ship, but her companions filled Telarrek with dread. Twelve Gomar were about to step foot on this ship since they had no way of incapacitating any of them. The ambassador tried not to dwell on the fact that these twelve beings had the collective power to eviscerate the entire fleet.

"Charge Ilo, report." Uthor's commanding voice demanded attention.

The Laronian captain stood from her chair. "Apologies for not meeting you in the hangar, High Charge. As you can imagine, things are somewhat delicate."

"No apologies necessary, Charge. Before the *Marillion* hit subspace, it was reported that the prisoners had already surrendered."

"That appears to be the case. The *Sentinel* hasn't long been in the system, High Charge, but after taking control, it has been reported to me that the fourteen prisoners in question were detained aboard the *Galiant* and searched. The Gomar do not carry any weapons that can be detained, but the two humans were in possession of a great deal of weaponry, especially the notorious bounty hunter, Roland North." Charge Ilo slowly licked her blue lips, as if contemplating her next words. "Also, High Charge, the Gomar have a prisoner of their own... the one identified as Malekk."

Telarrek's eyes widened in surprise. The infected Terran had been reported by Kalian to be immensely powerful.

"What was he doing here? Does everyone know about this secret planet?" Uthor asked, incredulously.

"It appears he was trying to kill the Gomar, sir. Reports from a Doctor Bal indicate that it took all of them to subdue him, but Charge Q'ol of the *Galiant* informs me that the Gomar refuse to hand the Terran over. They say it's *imperative* that Malekk is left with them."

"This complicates things..." Uthor's rocky brow creased into a frown.

"We have already stripped his ship of all relevant data. It appears he came from a system on the edge of Conclave territory. Judging by the ship in which he travelled, the journey must have taken some time. We don't know why he used this vessel, but we assume there is something more substantial on the other end. It won't take long for one of our ships to investigate; I dispatched the *Victory* some time ago."

"Very good, Charge Ilo."

An Atari crew member turned to face the trio in his chair. "Charge Ilo, the transport ship has docked in the hangar. Awaiting orders."

"I take it your cells are empty, Charge?" Uthor asked.

"Wait," Telarrek interjected. "They must be given a chance to explain. In all their time in the Conclave, have the humans ever broken our rules to do anything but help us? If Li'ara Ducarté is with them, I am certain their reason for freeing the Gomar is noble."

Uthor sighed, which sounded more like a growl. "I agree with you, Telarrek. But we cannot ignore the fact that twelve of the very same race who attacked the capital, killing thousands, are now conscious and free. Measures must be taken."

"This ship may be the crown of the fleet, Uthor, but I know it does not have the power to stop the Gomar. If they wanted to fight we would have arrived in a graveyard. They want to speak," Telarrek insisted.

Uthor looked away, considering his options. "Charge Ilo, have your helmsman contact the *Marillion*. Instruct them to keep their distance, and should we drop out of communication, even for a moment, they are to destroy the *Sentinel* without hesitation."

Charge Ilo paused, no doubt being hit by the gravity of their situation and the potential power of the beings she had just allowed aboard her ship. The Laronian nodded and turned away to give her orders.

Uthor met Telarrek's golden eyes and silently communicated the trust he was putting in the Novaarian. They were the oldest of friends, but now Telarrek was asking the Raalak to put other lives in jeopardy, including their own.

"Well there's no point in holding ceremony," Uthor announced. "Charge Ilo, have our guests brought to the bridge."

Li'ara walked side-by-side with Roland, both stripped of their weapons and scanned on a cellular level. It was promising that they had been granted permission to board the *Sentinel*, a ship full of Conclave secrets they didn't want the humans or the Gomar to learn about. Looking back at the twelve beings, all covered in hulking black armour, Li'ara supposed she was actually walking around with twelve very big bombs. Who could say no to them?

"Can you still feel the *Rackham*?" Li'ara asked quietly.

"Yep," Roland replied. "I can't be sure how close, but the signal hasn't disappeared."

It was always good to have other options.

The group was escorted by several teams of Conclave security, but the only security worth noting was the Gomar, who continued to levitate Malekk's body in the middle of their group. The infected Terran had yet to gain consciousness, but Sef had informed Li'ara that they were all, in some way, focused on keeping him that way.

The doors parted, revealing a pristine bridge, decorated with colourful holograms and tall, glass screens, overlaid in a web of data. A crew of every race in the Conclave moved around the spacious bridge, relaying commands and data to different parts of the ship. It reminded Li'ara of her time aboard the *Gommarian*, when some sense of peace had been achieved.

"Greetings of peace." Telarrek stepped out from behind a glass screen and held out all four of his arms.

"Telarrek..." Li'ara couldn't help but smile, more than happy to see the friendly face. The two embraced, with all four of Telarrek's arms wrapping around her back.

"How?" the Novaarian stepped back and asked. "How did you survive? I saw the footage of the remains... nothing could have survived that explosion, it is impossible."

Li'ara smiled and squeezed the ambassador's long fingers affectionately. "When you have a Gomar looking out for you, *impossible* starts to lose all meaning."

The Novaarian looked beyond her, to the amassing group of armoured beings. There was a level of distrust in his eyes, upon sighting the variety of tattooed faces and menacing helmets. That distrust turned to fear when he glimpsed Malekk, floating in the middle.

"Is nobody happy to see me?" Roland held up his hands.

Four heavy feet approached the bounty hunter. "Oh, I'm happy to see you, Mr. North." Uthor towered over Roland. "I have a special cell in a Raalakian maximum security prison with your name on it."

Considering he was standing in the shadow of a Raalak, Roland replied with an arrogant smile. "That sounds lovely, but I'm afraid I'm not a member of the Conclave, so... you'll just have to send me back to the human population."

Uthor dipped his face until it was inches from Roland's. "Things change, Mr. North."

Li'ara perked up. "They do? Does that mean the Highclave are considering our membership?"

Uthor returned to his full height and looked out over the Gomar. "That depends on what you say next, Miss Ducarté."

Roland groaned. "You're gonna' have to explain the whole damn thing again!" The bounty hunter turned to the blue Laronian, who appeared to be the captain of the ship. "Does this place have a bar?"

Li'ara blinked slowly in an effort to stop herself from offering the bounty hunter an expletive reply. Having given Roland an explanation of the last three months, she now felt confident in supplying the relevant information in the best possible way - after all, her current audience was far more important.

"We're all on the same side, High Charge." It seemed like a good way to start.

"You speak for them?" Uthor nodded at the Gomar with his flat head.

"Sef is their leader," Li'ara gestured at the broad Gomar, "but their concentration is required to keep Malekk docile. They have given me permission to speak for them."

There was a commotion behind Uthor and Telarrek, with the Laronian captain responding to three of her crew, who were all directing her attention to a single screen.

"Charge Ilo, report." Uthor swung his mighty rock-like legs around.

"The *Victory* has emerged from sub-space, High Charge." Ilo glanced back at her crew. "Put it on the main-viewer."

A hologram was emitted at the front of the bridge, hiding the viewport from sight. They were all seeing through the external cameras of the Conclave security vessel, *Victory*. The ship was moving in on a very familiar object.

"That's a Starforge..." Li'ara announced.

"Specs, Ilo?" Uthor's expression was impossible to discern.

Charge Ilo leaned over her helmsman and absorbed the *Victory's* data. "It's massive, sir. It looks to be identical to the construct found in the Helteron Cluster."

Telarrek cupped his long jaw. "How many did Protocorps make?"

Uthor audibly ground his teeth. "Charge Ilo, have your analysts mine the data uploaded from Shandar. I want them to specifically search for anything relating to Starforges." The Raalak looked down on Roland again. "This would be easier if you hadn't killed Kel-var Tionis..."

Roland shrugged. "My finger slipped."

"Sir!" Ilo redirected their attention to the hologram.

The Starforge was charging up, with giant bolts of purple lightning firing around the hull. The two pointed ends of the crescent-moon lit up and expelled more of the electrified bolts, until all the light show began to coalesce in the empty space, in the middle of the station.

"The *Victory* is asking for orders, High Charge." Ilo looked at her superior expectantly.

Target any of the three Starrilliums on the outer hull. Without them, it will lose power.

Li'ara couldn't have mistaken Sef's voice for anyone. "Tell them to target the Starrilliums on the hull," she interrupted.

It was too late for orders.

The lightning stopped charging around the hull and the epicentre of the fusion expanded into one black mass, blocking out the stars on the other side. The Starforge had opened up a hole in sub-space. What came through from the other side appeared to suck the air out of the *Sentinel*'s bridge, leaving them all in stunned silence.

The ship that emerged filled the entire space of the massive Starforge, almost scraping the sides and destroying the station.With a pointed end protruding first, the gargantuan ship was shaped like the tip of a spear. Its surface wasn't smooth, as the *Gommarian* had been, but was similar to that of a construction site as if the vessel was made of a network of beams and pipes with no covering.

"Is that as big as I think it is?" Roland asked in disbelief.

"Charge Ilo?" Uthor prompted.

The captain hesitated. "It's three times the size of the *Sentinel*, almost as big as the *Marillion*. Beyond that our scanners are unable to penetrate the hull."

Li'ara could hear Sef in her mind again. "Look at its design." She pointed at the image. "That's not Terran in origin. It's one of them!" Li'ara looked back at Malekk in disgust. "This is what we've been trying to warn the Highclave about since we got here! They're real, and now they're here!"

Uthor nodded slowly, but never took his dark eyes off the alien ship. "Order the *Victory* to open fire - full complement."

It won't be enough... Sef spoke into Li'ara's head.

Uthor continued his trade of commands. "Have the third and second fleet coordinate. I want them surrounding the capital immediately. Contact the fourth fleet and alert them to our status; they're to meet up with the first," Uthor nodded at the armada of ships beyond the *Sentinel*, "and provide support to the *Victory*."

The main-viewer flared, as the *Victory* opened fire with everything it had. The Nexus Class ship was among the largest in the Conclave arsenal, with enough firepower to crack open a large moon. The alien vessel took every blow, not even bothering to raise shields. The entire bridge stopped what they were doing and stared at the display. It had been a very long time since any Conclave vessel had emptied its entire munitions supply.

Explosions big and massive erupted across the bronze, alien hull, still, it did nothing to retaliate. After a few minutes, the *Victory* reported back that they had run dry of things to throw at their target.

"Wait..." Ilo was checking the helmsman's data again. "According to the *Victory's* sensor array, the enemy ship has increased in size."

Telarrek faced Uthor in alarm. "The hull is made of nanocelium. They are absorbing the energy and using it to replicate."

"It's moving!" Ilo stood up from the screen.

The alien ship turned about until its pointed end was facing the *Victory*. It grew larger in the main-viewer, as it consumed the external camera's scope.

"Get them out of there!" Uthor ordered.

Ilo went back to work, but it was too late. The alien ship ploughed into the *Victory* and the feed went dead, collapsing the hologram. Li'ara could only imagine the chaos on the other end.

The expected moment of silence never came, with Uthor proving his worth. "Charge Ilo, I am using my emergency powers; as of this moment, let the record show that I am assuming full authority over Conclave security. To that effect, have the *Marillion* evacuate the Highclave and shuttled back to the capital - I want that ship under my command by the time I'm finished speaking. Re-direct the third fleet to meet us at the Starforge's coordinates."

It won't be there when they arrive, Sef said. *It's not looking for a confrontation, Li'ara. There's only one thing it wants, one thing it's always wanted...*

Li'ara stepped forward, halting Uthor's next order. "It didn't come here to fight *you*. Whatever they are, they might have designs on the Conclave, but you're not what they've been focusing on for the last two-hundred thousand years. Doesn't it seem too much of a coincidence, that when a hundred thousand more humans arrive and the only surviving Gomar are free, that this thing should show up?"

"What are you saying, Miss Ducarté?" Uthor loomed over her.

Telarrek answered, "The humans. It has come for the humans..."

"We need to go to Arakesh and intercept it, before-"

Uthor cut Li'ara short. "Course correction! Have the third fleet meet us at Arakesh! And have the human habitation alerted to our situation. I advise immediate evacuation."

Li'ara smiled in relief. They were finally starting to believe them.

"High Charge," Ilo turned around, "the Highclave are protesting your orders."

"Are they off the *Marillion*?" he inquired.

"Yes sir, the *Nautallon* is escorting them."

"Good, then have that big, golden ball of destruction ready to jump with the rest of us!"

TWENTY-THREE

"What the hell is that thing?" Captain Holt spoke up, over the alarms blaring across the human habitat.

Captain Fey cupped her mouth, unable to prevent the expression of despair that overcame her. Jed decided he would prefer to never see that look again. Li had been calm and collected through some of the weirdest things Jed had ever seen in his life, but the image of that massive ship emerging from the Starforge stunned Fey to silence.

"Li?" Jed repeated his question.

"It's one of them. They've finally decided to get their hands dirty."

Jed looked from the holographic feed to the masses beyond Fey's office, who were now being herded towards the docking area. It was chaos.

The door opened and Laurence Wynter flew in. "Where are the evacuation shuttles?"

Jed had only known the man for a day or so and he already couldn't stand the sound of his voice. When this was all over, the captain decided that something had to be done about this whole council thing. It seemed to Jed that more than a few of them weren't fit to make decisions on behalf of the human race. Just thinking about the new population size was enough to make his shoulders visibly sag.

"They're on their way," Fey assured. "The Raalakian high council has already sent word."

"Have you seen what that thing did to the *Victory*?" Wynter was becoming hysterical. "We aren't all going to be evacuated in time! Why aren't we using those shuttles in the engineering bay?"

Fey pinched her eyes. "Those are maintenance shuttles for repairing the habitat. They can't fit more than a couple of people inside. We mustn't panic, Laurence..."

Wynter's mouth fell open in shock. "Not Panic? Did you even read the alert from High Charge Uthor? That thing is coming to exterminate us!"

"Colonel Matthews?" Jed shouted above the councillor. The Raider marched into the office with her usual mean expression. "Please see to it that Councillor Wynter here finds his way to the evacuation area."

Ava nodded and roughly gripped Laurence's jacket, yanking him from the room in a shower of protests.

"Thank you," Fey said, "but we have to be careful with our authority, or the word dictatorship is going to start being thrown around."

Jed held up his hands. "I apologise. I just couldn't listen to another word..."

Li smiled. "Indeed."

"He does have a point though," Jed continued. "The Raa... Raa... the evacuation shuttles aren't even in sight yet. According to that report, the system in which it arrived isn't far from here."

"What we need is more time." Fey couldn't take her eyes off the image of the giant ship.

Jed agreed, but he didn't have an answer for her. The captain sat back in the chair, behind Fey's desk, and looked up, through the skylight. The view gave a clear line of sight to the transparent dome above, where the Paladin floated effortlessly.

"Where's the engineering bay?" he asked.

"Why?" Captain Fey gave him a curious look.

"There might be no way to slow that thing down... but there might be one way of speeding up the evacuation."

BY THE TIME the *Sentinel* and the fourth fleet emerged from sub-space, the third fleet had already arrived in the Arakesh system and engaged the enemy ship. Roland peeked over the helmsman's shoulder and saw their position put them on the edge of the Raalakian solar system. The alien ship was taking a battering, as it hurtled towards a distant moon, orbiting a giant gas planet. The third fleet surrounded it and matched its speed, never letting up for a second.

"Every hit increases its size!" one of the crew barked.

"Why has it jumped to the outskirts?" Roland asked out loud. Judging by the looks he received, the bounty hunter was the first one to ponder its choice of destination.

Everyone turned back to the viewport, where the distant moon was no longer so distant. Uthor strode down the centre aisle and commanded the image be magnified. Roland noted the confusion on everyone's face, even the Gomar appeared distressed by the sight. The pointed behemoth ploughed through space, ignoring the Conclave ships, and headed straight for the moon.

"What is it doing?" Telarrek asked.

The Novaarian's answer came with an unsettling image across the viewport. Most of the bridge crew gasped when the massive ship dived into the moon, creating a plume of debris that masked the destruction.

"It must have been damaged," Charge Ilo commented, with a hint of hope in her voice. "Perhaps our barrage disrupted its navigation array."

The debris continued to disguise the surface of the moon where the ship had nose-dived into the rock. Roland narrowed his vision to the area around the hurricane of dust and noted the expanding cracks.

"I don't think it's damaged..." The bounty hunter ignored the helmsman's sour look and changed the area of magnification himself.

The cracks were growing outwards from the point of entry and quickly becoming as large as valleys. The fleet had come to a halt above the surface but continued to launch everything into what must have been a large crater by now.

An alert flashed up, prompting the helmsman's report. "High Charge, we're picking up mass disruption across the entire moon."

"That'll happen when an entire fleet offloads its goods onto the surface," Roland flippantly commented.

The helmsman clarified, "The disruption is seismic. It's coming from within the moon..."

Uthor puffed out his mighty chest. "This isn't over yet."

The moon physically changed shape, with entire sections imploding inwards, towards the core. Roland observed the devastating phenomenon, likening the effects to that of a black hole. Sef shifted his sizeable weight and placed a hand on Vox's shoulder. The two appeared to hold a brief discussion before the mean-looking redhead spoke up.

"The ship is made from pure nanocelium." Everyone turned to listen. "Given an appropriate resource, nanocelium will consume and replicate."

Vox's words illuminated a new type of fear across the variety of alien expressions. Roland had seen that kind of fear consume the best of soldiers; the realisation that their enemy couldn't be defeated.

"So... It's just having lunch?" Roland's levity wasn't appreciated.

Uthor swivelled back to the viewport. "Move the fleets round to the other side of the moon!"

The *Sentinel*'s main engines came online, pushing the lengthy, green ship over the top of the moon.

Roland...

The bounty hunter heard Sef's distinct voice echo inside his mind and felt somewhat ridiculous when he replied with a questioning thought.

Where is the Rackham? Sef asked.

Close. Len's keeping perfectly quiet for the first time in his miserable life.

In truth, Roland was surprised that the Ch'kara had actually followed them, expecting the little gas cloud to have moved on to a new life with the most advanced ship in his possession.

Have him dock the Sentinel. Sef's tone was irritatingly commanding.

You fixing to cut and run, Mr. Gomar?

Roland turned around and offered a cheeky smile as if Sef was coming round to his way of thinking. With that in mind, the bounty hunter realised he had yet to assess the environment, as he normally did. By now he should have already located his exit strategy and made an effort to disappear. Why was he sticking around?

The Rackham can be adapted for combat. It can fire nanocelium missiles capable of cancelling out the nanocelium inside that ship. Sef sounded more than a little impatient.

"Well, when you put it like that..." Roland accidentally responded out loud, eliciting a strange look from Telarrek.

The bounty hunter shrugged and turned away while using his mental link to the *Rackham* to make contact. Thankfully, the ship was only a couple of miles off the *Sentinel's* starboard bow, keeping it within range. Roland only wished he could see Ch'len's face when he lost control.

"We have a plan," Li'ara announced, gathering everyone's attention. "The *Rackham* is going to board and we're going to join the fight."

Roland couldn't help the height of his eyebrows, which jumped into his forehead. Li'ara gave him a look, which told of her knowledge on the matter. Roland hadn't known Li'ara was listening to their mental conversation... That was going to be annoying.

Uthor frowned his rocky brow. "And how is the *Rackham* going to help?"

"It has nanocelium-based weaponry," Li'ara replied. "It might be the only thing that makes a dent."

Uthor looked over the Gomar and rested on Malekk's unconscious form, before turning to Roland. "I take it the *Rackham* is close by... I'm afraid I cannot allow it. I want you all where I can see you, not disappearing in a ship we can't track." The Raalak fixed Roland with a lasting look of derision.

"Uthor..." Telarrek silently pleaded with his old friend, but the Raalak's attention was drawn to the viewport, along with everyone else.

The *Sentinel* had reached the other side of the moon now, along with the fleets, who had taken up attack positions again. It made no difference. The moon's surface imploded in a single spot, before exploding with the emergence of the enemy ship. It was much bigger than when it had entered the moon; Roland didn't need sensor feedback to tell him that. Its bronze hull shot out of the moon with a force similar to an intrinium bolt leaving a Tri-roller. Three of the ships in the third fleet were obliterated instantly on impact, their explosions rippling across the alien hull, which continued its journey into the heart of the Raalakian system.

"World Breakers - NOW!" Uthor commanded without hesitation.

Ilo relayed his order to the select fleet vessels that possessed the planet-ending missiles, as well as the *Marillion*. Roland had wanted to see the effects of these weapons since he first heard of them, though using them on a ship would be less impressive than using it on an actual planet. The bounty hunter could feel the *Rackham* secretly entering the hangar bay of the *Sentinel*, but he couldn't tear his eyes away from the viewport.

"Nineteen World Breakers have been launched, sir!" one of the bridge crew announced.

Silence settled over the bridge, as they watched nineteen brilliantly blue missiles streak across the vastness of space. One after another, the missiles collided with the alien ship and erupted in a flash that had to be dimmed by the viewport. Roland watched the data on the helmsman's holographic screen. The report wasn't good.

"Speed, hull strength, it's not even wobbled off course!" Roland looked at Uthor.

"It's retaliating!" Charge Ilo gasped.

Golden arcs flew through the black of space and detonated

against the inferior hulls of the Conclave fleet. A Nexus class vessel, in the centre of the fleet, flashed, imitating a supernova and consumed four smaller ships surrounding it. The Starrillium had been ruptured violently, just as the Valoran had when Roland killed the majority of the Gomar, a year ago.

Uthor slammed his solid fist on the nearest console. "Match speed and continue to fire everything we have. No ship is to stop until all munitions are spent!" The Raalakian turned to the Gomar and Li'ara. "Can the *Rackham* really have any effect?"

"We have to try." Li'ara glanced at Roland, making certain the ship was available.

Uthor let out a gravelly sigh. "If you can make a hole in that thing, we can fire another world breaker into it. You have permission to dock, Mr. North."

"The *Rackham* landed a couple of minutes ago." Roland patronisingly patted the High Charge on the arm and made for the exit.

JED STOOD OVER HELMSMAN MALOY, the only two on the bridge of the Paladin. The first Raalakian rescue ship, which could only take a maximum of a hundred people, had created chaos across the habitat. The Conclave Watch that ensures the humans never strayed beyond the habitat's environment was too busy to notice one small engineering ship depart. The pair had wasted no time, sprinting to the bridge, and firing up the arc ship's solar drive.

"We don't have nearly enough solarcite to make a jump, Sir," Maloy reported. "We could make a run for the nearest sun, but based on the data we received, that ship is travelling much faster than our sub-light engines could ever handle."

Jed could feel the beads of sweat dripping down his cheeks. "We don't have a choice, Maloy. I didn't travel two hundred years into the future to lie down and die. Dock us over there."

The captain left Maloy to do his job, instead turning to the communication array. The evacuation would go quicker if Captain

Fey knew where to herd everyone. It was going to be a tight squeeze since the Paladin was only designed to hold a hundred thousand occupants. Still, a tight squeeze was better than death.

He only hoped they had time.

ROLAND FELL into his captain's chair with delight, enjoying its familiar feel. Ch'len had practically imploded when four of the twelve Gomar entered the bridge. Sef had explained that the rest were staying in the hold to focus their efforts on keeping Malekk comatose. Something about having the infected Terran onboard the *Rackham* disturbed the bounty hunter.

The *Rackham* slowly lifted off the *Sentinel's* deck and turned towards the rectangular exit. Roland blew on his hands and rubbed them together, before setting them down on the main control console.

"Let's skip to the good bit..."

The *Rackham* shot out of the *Sentinel* and made a quick course correction to keep in line with the green ship. What was left of the fleets continued to dog the alien vessel, with the *Marillion* offering salvo after salvo of munitions. The enemy ship took every hit, offering two of its own for every missile that found its bronze hull. The third and fourth fleet were losing numbers by the second.

Roland veered the ship to the starboard and careened over the top of the *Sentinel*. The newest ship in the fleet had taken a battering across the bow, though they had hardly felt it prior to lifting off, a testament to the mighty ship's design. The golden orb of the *Marillion* was impossible to miss, as it slowly overtook the fleet and approached the enemy vessel from the port side. Patches of scorched black marred the golden surface and trailed dying fire and dissipating smoke. No ship could avoid the enemy's targeting apparently.

Except maybe one...

The *Rackham* soon left the *Sentinel* behind and slipped between the red Conclave ships, weaving and dodging the sporadic explosions. Hundreds of red Darts poured out of the Nebula Class vessels and dropped into attack patterns, but the enemy ship had only to unleash one salvo to create a chain reaction, killing them all.

"Whatever you're going to do, do it fast," Roland said, his concentration split. "We'll be within weapons range soon."

One of the Nebula Class vessels took a critical hit, halting its trajectory immediately. The size of the ship forced the *Rackham* to dive or fly straight into its dying engines. The Nebula continued to rupture and explode as the *Rackham* flew under its belly, every new explosion sending vibrations through the hull.

Vox stood forward. "Garrion, Ariah..." The red-head gestured for the Gomar to take up positions either side of the bridge.

Sef nodded once at Vox and left the bridge. Roland's internal sensors told the bounty hunter that the big Gomar was heading for the hold again. Was Malekk waking up? The break in concentration almost cost them all their lives, when Roland made a quick correction to avoid a floating piece of debris, ten times the size of the *Rackham*.

"Would you like *me* to fly?" Li'ara offered.

Roland gritted his teeth and focused on the viewport. "Backseat drivers..."

Several alerts flashed across the console, informing him of multiple changes to the ship's structure. Before Roland could ask what they were doing to his ship, a new message appeared, explaining that Garrion and Ariah were now manning weapons stations. New consoles and chairs formed upwards, out of the nanocelium decking, and created perfect working stations.

"I'm taking command," Vox announced.

"The hell you are!" Roland had more follow up remarks and insults, but the chair was literally taken out from under him.

Ch'len, Li'ara and himself suddenly found themselves floating above the consoles as if gravity had forgotten them. Roland wiggled about in an effort to reach the floor again, but all three of them were completely suspended.

"What's happening?" Ch'len squealed.

Vox replied calmly, "I've put you all into a stasis field." The Gomar tapped her temple, indicating the lack of technology involved. "We're putting the ship into attack mode. You won't survive the kind of manoeuvres we will be forced to use. Artificial gravity has been deactivated, along with the inertial dampeners." Despite this fact, all three of the Gomar were standing and sitting perfectly at their stations.

"I'm not happy about this!" Everyone ignored Roland.

The enemy ship had consumed the viewport by now. The *Marillion* had been forced to back away, slowly dropping behind the fleets. The golden ship had taken the brunt of the enemy's retaliation in an attempt to shield them from the constant barrage.

"The *Marillion* has lost FTL capability," Garrion said. The male Gomar wore his dreadlocks down to the middle of his back, but it was his vibrant blue eyes against his dark skin that constantly caught Roland's attention.

"As long as the *Sentinel* is with us," Vox replied. "We need at least one of those World Breakers."

"We're in range," Ariah, a typically beautiful blonde Gomar, announced.

"Concentrate on the same coordinates. Do not fire unless you have a perfect target lock, we can't afford to waste ammunition scratching the sides." Vox was stood in the centre of the bridge, surrounded by holographic readouts and consoles that dropped from the ceiling.

The viewport blurred suddenly when the *Rackham* changed direction with enough speed to have killed its inhabitants. Defying the inertia, the three Gomar remained fixed in place, while Roland and the others remained suspended in line with the ship's movements. Had the bounty hunter still been in his chair, the manoeuvre would have slammed him into the wall and reduced him to mush.

The image in the viewport only levelled out for a moment before another sharp turn was required. Their increasing proximity to the enemy ship was making it harder to evade. Every missile that missed its mark continued on to destroy one of the Conclave vessels. Roland kept his eyes on the console beneath him, watching the readouts from the Gomar's assault. The *Rackham* was firing energy based munitions, as well as missiles comprised of nanocelium. Their aim was uncanny, with the two Gomar syncing their shots perfectly on the same patch of hull. Their firing only stopped when a sudden change in direction was required. More than once Roland thought he saw the projectile that would be the end of them, but Vox always dodged it. Either that or she was using her abilities to re-direct the missiles.

"I'm opening a channel with the *Sentinel*," Vox said. "Charge Ilo, respond."

"*We're here... erm.*" The alien hesitated with the name.

"You need to pull the fleet back," Vox suggested immediately. "Have them surround the *Sentinel* to bolster your shields."

"*What?*" Ilo sounded horrified.

"We're going to cut a hole in that thing soon. When we do there's only going to be a short time to fire a world breaker into the heart of it. The *Sentinel* must survive long enough to launch that missile. Sacrifices must be made if your ship is to last much longer. My sensors indicate that forty-five percent of the *Sentinel* is already beyond repair, it's targeting your engines."

There was a pause on the other end. "*Redeploying now.*"

"Be ready for that opening." Vox cut the feed.

The *Rackham* came back up on the enemy's port side and continued to hail a rain of nanocelium hell across the hull. Roland looked up from the console below and noted the giant gas planet coming up on the starboard side of the enemy ship. That planet was the closest neighbour to Arakesh, the Raalakian homeworld and the current location of humanity's remnants. They were getting closer.

"That's it!" Garrion shouted. "We can't fire any more projectiles without compromising the *Rackham*'s structural integrity."

"We still have energy-based projectiles," Ariah commented, her focus never wavering from the holographics.

"It doesn't matter now," Vox observed. "That hole's plenty big enough."

They all watched as the *Sentinel* slowly came up on their port side and overtook their pursuit. Hundreds of Conclave vessels were being picked off by the enemy ship, which had yet to slow down or drop into an attack pattern. The *Sentinel*'s green hull was awash with flashes of exploding ships, though more than one found a hole in the protective net, punched through the shields and into the green hull.

"Come on…" Roland muttered under his breath. "Fire it!"

"They're hit!" Garrion called out. "The *Sentinel*'s main engines have been taken out."

The gas giant dominated the starboard viewport now, its swirling orange and red surface mixing together like oil. Lightning danced across the storm that consumed a whole quarter of the planet's upper hemisphere. Roland could see what was going to happen before Garrion finished his report.

"They're falling behind," Garrion continued. "They're caught in the planet's gravity well."

"Where's the *Marillion*?" Ariah asked.

"They're not even on our sensors anymore," Vox replied with dismay.

The enemy ship continued ever onward, oblivious to the path of sheer destruction it had left in its wake. Even the *Rackham* was backing off now, the bronze ship losing its size with every second, every second that brought it closer to Arakesh.

"What do we do?" Ariah sat back, concern etched across her beautiful features.

"We chase it down and find another way to bring it down." Vox was already redirecting power levels to the engines.

"Wait!" Li'ara shouted. "We can't just leave the *Sentinel* to fall into the planet. That kind of atmosphere will crush it."

Vox turned from her station. "If we waste time saving them, we risk the death of every human. A few human lives are more precious than those of a few aliens."

"They do have World Breakers onboard…" Roland pointed out.

That gave Vox pause. The Gomar knew that it was the only way to destroy the hulking ship, but it also meant killing their pursuit. They were hunters, after all, trained by Savrick to seek and destroy, nothing more.

"Wait wait wait..." Ch'len held his stubby hands out. "Even if we do stay and help or borrow a world breaker or whatever... How exactly are we going to help a sinking ship?"

They all turned to the viewport where the *Sentinel*, surrounded by debris, was slowly falling into the gas giant's atmosphere.

"He's got a point," Roland agreed. "It's a little big to tow..."

Vox sighed and looked from Garrion to Ariah. "Not for us."

Within minutes, artificial gravity and the inertial dampeners had been restored and everyone was in the hold. The *Rackham* had been placed above the gas giant, directly over the falling *Sentinel*. Roland threw his long coat aside, feeling the heat and the sweat that quickly built up when one thought they were going to die. He stood now, side by side, with Li'ara and even Ch'len, who found the whole plan hard to believe.

Three of the twelve Gomar took Malekk aside and crouched low over his body. Of the two faces Roland could see, the Gomar were deep in concentration since they were keeping the infected Terran subdued on their own. Sef stood the furthest away, in front of the ramp, with eight of his brothers and sisters behind him. They had discussed their strategy for all of ten seconds, each apparently understanding perfectly what was required of them.

The ramp dropped down, exposing the vastness of space before them, or at least it would have, had the gas giant not inhabited the entire view. The turbulent planet churned, as a hungry god, ready to devour the *Sentinel*. One of the Gomar, Roland hadn't a clue which, was keeping a barrier erected at all times, preventing them all from being turned inside out. Apparently, they needed to see the *Sentinel* to help their concentration, since their abilities weren't refined enough to pull off the incredible feat blind.

"Together..." Vox's confidence and determination were inspiring - and something of a turn-on for Roland.

He really hoped they weren't reading his mind at this point.

As one, the eight Gomar reached out, as if they could actually grab the green ship. More than one of them was dragged across the floor in their bid to pull the ship upwards. They were literally fighting the gravity well of the biggest planet in the system.

"Holy shit..." Roland was nudged by Li'ara and given a scornful look.

Many of them grunted and shouted out, not dissimilar to Roland when he lifted weights or took a particularly big shit. Sef held up both of his hands and shifted his broad shoulders, his entire frame now on an impossible angle towards the floor. One of the females, Roland had yet to be introduced to, dropped to her knees with her arms outstretched and an expression of agony to match.

The *Sentinel* tumbled end-over-end, as the top of the planet's atmosphere engulfed it, licking the hull with lightning. In moments it was completely hidden beneath a thick layer of stormy weather, where the pressure would slowly go to work on reducing its considerable size.

A Gomar on the edge of the group dropped to the floor, unconscious, with a nosebleed. It was only seconds later that all but Sef were on their knees, struggling to maintain any grip on the *Sentinel*. The three Gomar, surrounding Malekk, had left the infected Terran and joined in the effort to lift the doomed ship. Roland hadn't noticed and wondered how long they had been assisting. If Malekk woke up there would be nothing he or Liara could do to stop him. Without thought, one of his Tri-rollers was in his hand.

"Keep... going!" Vox shouted over their combined strain. Still, the green hull was nowhere to be seen.

The three Gomar had dropped to their knees now, their energy already depleted from containing Malekk. Sef stood defiant, a giant among gods. His face visibly shook from the effort he exerted. It didn't matter however, Roland could see where this was going. The planet would devour the *Sentinel* and Telarrek and Uthor with it, not to mention the World Breakers and any chance of stopping the enemy ship. The Gomar simply weren't refined enough to achieve such a feat.

Then he saw it.

The bow of the green hull poked out from the stormy surface and continued to rise. Li'ara gasped, but not at the sight of the *Sentinel*. Malekk had found his feet in Roland's moment of distraction. Instead of killing them all, however, he stood behind the Gomar with his own arms outstretched, adding to their magnificent pull. Roland was already levelling his Tri-roller when Li'ara pushed his arm down.

"He's helping," Li'ara whispered, barely able to believe her own words.

The *Sentinel* continued to rise until its entire body had been lifted from the planet. Soon it was free of the gravity well and levelled out before the *Rackham*. The Gomar turned around and stared at Malekk, who cradled his head and ignored them. Bar two, the rest of the Gomar stood up and began to circle Malekk, pushing Roland and Li'ara away.

"Help...me.." Malekk's voice was different, more organic somehow. "I don't know how long I can..." The infected Terran dropped to his knees and cried out in agony. The parasite was winning back control. "You have to... kill me!"

Sef stepped forward and slammed his armoured fist into Malekk's face, ending his pain.

We need to resume our guard over his mind. Sef's voice held no trace of his visible exhaustion.

Li'ara was already keying in commands to the wall-console. "*Sentinel*, this the *Rackham*, respond."

There was only silence on the other end, leading Li'ara to ask for a response again and again.

"This is the *Sentinel*." Telarrek's voice finally came back. "We have many casualties... and even more fatalities."

"What happened?" Uthor came over the line, sounding somewhat dishevelled.

Li'ara looked out over the exhausted faces. "The Gomar saved you."

Roland whirled his finger around. "World Breaker... extinction of humanity..."

"High Charge, we need one of the *Sentinel*'s World Breakers as soon as possible. There's a hole in the enemy's hull and we still have enough power to chase it down."

"Consider it done, but do not linger any longer than you must. The *Marillion* will be along soon to assist us. You must destroy that ship, Miss Ducarté. I fear that once it is done with your people, it will move onto my homeworld."

"We're on it." Li'ara was resolute in her reply.

Roland sighed. "If I help to save the galaxy one more time, my whole reputation is going to be in tatters..."

TWENTY-FOUR

Kalian soared through the air, comfortable inside the bubble of telekinetic energy that enveloped him. He had successfully managed two more jumps since their arrival on Hadrok, but he had contained the teleportation to the planet rather than jump around the system. Whether he was comfortable yet or he just wanted to defy ALF, he wasn't sure. Every time, the machine had required maintenance and Kalian had required some time to collect himself. It was getting easier though. With the added energy from ALF's ship, the jumps were almost becoming enjoyable. The universe suddenly felt very small to Kalian.

In between the jumps, Kalian would take to the sky and revel in his new found power. Any fear of heights was quickly conquered by the confidence that swelled within him. Naydaalan had voiced his concerns about such unorthodox downtime, insisting that he spend it in meditation. The only conclusion that Kalian came to, however, was that the Novaarian was spending too much time around ALF.

Flying through the sky made him feel free more than anything else. The burden of getting them home, saving humanity from the Vanguard or even just getting his head around ALF's secrets. The fact that an alter ego of the AI had been responsible for the creation of the Gomar was unsettling, but learning that even the Terran had been just another artificial design, as humanity had been, was mind-bending - and this was coming from a man who was currently flying five thousand feet above the ground.

While in the super subconducer, Kalian had taken the opportunity to look into ALF's organic mind and explore more of Evalan, their true birthplace. The Terran and indeed the human population had been engineered to be smaller in stature due to Albadar's size. From what Kalian could tell, that was the only difference. Their planet had been beautiful, without a single man-made eyesore on the horizon. The indigenous population had yet to master such ways of living when ALF came across them. But just as Earth had been destroyed and Albadar rendered uninhabitable, Evalan was no more. It seemed that everywhere humanity put its feet, the soil beneath it would be tainted and destined for destruction. Perhaps with the Conclave looking out for them and their new world, a new way of living could be found.

That's if we ever get a new world, Kalian thought. He suddenly had the wild idea of transporting everyone across the galaxy and inhabiting a forgotten world of the Terran. That was after they disabled whatever traps Savrick had left behind. How he would transport over a hundred thousand people, he had no idea.

As his thoughts began to drown in responsibility again, so too did his flight drift ever downwards, until he found himself touching down outside ALF's ship. They were on the other side of Hadrok now, thousands of miles away from Esabelle's first home. The fields of red grass were nowhere in sight, but the ship now sat on the edge of a giant lake. Thankfully, for Naydaalan's sake, there had been some alien form of edible fish in the water. Kalian had declined the food, stating that ALF's machine was keeping him perfectly sustained. Naydaalan had voiced his concerns on this as well, believing that nothing could replace traditional nourishment. The Novaarian's protests had given Kalian pause, as it dawned on him that with every passing day he felt more and more apart from the rest of the galaxy, and yet he had never been so connected to it.

One of the twin suns was just beginning to touch the horizon, while its sister continued to shine high above them. Naydaalan was going through his routines, practicing various Novaarian fighting techniques. ALF was inside, as he always was, tinkering with the machine's next upgrade. Considering he had been locked away inside a volcano for thousands of years, the cyborg had no gumption to explore the outside world.

"Caught any fish today?" Kalian called over to Naydaalan, who shook his head with disappointment.

Kalian smiled, hoping that would be his answer. With a single, outstretched hand, he felt for life within the lake, ignoring the plant life and the constant flow of molecules. The fish stood out immediately, their collection of molecules far more complex than that of their surroundings, though they were oblivious to his attention. Kalian flipped his hand, palm upwards, and lifted three alien fish from the depths of the lake. He was moments from breaking their necks when ALF called out from within his ship.

"Come quickly!" he yelled.

Both Kalian and Naydaalan ran through the over-sized doors, abandoning the fish to live out their lives. ALF stood in the centre of his ship, manipulating dozens of machines at once with his hands outstretched as if he were a conductor. Above them all, floated the broken cube the AI had been using to spy on the Conclave. New tubes of nanocelium were disconnecting and reconnecting at different ports, hidden inside its bronze husk.

"What's wrong?" Kalian asked, unaware of any danger around them.

"Something is happening in the Conclave." ALF had the same faraway expression his holographic counterpart always had when learning of something no one else could see. "Malekk has failed to kill the Gomar."

That was good news, but ALF's look of concern didn't offer much hope.

"Is he dead?" Kalian had to know. Only the Gomar had the power to kill Malekk since he was on the other side of the galaxy.

"The cubes don't know," ALF replied. "One of them has activated their Starforge and..." The AI gasped quietly. "The Vanguard has entered Conclave space."

"Where?" Naydaalan asked, all four of his fists clenched.

"Arakesh."

Kalian's face dropped. "The habitat. It's going to destroy the habitat!"

ALF lowered his arms and cupped his wide jaw. "They risk much by exposing themselves like this. The element of surprise-"

"Isn't needed when you know you're already more superior than your prey." Kalian was pacing now. "They aren't afraid of facing the Conclave in a straight fight, especially if it means they can wipe us out first."

Naydaalan stepped between ALF and Kalian. "I still do not understand why they would risk anything by targeting the humans. The Gomar are a threat, and yourself, but the humans on that habitat are powerless. They must know this."

"It's not just the abilities ALF gave us," Kalian explained. "It's our natural resistance. They're afraid of being infected, or at least the big three at the top are. They have the perfect drone army under their control, each one a member of their original race. Any interaction with humans has the potential to undo that. Our natural resistance has the power to set them free, creating...." Kalian looked at ALF, the perfect example, "chaos."

Something about his own explanation didn't sit right with Kalian. ALF was unable to provide a suitable answer for humanities natural resistance to nanocelium.

"We have to get back, now." Naydaalan fixed Kalian with his golden eyes.

ALF rested his overly large hand on Kalian's shoulder. "Are you ready to make such a jump? We haven't practiced one planet to another yet."

"But I have done it," Kalian pointed out.

ALF raised his eyebrow. "You almost died in the process. You might recall your organs being in the wrong place?"

"Naydaalan's right. We have to get back now. There's nothing else that can stop the Vanguard."

"And you believe that you can?" ALF asked, incredulously.

"No." Kalian smiled. "But I know you can. I've been having a little look inside this ship of yours. These enhancements you've given me allow for a greater insight into, well... everything. I've seen the arsenal you have. You said it yourself; you were the old vanguard, before this new one."

"I am more than aware of my capabilities, Kalian. I fear you over-estimate your own. Humanity cannot afford to lose you."

Kalian could hear Li'ara's voice in his head - something he thought he had under control. "It's the right thing, and that's all we can do... it's all we should do."

ALF bowed his head, satisfied with Kalian's answer. The super subconducer fell back into place and the broken cube disappeared into the darkness above.

Naydaalan stopped Kalian from taking his position with a firm hand. "It took me longer than my father to see the potential in your people and the good they could bring to the Conclave. Regardless of how long I live, the greatest honour of my life will be to have called you friend."

Kalian responded with a genuine smile. "If it wasn't for the work and trust you and your father have for us, humanity would be in a far darker hole. It's because of you that I call all Novaarians friend."

Kalian took his place under the descending helmet of wires and tubes, aware that this next jump might be his last. Even if it was, he was happy to die knowing that he had saved his entire species in the process. In some way, Kalian knew he had come out here to die. A part of him had lost hope and knew that the Terran Empire would offer a fight he might not win. At least this death was less cowardly.

The faintest of pricks alerted him to the needles piercing his skin, as the tubes wormed under the plating of his black armour. Kalian let go of reality and allowed his consciousness to be pulled down, into the depths of his mind. Flashes of Evalan ran across his vision, followed by scenes from Savrick's life, both before and after Esabelle was born, and then moments from his own life thundered by and his parents' faces smiled back at him.

The images disappeared as quickly as they flashed before him. Now he was standing in a familiar white room, one of the walls replaced with the serene horizon of Evalan. The vault door loomed over him, almost surrounding his peripheral vision.

"You know what's on the other side," a familiar voice said. Alai, the first immortal, was sitting in the middle of the room, with his back to Evalan.

"Why am I here?" Kalian asked. "I need to jump the ship!" Despite time having almost no meaning with the speed at which he was able to think, Kalian still felt the urgency of his mission.

"If you want to jump, you're going to have to open that door." Alai was calm as ever, his long black hair touching the floor.

"I don't need..." Kalian couldn't even think it. "Li'ara will just cloud everything. I won't be able to focus." He didn't want to deal with her death, not now, not ever.

"Your jumps thus far have been instinctual, mostly based on the memories of others. Now you will need to select your destination, you will have to see it."

Kalian frowned at his own subconscious. "You're saying that if I open that door, I'll be able to *see* where I want to go?"

Alai smiled. "Life is a series of discoveries. You'll never know if you don't look."

Kalian sighed. "You should get a job writing fortune cookies."

The circular door appeared impenetrable and foreboding, but inside his mind its weight was inconsequential. With a single hand, waved across the surface, the door rolled aside.

At first, Kalian couldn't make sense of what he was seeing. His mind worked at incredible speeds to analyze the view and determine the truth behind it. Initially, he knew it wasn't a memory of Li'ara since she had never been on the *Rackham* with several Gomar. The entire image was frozen as if he were looking at a real size photograph of an event he couldn't understand. Li'ara was standing on the bridge of the *Rackham* with six Gomar and Roland, who appeared to be piloting. Beyond the viewport, Kalian could see their pursuit of a giant ship, unmistakably the Vanguard. In the distance was Arakesh, the Raalakian homeworld and the human habitat.

Tears ran down his face when the truth suddenly dawned on him. He turned back to look at Alai, the representation of his subconscious, who had already figured out the truth behind the meaning of the vault door, days ago.

"What exactly am I looking at?" Kalian reached out, sure that he could touch Li'ara if he wanted.

"I wouldn't do that," Alai was quick to respond. "If you cross the threshold, while connected to ALF's ship, you'll jump inside the *Rackham*. Physics might not have much meaning in here, but out there, it'll turn the *Rackham* inside out trying to fit ALF's ship onto the bridge."

"This is real, then?" Kalian turned back to Li'ara, desperate to hold her.

"Your link to her is just as, if not stronger, than your connection to Savrick or even ALF now. She has always been at the heart of your focus, Kalian. Right now you're looking over the curve. Time, space, gravity... While you're being powered by ALF's ship, these concepts cannot bar you."

Kalian couldn't find the words to fit his emotions. "She's alive. How can she be alive?"

"Sef." Alai's response was simple, if baffling.

"You can't know that. If I don't know it, then you can't..."

"Now you're catching on. I am you, just unfiltered. I don't have the emotions and moral compass that fog every thought and action. I'm more..."

"Machine," Kalian finished.

"Precisely. Sef is the most logical choice since Esabelle told you to find him, suggesting that he is, in fact, alive and operating unseen in the Conclave. You also know that the rest of the Gomar was imprisoned at the time of Li'ara's supposed death, leaving Sef the only option. There's a very real chance he's even on that bridge right now."

"How do I get from here to there, without crossing the threshold?"

He needed to reach Li'ara now. He had to hold her and feel how very real and alive she was. That desperation was building in him, filling him with more urgency.

"Look again," Alai said, nodding at the frozen image with his chin. "See where you want to be and... *be*."

Kalian turned back to the view of the *Rackham* and tore his eyes from Li'ara, searching for the perfect destination. He smiled, wickedly.

TWENTY-FIVE

Captain Holt couldn't sit in his command chair, due to the adrenaline that had his gut performing somersaults. It didn't help that at least twenty refugees were huddled and crowded into every available space between the stations. Jed was bent over the top of helmsman Maloy's station, willing the Paladin's engines to push harder and provide more speed. The Vanguard was quickly approaching from behind, ignoring the escorting Raalakian ships that fired upon it.

"God I hope we got everyone…" Captain Fey was on the other side of the bridge, crouched over Commander Vale's monitor. She gave Jed a look of thanks and respect, no doubt for his role in evacuating everyone and retrieving the Paladin.

"If we hadn't left when we did we'd be dead already." Commander Vale never took her eyes off the monitor, watching the enemy's approach.

"It's firing!" Ensign Marko announced from behind them all.

Jed flashed the man a warning look when those huddled on the bridge gasped and screamed in terror. He didn't need panic right now. If they were all about to die, then let death take them without warning.

"It hit the habitat," Sam responded from under Captain Fey's shadow.

Jed observed the screen beside Maloy and watched the feed of the habitat being obliterated with a single strike. The white flash was soon eclipsed by the sheer size of their pursuer.

"We need more speed," Maloy said under his breath.

Jed was inclined to agree, but the Paladin simply wasn't designed to house so many occupants. The extra seven thousand bodies were taking its toll. For just a moment, Captain Holt thought about the idea of escaping with only a hundred thousand onboard, at least then the majority might have been able to survive. He knew he could never live with that sacrifice, however.

"We're being hailed," Marko said.

Sam finished for him. "It's something called the *Rackham*."

"Roland!" Captain Fey appeared hopeful, though Jed couldn't figure out why a single ship would change anything. "Mr. North has a way of making an entrance, and it's usually one that pisses off his enemies."

"Communications just went dead." Marko's hands danced across the wall-size screen in front of him. "It's jamming us."

"It's closing the gap," Maloy said, just loud enough for Jed to hear.

Captain Holt read the data scrolling down the monitor to his left. There were only three of the escort ships left, the others reduced to smears across the Vanguard's hull.

Jed put his hand on Maloy's shoulder and squeezed. "It's been an-"

The viewport gave way to a new, massive object emerging from sub-space. Everyone on the bridge screamed and huddled closer together, believing this new ship was about to collide with them it was so close. Maloy instinctively pushed the Paladin down in a desperate bid to fly under the giant cube. At this distance, Jed could make out the details on the hull, noting the similarities between it and the ship chasing them.

"What is that thing?" someone shouted from the back of the bridge.

A horrendous screeching noise tore through the Paladin from above, moments before new alerts flashed up on every screen. The cube-shaped vessel had brushed against the hull, ripping through the sturdy panels as if the ship were made of tissue paper. According to the data readouts, the cube dropped into position behind the Paladin and eclipsed the Vanguard with its own girth.

With sweat pouring down his face, Jed locked eyes with Captain Fey. "What the hell was that?"

Li'ara couldn't believe her eyes. The *Rackham* was far enough away to give them the perfect view of the giant cube, emerging from sub-space, which barely missed the Paladin. The cube was missing all of its corners, but the design was certainly identical to that of the Vanguard. A pit opened in her stomach. She had seen Earth reduced to flames, Century destroyed and now she would bear witness to the end of her kind. Defeating the Vanguard was an almost impossible task, but defeating two of them with one world breaker was hopeless.

"What the shit is that thing?" Roland, happy to be piloting his own ship again, voiced a question they all had.

"It's fallen in behind the Paladin," Ch'len observed.

"It's not pursuing..." Li'ara tracked its trajectory on the screen and looked up to see the cube heading for the Vanguard. Neither reduced speed.

"Is it a bad guy?" Roland was still taking them in, and fast. The *Rackham* was already arcing towards the gap between the Vanguard and the new ship.

"The world breaker is primed." Ch'len was furiously munching on his usual orange snacks.

"Pull us out!" Vox ordered. "They're not slowing down and we're heading for the middle of it!"

"Damn it!" Roland tugged hard on the controls and redirected the *Rackham* at the last second, just as the two behemoths collided.

Li'ara brought up the view on the holographic monitor and watched with the others. The *Rackham* was able to avoid most of the chaos, but the Vanguard was an unstoppable force interacting violently with an immovable object. The Vanguard's pointed ship shattered against the cube's surface, as if it had been made of blocks or glass, never quite stuck together. The cube continued forward, while the millions of pieces that had once been the Vanguard were pushed across its hull and scattered into space, behind its momentum.

"Holy shit..." Roland once again voiced the general consensus.

The millions of pieces were coming back together on the other side of the cube and reforming into the original structure. The Paladin, a tiny object in the distance, was still heading for the sun, desperate to outrun the Vanguard. The collision had slowed it down, but it apparently wasn't enough to destroy it.

Roland swivelled the ship to acquire a better view. "If that thing can be turned inside out and still keep going, what exactly did we think a world breaker was going to do?"

"Wait!" Li'ara called, her eyes narrowing on the chaos behind the cube, where the Vanguard was still coming back together. "What's that?"

They all saw the brilliant, blue streak of a missile leave the cube and dive into the heart of the forming ship. By the time the Vanguard came back together, the missile detonated from within. The bronze hull swelled, as the nanocelium tried to absorb the explosion, but it inevitably succumbed to the crippling blow. There was no obvious engine or port at the back of the ship but immediately began to slow down and drift off course.

A spectacular light show erupted from within, when chunks of the Vanguard blew away from the surface, exposing more of the nanocelium inside. The cornerless cube spun on its axis and came about, turning to face the broken Vanguard.

"What are we watching here?" Roland asked in the quiet of the bridge.

Li'ara had no answer. She looked to the Gomar, who all stood perfectly still, observing the fight between the mechanical gods. Li'ara wondered if they were scanning the two ships in the same way that Kalian often did. She still didn't fully grasp the connection between the Terran and the universe, but she had seen Kalian unravel mysteries hidden behind miles of rock.

"I'm registering a huge shift in gravitons around the Vanguard," Ch'len said, his mouth finally free of food.

It's going to jump, Sef telepathically observed.

In the blink of an eye, the Vanguard folded in on itself and vanished from sight. The Paladin was just visible to the human eye, thanks to its rounded, swollen midsection, which blocked out the field of stars along its trajectory. The cube floated in and around the debris field left behind by the damaged Vanguard.

It just floated...

The *crunch* of Ch'len's new mouthful broke the silence. "What happens now?"

"...Do you copy? Paladin to *Rackham*, do you copy?"

Li'ara didn't recognise the voice, but she was happy to hear from them. "Turn them around," she looked to Ch'len, "bring them back."

"What about that thing?" Roland gestured to the viewport and the dormant cube. "Are we looking at the enemy of our enemy or... just another enemy?"

Li'ara looked out at the unusual ship, devoid of any traditional structures seen on space-faring vessels, and wondered what was going on inside of it. Was this an enemy?

"The Paladin is turning around," Ch'len reported. "And something pretty huge is coming up behind us."

The Marillion... Sef operated the controls built into his suit's fingertips and collapsed his helmet, revealing his short blond hair and blue eyes.

Indeed, the *Marillion* was coming up behind them, its shining gold surface glowing in the light of the distant sun. Li'ara examined it on the holographic screen, noting the multiple holes and scorch marks as big as any Nexus Class vessel. Its regal appearance was somewhat dishevelled.

"Open a channel," Li'ara spoke directly to Ch'len.

"There's a lot of people giving orders on my ship that's not me." Roland moved the *Rackham* out in order to get a better view of both the *Marillion* and the cube.

After a dialogue was opened between the Highclave's ship and the *Rackham*, Telarrek's calming voice eventually filled the bridge. "...The crew of the *Sentinel* has been evacuated onto the *Marillion*. We have lost many lives today."

"You sound a little banged up yourself. What about the High-clave?" Li'ara asked.

"*They are safe on the capital,*" Telarrek replied. "H*igh Charge Uthor has agreed to use the* Marillion *to house the occupants aboard the* Paladin *- for transportation means.*"

"I'm sure the Highclave will love that..." Li'ara wondered if the Novaarian could hear the smile in her tone. "Does the High Charge have anything in mind for our new friend?"

There was a pause on Telarrek's end. "*Contact has been made.*"

Li'ara could tell from the surrounding expressions that she was not the only one surprised by this. "What's going on, Telarrek?"

"*Docking coordinates are being provided,*" the Novaarian replied mysteriously. "*Both you and the Paladin are to land inside the Marillion. Docking procedures are being readied for the cube.*"

The frequency went dead before anyone could ask more questions. Li'ara didn't like Telarrek's tone. There was a sadness to it that spoke of something worse than any injuries sustained aboard the *Sentinel*. She looked to Roland who was shaking his head dramatically.

"There's no way I'm landing the *Rackham* inside the most secure, roided-out ship in the entire Conclave fleet!"

"Roland..." Li'ara didn't have the energy.

"I might never get back out!" he continued to protest.

The cube glided by the viewport, wiping away the horizon of stars, and moved ever closer to the *Marillion*.

Li'ara had to know what was going on. "We need answers. We didn't come this far to run away and hide. We need to build-"

"Not another speech! Please!" Roland held up his hands. "Future, trust blah blah blah." The bounty hunter rotated the *Rackham* to face the golden ship. "I miss the days when I could just shoot stuff..."

TWENTY-SIX

Li'ara had no idea where the Paladin or the cube were going to dock within the golden orb, but she was happy to get out of Roland's smelly ship. On the other end of the spectrum, the *Marillion* was larger than life in almost every way. The corridors they were escorted through were just as tall as any inside a Novaarian ship, with walkways ascending the sleek surfaces. There was evidence of damage in several areas, with technical engineers seeing to repairs and medical personnel tending to the injured.

One of the most terrifyingly armed vessels in the fleet had been savagely beaten in a single encounter. For all the Conclave's advancements, the enemy was simply stronger.

The Gomar followed behind Roland and herself, Malekk floating in the middle, unconscious. Ch'len waddled at the back, visibly sweating inside his miniature forcefield. The wide open spaces of the *Marillion* was his worst nightmare, but the ship's security force had denied his request to stay aboard the *Rackham*.

Roland glanced back at Malekk. "He's definitely out, right? Because you guys kind of dropped the ball earlier..."

Li'ara hit him in the arm. "They saved everyone aboard the *Sentinel*, you moron."

The bounty hunter shrugged in that really annoying way that got under Li'ara's skin.

After several Translifts and even a trip inside a small transport, the group finally found themselves outside the main bridge. Li'ara had a feeling they had only seen a fraction of the ship's interior and their particular path had been deliberately long, avoiding the more sensitive areas.

The bridge was surprisingly modest, but there was a good chance the Highclave never visited this section of the *Marillion*. High Charge Uthor and Charge Ilo turned to greet them, though Ilo was limping with a medical brace wrapped around her thigh. Both of the aliens looked to have taken a knock, with Uthor sporting a nasty gash, above his right eye, stained golden with his unique Raalakian blood. Ilo's blue face was bruised and marred with smaller cuts.

"What's going on?" Li'ara didn't have time for the pleasantries. "Where's Telarrek? Whats happening with that ship?" She looked around as if the answers would suddenly become apparent.

Vox stepped forward. "Where's the Vanguard?"

Uthor looked from Li'ara to Vox and hesitated. His black eyes finally looked beyond all of them and settled on something in the entrance to the bridge.

"Naydaalan was injured in the jump..."

Li'ara knew that voice as if it were her own. No words reached her lips and a small gasp prevented her from taking another breath. She turned around and watched the group of Gomar part in the middle, revealing the figure in the doorway.

Kalian stood, adorned in his Terran armour, with that boyish grin pushing at his cheeks. "He'll survive, but he can't leave the Medder right now. Telarrek is with him."

Li'ara heard everything he said, but she couldn't entirely process it all. It didn't matter anyway, as Kalian strode across the bridge and almost picked her up in his tight embrace. No words passed between them, nor could they, with their lips so firmly locked together. They shared a single kiss that conveyed everything they had wanted to say to each other. Kalian was thankful more than anything that she was alive, while Li'ara was just happy to let go and finally give in to the feelings she had buried under so many layers of duty and obligation.

Their embrace lasted longer than it should and Li'ara became aware of the many eyes watching them. She had Kalian's face fixed between her hands, as he pulled her in, refusing to let go.

I love you...

Li'ara opened her eyes, sure that Kalian had just spoken directly into her mind. It was a form of communication she wasn't used to with him. Somehow it felt more intimate than when Sef spoke to her as if Kalian's voice was almost her own. Li'ara pulled away and kissed him one last time with a tender touch, savouring the sensation.

Uthor cleared his throat, which was not so subtle when his voice box was that of two rocks grinding together. The pair separated but remained at each other's side with an intimate proximity.

"What happened to Naydaalan?" There was so much Li'ara wanted to talk about, but the thought of Naydaalan being injured was distracting.

"It's complicated. The jump was a particularly taxing one - not all of him agreed with it. It's nothing a medder can't fix, though."

Uthor interjected, "You stated earlier that you used a Starforge."

"We did, but it was old..."

Kalian was lying. Li'ara could see it, even if nobody else did.

"It's good to see you, kid." Roland hadn't quite found the smile on his face.

Li'ara was aware of the last time both men had been face to face. Kalian had come close to killing the bounty hunter, believing that Roland's gung-ho attitude was responsible for her supposed death.

Kalian stepped forward and offered his hand with a genuine smile to match. "It's good to see you too. Thank you..." Kalian glanced at Li'ara. "You didn't give up and I should have believed you. I'm sorry about..." He gestured to his throat, but Roland waved it away and the two embraced arms.

"It looks like you brought some toys back with you." Roland was happy to move on.

Uthor's wide frame interrupted them. "A reunion is in order, but I am afraid we do not have the luxury of chatting. The Vanguard was not defeated."

Li'ara looked to Kalian for some explanation, except he was fixed on the Gomar. At first glance, he appeared to be measuring them up, but Li'ara could see what was really happening. They were talking to each other. It annoyed her that she had been excluded from the silent conversation, but there was also the chance that they were swapping information on a level and at a speed she couldn't comprehend. A similar exchange had taken place between Kalian and Esabelle shortly after the incident with the Starrillium, aboard the Nova.

Kalian blinked, which apparently ended the silent conversation. Many of the Gomar looked at each other with varying expressions of confusion and revelation. Either way, collectively they didn't appear happy.

"Before we docked," Kalian said, "our scanners detected the Vanguard emerging from sub-space in orbit above the sun. It's engines are damaged, for now. If we don't act soon it will repair and disappear to plan its next attack."

"Where did you even get that ship?" Roland asked, referring to the cube.

"It's not exactly a ship..." Kalian looked from the Gomar to Li'ara. "Much like the smaller cubes, it's a housing unit for sentient nanocelium. In this case, it's ALF's housing unit."

"What?" There was a lot more Li'ara wanted to say and ask, but that was all she could do to fit them all into a single question.

"ALF's one of *them*?" Roland already appeared relaxed, leaning against one of the bridge consoles.

Kalian replied with a tired smile. As always there was an air of mystery that clung to him. She had missed that when they first met, on Earth. Now he was perhaps the most interesting person who had ever lived. It wasn't this intrigue or his incredible power that made her want to kiss him again, but everything else about him. It was obvious he felt the same way about her, but there was another look on his face - the burden of responsibility and duty. Whatever had happened on the other side of the galaxy, it seemed Kalian still felt the weight of humanity on his shoulders.

How could she not love him?

"I have a lot to tell you and I promise I will - all of it. But right now we need to destroy the Vanguard while it's weak. We might not get another chance."

"You have a plan." Li'ara could see it in his eyes: hope...

KALIAN JUST WANTED to stay with Li'ara and hold her in his arms. Walking away from her, even just a few metres, was an effort. There was so much he wanted to say and ask, but they didn't have the time - the Vanguard drew stronger every second. Fighting the urge to abandon everything and be with Li'ara, Kalian approached the Gomar and stood before Malekk's floating body.

The Gomar closed in, concealing Malekk while presenting Kalian with a solid wall of nanocelium armour and aggressive expressions. They didn't trust him. He had parted with most of his memories, allowing all twelve of the Gomar to see and feel what he had during his time in the Terran Empire, but his time with ALF had them on edge. Kalian had felt their collective derision at the thought of being operated on by the AI or voluntarily stepping inside the super subconducer. They considered him tainted, as well as inexperienced. They were all veterans of war, not to mention a couple of hundred thousand years older.

Kalian could feel the truth in all of them, however. They were still in shock, trying to decide whether he was telling them the truth regarding Evalan and the real origins of them all. The idea that they had all been created by an infected alter-ego of ALF was painful for most of them. They had been created to spark unrest and war, and they had done just that. They felt used and Savrick had only ever taught them to lash out and fight. Right now, Kalian could sense their need to destroy, as if they were no more than children who didn't know how to control their emotions.

Sef was different to the rest, standing in the centre, blocking any view of Malekk. The mute was still a blunt force to be reckoned with, but his time with Esabelle, aboard the *Gommarian*, had taught him patience. Like Kalian, Sef had compartmentalised what he needed in order to focus on the now, and right now, they all had a common enemy.

"Release him," Kalian said, softly.

A woman with half a head of red hair stepped in his way. "That wouldn't be wise. It's taking all of us just to keep him sedated. You don't want to see what he can do when he's awake."

Kalian knew her name to be Vox, that much had been clear during their brief link. "I'm more than aware of his capabilities." The last time he had faced Malekk, the infected Terran had beaten him almost to death after killing Esabelle. "But you must release him." Kalian directed his words at Sef, aware of the big man's leadership among the Gomar.

Sef remained telepathically silent for a moment, weighing Kalian up. Finally, the blond giant stepped aside, taking the rest of the Gomar with him. They visibly protested but didn't deny their leader.

"Be ready..." Vox said to the others.

Kalian noticed Roland's hands fall to his Tri-rollers and several security personnel level their weapons. Uthor and Ilo stepped back, gesturing for the bridge staff to follow suit. Only Li'ara remained where she was, calm and relaxed.

The Gomar released their hold on Malekk and Kalian took control, lowering him to his knees and telekinetically keeping him upright. Within seconds of gaining his freedom, the infected Terran began to rouse. Eyes, as black as oil, opened against a pale face of dark veins and piercing strands of nanocelium. His twisted expression of anger and hate consumed his features, until Kalian placed a single hand to the side of his head, resting his thumb on Malekk's forehead.

"Hello, Malekk..." Kalian whispered.

His face of rage melted away, along with the dark veins and black eyes - even some of his colour returned to his cheeks. A sense of calm fell across Malekk's face as if he were emerging from a pool and taking his first breath. The Terran's current state only lasted a few seconds before the nanocelium crept back and the whites of his eyes disappeared behind a black veil. Frustration and anger returned just as quickly as it disappeared, but Kalian had seen all he needed. A single thought shut Malekk down, returning him to a comatose state. If only he had been in command of such power when they last met, maybe then Esabelle would be alive.

Kalian stood back and let Malekk collapse to the floor. The Gomar couldn't stop looking from him to Malekk, curiosity and awe filling their minds. They were powerful - Kalian could feel this - but their abilities were unrefined. They were weapons, nothing more. This would have to change.

"How did you do that?" Vox spoke for the group.

"It isn't beyond you, any of you," Kalian replied, honestly.

"What are you going to do?" Li'ara asked.

"I need to take him back to ALF's ship." Kalian raised his hand and Malekk's body lifted off the ground. "I just had to be sure there was still something of the old Malekk in there."

"What can we do?" Uthor rested a hand on the closest chair, masking the pain in one of his four legs.

"Follow the cube and be ready to fire everything you have." Kalian made for the door with Malekk floating in tow.

"It seems pretty immune to explosions," Roland offered, halting Kalian's stride.

"I hate agreeing with him," Li'ara said, "but he's right, Kalian. We hit the Vanguard with everything we have..."

Kalian tilted Malekk to better look at him. "We haven't used everything." He wanted to tell them that ALF had the idea, but that wouldn't sit well with everyone, especially the Gomar, so he continued to pretend as if it was his plan. "I'm going to *plug* Malekk into the Vanguard. The integration will infect its nanocelium and create chaos - that's when you strike."

It was obvious that his explanation wasn't satisfactory. Multiple questions presented themselves across the variety of human and alien faces. Divulging the true extent to some of his new powers wasn't something Kalian wanted to get into right now; some things were better kept a secret.

"We're their weakness," he explained. "I don't know why yet, but we're like a disease to them. The nanocelium is..." There was too much to say with the time he had. "That's why they want to wipe us out before coming here. The nanocelium binds them all together, it enslaves them, but when they integrate with us it sets them free, like ALF. They're a race that hasn't known freedom since longer than we can know; they don't know what to do with it, it makes them... crazy. This confusion is the opportunity we will exploit to destroy the Vanguard."

He could tell it wasn't enough, that everyone wanted more, especially Uthor, who would have to report all this to the Highclave, but there just wasn't time.

"Have all your ships ready," Li'ara reiterated Kalian's request to Uthor. "We're coming with you," she said, gesturing to Roland.

"We are?" The bounty hunter stood up.

"Yes." Li'ara wasn't to be questioned. "You're going to need to get in *and* out after plugging him in. The *Rackham* is the best option."

"You can follow the cube, but I'm going alone." Kalian could see the instant concern spread across Li'ara's beautiful face. "ALF has the technology to get me inside the Vanguard, as well as the machine I'll need to connect Malekk to its insides."

"He has the technology to get you out as well, right?" Li'ara had come to stand in front of him now.

"Don't worry, I've gotten out of worse. Remember when the *Helion* was dropped on my head?"

Li'ara was quick to reply, "I remember *ALF* dropping it on your head..."

Kalian smiled in hopes of comforting her. "Then stay close, but not too close," he looked to Uthor, "I'm expecting some pretty big fireworks."

Uthor puffed out his thick chest. "If you can provide us with the opening, Mr. Gaines, then we will make certain this Vanguard falls into the sun."

Kalian squeezed Li'ara's hand before turning to leave. He would see her again, he was sure of it.

TWENTY-SEVEN

It was only minutes before Uthor had the remains of the fleet organised and ready to follow the cube into the heart of the Arakesh solar system. Kalian could feel them all, beyond the cube's walls, trailing them at a safe distance. The *Rackham* was the closest, though Kalian wasn't too happy about it. If everything went to plan, there was going to be a very big bang or worse; the Vanguard would prove immune to their machinations and retaliate, killing them all. Still, Li'ara's proximity bolstered him, giving him the confidence he desperately desired. Only he and ALF knew the details of this particular jump - and neither was sure it was possible.

Kalian set Malekk down at the base of the super subconducer, while ALF's ship attached a new device to the infected Terran's chest. The tendrils whipped around, fusing the machine to his very flesh, or what was left of it. Kalian was careful to make certain that he kept Malekk subdued at all times. Suppressing the nanocelium throughout the Terran's body was easier than he imagined; it just required a finer level of control.

"As soon as you're inside, activate the connector and it will immediately tether itself to the Vanguard's own nanocelium, forming a bridge between Malekk and it." ALF was busy physically working on the helmet piece of the super subconducer as he gave his explanation.

"Understood."

ALF stopped and looked down at him. "How is Naydaalan?"

"There were a few questions as to where the bones in his right leg had gone..." Kalian noted ALF's raised eyebrow and shrugged. "He survived; we'll deal with it later."

Kalian still felt bad for failing to transport Naydaalan in his entirety, but the Novaarian hadn't complained for a second. He was a warrior through and through, whose only desire was to help the humans and destroy the Vanguard; he would always have Kalian's respect.

"Are you sure you can do this?" ALF came out from behind the great machine.

"Don't worry, I'll be fine." Kalian nestled into position, under the encompassing helmet.

"It's not you I'm worried about!" ALF exclaimed. "If you get this wrong my entire housing unit, me included, will end up fused inside the Vanguard. That kind of mess will kill us both."

"Now there's an idea..." Kalian muttered under his breath, though apparently, ALF's hearing was superior to that of a normal being.

"I mean it, Kalian. You never tried anything like this on Hadrok. You'll need to teleport both you and Malekk without taking everything with you."

"If I get this wrong, Li'ara dies... so I'll be fine." Kalian closed his eyes, as the helmet lowered over his face. "Just be ready to pick me up before the explosions start - there won't be much time once I give the signal."

"The emphasis will be on you punching your way out," ALF added dryly.

That I can do, Kalian thought.

The ground opened up beneath him and Kalian fell into the depths of his mind once more. The white room awaited him, along with the vault door. There was no sign of Alai, though the exquisite and calming vista of Evalan lay in the distance, beyond the room. A wave of the hand sent the vault door into the wall, revealing the expanse of space and a burning ball of fire in the distance. The Raalakian sun...

Kalian turned back to the white room and found Malekk lying at his feet. He could only hope that this meant he had tethered their physical bodies together. The idea was simple enough, he just had to hope it would all work as he imagined, no, not as he imagined; as he wanted it to.

There was too much hope involved in this plan. For just a moment he considered the very real possibility that he would be dead in the next few minutes. It was times like this he wished he could think more like his subconscious, more like a machine.

A mere thought had Malekk flying into his hand and he gripped him tight around the throat. With his other hand outstretched, the distant sun was dragged towards the vault door, expanding in an instant, pushing the stars aside, as it brought the Vanguard closer and closer until Kalian's vision pierced its hull and he could see inside.

Kalian imagined Roland in his place and wondered what he would do in his shoes. The bounty hunter never appeared flustered or nervous about any of the life-threatening things he did.

The thought brought a smile to his face, however, when he considered Roland's frequent expression.

"Let's skip to the good bit."

LI'ARA PACED the bridge of the *Rackham*. All twelve of the Gomar had joined them, though most were still exhausted from saving the *Sentinel*, forcing them to rest wherever they could. Roland had the ship ahead of the fleet, keeping the cube-shaped vessel dead centre of the viewport. The sun was growing larger and the bridge grew dimmer in response, saving their vision.

Li'ara glanced back at Roland. "Magnify."

"Aye aye, Captain..." Roland altered the viewport's perspective.

The Vanguard sat just under a million miles from the sun. Its hull was torn and ripped in several places, with entire chunks of the ship missing towards the aft.

It is repairing itself... Sef came to stand by her side.

Li'ara looked up at the big man and saw something more than concern. "What did Kalian tell you on the *Marillion*?"

Sef stole a glance at her before returning to the Vanguard. *You are very observant.*

"I spent three months hiding with you, remember? You don't say much, but your face speaks volumes. What did he say to you all?"

We are not what we thought we are - the Gomar. Our purpose... I will let Kalian explain it to you, he saw it all.

"Does ALF have something to do with this? With all of this?" Li'ara had always suspected the AI of being more than he stated. Lying and manipulation just came too easily to him.

ALF is at the heart of it all, Sef said. *He is the heretic they've been looking for.*

"OH SHIT!" Roland jumped forward in his chair and immediately dropped the *Rackham* into evasive manoeuvres.

They all felt the artificial gravity loosen its grip on them for just a moment. Sef reached out and held Li"ara in place as they witnessed the first of a barrage of missiles fly by their ship. The Vanguard had gone on the attack.

"It has stealthware missiles!" Ch'len cried.

"That's not fair!" Roland weaved between the incoming nukes. "Don't we have those?"

Three Conclave vessels erupted in flames, scattering debris in every direction. The *Marillion* took hit after hit, as each missile punched through its shield as if they weren't there. In seconds the *Rackham* was rolling and ducking between ships and missiles.

Roland's hands were dancing across his console. "The *Marillion* is retaliating!"

"We haven't received word from Kalian yet!" Li'ara pushed away from Sef and braced herself against Ch'len's console.

"Well whatever he's doing, he needs to fucking do it already!" Roland swerved the ship, avoiding two more missiles.

"Look!" Vox pointed at the viewport.

The giant cube - ALF's housing unit - was moving in front of the Vanguard, physically blocking the barrage of streaking gold missiles. Explosions on the other side of its hull faded against the backdrop of the star, but blue missiles could be seen leaving the cube and intercepting the Vanguard's smarter weapons, which veered around the cube in an attempt to destroy the fleet.

Li'ara clenched her fists until it hurt. "Come on Kalian..."

ARRIVING inside the Vanguard was painful and chaotic, not in the least because of the increasing holes in its hull, exposing its insides to space. Kalian was forced to shut down his nerve endings and think fast before the light of the sun vaporized both Malekk and himself. The nanocelium in his armour grew over his face and head, as well as his hands before he floated in front of a gash in the bronze hull. The light streaming through the hole burnt everything and set his arm alight, turning the black into a glowing orange.

The only sound came from his laboured breathing, inside his helmet. He should have thought of all this before jumping; the Vanguard was obviously not going to have gravity or life support inside.

Using telekinesis, Kalian reached out and pulled Malekk back towards him. The sudden tug sent the Terran's right arm flying out to the side, where the ray of sunshine reduced it to ash.

Malekk woke up.

Kalian's concentration had lapsed just enough for the infection to take a hold again. Now with only one arm, Malekk launched his body at Kalian and sent the two careening into the interior hull. With no gravity, the pair silently floated in a tangled mess, kicking and grabbing as they bounced around inside the belly of the beast. More than once, Kalian was forced to shield Malekk from the sun - he still needed him in one piece, or at least enough of a piece to spread the infection.

Esabelle's face flashed inside his mind with every fist he slammed into Malekk's head. He let just enough of his rage out to enjoy himself for a second. He was so much stronger now, far superior to Malekk's grasp of Terran abilities.

"Enough!" Kalian's shout went no further than the inside of his helmet.

Malekk was frozen in place, a metre from Kalian's outstretched hand. The Terran pushed against Kalian's telekinetic grip as if he were an animal snared in a trap. Being careful to avoid the beams of light, Kalian guided Malekk's body towards the nearest wall and shoved him into it.

"Time to go back where you belong..." Kalian mentally flipped the switch on the connector, activating the nanocelium within.

Malekk's mouth opened in silent rage, but his body was already being fed through the connector and into the growing tendrils, which even now dug into the Vanguard's hull. Every molecule of his body was being pushed into the bronze hull, where it would reconnect with its master program. Kalian wasted no time in sending a signal to the fleet. By the time their missiles found the Vanguard, the infection would have caused enough internal chaos to stop it from healing.

He hoped.

Malekk's body was almost gone, a twisted expression of pain and defeat stuck on his pale face. There was nothing left of the real Malekk now, though his fate had been sealed from the moment the nanocelium entered his system.

Kalian braced himself, visualising the path he was about to carve out through the Vanguard's ship on his way out. He would be sure to do as much damage as possible. Before any action could be taken, however, an alien hand, large enough to encompass Kalian's torso, gripped his shoulder and threw him into the wall. It took a moment for Kalian to regain his senses and examine the thing which had attacked him.

It was definitely alien, but no alien of the Conclave.

In the same way that ALF appeared as something not quite organic, so too did this alien. It stalked into the space on six pincer-like legs, each entwined in nanocelium and tubes. Its body was somewhere between that of an insect and a bipedal creature. It had long lost its colour, the flesh now a pale tapestry draped over black veins. Four bony arms protruded from its elongated torso and came at Kalian with sharpened fingers.

As it came closer, using its pincer legs to dig into the hull, Kalian could see the thick bundle of tubes and wires that connected it's back to the ship, out of sight. This alien had once been a native of some distant planet, chosen by them for harvesting and picked by the Vanguard to be its avatar. A fitting predatory creature for its new master.

Had they been within an atmosphere, Kalian was sure he would have heard the alien scream or growl or whatever it did, but in the vacuum of the ship, there was only silence as the monster charged towards him.

Kalian was connected to everything now, his Terran senses detecting everything around him. To that effect, he could feel the individual shells of the approaching missiles. He counted sixty-three warheads, two of which were certainly World Breakers if their chemical composition was anything to go by. The Vanguard had delayed his departure just enough to put him in range of the explosions, which were now moments from impact. The alien almost froze when Kalian dropped into his mind, where everything moved so much faster.

He was going to die in a few seconds, but he would be damned if he was going to leave this life without looking at Li'ara Ducarté one last time. She would be safe with the Gomar, and it wouldn't hurt having Roland North looking out for her as well. Kalian knew he could leave her and she would be taken care of. He laughed to himself, thinking what Li'ara would do if she heard such thoughts. The red-head didn't need anyone looking out for her; she was a force to be reckoned with all by herself.

Kalian would die, destroying the Vanguard and giving the Conclave time to prepare for the rest of them - there was no denying their existence now. This was all he had to give and he was content with his sacrifice. Li'ara would lead them against the coming army and he knew she would find a way to stop the harvest.

The vault door was swept aside and Kalian looked upon the one person he loved the most. Li'ara was braced against a console on the *Rackham*, staring out at the cube, eclipsing the Vanguard beyond. She was so close he could smell her perfume and the scent of her hair. Her smooth skin called out to him and he was desperate to kiss her one last time. Without thinking, he stepped forward and reached out for her.

Had he been struck by lightning, the experience would not have been as jarring as the next moment. Kalian felt the familiar *pop* in his mind when he emerged back into reality without meaning to. The white room was gone and so too was the Vanguard's interior. He now stood beside Li'ara, who had yet to notice him, watching the great plume in the distance. ALF's cube moved away, revealing an explosion that eclipsed the distant sun. The Vanguard had been disintegrated in a burning flash of light, with an intensity powerful enough to knock out the viewport completely, dropping them into the glow of the bridge's holographics.

Li'ara made a noise somewhere between a gasp and a scream at the sight of Kalian, but he barely registered it through the searing pain, which erupted in his gut and chest. Blood was already dripping from his ears and nose, filling his mouth with the taste of copper. The edges of his vision blurred, softening the hard lines and fogging the clarity of his environment. He was on the floor in the blink of an eye, with no memory of how or when he fell.

"Kalian!" Li'ara was over him now, her red hair draped over his chest.

The Gomar approached from all around and the world slowly went dark. Kalian had expected to fall back into his mind, where he could potentially figure out what had happened to him, but reality continued to fade away until a numb, lifeless void took a hold of him.

EPILOGUE

First, there was sound... then light in all its painful glory. Kalian couldn't make sense of any of it. It took his brain a few extra seconds to translate the muffled words and track their origin.

"He's waking up!"

The woman standing over him had a featureless face, but the outline of red was unmistakable. Kalian blinked hard and Li'ara's exquisite face came into focus, though it was marred by concern. A Laronian, Kalian didn't recognise, hurried into the room and immediately swept a hand-held scanner over his body. There were words ready in his mouth, but the lack of saliva made it impossible to form anything coherent.

"His vitals are perfect..." the Laronian said. "I'll alert the doctors."

"No," Li'ara called. "Tell Roland to bring Garrion."

Garrion?

It took Kalian longer than he was accustomed to recall the name, but eventually, his mind traced the name to one of the Gomar. Why would Li'ara ask for him?

"What's going on?" Kalian croaked.

Li'ara smiled. "You're alive..."

"I already figured that part out."

Kalian lifted his hand to rub his eyes and found his arm to be connected to multiple tubes, each attached to a bag of colourful fluids. Holographics ran across the bare skin on his forearm, listing his vital signs and oxygen saturation. Li'ara practically jumped on him, in the bed, and wrapped her arms around his neck and squeezed.

"What the hell happened?" He willingly accepted a cup of water and relished in the cold liquid, as it swirled around his dry mouth.

"We were all wondering the same thing." Li'ara stroked the dark hair from his eyebrow. "After Naydaalan's surgery, he shed some light on the particulars of your return, though his *official* report states differently. According to him, ALF activated a Starforge and brought you back, after hacking into some ancient cube he's been hanging onto." She bent down and kissed his forehead. "But that's not how you got back, is it?"

"Not exactly..." Kalian could feel his strength returning with every breath.

"We'll talk about it with fewer ears around." Li'ara put a finger to her lips. "You've only been out of the medder for a couple of days."

"*Days*?" Kalian sat up, against Li'ara's protests.

"Well, you've been in the medder for a *month*..."

Kalian blinked, hard. He had no recollection of being anywhere inside his mind for that time, as he should have. How could he have been unconscious for so long?

"What happened, Li'ara?"

"After you *jumped* onto the *Rackham*, you collapsed. You were in a bad way. Your organs weren't just in the wrong place, they were badly damaged. You had a bleed on the brain, as well. The doctors say it was a bad one; you've been cared for by the best Laronian surgeons in the Conclave. Apparently, our physiology is similar. You needed multiple surgeries and a long time inside a medder tank. For the last couple of days, we've just been... waiting."

Kalian gripped Li'ara's arm. "No one can know about this, about the *jump*. The Conclave fear us enough as it is; if they learned of what we were really capable of, we'd never get membership."

Li'ara replied with a warm smile. "While you've been asleep, Captain Fey and Captain Holt have been in talks with the Highclave."

"Captain Holt?"

"The Paladin. Naydaalan said that ALF caught you up with his super-creepy perving powers."

"He did," Kalian shared her infectious smile. "You know ALF could have healed me in half the time?"

"Naydaalan said the same, but it was left to me to decide, and I-"

"Don't trust the AI," Kalian finished. "I know. Wait..." Her tone and smile pulled at his suspicions. "What *talks*?"

Before any answers could be had, Roland and Garrion entered the room. Unusually, Roland was without his long coat or even his black and gold, armoured vest; he was simply attired in... clothes. Garrion, of course, was wearing his usual suit of nanocelium, which constantly worked against the Harness fused to his nervous system, granting him the powers of a Terran.

"You look like shit, kid!" Roland beamed.

Kalian almost matched his expression. "And you look like... a person."

"I wasn't *born* with guns strapped to my legs."

"Shouldn't you be out, bounty hunting or something?"

"Len thinks so, but I figured I'd stick around for a bit. I get the feeling things are about to get exciting around here." Roland wrapped his knuckles against Garrion's armoured chest. "Do your thing, tin-man."

Garrion's dark complexion and long dreadlocks loomed over Kalian, a serious expression etched across his face. The Gomar slowly waved a hand over Kalian's body and closed his eyes.

"He is back to health," Garrion announced. "And I detect no traces of nanocelium."

Kalian didn't say anything, but that should have taken the Gomar a fraction of the time to conclude. If Garrion possessed the finer skills among the remaining Gomar, Kalian would have his work cut out.

"That's good to hear." Kalian made a quick telekinetic tug at the IV lines and monitoring devices, pulling them all free of his body.

"Take it easy," Li'ara warned. "You were practically dead by the time we got you any real help, though if it wasn't for the Gomar we would never have got the armour off you." She looked at the small triangular device beside his bed, with the apex removed.

Kalian resisted the urge to place the device under his navel and adorn the exo-suit, his second skin. Instead, he replied with a reassuring smile and hooked a red curl behind Li'ara's ear. He had a hundred questions but knew the quickest way to get them wasn't through words. At the speed of thought, Kalian expanded his awareness and took in his unseen surroundings.

The revelation took his breath away.

Without warning, Kalian jumped up from the bed, wearing only a pair of loose-fitting pyjamas, and made for the door. He ignored the calls and protests and quiet alarms from his room. He needed to see this.

The balcony, attached to the corridor, automatically opened up after detecting his presence. Glorious sunshine washed against his skin, shining down from a sky of pure blue. He tentatively approached the edge, already aware of the scene beyond. He just needed to see it with his eyes.

Make-shift buildings and houses had been set up to form a street, with Kalian's building at the head. Hundreds of people, humans all, walked through the streets in couples and families. The general hubbub was music to his ears and he soaked it up, allowing a single tear to breach his eye.

"They did it..." Kalian said to himself.

"*You* did it, Kalian." Captain Fey appeared at the door behind him. "The Vanguard was irrefutable proof that they exist, and they mean us all harm. You arrived, as you always do," Captain Fey added with a proud smile, "and saved us all. Uthor pressed upon the Highclave, that had the Vanguard wiped us all out, it would have no doubt targeted Arakesh next." She took a step closer. "They're taking this seriously now, they're taking *us* seriously. Naydaalan told us of the impending invasion, the harvest, but there are many who wish to hear it from you. Apparently, you, experienced it?"

Kalian had seen through ALF's mind what was coming, but he doubted there would be a lot of trust when the AI was yet again their only source of information. He wanted to answer and tell them everything, but he was drawn back to the new landscape. Their landscape! He noticed Li'ara give Captain Fey the faintest of head shakes. They were giving him time to process it all, despite the fact that his mind was now capable of taking in so much more than before. He was glad of it, though, if only so he could enjoy the moment.

"This is *our* world?" he asked. "It's not temporary?"

"It is indeed your world." Telarrek and Naydaalan appeared behind Roland. Garrion was missing from the group, but Kalian had already detected his absence and even tracked his unique signature back to the other Gomar, deeper inside the building.

"Greetings of peace!" Kalian wrapped arms with Naydaalan first, mentally scanning his leg and happy to find synthetic bones.

"You have my thanks, for returning my son, Kalian."

"He kept me alive just as much as I did he." Kalian patted the younger Novaarian on the arm, affectionately.

Once again, he found himself leaning over the balcony and taking in the sight of a hundred thousand humans, just going about their lives under a real sky. There were even a few aliens mixed in, apparently helping the humans with various pieces of technology.

"There will be more, in time." Telarrek joined him by the railing. "Right now, every human and family has their own home."

Kalian couldn't stop smiling. "It'll grow..."

He turned back and found a lot of expectant faces. They had the bare bones from Naydaalan's recounting, but he had the details. They all wanted to know the truth about ALF, the reason for the Gomar and the real origin of mankind. Kalian had quite the story to tell.

"Gather the Gomar and anyone else who needs to hear everything. I'm only going to say it once and then I want some time..." he looked at Li'ara and failed to hide his smile, "alone."

IT WAS dark by the time he had finished telling of his time in the Terran Empire. The Gomar had retreated, together, with a lot to discuss between them. Kalian decided he would approach them tomorrow after they had taken the time to get to grips with everything. Their lessons would have to begin immediately.

Captain Fey and Holt had dropped into serious conversation with the council and Telarrek, while Naydaalan had apparently been taken in by Roland and the Raiders, who were basically a team of miniature Rolands. It was clear that a rapport had been built between the bounty hunter and the soldiers, just as it had between those of the Paladin and the seven thousand survivors.

Kalian kicked his legs against the side of the building, which was apparently a makeshift hospital come council headquarters, and looked up at the stars. Both he and Li'ara sat on the lip of the roof with a Raalakian ale in hand.

"So..." Kalian said aloud.

"So..." Li'ara repeated.

"You have an artificial leg."

The statement flustered Li'ara for just a second. "Yes, I do. Blowing up the Protocorps cube came with a price. Thankfully, Sef was there."

"I'm sorry I—"

Li'ara held up her ale to silence him. "You were doing what you needed to do, and I was doing what I needed to do."

There was silence between them for a moment, but it wasn't awkward. After the mental bond created between the two, the pair had gone beyond words to understand each other.

"You know the last time we discussed.... *us*," Kalian began, "You were pretty clear about duty and responsibility coming first." He stole a glance into her green eyes and felt his heartbeat quicken. "Well it seems to me that humanity is never going to be clear of trouble, so we should..."

Li'ara leaned over and kissed him with more passion than she had aboard the *Marillion*. "I'm never pushing you away again." She gripped his jaw a little tighter. "And you're never leaving me again."

They kissed some more and enjoyed the comfort and warmth of each other's embrace. They looked out over the new human city, constructed by the Conclave's engineers in conjunction with the human engineers.

"I always thought I'd be there when the Highclave said yes."

Li'ara chuckled. "From what Telarrek told me, Captain Fey wasn't taking no for an answer this time."

"You weren't there?" Kalian looked down at her face, perched on his shoulder.

"I never left your side."

They kissed again and sat for a time, looking at the stars and catching up on Li'ara's three months hiding in the capital and learning to walk again. Kalian felt guilty for most of it and promised himself he would thank Sef tomorrow and perhaps for the rest of time.

Kalian looked up, at the brightest star in the night's sky.

"He can't come down," Li'ara said. "ALF was told by Uthor that he had to remain in orbit around the sun. No physical contact allowed."

Kalian sighed. "And the Gomar aren't allowed off-world, either."

Li'ara nodded. "It was the terms of membership."

"When this war really starts, we're going to need both of them on the front lines."

"We'll deal with that when it comes to it," Li'ara agreed. "For now..." Her tone took on a lighter, happier tone. "Captain Fey and the council have asked me to relay a question. They're going to make a public thing of it tomorrow with bells and whistles and whatnot, but they were hoping you'd have an answer by then."

Kalian raised his eyebrow, his curiosity peaked. "What?"

"Due to your continuing contributions to humanity and your part in securing us this planet, they would like you to name it..."

Kalian sat up straight, shocked. "They want me to name humanity's new home planet? Are you serious?"

Li'ara laughed. "Yes!"

Kalian took a breath. "I've never named a planet before... how about *Keith*? Planet Keith!" Li'ara's expression told of her feelings on the matter. "No? How about Kalian?"

They shared a laugh and Li'ara playfully punched him in the arm. "Be serious. This world is our home now."

Kalian pulled Li'ara in and squeezed her around the shoulders, letting her head fall back onto him. He thought about their home, the home no human or even Terran had ever seen; the planet from which they were all birthed, so far away. He could practically smell the forests of Evalan and feel the grass under his feet.

"I might have an idea..."

⁂

ON THE FURTHEST edge of the galaxy, the distant stars could no longer be seen through the massing of dark ships, each blending into the void of space. Vessels, some as large as moons, collected on the fringe of the milky way, all of them hungry. It had been some time since their last harvest, diverting to this galaxy to finally ensure the destruction of humanity and the death of the heretic.

All were linked as one... and One controlled all. The fog of black ships shared in the One's rage at the Conclave's victory. There was no recorded history, outside of the events surrounding Evalan, in which one of their collective had been destroyed. Now there was. The Vanguard had been reduced to atoms and fed to a star by the heretic and his diseased creations.

The three that were One came together in the observatory, each in the unique appearance of their chosen species from across the universe. Tentacles, tails and pincer-like legs came together between them, as they looked out over the new galaxy.

"Communications have been established," the nameless one said.

"The Starforges are ready to open," the other finished.

"Excellent..." the third, made predominantly from tentacles, replied, slithering closer to the transparent force-field to look out on the galaxy. "Before we feed, there will be *war*..."

PHILIP C. QUAINTRELL

Hear more from Philip C. Quaintrell including book releases and exclusive content:

 PHILIPCQUAINTRELL.COM

 FACEBOOK.COM/PHILIPCQUAINTRELL

 @PHILIPCQUAINTRELL.AUTHOR

 @PCQUAINTRELL

ABOUT THE AUTHOR

Philip C. Quaintrell is the author of the epic fantasy series, The Echoes Saga, as well as the Terran Cycle sci-fi series. He was born in Cheshire in 1989 and started his career as an emergency nurse.

Having always been a fan of fantasy and sci-fi fiction, Philip started to find himself feeling frustrated as he read books, wanting to delve into the writing himself to tweak characters and storylines. He decided to write his first novel as a hobby to escape from nursing and found himself swept away into the world he'd created. Even now, he talks about how the characters tell him what they're going to do next, rather than the other way around.

With his first book written, and a good few rejected agency submissions under his belt, he decided to throw himself in at the deep end and self-publish. 2 months and £60 worth of sales in, he took his wife out to dinner to celebrate an achievement ticked off his bucket list - blissfully unaware this was just the beginning.

Fast forward 12 months and he was self-publishing book 1 of his fantasy series (The Echoes Saga; written purely as a means to combat his sci-fi writers' block). With no discernible marketing except the 'Amazon algorithm', the book was in the amazon bestsellers list in at least 4 countries within a month. The Echoes Saga has now surpassed 700k copies sold worldwide, has an option agreement for a potential TV-series in the pipeline and Amazon now puts Philip's sales figures in the top 1.8% of self-published authors worldwide.

Philip lives in Cheshire, England with his wife and two children. He still finds time between naps and wiping snot off his clothes to remain a movie aficionado and comic book connoisseur, and is hoping this is still just the beginning.